Singinnary

"A virtuosic, richly layered saga, *Singing Lessons for the Stylish Canary* is a remarkable achievement. With prose dipping effortlessly into deeply drawn characters, Stanfill strikes the notes of the human condition so deftly that outrage and empathy harmonize in an intoxicating rhapsody. Every turn of this intricate music box produces heartache and wonder."

—Eli Brown, author of *Cinnamon and Gunpowder*

"With delicacy, precision, and a luscious sense of place, Stanfill captures the once-upon-a-time moment at the end of an era, and an unforgettable family. I can't wait to read what Stanfill writes next!"

—Michelle Ruiz Keil, author of *Summer in the City of Roses*

"Enchanting historical fiction that pulls you into its world from the very first page. Alive with complex characters and mesmerizing settings, *Singing Lessons for the Stylish Canary* is a spellbinding tale of love, art, and growing up."

—Juhea Kim, author of *Beasts of a Little Land*

"Honest, warm, and heart-shattering all at once; this is the kind of book that makes you happy to be alive. A joyous experience all around!"

—Jonah Barrett, author of *Moss Covered Claws* and bookseller at Orca Books Co-op

"Families of vivid characters, carefully detailed scene setting, and delicately gilded writing...create a cozy and enjoyable environment. Fans of Joanne Harris will find plenty to admire."

—*Publishers Weekly*

"Stanfill's deft plot, laced with sparkling flashes of magical realism, keeps us turning the pages, and her prose thrums with the joy she has found in creating this charming, masterful fable."

—Stevan Allred, author of *The Alehouse at the End of the World*

"A rollicking and tender family story of strong-hearted women, misguided fathers, and rebellious youth that leaps joyfully through generations.... I was entranced from the book's overture right through to the final coda."

—Joanna Rose, author of *A Small Crowd of Strangers*

"*Singing Lessons for the Stylish Canary* is a bird's-eye view of how rule-breakingly imaginative a modern novel can be."

—Robert Hill, author of *The Remnants*

"The writing is whimsical but transcends whimsy. The story is magical but transcends magic.... Deceptively delightful, exploring real-world themes of connection, loss, feminism, death, and identity, all wrapped up in lyrical language, bountiful cleverness, and endless wit."

—Gigi Little, bookseller at Powell's Books

Singing Lessons for the Stylish Canary

Laura Stanfill

LANTERNFISH PRESS
Philadelphia

Lanternfish Press
21 South 11th Street, Suite 404
Philadelphia, PA 19107
lanternfishpress.com

Cover Design: Kimberly Glyder

Printed in the United States of America.
25 24 23 22 21   1 2 3 4 5

Library of Congress Control Number: 2021944624
Print ISBN: 978-1-941360-61-3
Digital ISBN: 978-1-941360-62-0

To my parents

And in memory of Dr. Priya Khanna

Singing Lessons for the
Stylish Canary

Overture

In *Avril* of 1718, a traveling salesman visited the drizzly village of Mireville, France, to sell the locals on the charms of the flageolet, a reedless predecessor of the clarinet. He kept his demonstration instrument tucked in a loop his wife had sewn onto his pants, lest it get mixed up with the ones in his pack. He decided not to write home about how the flageolet banged his thigh and knee when he walked, nor did he remove it from the loop, because he missed his wife, who did the best she could.

On this particular day, nearly a century before our story starts, it rained. It always rained in Mireville. The seasons cycled from foggy to gloomy, with an occasional spell of heartening summer haze. Most crops sluiced themselves off their roots and died before producing any sort of yield, leaving limited options to the farmers: peas, watercress, the heartiest of tubers.

The rain encouraged work. The women of Mireville embraced their feminine calling to turn thread into bobbin lace: thick, sturdy pieces suited to tables and windows. The men made musical instruments, violins and violas and violoncellos and barrel organs. Every day the villagers snapped, nailed, or stitched parts of their work to someone else's in an effort to export beauty to kindlier climes. They thought of the future owners of these goods with wonder: to want something—and have the means to send away for it!

Mireville's reputation lured our traveler to the old stone bridge, which he crossed with hope, flageolet banging. Perhaps these music lovers would buy the rest of his inventory. Then he could go home to his wife. He missed her footsteps, how she meandered from room to room, hunting for her comb or extra pen nibs. The traveler worried she might replace him if he stayed absent too long.

In the town square, he announced to the assembled men that he had brought the latest fashion: an instrument for training canaries to recite popular *chansons*. He pulled the flageolet out of the loop and launched into a prickly little étude, followed by a sprightly march—and then he quit, for the rain was getting in his ears.

The men applauded. The traveler proceeded to lecture them about which canaries could best be coaxed to memorize such music. "London Fancys, Lizards, Yorkshire Spangles, Norwich Yellows, the Belgian Fancys, Border Fancys, Glocester Fancys, the Turncrest, the Green, the Cinnamon, the Yellow, the Pure White," he said. "I myself prefer the Cinnamon. My wife keeps a pair."

It was as if the traveler spoke of something as farfetched as the sun—London Fancys and Norwich Yellows!

"You are much mistaken, sir."

"We don't have any canaries here."

The traveler assured them that hatchlings could be ordered from Paris. "Your wives will love learning the fingerings of the songs so they can teach their birds."

The men looked wonderingly at each other. The flageolet was

obscene in shape, and they didn't dare imagine their wives putting their mouths and fingers on it.

"We have no time or money for such amusements."

"Why would anyone want to train a bird?"

"Canary contests," the traveler said. "You want your wives and daughters to be winners, don't you?"

The music-makers did not. But fulfilling whims had always proved more lucrative than questioning them, so they conferred among themselves. What if they could invent a mechanical alternative to the flageolet that didn't need lips, training, or breath control? Surely such an instrument would please the husbands: no wrong notes. Barrel organs with short pipes would produce a high-pitched, piccolo-like tone. If they could invent such an instrument, they could add one more pleasure to their list of exports; the traveling violin and lace salesmen who frequented the village could spread the word to their wealthy clients. Whispers attached one person to another—*an idea, we have an idea.*

"You're not lying to us?" they asked the traveler. "Canaries are popular?"

"*Absolument.* Especially across the ocean."

The men pooled their money to buy one flageolet. After securing the lousy payment in his pack and slipping his demonstration instrument back in its loop, the traveler sighed and made his way toward the next town, hoping for better luck.

The music-makers tinkered for a fortnight, each contributing spare parts, much like their wives gathering ingredients for a communal soup. The men sawed barrel organ pipes in half to produce higher pitches. They passed cups of pins around to add jaunty ornamentation to a favorite *danse.* They experimented with the size of the bellows and soon enough produced a prototype barrel organ with ten tin pipes. The men named it the serinette, for *le serin*, the canary. With the turn of a crank fitted into a notch in the back of the case, the instrument poured forth twittery versions of ten concise but well-known songs. The local terns, grebes, and wagtails gathered to listen when the music-makers tested it outdoors.

A marvel of engineering.

As close to birdsong as anyone had ever manufactured!

One more thing to make.

I.

The Mechanics of Birdsong

Chapter One
An extraordinary occurrence.

Our story begins with the grandparents of our hero, who believed their village to be as normal as any other, despite its pervasive gloom. Mireville had a tailor, a jail, a church, a baker, a doctor who did the best he could, and a midwife who did better. *Violon* scales mingled with the waftings from the baker's oven. The nuns patrolled the perimeter of the convent, keeping their eyes peeled for miracles. Gallant music-makers wooed pretty lacemakers, producing another generation.

An ascending path on the west side of the river curved upward alongside the Cocteau farm, forged its way through a small wilderness of scrub and damp loam, then passed by the Rigoniet cottage, steepening its climb. Close to the German border, where travelers often paused to take stock of how far they had come, perched the Blanchard home, adjacent to the family's serinette workshop.

Upstairs, in the bedroom, Cérine Avieux Blanchard stuffed her fist in her mouth. Between squeezes, she inspected her knuckles, watching the color come back to the spots she had bitten until waves of pressure began pounding her hips—how odd for her hips to bear so much when they had little to do with this predicament—and in mid-thought, more pressure came until an embarrassingly long wail burst from her lips, and it was this that alerted the servant girls, one of whom rushed down the hill for the midwife.

Pregnancy had turned her body into a mechanical instrument, each part with an intended purpose: producing the next generation. Cérine realized she had no choice but to continue what had begun as a painless—though also mostly pleasureless—procedure nine months ago. She pointed at her mouth, and the remaining servant girl found a cloth and gagged her. Only the worst sounds proceeded past the cloth, through the door, down the stairs, past the kitchen hearth, and into the parlor, where her husband, M. Blanchard, kept himself busy by stitching white leather that would soon become a bellows.

It was easy work, sewing, something he usually made the new apprentices do, but today it soothed him, this pouch, and the air that would soon be expelled from it. Turning the serinette's C-shaped crank inflated the bellows while the worm gear rotated a barrel studded with pins and bridges—each poised to sound notes of varying length and temperament. As the pins brushed against a suspended wooden bar of keys, those keys opened the slender passages to the pipes, letting the air transmute itself into melody.

Monsieur imagined this slender passage from downstairs in the parlor while listening to his wife's accelerating bellows from the bedroom upstairs, a clean white run of sound, which was nevertheless unnerving enough to make him prick his finger and bleed all over the leather. It took courage to listen, but he would think less of himself if he left. Soon his child would be born, on this, the very auspicious last day of 1815. With several turns of the crank, this babe will grow to father our hero, but M. has his role to play yet, and hurried songs do not linger as sweetly in the heart.

Upstairs, Cérine pressed her hands against her hips to keep them from flying apart until it struck her that the midwife would not arrive in time. She plunged deep into the currents of her body, imagining the river coursing through her veins, pumping silt and algae through her desperate heart, riding the bright crescendo out of the liquid center of her very own self.

Soon—though not fast enough to circumvent a series of shrieks, grunts, and insults to the poor servant girl (who perched by the bedside, legs firmly crossed)—the baby's head was followed by the shoulders, the shoulders by the torso, the torso by the bottom, the bottom by the feet, the feet by the spongy placenta. When she had completed the process, Cérine found herself as saddle-worn as if she had ridden a head of cabbage down a waterfall.

The servant girl slid downstairs on her stocking feet to deliver the good news.

"*Un fils*," she said. "Your wife apologizes for the ruckus."

"No matter," M. said, feeling suddenly charitable. "I shall name him Georges."

Monsieur's tolerance did not last. Want, want, want—his infant son filled the house with unfulfilled desire. Had his young wife made this ill-tempered child with another man? It seemed *that* unlike him. Even serinettes, with all their complex mechanical parts, had such a fluid, pleasing tone that the listener hardly heard the clicks of pipes opening or the subtle puffings of the bellows.

This baby, though, made all his noise at the same impossible pitch and timbre. Monsieur couldn't stand it. He held the boy at a forearm's distance and half-hoped his wife would leave the room so he could let those tiny fingers dangle into his mouth and bite them off. Give the boy something real to cry about. Yet he was not a cruel man; M. knew this about himself. Which meant, of course, that he ought to blame his wife for such barbaric fantasies.

"You welcomed him with your own screaming," he told Cérine on their third night as a family of three. "If you had been more restrained—"

"You are chastising me?"

"*Pas du tout,*" he said, "but pray tell—how would the boy know loud sounds if not from you?"

"My other lips were more involved," Cérine said, straightening her back against an unaccustomed milk weight, "and if you had borne witness to the bearing up those lips had to do, you would think me restrained. Besides, I apologized."

Whenever she cooked, Cérine used wooden spoons in her metal pots to minimize the scraping, as per her husband's instructions. She checked her kitchen broom for debris lest it eke scritching noises from the floorboards. When it was time to eat, she placed each plate on the table by easing one edge down first, then the other, avoiding a percussive thump. Surely, M. thought, with such a quiet example as a mother, their baby would soon keep to itself with an occasional shushing, perhaps a blanket held over its face as a reminder, after which he and Cérine would do the same as every family in the village: make more babies.

Except Georges kept crying. Monsieur soon removed himself to sleep beside his apprentices in the back of the workshop, isolating himself from that tinny, needy, greedy voice, which in those fragile days of early life had shifted from outraged gulps to all-out cacophony.

Cérine spent much of each day holding her son and sobbing with as little sound as possible, as did her favorite servant, who was too skinny a thing to bear so much anguish from baby and mother, their sniffles like the sound of cloth being ripped down the middle. During mealtimes, Cérine forced herself into some measure of false cheer. When M. returned to the serinette workshop, she and Georges and the servant girl recapitulated their miserable trio.

Of this state of affairs, the new father complained to his friends, who gossiped to their wives, who identified M.—despite his status as a master craftsman and owner of his own workshop—as a lout. The lacemaking ladies of the town flocked in damp quartets to Cérine's hearth to help her. They could not afford to miss work, so they secured their projects-in-progress to the tops of their sawdust-stuffed lace pillows, then tied the bobbins into a neat bundle lest one get loose and unravel all the way down the hill.

At her friends' arrival, Cérine exchanged Georges for a drizzle-soaked lace pillow, which did not scream, cry, or snot. She slid it between her knees and began twisting and crossing the bobbins, trying not to shiver from the chill. Each pillow she borrowed blocked the secret place she blamed for her son's loudness, that hideous place that kept on bleeding and cramping and forcing sobs out of her mouth that would, for the sake of domestic harmony, be better held in. It helped to concentrate on the threads, her training taking over. As the women took turns holding Georges, Cérine moved from pillow to pillow, trying to match the tension of each lacemaker's work.

"That's a colicky one, all right."

"Have you tried a spoonful of strong coffee?"

"Not coffee—Magnalle's Sedative Solution."

"Nonsense, it's gas. Give him here."

Between them, the women discovered what worked: holding Georges upright while jigging a hop-foot dance, coupled with a singsong *eh eh eh* close to his left ear, and a finger stuck between the boy's lips so he could suck.

Soon, though, the lacemakers tired of their own kindness. Getting to the Blanchard home entailed walking uphill in the rain with a heavy pillow and gathering enough green apples to share, there being never enough sun to redden them—all for the sake of a male born into more privilege than their own children. It was not Cérine's sadness that bothered them, or the baby's, but the pretense. Why couldn't she admit failure? Her husband, so quick to brag, had begotten a woeful baby—and worse, Cérine stood there with her mouth tucked up at the corners, her smile as gracious as a princess's tablecloth.

The lacemakers pushed the baby back into her arms, apologizing that they would not be able to return tomorrow, or the next day, or the day after. The lace cutter would soon return to Mireville. He would measure their pieces' progress and pay accordingly on the cutoff date. Cérine said she understood and thanked them. She closed the door with her sobbing baby on her hip. Her friends should have known her smile as a poor attempt at bravery, but they didn't.

How had life narrowed to these tiny shoulders?

Whatever it was that Georges desired, Cérine did not come equipped with it. She spent her days indoors, letting the boy suck on her breasts, her fingers, and, when she could not bear his needy lips any longer, a parsnip from the root cellar. Her favorite servant girl quit, and the other one too. Cérine put a notice in the paper, but no replacements arrived. Neighbors left parcels of food on her doorstep—but never when she was looking. Monsieur quit appearing for meals, or even a change of clothes. Dust collected. Garments wrinkled in the mending pile. Cérine grew accustomed to the sticky heat of Georges's red wet face pressed against her bodice while she tried not to ruin the stew with the salt of her own misery.

Sometimes she regarded herself in the parlor mirror to make sure she still existed. The baby had sucked the pleasing fat out of her once-plump cheeks and into his thighs. She did not bother to cut nor comb her hair; now it fanned over her shoulders like dirty sunlight. Her blue eyes seemed to be filled with smoke. Bags had formed beneath them, dark sunken cups of skin. She half-suspected tying her hair up would help her look more like herself—with it down, her face seemed short—yet she did not make the effort. Nor could she change her face, though a few times, exhausted, she yanked on her chin, willing the bones to descend.

Sleep came only when she and Georges were together, naps and overnights with Cérine's body curled around the baby so he could not roll. Her fingers grew wrinkly from his sucking, the cuticles peeling away from the nails, her breasts a place he could safely express his fury. Sometimes she stayed awake to inhale his sweet milk breath and rub the rims of his ears, and she did not regret taking this quiet for herself. She imagined streams of rain pouring out of her nipples and into his belly, finally, *finally*, satisfying him.

"LET YOUR FATHER STINK!" she shouted one exasperated afternoon, when another set of hands would have been welcome.

"I WILL NOT WASH ANOTHER STOCKING OF HIS UNTIL HE MOVES BACK IN."

Georges opened his mouth, and he burped, then rewarded her with a puckish smile.

"YOU LIKE THIS?" she asked. "WHEN I AM LOUD?"

The baby hiccupped. This was a start—startling him with her own voice—and more satisfying to both of them than the parsnip. The louder Georges became, the louder he gave his mother license to be. Her occasional humming bloomed into constant singing—both nonsense words and real songs that cheered Cérine's lonely heart. She began using metal spoons in her metal pots. She donned her boots to stomp sturdy rhythms on the stone hearth, telling herself it would be okay, her son would be okay.

"YOU ARE A FINE BABY!" Cérine shouted at him. "I LOVE YOU EVEN IF YOUR FATHER DOES NOT."

At last, on a day that seemed as far from the child's birth as the moon itself, Georges's loudness ended.

For the first few minutes, Cérine blundered about the house, sure she had misplaced something. Then she noted the wheeze of air moving through her nose. It had been there all along: her breath. She stood at the open bedroom window and filled her lungs with a moist glad gulp of the world. She felt charmed by the mechanics, how her body had kept going even when she didn't pay it any mind.

Not that she regretted motherhood, but—oh! *Silence!* Had the baby suffocated?

Cérine twisted her ankle as she pivoted away from the window. Pain streaked through her leg. She hobbled to the nursery and found Georges happily gnawing on his thumb.

Cérine had pushed that digit into his heart-shaped mouth count-less times, even sucked on it herself, trying to demonstrate its potential for comfort. Had her persistence paid off? She rubbed a finger against his hair, which was growing in blond as the dark baby fuzz rubbed off.

"FEELING BETTER?" she shouted, out of habit.

The thumb popped out. His lower lip quivered and turned down, so she scooped him up and prepared to launch into the hop-foot routine despite her throbbing ankle. Georges calmed quickly in her arms.

"I won't be loud anymore if you don't like it," she told him.

He grinned. She had waited four months for this: a quiet, happy baby, the kind all the other village women took for granted. That day Georges took six naps. He only fussed from hunger and needing his cloth changed. He giggled before spitting up and after spitting up. Cérine's body prickled with gratitude. Perhaps she would like motherhood after all.

One good day—and a six-hour stretch of sleep—led to another. Cérine caught up on laundry. She spent the next three afternoons resting her ankle, still a bit swollen, on M.'s bed pillow, which he hadn't bothered to take with him. This routine pleased her, especially when she left bits of dirt and pulverized leaves on the surface where, as soon as she told him of their son's recovery, her husband would once again rest his head. She would wash it before he came home—of course she would.

A week went by. She knew she should fetch her husband, but she didn't need him around now that Georges had become so companionable. She began tying her hair up. Her cheeks began filling back out as she took the time to feed herself better. Another week passed, then another. Her ankle healed, though the constant rain made it ache.

"Do you remember your father?" she asked the baby, who cooed. Monsieur had been absent for three whole months, an eternity of sobbing and cuddling. She decided she must fetch her husband. Today. Before she changed her mind.

With Georges napping in his cradle, Cérine changed into her best dress, pinched her cheeks for color, added a bonnet for the rain, checked the baby one more time, and proceeded to leave the house. She scurried along the short muddy path—spring showers in Mireville being slightly wetter than summer, fall, and winter ones—to the serinette workshop next door. She entered her husband's domain without knocking and started down the center aisle of workbenches. The apprentices' heads bobbed at the disturbance, and three concerned young men rushed over to block her way. She remembered, suddenly, that she had not washed M.'s pillow. No matter. She would once again sleep beside these boys' master, while they slept on their pallets and dreamed of the future.

"Fetch my husband," she commanded them. When they didn't respond, she added, "*Maintenant*," at which point one rushed off while the other two stood guard. She wondered what M. had told his apprentices when he moved in with them. Had he complained of the child? Of her? Had he asked one of them to give up his pillow?

Monsieur took his time responding to her summons. He bent over apprentices' workbenches, suggesting tweaks, offering an exaggerated laugh here, a punch on the shoulder there. Perhaps this show was for her benefit? Or perhaps it was for the apprentices, a reminder that he ruled here and would not be rushed, especially not by his wife. When her husband finally approached, Cérine nearly laughed to see the bigness of his pores. He had a brown stain on his shirt collar. She had never liked his nose. Now it protruded over an untrimmed beard like a warning sign—of what, she would surely find out.

"Georges has quit crying," she reported.

In a swell of affection that surprised both of them, M. grabbed his wife's hand and let her lead him back to the kitchen. His house existed for him, it belonged to him, its floorboards ready to absorb his weight, its walls meant to amplify his decisions, its windows to frame views he might find pleasing. How stuffy its air seemed, how unfamiliar. Apple mush and fried meats and an overlay of sour milk. Had she forgotten to air it out once a week?

Cérine pointed up the stairs, wordless, though she wanted to say, "Don't you dare wake him."

Monsieur trudged up the stairs and stopped at the transom of the nursery. He balanced there, hands on the doorframe, lifting one foot, then the other, an exercise he performed to clear his head after staring at serinette parts for too long. Better go on, then. He ventured into the room and peered over the plain wood sides of the cradle to find not the red-faced blast of fury he remembered but a small child with uneven tufts of blond hair and blue eyes much too big for his face. He would grow into himself—and those ears—in time.

"Georges," M. whispered.

The boy had a tiny nose, high cheekbones, and the characteristic blond Blanchard ringlets. Monsieur's locks, once a brilliant gold, had turned a premature gray. In eyeing his son's hair, he suffered a pang of jealousy. The boy would grow strong and replace him. Until this moment, he had not thought much of death, but here it was, in his own house: a promise that the future would parade forward without him.

He reached into the cradle and lifted Georges, pulling him tight against his stomach in the horizontal position babies favored, just as Cérine joined them. The boy opened his eyes, fluttering tiny eyelashes. His little mouth turned to a tiny heart that parted in the middle until an ill-tempered chord of frustration flew through the opening and struck M. deep in his chest. He tried to hand the boy to his wife, but Cérine crossed her arms over her bodice and would not take him.

"He prefers a vertical hold," she said.

Ah, of course. Nothing to cry about! They did not know each other yet. Monsieur took a deep breath and pulled his son upright, smashing him tight to his torso with one hand on his head and the other supporting his rear. The baby reached out and tweaked his nose with obvious pleasure. Monsieur gasped from the unexpected violence. It would serve the boy right if he dropped him—but dropped babies often grew up to be defective, dim-witted adults, and he couldn't risk that with his firstborn.

"You don't have to support his neck anymore," Cérine counseled. "He's four months old."

He adjusted again, this time letting his son recline against his forearm. Georges emitted a quiet string of nonsense syllables, steady beats of *bah* and *dah*. His chubby legs dangled and kicked. The boy would soon realize his place in the world: he was a future master craftsman.

Monsieur decided to introduce his child to the music-making men in the village that very afternoon. Cérine seized the baby to bonnet him. This was harder than she expected, since his ears had to be pinned back in order for the hat to fit, but she accomplished the matter nonetheless.

For weeks, she had needed to put Georges in his cradle or on the floor to get anything done. Recently she had taken to knotting a length of old curtains to tie him against her chest. Soon he would be able to crawl away—and just in time, another set of hands had presented itself. Cérine handed the baby back to her husband while she donned her cloak and laced her boots.

The couple set off for the village, M. making conversation about a ladies' society in Bedfordshire, New Hampshire, which had decided to raise and song-train canaries as a fundraiser for a new town hall. They had put in an order for forty serinettes. As they passed the Rigoniets' house, Monsieur passed the baby back to his wife, his arms already starting to ache.

Heat flamed through Cérine, sparking up and down her arms, welling in her belly with a desperation that intoxicated her. Touching her husband's forearms, even accidentally, had sprung desire free from the dark corner where she kept it hidden. This reawakening did not belong to her husband or their child. It was hers; a secret. Monsieur would come to bed tonight. She would have to remember to turn his pillow over because of the foot dirt. Maybe this time, she would be brave enough to whisper that he should touch her *here*, and *here*, and *there*.

As they descended the steep path, a curious line opened in the sky over their heads, snipping the gray clouds apart with the efficiency of a practiced seamstress. Monsieur charged downhill, eager to meet the praise and good-natured back slaps waiting for him. He paid no mind to the brilliant blue seam overhead or the sun streaming through the new opening.

Cérine paused to readjust Georges's bonnet; his ears had popped out. She marveled at the sudden vividness of each rock and tree, how each leafstalk leaned toward the new light, shaking off crystalline droplets with help from a friendly breeze. The heat searing her insides now warmed her shoulders and the rounded tips of her ears. She had expected adulthood to be like this—full of warmth and wonder, like the stars patting her on the head. She looked up and suddenly understood: sun! It blazed with an ineluctable joy. She gasped and pointed the sky out to her baby, who murmured his approval.

Cérine was glad her husband had rushed forward; this miracle belonged to her and Georges. She kept her own pace, chatting excitedly with the boy, marveling as they passed the Niçoises' and the Cocteau place. The gray continued to pull apart, letting the blue expand. The strange overhead choreography paused whenever the mother and child stopped to look around, and this became a game. She stopped, and the sky stopped above her head. Georges wiggled in her arms with delight. Eventually they arrived in the heart of the village, the cobbled town square, where M. stood checking his pocket watch.

"What kept you?" he asked.

"Everything's slower with a baby." Cérine grinned, too dazzled to mind her husband's attitude. She tilted her face toward the spectacular show overhead, marveling in the brisk and sudden brightness, the sting of unexpected light. She blinked back tears and focused on the irascible tufts of cloud floating across the German border. More dark clumps shouldered their way to neighboring Ambaville, while the new blue seam spread wider than a bolt of cloth—wider than five bolts—broader than the river, than fifty rivers. Gray gave way to blue with an ebullient gold centerpiece. It seemed impossible to call such resplendence *sun*, and yet incontrovertible proof held court above her, pressing warmth onto her shoulders. Cérine couldn't help it; she stared boldly up at the orb itself, holding its gaze, for if this experience of brightness was all she'd ever have, she didn't want to waste a moment.

Monsieur's mouth dropped open. He had a clear-headed view of the situation. Georges would be all right now—his colic had passed—and look! Here was the sun to prove it.

"Our son moved the clouds," he mused aloud. "It's a miracle!"

Cérine couldn't win her staring contest with the sky. A stabbing headache came with the light. She closed her eyes and rubbed them, wanting to argue with her obtuse husband. *Really—our four-month-old?* The whole village had yearned for the sun for years. The nuns prayed for it twice a day. Why would the sky listen to a baby?

Georges squinted and fussed and rubbed his eyes at this change in condition. He didn't even like the brightness! Cérine tugged his bonnet lower and soothed him with back rubs. She didn't dare correct her husband in public, though, and so his version of the story spread. Villagers out on errands called to each other. Lacemakers and music-makers, hearing the ruckus, ran outside to gawp. The three Blanchards stood in the center of the town square, dazzled by light, the baby tucking himself against his mother's chest. Everyone clustered around them. Adults peeked over each other's shoulders at their own leggy shadows. Little ones blinked and begged to be carried back indoors. And word of the miracle spread.

"The Blanchard baby quit crying."

"He moved the clouds."

"Cheered up the sky!"

Chapter Two
Georges makes a mistake.

The sun had never appeared in April, the most water-logged month in Mireville's oversaturated year, until Georges Blanchard quit crying, or so the story went. The newspaper editor coined the nickname *Sun-Bringer*. Villagers swore on the record that the sky had split directly above the baby.

"A coincidence."

"No, the baby's bewitched."

"Let's not complain—look at the sun."

Monsieur accepted all their praise and gifts on behalf of his family; the villagers thanked him for fathering such an extraordinary child.

Georges grew like the other sons of music-makers: with the dense efficiency of the boxwood tree. Boxwood was a favorite for violin pegs. Monsieur used it to build worm gears, which drove the air into the bellows of his serinettes. All but the oddest boys grew like boxwood: straight up, straight out. Within the first year, Georges's thighs lost their chub. His knees straightened when he began toddling.

And oh! The weather! It took a full cycle of seasons for Mirevillians to understand how much bounty that little boy's silence had earned them.

At last, apples turned fully red. Vines stretched and yawned and wrapped themselves around whatever they could reach. Berries raised their sugary heads and plumped. Corn tasseled and silked. Mint planted its roots in many beds. Men waited in line at the tailor to get waistcoat seams snipped and restitched, allowing their shoulders the freedom to straighten since they no longer needed to huddle against the constant gloom. Children freckled—even between their toes where their mothers used to find green fungus. Monsieur Papineau began carrying around a glass vial of cinnamon and sugar to dust vine-cooked apples. Work slowed for a few months as everyone flocked outdoors, but soon sunburns encouraged a resurgence of indoor productivity.

Mireville, by Georges's one-year birthday, had thoroughly dried out. Occasionally it snowed or rained, or a fog rolled through the village square, but even the wettest and coldest days held some measure of brightness. By two, Georges grabbed and pulled and hit. At three, he was allowed to walk the path from kitchen to serinette workshop, where he wagged his pointer finger in apprentices' faces.

"Do it," he said.

"Fix it," he said.

"Tune it," he said.

"You heard the boy," M. would tell whichever apprentice had received a command from the tot. "Do it, fix it, tune it."

Cérine's lacemaker friends began visiting again, apologizing for abandoning her. She didn't complain when they called Georges the Sun-Bringer, but she did wonder about the miracle. *Why would a baby change the sky?* Wouldn't it make more sense that *she* had done it—rejoicing that his colic had subsided? She now delighted in braiding her locks and affixing false side curls made out of her mother's hair, and she fixed lunchtime picnics for herself and Georges once a week.

As was expected of all music-makers' wives, Cérine raised Georges to stifle skinned-knee yelps and to lift his chair away from the table, lest the scuffs trigger his father's temper. Silence was sacred—not for women or children to break. But sometimes she hummed under her breath, or dropped a knife on the stone hearth, or smashed a plate just so she could pick the pieces up and throw them down again, allowing herself a lingering measure of joy at each small thud and crack.

If one of her friends labeled these acts a rebellion against the institution of marriage, against the silence Mireville music-makers expected of their wives, Cérine would deny it (crash), refute it (clang), and shoo her from the kitchen (slam).

Had Georges Blanchard been born a girl, the clouds' disappearance surely would have been attributed to a strange wind or a celestial hiccup. But he was a boy—and the only child of a master craftsman. The sun rested on his shoulders.

So did blame for the frequency of sunburns. Noses peeled. Moles grew fat on necks and arms and the backs of farm boys who took their shirts off. The river shallowed despite occasional rainshowers. Everyone ate meat and bread for dinner, little else. Those who remembered told stories of how fat drops once plinked on their cheeks, plunked on their sleeves, and made sieves of their socks.

Despite their efforts over the next five years, Cérine did not become pregnant with a second child. Monsieur suspected their firstborn of being so exceptional that all the nutrients in the womb-soil had been depleted. He abhorred wasted effort, so he quit his conjugal attentions, which pleased Cérine. She liked her husband best when he stayed in his own bed, a broom handle's length away, so she could nudge him with the bristles if he snored.

At six, Georges had high cheekbones and what his mother could only term a weak chin, and this she loved most, because it was least like her husband. (Monsieur wouldn't have tolerated something so puny on his own face.) The boy survived his childhood at a meandering *lento* pace, his eyebrows often lifted with a sense of expectation that he might split the earth or make the river boil if he refused a chore or argued with his mother. Once little Rina Rigoniet slapped him, trying to make the clouds come back. Georges was more stunned than angry, not to mention disappointed when nothing happened. Rina's braids swung with outrage.

At twelve, after completing his schooling in the village, Georges joined the serinette workshop, his father's domain. Amid the noise of hammerings and the twitterings of half-finished birdsong, he learned the family art as his adolescent body continued to sprout. His arms shot out like branches in need of a trim, and patches of ill-tempered whiskers appeared on his jawline, his chest, his knuckles, and even his knobby toe joints.

By fourteen, Georges had tired of his nickname and wished to be normal—or at least to have earned his reputation by actually *doing* something. It frustrated him to be famous for something he didn't remember. Once, after church, he made the mistake of mentioning the burden of the sky to Geneviève Rappatout, an older girl with wavy sandy hair that hadn't quite made up its mind to be curly.

"You have the privilege of being a firstborn son in a successful family," she told him. "There are worse fates."

"But the drought," Georges insisted. "And the lack of fresh vegetables. It's all my fault."

He imagined, in pressing his case, that Geneviève would appreciate the tragic burden and want to comfort him. Reassure him. Perhaps even take his elbow and lean in closer.

Instead, she let out an ungirlish snort, her shoulders quaking with mirth, her new breasts bouncing beneath her corset. "I think it's the soil's fault, not yours."

Georges didn't understand. All the other villagers considered him culpable for the change in weather, as if the sun were a flaw in his character.

"Or the vegetables. Conditions changed, but the carrots and onions and beans haven't yet adapted," Geneviève added.

Georges nodded but could not help listing more losses—leeks and rutabagas, peas and lettuce—until Geneviève made a hurried excuse to turn away and find her parents. He stared after her, thinking about what she had said. He and the other villagers had adjusted to the sun, living brighter lives, so why not carrots and beets? He hadn't thought of it that way before.

Meanwhile the enterprising farmers of nearby Ambaville carted their crops six miles down the road to sell in Mireville. A sun-ripened apple out of season, once a prize, could be traded for a mere half carrot. Monsieur Papineau still carried cinnamon in his pocket, but he rarely bothered to pull it out. He had gotten bored of vine-cooked apples. Only the residents in the vermillion-roofed houses by the river could afford chard, spinach, parsnips. Sometimes a local family who missed the taste of beets trekked up the hill to rap on the Blanchard door, begging Georges to return the clouds.

He told them, "I'm sorry. I don't know how. Maybe you should ask the beets."

Monsieur refused to cede control of the workshop when Georges turned eighteen, then nineteen, then twenty. His father's pronouncements came on the last day of each year—Georges's birthday—and thus, the young man carried his relief into the new year. His mother managed the kitchen and the servants. His father ran the workshop. Georges preferred tinkering with new songs and memorizing the apprentices' birthdays so they would feel appreciated. He didn't feel ready to become a leader.

All the serinetters touched the canary illustration on the workshop wall for luck each morning, including Georges, who followed that ritual with more routines: checking the supply of crank shafts, sorting pins and bridges, and keeping his workbench dusted.

By twenty-one, Georges's face had filled out and his belly had plumped: the marks of prosperity. He kept his ringlets chin-length to disguise his ears, which were still too big for the rest of his face. He shaved every day. His parents had provided him with food, lodging, and a solid future. The only thing he needed now was a wife.

But the local girls, more interested in boys who knew how to use their capes and words, refused to be courted by a man responsible for the weather. When their mothers urged them to reconsider, the girls complained:

"Would our firstborn move the moon?"

"Erase the stars?"

"Raise the dead?"

Whenever threads of these speculations wound around the bobbins of his ears, Georges pretended not to notice. The apprentices acted aloof with him too, though, and this was a harder situation to ignore. Oh, they said hello all right, and spoke of the abundance of limewood or the benefit of adding gum arabic to a varnish, but never of the weather—never to him! It felt quite unfair. Nobody had proof that his lungs had caused this drought. He imagined his mother must have spread the story. His father didn't think him capable of running the workshop, let alone performing miracles.

"I do not wish to be the Sun-Bringer anymore," Georges told her one day. "I wish to be married."

"It only takes one girl," Cérine said.

Georges knew how to pin an étude on a cylinder, and how to cut tin pipes without getting metal shavings stuck in his skin, but he didn't know how to tell if a girl fancied him. He had an interest of his own, though. Geneviève Rappatout knew her way around a workshop; her uncle was one of the most famous luthiers in town. She knew what to do with boxwood, *certainement*. In fact, several boys claimed she had whittled and sanded a leftover piece into a *pénis*. The thought excited Georges. A quiet girl wishing for pleasure. Not just wishing—but creating it for herself! That Sunday after church, he spied Geneviève leaning against the outside wall of the herbalist's garden. Georges stationed himself a respectable distance away to fidget with a crank he had stashed in his pocket. He liked that she had challenged the story about his colic and the cloud-moving. Perhaps she wouldn't mind if they had children who erased the stars.

It took the rest of the week for Georges to find the courage to mention her to his mother, and when he did, Cérine gave an exaggerated sniff. She had always thought of Geneviève as too brash, but other women in the village had warned her: the more she protested an early romantic attachment, the longer it would linger. She was glad when M. blustered into the kitchen, wearing his church clothes.

"It's time to go," Cérine said. "We can discuss this later."

After church, the Blanchards followed the other congregants into the town square, where they greeted each other with kisses on the cheeks and charming hand squeezes. Georges broke away from his parents so he could consider saying hello to Geneviève. This amounted to leaning against the bakery wall twelve paces away as she twirled her hair for an eager cluster of barrel-organ makers. Geneviève looked left and then right and then left, an imprecise metronome, responding to each admirer in turn. Georges, uncertain whether to join them, swirled fallen leaves with his foot—shades of apricot, persimmon, and garnet, all well-toasted.

"Sun-Bringer." A luthier's son interrupted his ruminations with a merry wave. "Have you tried the grapeseed oil M. Pignon has been selling? It might be useful to lubricate crank shafts."

Geneviève stopped talking. She frowned. *Had she heard?*

Georges's anger snapped like a too-taut bowstring. "DON'T CALL ME SUN-BRINGER!"

The young men courting Geneviève chimed in.

"You've never minded before."

"My father remembers the seam of blue."

"It's only a story my mother made up," Georges said. "There's no proof it was I who moved the clouds."

"See? Even his mother says it happened!"

Georges kicked at the fallen leaves. He was not extraordinary. He wasn't even special—at least, not the way they thought. Short of calling the other boys *imbéciles*, how could he make his point? Then he had an excellent notion.

"My mother," he announced, with a grand flourish of his hand to attract his potential sweetheart's attention, "is a liar."

Genéviève's mouth dropped open. The nearby luthiers gasped, clutched their hearts, and stepped back in concert, loosening the circle that had formed around Georges. At their stricken expressions, he pressed his lips together and wondered, *What have I done?* He loved his mother, he did. She could have let him wail through his colicky days alone, abandoning him between wilted rows of cabbage in the back garden, slug trails on his arms. He reached for the crank in his pocket and spun it backward with his other hand, trying to reverse the course of his words.

The boys told their fathers and uncles and older brothers what Georges had said. The bit of gossip threaded its way through the crowd, one cottony whisper at a time. The music-makers thought nothing of complaining to their wives of a poorly mended sleeve, but they would never insult their mothers. They wiped their eyes, either from the brightness or from trying to see Georges as he really was: a young man who called his mother a liar. One by one, the boys and their fathers and grandfathers turned their backs on Georges and walked away, crunching leaves and pulling their conversations along like kites.

The lacemakers picked up the thread of news from Genéviève. Her sisters and friends told their friends and aunts, the news flashing between tight-knit rings of women, until it reached Cérine, whose mouth crumpled as if a string had drawn it closed. Her friends murmured reassurances. They took turns touching her on the back, the arm, the shoulder.

"Don't listen to him."

"He didn't mean it."

"Perhaps some other Georges said it?"

Cérine and Georges had fused their selves together in those relentless years of childhood. She could still see the baby in him; he continued to have a fondness for parsnips and bought one for himself per month from the Ambaville farmers as another child might save up for candy. Had Georges forgotten how he and his mother used to bang metal spoons on pots, terrified that M. might barge in and catch them? She knew her son ought to grow like boxwood in the mold of his father—and he had, he had!—but she had hoped to provide a kinder counterpoint to M.'s harsh ways. And until this too-public moment, Cérine believed she had succeeded. Georges fit in with his peers, but he did not taunt or tease. He had learned his father's harsh way of issuing orders as a toddler but soon outgrew it. Yet now—this winsome son of hers had called her a liar. All because she did not approve of Genéviève Rappatout.

Cérine excused herself from her friends and turned toward home. She heard Mme. Papineau calling after her, asking if she was all right.

How could she be?

Georges plopped down in the very place where Genéviève had been standing before she found herself in possession of such excellent gossip. He traced circles in the dirt where her feet had been, pressing his forehead against his bent knee. In the workshop, M. Blanchard and his apprentices built serinettes *sans variation*. A part was good or not good. This part needed to be thrown out and remade, but Georges did not know how.

When M. finally spotted him and urged the young man to come along straightaway, to apologize to his mother, he didn't budge.

"She will forgive you," M. said, "but we must go home to her immediately."

Genéviève Rappatout won't forgive me, Georges thought, tracing another circle, this one faster, and looping into another one, and then another. *She loves her mother.*

By the time he and his father made it up the hill, Cérine had locked herself inside the master bedroom.

"*Chérie*," M. said through the door, "Georges wants to apologize."

Silence from the room.

That night M. slept fitfully, imagining his wife red-faced and colicky, her hair matted from rolling back and forth on the small hard bed.

Georges visited the closed door twenty-seven times over the next few days, reporting on the chores he had completed and renewing his apologies, marking each one with a scratch in the wood of his desk so he could prove his chagrin when she finally emerged. He had meant to lift the Sun-Bringer yoke off his own reddened neck, not to make Maman sick with—what, grief? In one of her British novels, a servant girl died from being called a terrible cook. How had he not recalled this story before calling his mother a liar?

When he mentioned his concern at dinnertime, M. replied, "If she were going to die from you, your colic would have killed her."

Georges burst into tears and fled the table, which might have soothed Cérine—his vulnerability an echo of his babyhood—had she been awake to hear him.

❋ ❋ ❋

When M. couldn't coax his wife out of their bedroom, he left food outside her door, mostly seeds and bread, as if she had turned into a bird. He tried triggering the lock mechanism with a straight pin but that came to naught. He had no wish to bash down the door with an axe, for he had a temperamental back and did not like to lift things over his head. By the third day of his wife's reclusivity, he admitted to himself that he had failed to cheer her. *Ça suffit.* He would not wait around feeling inadequate. Monsieur sent Georges to his room to pack.

"Where are we going?" Georges asked.

"Away," M. said.

"What if Maman comes out and finds us gone?"

"That's what she deserves," M. said. At the horrified glance from his son, he amended: "Some time alone. Some privacy."

❋ ❋ ❋

Our story must cycle through one more rotation of the barrel before Georges settles into the background and lets his son—our hero—take over.

To know a place, one must leave it. Georges consoled himself with this thought as the jostling of the carriage made his buttocks sore and his spirits sorer. October meant an unexpected dourness in the lands beyond the charmed, light-soaked village. The leaves did not fall in cheery bursts of color. They dripped themselves to the ground in soggy shades of hazel, umber, and ginger. He shivered constantly. How Georges missed the bright side, the gloom-free idyll, his real life. He had never known the discomfort of his coat getting soaked without having the sun bake it dry within a few minutes, nor the particular squidging of a wet sock within a flooded shoe. He missed his bed. He missed the sun on his neck. He missed his mother.

Two days into the journey, M. explained why he had stacked and secured fifteen brand-new serinettes in the back of the carriage. They were headed to the port of Le Havre, where the biggest oceangoing ships docked between trips to the Americas. Usually M. hired a traveling salesman to accompany his beloved instruments all the way to New York City, whereupon the local merchants would purchase them to resell to wealthy women in New England, at which point the salesman would make the trip back to Mireville with enough money to buy more wood, crank shafts, and the occasional treat of a carrot or parsnip.

This time, M. told his son, instead of having a salesman take the new instruments to New York, the Blanchards would go together. Georges would learn how to study the departure timetables, pay fees, and sign the proper *billets* of transport to take the serinettes to their new homes. Alongside the instruments, father and son would float away to the New World, then return with money in their pockets and perhaps a story or two to share.

"Someday, overseeing the distribution of our instruments will be your responsibility," M. added. "You cannot manage a man's journey if you don't know what it's like to travel there yourself."

"But not by myself yet, *ça va*?" Georges said. "I am not ready."

"And I am not ready to be unnecessary," M. agreed. "That's why we'll go together this time."

His father didn't complain about the dreary conditions, which gave Georges no license to do so, although he couldn't help voicing an occasional observation. He allowed himself one per hour. His back itched. Rain flowed down the back of his collar and soaked into his undershirt. His left buttock turned tingly. A piece of dirt flew into his eye. A piece of dirt flew into his other eye. Monsieur allowed his son short respites inside the carriage, amid the stacks of serinettes, but these never lasted long enough to dry his clothes thoroughly.

By the time they arrived in Le Havre, M. had decided he couldn't bear the relentless tempo of Georges's grievances any longer, let alone all the complaints sure to be issued during an ocean crossing. Monsieur left his son gape-faced to tend the carriage at the curb for an hour until he returned. Georges amused himself by eyeing different carriages, hats, and the occasional loose hound.

Monsieur returned with a just-purchased *billet* along with a sack of cooking supplies and a bedroll he hoped didn't harbor mites. "Georges," he announced. "I'm not going with you." He thrust the ticket toward his son.

The trees picked up a gust and played their leaves into a lingering and haunting symphony, and there stood Georges, trembling, with a piece of paper that meant his father was really, really angry. Twenty-one, old enough to be married—and banished.

"I cannot carry so many instruments!" he protested. "I only have two arms."

Monsieur sighed. "Fine. I'll hire someone else to do it."

Georges couldn't believe he had so easily convinced his father not to send him after all. He let out a deep, relieved breath, only to realize his error when M. did not take back the ticket but instead handed over another piece of paper, this one labeled *Mrs. Delia Dumphries Stanton*, with an address in Pleasant Hill, New York.

"You'll carry just the one, then. It shouldn't be too taxing. Mrs. Stanton is one of our best clients," M. said. "Visit her operation, ask questions about her needs and preferences, and bring the answers back to us."

Georges was still being sent away, just with less responsibility. Somehow, this made him feel even worse.

"I don't want to go." Georges heard the whine in his voice but didn't bother to correct it. "Please, Father."

"I already wrote to Mrs. Stanton from Paris. She's expecting us both, but she'll make do with you."

Monsieur handed over the best serinette of the lot: a gift for the lady of the house. Georges wrapped his arms around the small wooden box, hugging it against his damp chest. He thought of Geneviève. Of Maman. Of the certainty of the weather back home: sun, with 100% chance of more sun. Traveling this far had been enough of an adventure. He wanted to go back.

Instead he climbed the gangplank. At the top he looked back to wave goodbye, but his father had already turned to go home.

Chapter Three
Whereupon boy meets birds.

*G*eorges crossed the ocean in a second-class cabin, plagued by dreams of water draining from a hole in the wash-basin. He secured the serinette and the suitcase beneath his bunk, then unfurled his bedroll and climbed in. The ship pitched to the rhythm of his sorry heart: *Maman, Maman.*

Monsieur had booked him a ticket not because he called his mother a liar, but because he'd moaned about the rain—*like a girl*, Papa had scolded when they hugged goodbye. Perhaps if Georges had kept his disappointment to one comment every two hours, Papa would have let him return home. But it was too late. He had been set adrift.

At last Georges had ample justification for his complaints, but he did not have the oomph to make them, nor anyone to listen. He had never conversed with strangers: everyone in Mireville knew each other's great-grandfathers' middle names. On the ship, Georges took one meal per day in the single men's dining room. Occasionally he went for a promenade on the deck. When others smiled at him, he did his best to return the kindness, though he wanted to grab their lapels, shake them, and shout, "ISN'T THIS WRETCHED?"

If Georges had not tried to change his reputation to please Geneviève Rappatout, he would be at home now. At least here—rolling around mid-ocean—nobody knew to call him the Sun-Bringer.

The fact that Mrs. Alastair Stanton insisted her given name, Delia Dumphries, be calligraphed on her calling cards was only one of the things her neighbors held against her.

The other reasons included, but weren't limited to, the following: She had unkempt fingernails and refused to wear gloves. She went for walks unaccompanied. She contained her hair so poorly that bits of it stuck to her lips when she greeted other women. Occasionally she left the house too soon after showering, and this led to accusations of her having ruined a Gilbert Stuart portrait hanging in the Hamden family's front hall. The misunderstanding occurred due to an ill-timed shake of her damp locks, attested to by the Hamdens' cook; more likely, the spots had been inflicted by a careless housemaid, the cook herself, or the sons, known for their uncouth spittery. Still, the women welcomed Delia into their least-formal parlors or, if it could not be avoided, the formal parlor—after its best decorations had been stashed behind the curtains.

The women of Pleasant Hill, New York, also held Delia's business against her. Her husband owned a coal mine in Pennsylvania, so she did not need to work. Yet she had the gall to raise prize-winning canaries, not bothering to hide behind her husband's name. The ladies who fretted over the condition of her hands and hair paid her prices, though, because they wanted to win a canary contest. Every community in upstate New York held at least one per year. Women toted cages full of their favorite

London Fancys, Yorkshire Spangles, and Norwich Yellows to the town hall or the garden club or the school, whereupon men with monocles would judge them on color, crest, beak, wingspan, height, and Delia's specialty: voice. She reserved her very best specimens for women who hadn't won in the past three years. It only seemed fair to distribute the luck.

Not only did Delia select which birds would learn which songs, she often cranked the serinette herself, unlike women hobbyists who hired male servants to exert themselves. She purchased several instruments from the Blanchard workshop every year, not because she longed for the latest tunes but because she had the money. If the bellows seam failed, or a few pins fell off the limewood barrel, she could replace the instrument with a fresh model. Besides, she liked new possessions. They entertained her.

New York City surprised Georges with its frenetic energy. It was snowing and blowing when he arrived, and almost immediately, he couldn't wait to leave. He hired a small carriage with a canvas top to take him to Mrs. Delia Dumphries Stanton. Three hours later, the coachman halted in front of a mansion, a few lengths in advance of a porte cochère instead of beneath it. Fine—Georges would get his curls snowed on *again*. The coachman hopped out and gazed upwards, his mouth dropping open. Georges adjusted his boots, picked up the serinette he had brought, and hopped out. Above the porte cochère, like a tower perched atop a bridge, soared a structure made of glass. The walls reflected the land— the pebbled drive, the gardens—but also contained a strange and vibratory energy, a streaky mix of sunset colors, as if an invisible giant had leaned down from the sky to shake them.

"What is this place?" he asked.

"I have no idea, sir," the coachman said.

"All right—you'd better wait while I knock."

When a servant answered, Georges introduced himself.

"Are you here for the man of the house or the woman?"

"The woman."

"She's unavailable, but you may wait."

Georges dismissed the carriage, sure that another could be found to escort him to a nearby rooming house after his visit—or perhaps he could save his father's money and walk, if it ever stopped snowing. The servant installed him in a fine parlor with high ceilings, wainscoting, and golden striped wallpaper. A girl brought him a small brass platter of powdered tea cakes that put him in mind of old wigs. Georges believed his family to be wealthy, and they were by village standards. But this? He had never imagined such luxury.

After he finished the cakes, Georges spit on his palms to loosen the powder and rubbed the resulting paste onto his trousers. This rudimentary cleaning satisfied him, so he opened the lid on the serinette, pulled out its brass C-shaped crank, and inserted the pinned end into the walnut shell of the box, making sure it engaged.

Every serinette featured ten tunes, each a maximum of two minutes in length, but most were closer to ninety seconds. At the conclusion of the first song, Georges shifted the barrel over by one place to play the next one. Home in a box—the sound of it, the smell of it, the sense of purpose found in handling the instrument he had learned to make from his father, who had learned from *his* father, who believed in luck. When he tired of cranking after the sixth tune, Georges slumped on the settee, tipped his head back, and napped.

He woke groggy, with an aching neck, when the *madame* of the house appeared in a plain brown traveling cloak, snowflakes dotting her long brown hair. She asked him to call her Delia. She had rouged cheeks and thin eyebrows that connected above her nose, and she appeared to be around his mother's age. This reassured him.

"You brought a serinette?" she asked.

Georges stood, then rubbed his eyes and smiled. "My father sent it with me. He was, ah, unable to come himself."

"You must be Georges Blanchard, then." Delia took the instrument from him, lifted the lid, and inspected the fittings and the bellows. She nodded, pleased, and set the box on a side table before fiddling with the ribbons of her cloak to shuck it. A servant stepped out of the shadows to grab it.

"My father said you could show me a canary," he said.

Delia motioned for him to follow. He trailed her to the foyer. She turned down a sumptuous hall and mounted a dark set of stairs. On the second landing, she proceeded down another corridor. Georges wondered what Geneviève Rappatout would think of this house. She had probably never imagined something so grand. By the time he turned the corner and caught up, Delia stood poised with a hand on her hip in front of an unlikely structure—more tower than room, constructed of soldered panes of glass with one sturdy brick side to the south. Even the ceiling was glass. Monsieur had made a few prototype serinette cases with glass tops, but they broke too easily in transit. And this woman had made a whole building of glass! Georges rested his palm against one of the panes and found it slightly warm.

"The downstairs hallway, the men's smoking parlor, and the porte cochère form the floor," Delia explained, which, as far as explanations went, merely created more mystery. She fiddled with the long string around her neck, procuring a key.

"Is it safe?" Georges asked. "What about high winds?"

"The panes are reinforced." Delia inserted the key into the lock, which was set in a wooden rectangle in the mostly glass door.

A pungent blast of humid air greeted Georges's nostrils, and he sneezed.

"Quickly, go in," she said.

She followed him and used a padlock to secure the door from the inside, then left the two keys to bob on a string that dangled between her bosoms. A whapping blur of wings frothed the sour, musty air. Georges shut his eyes. He took a few reluctant breaths, wondering whether it would be impolite to ask Delia to let him out. He did not belong in this glass cage in Pleasant Hill, New York, with snow swirling outside. He belonged at home. With his mother.

After a few more breaths, he opened his eyes to birds in brilliant hues of yellow, green, white, and flabbergasting orange. They flew in compact bursts around the room in response to the interruption. Some settled on Delia's shoulders and outstretched arms, cocking their heads and tweeting. Others sang to their own reflections in mirrors hung from the potted trees, which were strung with a curious sort of greenery that stretched from treetop to treetop and along the wooden beams that helped support the structure.

"Canaries?"

Delia confirmed this. "Surely they have aviaries in France."

Mireville villagers produced beautiful things, but they did not keep them. Each piece represented work, work, work. Not beauty; deadlines. Not pleasure; money. In the aviary, though, Georges found himself surrounded by beauty for the sake of beauty. A hundred by a hundred chirps bounced around inside the glass. This music could not be boxed or slowed down or sped up by a wrist. The accidentals could not be adjusted by moving a pin.

Georges cupped his ears to draw the full-throated chaos close, a mash of melodies, all the *chirrupping* and *seet-seet-seeting*, the sounds of wings reminding him of air being pushed in and out of a bellows. The birds were no more aware of their remarkableness than a slug of the luminescence of its trail. They sang not for him, or for Delia, but for themselves.

A frosted droplet landed on his cheek and he paid it no mind. His breathing had eased. What wonders this woman kept.

"You like them." Delia reached over and pinched the droplet off his cheek.

He touched where her fingers had landed. "Very much."

Delia explained that she had designed the aviary with an architect—"no help from my husband," she added. The roof featured tin lined with felt, so the rain wouldn't pound too loudly. Brick towers, each about as wide as a fireplace, framed the corners. Wooden side beams ran between every six panes of glass, and iron bars—called *cames*—held the panes together like the bits of an enormous stained-glass window, but clear, so the birds could enjoy the view. The fat lines of green that draped from the wooden supports and into the tops of the smaller trees were not vines at all but crochet work done by servants. This was what he and the coachman had stared up at when they arrived, such magnificence that they couldn't understand it from the ground. Here—amid the pleasure—Georges felt guilty that he hadn't asked the coachman to come inside and experience this too.

The southern wall, all brick, offered stability in case of fierce windstorms, Delia explained. The fireplace in the men's smoking parlor below heated the bricks, pumping extra warmth into the breasts of the tiny-feathered beasts whose lights might otherwise be snuffed out by cold weather. For the aviary's flooring, she had chosen slate for its absorbency, then smothered it with dirt laid thick enough to sustain live grasses and assorted herbaceous plants, the watering of which caused some troublesome drippage below. Alastair did not complain of the water running down the walls; he simply dragged his chair closer to the fire. Delia rather liked the effect of the water lines marring the cheerful green wallpaper downstairs, as if her husband had retreated to a subterranean cave while she controlled the sky above.

"Do your birds have names?" Georges asked.

"Not the cocks, they're the singers—and their owners will pick names once I sell them—but these are hens." Here Delia paused to wave her hand around the aviary. "They all have names. Many are past the age for breeding, but it doesn't cost much in seed to keep them happy."

Sturdy, Georges thought, listening to her business plan and eyeing her ample hips. Her arms sliced through the fowl-scented air, swooping with the flying creatures as if they had rehearsed. *Nothing skittish about her. Nothing girlish.* He wished he felt as impassioned and certain about something—anything—as Delia did about her aviary. Geneviève Rappatout inflamed Georges's curiosity; serinettes would be his work. But neither made him wave his arms around with confidence, with the kind of surety that this American woman possessed as she told him about her birds.

He thought he ought to ask a question. "Where do you keep the males?"

"Cocks," Delia corrected. "In small cages all around the house, separated by whichever song they learned, otherwise they would incorporate the hens' natural calls or snatches of other songs.

We have London Fancys, Lizards, Yorkshire Spangles, Norwich Yellows, the Belgian Fancys, Border Fancys, Glocester Fancys, the Turncrest, the Green, the Cinnamon, the Yellow—"

"I have heard of Cinnamons," he interrupted.

"Would you like some time alone with them?" Delia asked.

She had observed him: not the son of a serinetter, not the Sun-Bringer, but *him*. Georges. He felt a rush of gladness. Perhaps, with practice, he would figure out how to be just Georges. In the same way Delia seemed to inhabit herself fully.

"Yes," he said, "I would."

"I'll come back for you later," she said.

Delia opened the padlock and let herself out, then locked the door again, keeping both keys around her neck. In effect she had added him to her flock, but he did not mind; of course she would not want him letting any of the birds out by accident. He held out his forearms to see if any canaries might take to him. They did, tilting their heads in approval.

Chapter Four

Delia lavishes attention on her latest acquisition.

Delia, who sold entertainment to women who despised her brazenness, had little to razzle her days into more interesting patterns. The servants obeyed her. Nobody visited for tea. Her husband Alastair preferred his coal mining reports and his pipe to her company. A few months earlier she'd barged into his smoking parlor and straddled him on his favorite chair, hefting her skirts up her thighs and thrusting her bodice against his chin so he could get the full effect of the sachet of dried roses she had crushed in there. Alastair had sneezed, then turned his head away from this display and said, "You're wrinkling my papers."

She'd met Alastair in her Pennsylvania hometown when campaigning to get him to release canaries after each had survived a month in the mines. For these creatures and their human counterparts, a lifetime spent in the dark passages seemed crueler than asphyxiation. Alastair seemed amused by her enthusiasm. He agreed to gift her eight canaries—five females and three males, which he explained were more accurately termed hens and cocks. She bred them, lending a cock at a time to his miners to scout for poisonous gases, because hens didn't sing as much. If a cock survived a month underground, the miners would return it and Delia would breed it. Her flock grew. Delia and Alastair married within the year. They had real conversations—he found her a better thinker than his business partners—and excellent, sheet-rumpling nights. They had no children, not for lack of effort. But as a butcher's daughter who had grown up accustomed to lamb's blood staining her aprons, Delia changed what she could and wasted no time on regretting what she could not.

For their fifth anniversary, wanting to spirit his young wife away from the coal dust, he bought the Pleasant Hill property. Delia had set about designing her aviary with the same fearsome concentration she applied to changing the miners' canary protocol. Head filled with architecture, she repelled Alastair's advances and mumbled *hmm* and *ahhh* and *oh* when he asked her questions about his business. Nothing mattered besides giving her hens a safe place to range. Two years later, when she completed the aviary and dismissed the builders, she turned once again to her dear husband, ready to lavish him with attention. She hadn't counted on his stubbornness, though. To punish her for ignoring him, Alastair refused her overtures in kind, feigning interest in his reports and his newspaper. When she asked him a question about the mine, Alastair grumbled *hmm* and *ahhh* and *oh*.

He had hoped this technique would elicit an apology, followed by the physical reunion he craved, but Delia misunderstood his intentions. She decided she had made a mistake—married a man like all the other men. He no longer valued her intellect. Well—fine. She did not need Alastair to fill her days. She would make herself and her birds happy. Delia ordered the very best serinettes from France and spent her days in the glass cage she had built.

Now, upstairs, waited an attractive Frenchman with leonine hair—a man younger than her husband, yet old enough to be an appropriate object for her flirtations. She could install Georges Blanchard in any one of the many unused bedrooms, if only he'd let her convince him. She could not predict what he might say or do, unlike her birds—and every other person in this too-polite little town.

Georges might have pitied Delia's cocks, cooped up in individual cages, some of them in chilly parts of the house, except the birds themselves seemed pleased with their conditions. Unhappiness would never inspire such singing. They embellished the melodies they learned from the serinettes with decadent trills and flighty accidentals—lush and passionate ornamentation that M. never would have dared pin on a barrel.

Delia insisted Georges stay for a few days so he could learn the fundamentals of canary training. On his first morning as her guest, after a repast of fresh bread with last summer's honey, she introduced him to her most populated room besides the aviary: a library full of cocks trained to sing "Marlbrough S'en-Va-t-en Guerre." Americans knew this jaunty 1709 folk song—an account of a man who dies in battle—as "For He's a Jolly Good Fellow." The cages rested on the floor along the walls. Both bookcases had had their shelves removed at eye level, allowing for more cages. A library of birdsong. Georges leaned toward a bird the color of hot embers. He cupped his ear and caught a triumphant snatch of melody in the key of F. He couldn't wait to tell his father. Perhaps Georges himself had stuck the pins into the barrel of the instrument that trained this bird. It was a momentous thing, to realize the reach of one's daily work. Its marvelous wingspan.

"That's one of our Cinnamons—they're good sellers." Delia opened the closet, bent over like a hen intent on displaying her tailfeathers, and pulled out a serinette. "Want to play?"

Georges nodded. Delia's fingers brushed his own when she passed him the instrument. He opened the lid. "Marlbrough" was the fourth song on the list. He slid the small front case panel up and out of its grooves to check the condition of the bellows. Satisfied that the leather had neither cracked nor been over-stressed at the seams, he unhooked the crank from its resting place above the bellows and fitted its nub into the notch in the back of the walnut case. He shifted the barrel over three places. Georges had tired of this particular tune long before his apprenticeship began. He would have chosen a traditional *danse* or even "Les Folies d'Espagne." But the library was the "Marlbrough" room and so he would play "Marlbrough." The music littered the air with predictable cheer. Delia sang along—"For he's a jolly good fellow, for he's a jolly good fellow"—and the birds sang along too, all in the same key.

Thus began Georges's canary lessons. At night, by lantern in the guest room Delia had assigned to him, he copied down what she taught him, so he could bring the notes home to his father:

> Breed in spring. The hen must be at least one year old, the cock no more than five. Pick pairs with care. Two birds of excellent crests often produce bald off-spring. Garnet-colored eyes at birth means the canary will be a Cinnamon. For best feather quality, pair frosted with non-frosted. Variegated plumage often, but not always, means a strong singer.
>
> The birds destined to win contests have light, lilting voices. Their eyebrows are not too bushy, nor

*their crests too floppy. They have vibrant coloring and
fine, fitted feather texturing. A small, compact bird of
five inches or less, as long as its wings don't cross, is
favored over a bird closer to six-and-a-half inches. The
preferred song stance is upright and eager, not hump-
backed nor with stilted legs. The neck angle must fall
within a pleasing midrange.*

*For breeding purposes, a pair must be introduced
in side-by-side cages once the hen begins tearing paper
and signaling willingness. If the birds are mutually
interested, cage them together. To the hen's usual mix
of millet, rapeseed, thistle, and grass seed, add dietary
supplements such as spinach, dandelion leaves, egg-
shell for protein, and a daub of digestible oil to lubricate her insides for the ordeal to come.*

Georges learned to tell rollers from waterslagers and timbrados.
He draped young birds' cages with dense black cloth before
playing songs for them, so they would learn *sans* distraction, and
decided when the birds had learned enough to be caged together
with others that had memorized the same songs.

His willingness pleased Delia, his hostess, his teacher, his
friend. If only Geneviève Rappatout understood him as well as
she did! Delia provided food and a blanket in her second-best
guest quarters—much finer than his room at home. She insisted
on accompanying him on bracing walks, for the humid aviary
climate had stimulated the pores on his face, causing unsightly
blotches; rain and wind acted as astringents. Outside Delia would
point out and name the native trees, shrubs, and birds. When
he told her he missed his family, she switched to an unsteady
French so he would feel comforted, and he was! He told her so.

She leaned her shoulder against his, and he felt their kinship. She wanted him to stay. Georges suspected she preferred his presence to her husband's.

And therefore he would stay another night and keep her company another day, though surely he must get going by Friday. Or next Tuesday. Or perhaps the following Friday.

Each day arrived and concluded with the ease of a well-lubricated egg-laying, with Delia and Georges often dining together, Alastair preferring to eat in the men's smoking parlor. Delia pampered her handsome guest, peppered him with informational tidbits, and untwirled locks of her hair to retwirl around her finger. She began wearing her best dresses. Alastair noticed this, having once been privy to such signals, but when he complimented her appearance she ignored him, so he went back to his newspaper.

Georges didn't miss his family until a letter from home arrived. He wished for his mother's cooking to waft out from between the lines of his father's writing, but it only smelled like paper.

> *Dear Georges,*
>
> *I hope you fared well in your travels.*
>
> *Madame Stanton has begged me to let you stay through the breeding season. She hinted that she will double her next order if I can manage the workshop in your absence. You have my permission. Learn as much as you can for as long as she'll keep you.*
>
> *Bonne courage,*
>
> *Papa*

Georges read the letter twice, seeking clues about his mother. Had she left her bedroom yet? Had she forgiven him? She had not added a postscript, let alone a paragraph, of her own, nor had she addressed the envelope. Papa had not passed along her regards nor asked him to write her.

That night at dinner, Delia inquired about the correspondence. In truth, she had steamed open the envelope, read the contents with glee—her serinetter would stay!—and pasted it back together. But it remained for the young man to bring up the subject.

"Papa has agreed to let me study canaries for as long as you wish," he told her.

Delia leaned over the wide table and grasped his hand. "We have made our case, then, haven't we?" Whereupon Georges squeezed back and said, "Indeed," though he found it curious that she assumed he had been hoping for this news when they hadn't ever talked about it. Delia ordered the servant girl to move his place setting nearer to hers so they could converse more intimately. Georges decided it suited him to be wanted here, needed by Delia, seeing as his father and his mother could live without him. He leaned into her words, asking questions and agreeing upon the tastiness of each course. At home they had one plate each; here, a rotation, with a servant girl whisking the soiled plates away before issuing the next delight out of the kitchen. Roasted winter carrots and peppery potatoes. The best cuts of meat laid like ships upon oceans of bitter greens grown in pots on the windowsill. Peach tarts made from the fruit the house staff had jarred and sugared over the summer.

❊ ❊ ❊

On the occasion of Georges's twenty-second birthday—the final day of 1836—Delia ordered her servants to roast a pig in the backyard despite the frigid temperatures. The smoldering coals melted a ring of snow around the pit. What warmth he had felt toward Geneviève Rappatout had begun transferring to his bustling, chipper hostess. He knew her. They lived together. She made him laugh. Delia understood so much more than any girl his own age. About making a guest feel at ease. About art. About cocks.

Delia suspected that if the young man placed a finger on her cheek, the whole of her would bloom, her breasts turning into camellias, her head a sunflower tipped toward the sky, every one of her organs, tomato starts. One finger—that's all she asked—and where would he put it to please her most?

The next day, as if he had read her mind, he reached out and touched her sleeve with not one finger but two. She made up her mind to advance on him before he changed his mind. Delia had no shortage of courage; the estate ale rubbed its warmth over her doubts and made it seem impossible to do anything *but* knock once on Georges's bedroom door and let herself inside. He sat at the walnut desk in the corner, poring over a breeding manual she had loaned him. Georges popped out of his chair— *her* chair, in *her* house—in his nightshirt and long underwear. He lingered against the wall, pulling at his ears, not daring to make eye contact.

"I've come to help you," Delia told him.

"I do not need anything," Georges said.

"Do you mind if I lock the door?"

Georges didn't know much about women but he recognized the request as the most efficient way to keep her husband *out there* and to keep the two of them *in here*. Delia's brashness turned the crank on the pulley he imagined in his stomach, elevating his *pénis*. To her request about the door, he said yes, *mais oui*. She turned the key in the doorknob, then told him to move the glass of water from the bedside table to the desk.

"We wouldn't want it to tip over," she added.

He followed her directions, ever the good pupil. She drew him to the bed, pushed his shoulders down, lifted the skirts and underskirts of her voluminous dress, and had a go at what she knew best: breeding.

The next morning, Delia found an apologetic note from Georges on the formal dining table. He was quite sorry that he had so overstayed his welcome; he needed to return home immediately. How could he leave her like this? Without even saying goodbye or thank you for all her tutelage? Fighting back unbidden tears, Delia burst into the men's smoking parlor without knocking.

"Did you tell him to go?"

"Of course not." Alastair smoothed his newspaper. "Perhaps you frightened him off."

Chapter Five
A firstborn son.

Georges arrived home in mid-March 1837 to find his mother in mourning, her best dress dyed black. The *someday* his father had mused about on their journey to Le Havre had arrived. Monsieur had swallowed a bone and died from it. Georges's turn had come. He would be the master craftsman from now until he bore sons of his own and raised them to take his place. Cérine told him, "Your father expired in silence, save the pound of his head against his dinner plate."

"He would have liked that," Georges mused. "No extra fuss."

Georges didn't want to inherit the workshop—not yet—but he didn't have a choice now. He had been selfish, staying so long in Pleasant Hill, reveling in what should have been a punishment. He should have been home to pummel his father's back and dislodge the bone. Perhaps Papa's letter about staying longer had been a test of loyalty. If so, Georges had failed.

In the bereft weeks that followed, he did his best to distract his mother with canary stories, omitting the truth of the final night. Delia had wanted him around not because she admired him but for the pleasure he might give her. She had appreciated his curiosity but never called him clever, nor invited him to accompany her on a bird-selling call. He stayed behind, sequestered in her house, another creature in her bright menagerie, flapping at the glass.

The sunburn Georges earned upon his return flushed his cheeks and forehead. It felt like relief. And also like shame. *His* weather. He had returned to the place he belonged so he could resume his role as a straight pin on the cylinder of industry. And his mother was there, cooking and cleaning for him.

Upon completing the three-month mourning period, Georges pursued Genéviève Rappatout with long glances, an occasional hand upon her sleeve, and other intimacies Delia had taught him. Since Georges had grown like boxwood and Genéviève like limewood, surely as a couple they would make boxwood boys and limewood girls. Strong and healthy replicas of their own goodness. Genéviève reminded Georges of a lace bobbin, stout at the shoulders and hips, and slightly less stout at the waist.

Georges proposed in the Blanchard family parlor, with his mother a few steps away, tending a stew in the kitchen.

"And what is my role," Genéviève said, "if I quit lacemaking to be your wife?"

"Being a mother," he said.

"To you? To our children? Or to your mother as she ages?"

Georges sensed a trap. "Which would you prefer?"

Genéviève lifted her chin and laughed. "*Ça suffit*, I will marry you."

"Maman!" he called. "She said yes!"

Delia soon enough recovered her pride and equanimity but was plagued with a lingering discomfort. At first, she suspected a noxious bout of gas, then a lingering flare of indigestion, then all-out poisoning, whereupon she fired three cooks in a row before the quickening alerted her to the truth. She had gotten pregnant. (With some assistance from the serinetter.) As Alastair had not plowed her fields in several years, she realized she needed to thrust that routine back into their lives or he would grow suspicious. She worried rigorous activity might hurt the baby, but having no close friends to confide in, and being more fearful of Alastair discovering the truth, she forged ahead. They both preferred the surprise of her arriving at the men's smoking parlor, her underthings shed, then frolicking under the threat of a servant girl popping in to tend the fire or fetch dishes. Sometimes Delia mounted her husband in his favorite chair, both of them impatient at the nuisance her body made on his lap; she needed to shift her increasing weight one direction or the other to free the appendage that interested both of them.

Then she began to show, and Alastair rejoiced at the good fortune. It had been so long since he and Delia had something in common. The pregnancy surprised Alastair less than her increased affection—one being the obvious product of the other. He hoped this reprise of the early years of their marriage might lead to some rich, ripe middle years, followed by a sweet and meaningful coda in which their solicitous child would be there to oversee the servants who fed and bathed them in their dotage. Perhaps the dear girl—or boy—would even push the paid help aside and press a sponge to the parents' brows with a patient, loving hand.

On October 7, 1837, Delia gave birth to a boy—six pounds, eight ounces—in a spare bedroom lined with cages. The cocks sang an unassuming waltz, comforting her during her thirty-five-hour labor. Alastair, grateful to his wife for finally providing an heir, let her name the child.

Robert Dumphries Stanton may not have been conceived in love, but he arrived to it. He had a squishy red face and the first kindlings of dark hair. He looked like any other baby. Alastair visited the nursery several times a day, setting his newspaper and mine reports on the rocking chair so he could pull the tyke out of his crib and admire him. He started taking meals in the dining room again so he could talk to his wife about Robert's smiles and his melodious, pitch-perfect gibberish. Sometimes he read the coal-mining reports to the boy, who seemed to enjoy them. When light-brown tufts replaced the fine dark baby hair, Alastair remarked on the development with glee. Fair children pleased him. They freckled with dignity—never as an afterthought.

Robert's eyebrows grew in nicely, two arches that met in the middle, just like his mother's. When his locks began curling, though, Alastair grew suspicious. He took stock of the wide-set caramel eyes, the proud nose, and the heart-shaped face, much rounder than his long one (or even Delia's), with a small nub of chin.

"How come our son looks like your serinetter?" he asked his wife that night at dinner.

Delia figured lying might best preserve the intimacy between them. But running a blade of truth there instead would prove how sturdy this new phase in their marriage was. If her husband shrank from the news, or struck her, they would need to untangle themselves. He would return to his smoking parlor, she to her aviary.

She took a deep breath and flashed him the sort of grin she usually reserved for the women whose houses she visited. A dare flashed across her face. "We wanted a baby, didn't we?"

The sharp words poked Alastair under the ribs, deflating the bubble of pride that had swelled since Robert's arrival.

"I can't believe you did this to me," he said.

"I didn't do anything *to* you," Delia corrected. "I did this *for* us."

Alastair reached for the child; Delia surrendered him. Tiny fists grabbed at his whiskers. Despite himself, Alastair smiled.

Delia took this as an opening to admit that she hadn't told Georges. "Robert will grow up with you as his father. That's what you want, isn't it? A family?"

Alastair *hmmed* his disapproval. His wife's methods had always been unconventional. He didn't mind the infidelity so much as finding out now, when he had grown so attached to the little child. Robert burbled. Alastair pressed him against his chest.

"You need to write to Georges," he told Delia. "If you seduced him—and I have no doubt of your powers—then it's your duty to keep him informed about his son."

"But he's married now," Delia said. "What if his wife finds out?"

"That's his concern, not yours."

Delia realized this was her husband's bargain: tell the true father of Robert's existence, and Alastair would forgive her trespasses. (Or at least the one that resulted in a baby.) And so she wrote to Georges Blanchard of Mireville, France, the first of a string of letters. Even though she used different adjectives and anecdotes as the baby grew, what she meant was this:

See what you're missing.
See what you're missing.
See what you're missing.

Chapter Six
The other firstborn son.

On May 3, 1838, Georges and Geneviève produced a child of their own, who wasn't stricken with colic (or Cérine would have moved out or died).

Henri Blanchard nursed and grew. His pupils, deep inkpools at birth, mellowed to a pretty blue like his father's. He reached for objects equally with left hand and right. The dimples in his elbows matched the ones beside his mouth, which lent him a mischievous attitude that contrasted with his sober personality. Geneviève had a hard time not giggling at his expense, especially when he became outraged by small grievances.

The sun followed the baby carriage around the village, making the metal handle so hot Geneviève had to wrap a strip of wool around it. She claimed she would rather park the darn contraption in the woodstove and let it burn, but she still used it, not wanting to hurt her husband's feelings. He had procured it from Paris to please her.

Geneviève began taking herbs recommended by Sibylle the midwife to avoid getting pregnant again too soon. She liked her family this size, and besides, they only had three kitchen chairs. Her husband's father had destroyed the fourth one, Georges had told her, during one of his tempers.

Once Henri quit nursing and learned to walk, he devoted himself to earning his father's attention. While his mother fed and bathed him, dressed and scolded him, his father spent most of his time in the workshop. Papa burst through the kitchen door every evening, as regular as the sunset. Before sitting to eat the evening meal, he planted himself on the floor, never mind the dirt on his trousers, and let little Henri crawl into his lap and smell the backs of his humongous ears.

The boy didn't know about his father's exalted reputation until his fourth birthday, when the baker handed over a free sweet roll and said, "For the son of the most famous person in the whole village."

Henri's mood soured. He didn't want to give his gift away. "Who's that?"

"You." The baker smiled kindly.

This puzzled Henri. "I'm not famous."

"*Pas du tout*," Maman reassured him, glaring at the baker. "Of course you're not."

On the walk home, Henri wouldn't quit asking questions, though, and his mother finally told him the legend of his father's birth. How everyone called him the Sun-Bringer.

"Papa is famous?"

Maman nodded and squeezed his hand, though she didn't look cheerful about it.

"I'm the son of the Sun-Bringer?"

"You are."

From then on, Henri interrupted her on walks to point out the latest cheeky crop of rainbows: proof of his father's greatness. After church, he noted how the other music-makers circled around Papa, speaking over each other, wanting to bask in his attention.

Henri wanted to be a Sun-Bringer too. Or maybe a Rain-Bringer, since it did get awfully hot in Mireville. He devoted hours to lying in the grass, staring at the sky, wondering if it might have a message for him. But no message came, so Henri took to stealing his father's shoes and stamping about the house until Papa lunged out of his chair to scold—a ritual proving that the Sun-Bringer belonged to him, that they belonged to each other.

Though Cérine kept a polite distance from her daughter-in-law, she loved having a little boy in the house again. She often called Henri, now age six, to the parlor to let him admire the family serinette, its white leather bellows and its limewood cylinder and its ten tin-slitted pipes. His curiosity delighted her. Before M. had died he'd refused to let her work the crank, claiming it to be men's work. But Cérine's wrists worked as well as anyone else's, and this was her house (or it used to be), and the shrill little box was intended to please women. Why shouldn't her grandson have this pleasure, this memory of her?

If she had been in better health, she might have packed Henri up and taken him on a real adventure. To Paris, perhaps, to hear a full orchestra. Or into the mountains, where she would teach him which mushrooms he could eat. An old lady's fanciful ruminations, nothing more. She would not take him to Paris, nor into the mountains. She blinked—tears. How had she come to be crying in the parlor, not at the end of her life but surely on the way to the end? She had—during a routine bath—noted a bulbous lump jutting from the folds of flesh around her belly. Not a baby, not at her age. The grand climacteric with its unpredictable bleeds had taken her fertility a few years back.

Cérine's hair had prematurely turned the color of silver

thread, the lusterless kind manufactured in Baudricourt (not the ostentatious brands from Paris). Since the discovery of the lump, she needed to sit more often, which made the serinette sessions more convenient than baking a loaf or bending over the washboard.

When her daughter-in-law left the house on errands, Cérine cranked the parlor serinette as fast as she could, encouraging Henri to flap his arms and pretend to be a giant stork. When she needed to rest, she recited incidents from Georges's childhood, not just the clouds parting but funny little things that only a mother would remember.

"It is an industry run by men," Cérine told her grandson, "but American women are the customers. When you become a serinetter, you must work hard to make them happy or they will not order more instruments."

"Serinette, like you," Henri said.

She explained the difference between Cérine, referring to a rare metal, and *serin*, canary, for which the serinette was named. "Though they sound similar."

"Do canaries not know how to sing?" Henri asked.

"Your father has heard them," Cérine said. "Ask him."

"He should make instruments for sparrows or storks," Henri said. "For birds we have here."

Cérine didn't like hearing Henri say this. "But it's cruel, *n'est-ce pas?* To want something to sound less like itself and more like you?"

The boy thought about this for a moment. "I don't want to be cruel."

"There's beauty in all music," Cérine amended. She did not want to sour his gentleness with the thoughts she played through her mind. "How about I play a *danse* next?"

If this new lump had it out for her, she would not be around when Henri began his apprenticeship at twelve. She only occasionally gave into curiosity when alone, poking at the mass with a finger, occasionally petting it, encouraging it to disgorge her energy, give it all, all, all back so she could have another go at life.

One afternoon that spring, Geneviève returned early from her chores in the village and caught her mother-in-law cranking the serinette for Henri. Cérine hadn't been eating as much as usual. Her flesh hung loose on her cheeks. Skin sagged from her forearm like a reticule as she played through a minuet. When Geneviève entered the parlor, Cérine let go of the crank so fast it popped out of the back of the walnut box and clanged against the floor. The extra skin jiggled in surprise. Geneviève sent Henri outside to play.

"I'm sorry," Cérine said. "I know I shouldn't—"

"Shouldn't introduce him to his future?" Geneviève offered a small smile. "It's better he learns to enjoy music before he must make it—but let's not tell Georges, ça va?"

This became a firm alliance of *deux* with an apt motto: *let's not tell Georges.* Cérine went so far as to stitch the phrase on a pillow. When all the wooden cooking spoons disappeared from the kitchen, Geneviève claimed they had broken, every single one; Cérine swore to it as well. Both women relished the ding of the new metal ones against the metal pots, something M. had long ago forbidden.

It was good to be loud.

It was better to be loud with someone else.

Had he not exited so swiftly, M. would have railed against such obvious collusion. Georges admired both women and pretended not to notice—even after he found an embroidered pillow proclaiming *"Ne le dis pas à Georges!"* with its emphatic exclamation point. It had been made by both their hands—he recognized his mother's elegant flourishes of thread alongside his wife's more clipped and efficient style.

"Thank goodness for my husband," Genéviève said, "who loves me anyway."

"Thank goodness for you," Cérine said, "now that I have gotten used to you."

Georges chopped off his abundant, chin-length ringlets for the first time since adolescence. The short curls sprung tight as sun-bleached snail shells around his head, a crown of selfhood. Georges had spent his life hiding his ears—and for what? They were ears. Everyone had them. He had expected his firstborn would be a grace note, an embellishment on his already fine life, but here he was, cutting his hair to show his son the importance of being yourself. Years before the child would understand or remember such a lesson, Georges taught it. Henri was not a grace note at all, but the music of his life.

Except, it turns out, another melody had taken root as well.

Delia Dumphries Stanton's first letter had arrived about a week after Henri's birth. It seemed absurd to Georges that a woman on the other side of the ocean would claim him responsible for what had grown in her gut.

"He cannot be mine," he scribbled with great haste, running down the hill to hand the missive directly to the postman. "I already have a firstborn son."

Weeks later: "Then you have two firstborn sons," Delia replied.

She enclosed a small, commissioned portrait, showing the boy's singular eyebrow, a heart-shaped face, and the characteristic

Blanchard ringlets. Was that the rim of an impressively large ear hiding behind the curls? Georges could not quite tell. It could be a painting of any infant. Then again, Delia would not have written if she believed her son to be Alastair's. She did not ask for money. Or for Georges to claim the child. And Georges had not seen Alastair touch his wife, not even a brush of the wrist, during all his months in Pleasant Hill. They didn't even take meals together.

Per Delia's regular correspondence, Robert Dumphries Stanton learned how to walk at ten months. He knew a hundred and twenty-seven words of English at eighteen months, plus eight French words. By three, Robert wrote cinquains; by five, he composed ballads.

"*A prodigy!*" Delia exulted in loopy script. "I would offer you an example except his compositions are much too valuable to be entrusted to the mail."

As Delia's letters amassed—one every few months—and the boy's accomplishments grew increasingly spectacular, Georges became desperate for proof of the sprout of greatness that had apparently sprung from his seed. Couldn't the child hand-copy a single song? Delia would merely have to invent someone waiting for a sample—a symphony conductor, for instance—and away the little hand would dance between inkpot and page. No songs arrived, though, to Georges's chagrin; the letters, effusive to the point that he worried Delia was spoiling their son, continued to arrive, sometimes out of order. The boy recovered from mumps before contracting them. He debuted a short étude at the Pleasant Hill ladies' tea before trying his hand at composition.

Georges pieced the tale together, arranging the letters in the intended order. At first he secured Delia's missives inside his pillow, eventually stuffing the growing collection into the leg of a pair of trousers in the bottom drawer of his chiffonier. Geneviève expected him to put away his own laundry after the servant girl scrubbed it and dried it. She would never think to look there.

Georges memorized each of his American son's milestones, conveyed in Delia's fine hand, and compared his French son, who was almost exactly seven months younger. Henri walked at fourteen months and had thirty words at eighteen months; he didn't pen cinquains, nor ballads, nor quartets. He had trouble pronouncing *le* and *les*, while his half-brother composed sincere little lullabies.

His firstborn. So smart. So far away.

Georges responded to Delia's letters, but Henri didn't have corresponding brag-worthy achievements, so he kept his notes cordial but brief. Despite his regular efforts, Geneviève did not become pregnant again. A few times he hinted she ought to consult with the midwife, but Geneviève pretended not to understand, and he blushed at the thought of having to spell it out. Besides, Henri would grow up fine, perfectly normal, his position as a master craftsman secure through being Georges Blanchard's firstborn son.

Normal might have pleased Georges, if it weren't so obvious that Robert Dumphries Stanton of Pleasant Hill, New York, though still in short pants, was the type of extraordinary—earned on his own merits—that his father the Sun-Bringer never had been.

Chapter Seven
Cérine becomes a cloud.

Besides his grandmother, Henri had only one friend: a girl. He didn't like to catch or race or fight like the other boys, so he trailed alongside five-year-old Aimée Maullian, a half-year younger than him but twice as adventurous. While the boys played the same boring games every day, usually in one of the older kids' yards, Henri never knew where Aimée would lead him. The cemetery. The old bridge. Into the bushes on the side of her house, where they pretended rocks into ice, licking the dirt off and exclaiming with delight that felt genuine, even though it was only dirt.

It became a common sight in Mireville: the two children holding hands and waiting outside the creamery, guessing whether their mothers would procure cheese or a cold slab of butter this time. Aimée didn't need to pull back her hair yet; she wore it tangled and uncut, an unruly beech color streaked with sun. Often strands flew into Henri's face when they stood next to each other. There was a gap between his two front teeth, and when he opened his mouth to speak on windy days, her loose hair slid in between. He never complained, just pulled it back out, glad for her companionship.

The adults didn't mind these two being companions, because they could never be betrothed; Aimée's father was not a music-maker, so his lacemaking daughters would marry builders, farmers, or butchers. Definitely not a Blanchard.

One afternoon, Henri fell into a sulk because Aimée kept her balance across a log that proved too wobbly for his legs. To mollify him, she ran home and stole a bobbin of coarse thread from her mother's lace kit, then led him to a small clearing in the woods past the violin-makers' workshops. Aimée instructed him on how to string the thread around tree trunks. He caught on quickly, creating complex knots at the base of one tree, then another. Aimée decided which tree to connect to which. Once they had four trees strung together, the children began tossing the spool to each other, letting the thread unravel in midair. They laughed aloud, feeling safe as the violin scales hid any noise.

"What if you get caught?" Henri said, meaning *what if we get caught?* Any adult discovering them beneath the leaves would surely blame them both. Not just the thief.

"Maman hates linen because it chafes her fingers," she told him. "I'm doing her a favor."

Henri sighed long and deep but was having too much fun to quit. They worked on their tree project until a few yards of thread remained. The clearing now held a low-slung knotty mess, and Aimée devised a new game of jumping between the rows, trying not to let the linen touch their bodies.

When they tired of that—Henri complaining of his thigh muscles aching—he and Aimée crawled under their threadwork and closed their eyes, pretending to be bugs caught and trussed by a spider. The violin workshops were quiet now, the apprentices gone to their rooms. Henri listened for footsteps. He wished he could be more like his friend. Fearless and strong. Even her legs—what he had seen of them the one time she hiked her skirts up and waded into the river—had more hair than his. And she didn't seem to be afraid of her older brother Guillaume; everyone else was. Sometimes Guillaume taunted Henri with the feminine pronoun, *elle* instead of *il*. Sometimes, Henri felt sure Guillaume was following him, although Henri had never quite caught him at it. Probably the boy just wanted to protect his sister. Make sure she and Henri weren't up to any mischief.

"Promise we'll always be friends," Henri told Aimée. "Even if you get sent to jail for stealing thread."

She laughed. "We're not supposed to be friends now."

Henri agreed that this was probably true, but lying under the mess of their making, she held out her pinky finger, and he hooked it with his. When they finally crawled out, they made a promise bridge of their arms, floating them above their heads in an arc. Then they wiggled their fingers down like rain sprinkles, a blessing in this sunny village. Henri smoothed his trousers as if they were a skirt. Aimée crossed her arms over her bodice as if it were a vest.

Despite his having a girl as a best friend, the musical families of Mireville looked upon the Blanchard boy as a prize future husband: a firstborn, a future master craftsman. The mothers of little girls visited Geneviève's kitchen, bringing soft cheeses and windfall apples and an occasional carrot, imagining tiny haloed tykes, their grandchildren ringed in gold. They hoped to lay claim not only to Henri but to the next few Blanchard sons as well. Geneviève still hadn't grown wide with another child, though. Perhaps her insides had broken, or perhaps she kept having miscarriages like Mme. Nanin, the doctor's wife. The hopeful mothers added apple cakes and custards to their baskets and trudged up the hill. Someday, all that effort would be worth it for one of them—but not the rest.

When Docteur Nanin diagnosed her with a tumefaction, Cérine didn't ask the doctor for a prognosis; she did not need a man to tell her what she already knew. Besides, the bigger the stomach lump grew, the less tethered she felt to the world, as if it might fill with air and let her soar away, petticoats billowing.

Occasionally the tumor whisked away the word she wanted. A well-bred woman might have quit trying to speak, hoping to conceal her muddlement, but Cérine became even more insistent, especially with her grandson. She wanted to leave Henri what dwelt in her own heart: how it felt to wake to the sound of rain on the roof, how simple noises can matter as much as music, the wonder she felt the first time her father showed her a bird's nest, how that wonder bloomed still, someplace inside her. Her grandson didn't need miracles or fame to have a good life, as long as he kept noticing the world. Paying attention.

By age seven, Henri knew that he was different from other music-makers' sons. For one thing, they had all grown out of crying in public, if not in private, but Henri couldn't understand why. If a person is sad, why not cry? This perspective endeared him to girls his age, who often begged handkerchiefs from their mothers to help sop up his sadness over a skinned knee or a dead baby bird.

For another, most of his peers had siblings—usually older and younger ones—who taught them about the world. Henri liked being an only child. If he had brothers, he felt sure his peculiarities would be even more obvious. He didn't like to race the other boys or turn branches into swords. He held utensils with a dainty grace, the way his grandmother did, and he loved his mother's lace kit. Maman refused to give him lessons, though. Farmers' sons were the only boys allowed to learn lace—and only until they were strong enough to work outdoors all day. Henri wished he were a farmer's son: lace and seeds, pins and weeds. Before she got sick, Grand-Maman often indulged his interest, letting him examine Maman's hand-carved bobbins, most of which used to be hers. She taught him to sort them by wood type with his eyes closed. The blood-red heartwood of pernambouc made the fingers on his right hand buzz. Ebony, dense and rich, offered a satisfying grip, almost as if it wanted to grip him right back. He loved rolling the rosewood bobbins along his cheeks. But his grandmother never said anything interesting anymore. Her mind wandered away midthought. Henri made a game of filling in the spaces, trying to guess at her meaning.

"When I was your age my father bought me..."

"A comb? A sweet? A *violon*?"

"Not a comb, nor a sweet, nor a *violon*," Grand-Maman said. "Quit pestering and then I will remember."

Cérine kept her health condition to herself until one night in February 1846, when her daughter-in-law discovered it.

On the way to bed, Geneviève noted the flicker of a lantern beneath her mother-in-law's door. Still awake. She knocked quietly before opening the door. To her surprise, she found Cérine on the floor, pins in her mouth, her legs stretched out and crossed at the ankles, hunched over a puddle of material: her everyday butter-colored dress, now with a seam open, her needle plunging in too close to the frayed edges, the resulting stitches too wide. Like the sewing of a child.

"That won't hold for long," Geneviève warned.

"Doesn't need to," Cérine said, the words muffled.

Geneviève sat down and reached over to pull the pins from her mother-in-law's lips.

"I need to alter it," Cérine said, more clearly now. She could have left it at that, because women's bodies change shape, thickening here or thinning there with age, but she trusted her daughter-in-law and did not see a reason to keep this secret from her any longer. "I have a lump."

Geneviève pressed her fingers against her jaw, as if forcing her mouth to ask a question she didn't really want answered. "Have you consulted *le docteur*?"

"*Oui*, back in July. There's nothing he can do." Cérine lifted a corner of her lips in a half-smile, meaning to be reassuring. She wished it wasn't her news; it was, though. Geneviève would have to handle it. Cérine didn't have the energy. She let go of the fabric and leaned back, putting her palms flat on the floor behind her so the tumefaction would pop out of hiding. "Docteur Nanin suspects it's toxic. If it burst or were cut open, it'd kill me faster."

Geneviève cupped the mass in her hands with tenderness, feeling its putrefying core beneath the blue fabric. It bobbed up, then back down, as Cérine breathed, as if it had its own heart and lungs. "Does it hurt?"

Cérine sat up and shrugged; the lump receded behind her dress. Geneviève removed her hands from the bulge and crossed them over her own stomach.

"I can't run this household without you."

"You must," Cérine said. "Hire another servant girl. Georges can afford it."

"But I'll be lonely."

Cérine shrugged. She could not solve this problem, either. "What did you need?"

Geneviève shook her head, not understanding the question.

"You knocked."

She had found a stash of letters in unfamiliar handwriting in her husband's drawer, but she couldn't very well mention those at a time like this. An ache in Geneviève's stomach, in the same exact spot where the tumor released its hot fecundity into her mother-in-law, pressed upward onto her heart until sound burst out as a sob. Oh, what a gaffe, to burden Cérine further! It was not Geneviève who was dying. Now the older woman would feel a duty to comfort her—except that she didn't react, didn't even lean in to offer a hug. That's when Geneviève knew for sure: Cérine would not be here much longer.

"You should tell Georges," Geneviève said.

"He'll know soon enough." Cérine made her promise to tell Henri that she'd died of happiness and become a cloud. "And let him have my British novels. He should learn English."

Geneviève agreed to these requests. "If we have a baby girl, we'd do well to name her after you."

"Flattery," Cérine said. "I have seen your herbs. You do not want another baby."

Geneviève took a deep breath. Her mother-in-law hadn't lied when confronted; she would not pretend either. "I don't—not yet, anyway. Are you going to tell Georges?"

"I've known for a long time and haven't told."

Geneviève reached out and took her mother-in-law's hand. "Thank you."

Cérine grinned, and Geneviève swept her up in an impetuous hug, leaning in and wrinkling the butter-colored dress on her lap, taking care that she didn't press against the lump. Cérine smelled of lantern oil and the rosemary butter she liked to apply to her hands.

When her time came, the men would grieve but go on working and sleeping and pushing food into their mouths. Geneviève, meanwhile, would have no one to confer with about whether the stew was done. Would Georges understand the depth of his wife's loss? Her own mother had died young, before they learned to understand each other. Cérine's friendship and love had come to fill part of that sore, empty place in her heart.

❋ ❋ ❋

When Cérine floated off to become a cloud over Ambaville that summer, Maman's grief made Henri feel terribly small. He drew her pictures with pigment sticks he made from soil and oatmeal. He picked bouquets of dried flowers—even occasionally a fresh bloom, if he could find one before the sun baked it. He sculpted mounds of wet river clay into shapes that might please her: a chair, a bowl of custard. But his gifts only made her sadder. Even the linen braids he made by tearing apart what was left of the thread labyrinth he'd made with Aimée. He thought his mother might wind one around her wrist or tie one into her bun, but instead she put them absently in a drawer in the parlor, her *thank you* a kind of hollow echo. His real mother would have asked, "Where did you get this thread?"

Sometimes Henri felt as if he should be sadder. He had loved his grandmother! But she had *wanted* to become a cloud. How could he be sad for her? Her wish came true. He missed snuggling into her lap and their serinette sessions and the way she said his name, drawing it out to make him laugh. But he did not want to be selfish by begging her to come back. She could go anywhere she liked now—Paris, even!—without paying any money for tickets. Henri hoped that she would stay in Ambaville, nearby, just in case he needed her.

Geneviève arranged for Madame Picoult to watch Henri during the burial. Let him keep his ignorance of death a while longer. Besides, Cérine *wanted* the boy to believe she had turned into a cloud. Georges, grief-stricken and glad his wife had a plan, agreed to the ruse. He placed the subversive embroidered pillow—

the only proof of collusion between the women he loved—in his mother's casket.

Now Georges would control the household with a firm hand, in accordance with his father's tutelage; his mother wasn't there to make the softer way work. Georges turned his attention to his son, who had spent too many of his formative years wandering around with that Maullian girl. It was time to enroll Henri in school and insist he accomplish assorted household tasks as proof of his value in their family.

Henri took the news of his new position rather well. After a blistering hot summer, walking to the village to sit inside the schoolhouse felt like a balm. He liked being with the other sons of local music-makers in the one-room schoolhouse. His hand-writing earned him praise from the schoolmaster.

M. Maullian enrolled Aimée in formal lace tutelage at Madame Oeuvriot's school that same fall. Henri and Aimée no longer had time to be friends. They would never again sit by the river for hours at a time, or trade boots, or try to stump each other with sums now that they both had to sit through lessons. Aimée had become a thread on the sawdust-filled pillow of women's industry, her life raveling away from his.

Henri appreciated the distraction of school. He missed Grand-Maman the way he missed his baby teeth, each carried off in the night by a little mouse, or so his parents claimed. Then he lost Aimée to her future. He couldn't do anything about these feelings except hope that he would grow up to become less susceptible to them. Or that more would happen to him, filling some of the emptiness back up.

For strength, Henri prayed not to God but to the clouds over Ambaville, believing his grandmother would be more likely to help. Perhaps she would even bring the clouds back to Mireville!

How he would love to look up and see her there in the sky. He felt sure he could be more like his father if Grand-Maman floated overhead. Encouraging him. Watching out for him. Alas: despite his prayers, every day the sun came back and blazed, just as it had all the days of his life, and the clouds remained stubbornly fixed over Ambaville.

Henri's classmates didn't like how often the schoolmaster praised his penmanship. They took to teasing him whenever they could get away with it. Henri stayed in the classroom for *déjeuner*, only crying into the crook of his arm when he felt particularly awful. Soon winter lessons arrived; though the sun remained as resolute as ever, the air turned too cold for the boys to go outside. Henri figured this would be his chance to make friends. He began bringing snacks from home to woo them. But the boys stayed at their desks, eating food from their own homes and passing insults back and forth among themselves like a dish of dried peas.

"You're a flat note."

"Who're you calling Accidental?"

"Out of my way, Blunder-Bow."

Henri didn't respond to their jibes with any nastiness of his own, so they invented special nicknames for him: *Petit Serin*, *Pin-Head*, *Crank-Head*, and *Bellows-Brain*; and, least inventive, *Son of the Sun-Bringer*.

Papa would be disappointed if he knew about the teasing, so when his parents asked about the day Henri always said fine, *bien*, as well as yesterday, and imagined the noxious words stuck between his two front teeth where they wouldn't ever pop out and upset his parents. Soon spring would arrive, and he would once again spend his lunches in an empty classroom, away from the mysterious rules by which his peers governed themselves.

Chapter Eight

The girls' council investigates a mystery.

To mark her eighth birthday, Aimée Maullian established a council of girls. They convened on Sundays after church, when they could sneak away from their mothers undetected. For their meeting space, Aimée chose a clearing in the woods behind Docteur Nanin's house. She improved it by tying some willow branches together so they'd grow into a dome, big enough for the whole group. The doctor and his wife did not have children, so they never looked out the window. Besides, the Nanins lived next door to the Maullians, which made this location quite convenient for Aimée. Less so for the other girls, perhaps, but that was what leaders did: accommodate themselves.

Aimée wanted to call their group The Council of Apprentice Lacemakers, but Margaux Vuillaume, eldest daughter of one of the most famous violin makers in town, argued for a bit of intrigue.

"How about The Shadow Council of Apprentice Lacemakers? Otherwise it sounds like it's a work group."

"It's supposed to sound like a work group so we don't get caught." Aimée didn't take well to correction. But even she had to admit Margaux's version had a better ring to it, and eventually they all agreed. Among themselves, they would call it the Shadow Council for short.

Henri suspected Aimée had a secret, but she refused to tell him what it was. They still liked to play together when they could, but they knew different things. On Sundays, after church, when he went looking for her, he rarely found her anymore. He felt certain she knew rules that nobody had bothered to teach him.

One summer afternoon, when Henri was helping sort pins in the serinette workshop, Papa sent him to the house in search of his courbette, a long-snooted pin-straightener. Henri checked the parlor and his father's coat pockets, then asked Maman for ideas.

"The bedroom?" she suggested.

Henri darted up the old wooden steps that led from the back of the kitchen to the hallway where his parents' room was. He opened his mother's bottom drawer, pulling out lengths of lace and stockings. He pressed a pair of wool socks to his cheek and imagined them being knitted, every dip of the needles, every length of yarn spooling through his grandmother's fingers. If he could not learn lace, Maman would not teach him knitting. But still, he could admire Grand-Maman's craftsmanship. The heels had been patched with yarn from a different sheep—almost a match but not. The next drawer held dresses. No courbette there either. Henri moved to his father's chiffonier, a much more likely prospect. There, stuffed in the leg of a pair of trousers, he found not the courbette but two stacks of letters tied with twine, from a Mrs. Delia Dumphries Stanton of Pleasant Hill, New York.

The letters had weakened along their seams, as if they had been read with frequency. Henri did not know English but he saw a name—*Robert, Robert, Robert*—repeated on every page like a sharp in a key signature. Not an accidental, but a sound that made the music special.

His father had a secret. He riffled through enough of the correspondence to see dates that went back to his own birth year. The whole time he had been alive, Papa had been receiving these mysterious letters. Henri hated *Robert,* whoever he was—this American in his father's drawer. He shoved the letters back into the trouser leg and returned to the workshop, his insides gummed with shame. He hadn't meant to snoop.

When Papa inquired about the courbette, Henri said, "I didn't find anything."

After church on Sunday, Henri pulled Aimée away from her friends. Her forearm was satisfyingly muscular beneath her sleeve. He kept a firm grip on it until they reached the doorway of the *boucherie,* whereupon he let go and pinched his own forearm for comparison. His bones felt like quills set in custard.

He described the letters in his father's trousers. All that English. "I don't know what they say."

"You must tell your mother!"

"I cannot—because what if…" Henri did not know exactly what he feared, or how to explain the wild bubbling in his gut at the mere mention of Maman. He could not fathom what could possibly be written on so many pages. Perhaps they detailed old serinette sales—but if so, Papa would keep them in the workshop, not in a trouser leg.

"You trust me?" Aimée asked.

Henri aimed his eyes skyward, whereupon he spied the sun luxuriating in its ineffable refusal to be dimmed, all because of the Sun-Bringer. It scared him, this new piece of his father's story. It felt as if he had discovered Papa had another leg. Henri blinked and tears rolled out of the corners of his eyes. Aimée paid his tears no mind; people looked at the sun all the time and made themselves cry, and her friend cried more than her and all the other boys anyway.

"You must trust me," Aimée added, "or you wouldn't have told me." She swished her beech-colored hair from side to side, scanning the crowd, until she spotted Henri's parents, his father in a circle of music-makers, telling a story, the men around him nodding as if they hadn't heard it before. "Go—run up the hill and bring some of the letters back to me."

Henri gaped at her. He couldn't possibly take them.

"It's not stealing, it's borrowing," she said. "You'll bring them back when I'm done with them."

Aimée had a plan. Even for this unthinkable situation. Of course she did. He scooted away to do her bidding.

✳ ✳ ✳

Sunday proved an ideal day for the council; none of the mothers made their daughters work after church unless the lace-cutter's arrival was imminent. Usually the girls met at an appointed time to trade threads and bobbins their mothers had given them, but today Aimée had a more enticing agenda. As soon as Henri left, she rushed back to her friends and told them, "We must convene."

"*Qu'est-ce que c'est?*"

"What happened?"

"Do tell us, Aimée."

She shook her head and grinned. "Meet me at our usual place, but go in pairs, so you don't all disappear at once. We don't want to make our mothers suspicious."

Aimée slipped off to find Odil Michaute, who was twelve or thirteen; nobody seemed to know for sure. The strange boy refused to make eye contact and his parents didn't make him work outside the house. When he came to church on Sundays, instead of conversing with boys his own age after the service, he climbed into the empty fountain, which put a stone barrier between him and the crowd of villagers.

Once last summer, Aimée had called him *stupide* when she passed by the fountain, not out of meanness as much as following her friends' lead. Odil didn't quit rocking or respond. In fact he didn't seem to notice at all, but she still lamented that lapse of grace and good manners. Perhaps adding Odil to the council would atone for her poor behavior toward him. Besides, she *needed* someone who spoke English. Anne-Jeanée had picked up some from her salesman father, but everyone knew Odil was fluent.

Aimée had asked her mother about what happened to Odil, and her mother had said, "God," which wasn't an answer at all, but she hadn't asked again, because she took *God* to mean *I don't know*. There was a lot her mother didn't know. Part of the girls' council was sharing information so they could grow up knowing more than their mothers.

Aimée found the older boy sitting cross-legged in the dry fountain like usual. Odil picked at his trousers and rocked his torso back and forth. Though he pretended to be invisible, everyone could see him; the fountain edges were low. Aimée usually ignored him, not because she wanted to but because her mother had told her not to stare. He intrigued her like a music box that could not be fixed with a hammer or better sealant, one that didn't play the tune everyone expected. Today, though, she needed his help. Aimée stepped up to the edge of the fountain, leaned toward him, and whispered, "I need you to come with me. To a secret council meeting."

Odil kept rocking, his hands folded over his body in mirror image to his legs. He had a fragile sort of beauty, especially when in motion. Aimée imagined a butterfly had flown into Odil's face and gotten stuck there. Wings—freckles—lightly spotted his cheeks, which scrunched in suspicion.

"You've never asked me before."

"You know English, *n'est-ce pas?*"

Odil said *oui*, rocking.

"Then you have to come with me. To my house. The one next to the doctor's house."

He was thirteen. He could decide to go or not. She couldn't make him go.

"I am not stupid," Odil said to Aimée's knee. "I know where you live."

She felt even sorrier that she had called him that last summer. As an apology, she held out her hand, and this gesture overcame his doubts. Nobody had ever offered him a hand, especially not a girl. Once he'd scrambled over the fountain edge, he let her lead him away.

Henri rushed down the steep hill with a few of his father's letters tucked into the waistband of his trousers. He had wiggled them out of the twine, careful not to bend the edges. His blond ringlets sprang up and down as his feet pounded against the dirt path. Perhaps he had taken too long, agonizing over which letters to steal, not knowing which ones Papa would miss or how long

Aimée would expect to keep them. Perhaps she wouldn't be there when he returned and he would have to smuggle them back into the drawer, this mad rush for naught.

At the bottom of the path, a few blocks from the village square, Margaux Rigoniet planted herself in front of Henri, arms akimbo, dainty shoes planted, sweat at her hairline. Aimée had taught Margaux and the other girls how to stand firm without flinching. Henri nearly skidded into her.

"Have you seen Aimée?" Henri asked.

Margaux—whose family owned the land two parcels away from the Blanchards'—grinned as she blocked his way. "Hand them over."

"Hand what over?" he asked.

"The letters."

Aimée had told his secret! He hurled his fists toward Margaux in frustration, and she caught his wrists neatly and squeezed them: another trick Aimée had made the council practice. Boys never expected girls to fight back.

"Ouch, let go, that's not fair!" Henri begged.

"You tried to pummel me," Margaux said. "Now give me the letters or I'll pummel *you*."

"Either I give them to Aimée myself, or I put them away again," Henri said.

Margaux sighed and removed her dress sash. Aimée had warned that he might not part with them.

"If you let me blindfold you," she said, "I'll take you to her."

Henri agreed, for it was a better solution than handing over the letters. Margaux pulled the slippery sash over his eyes and tied it tight, taking care not to catch his curls in the knot. Then she led him through the back alleys of the *violon* workshops— everyone was still mingling post-church—and over to the

vermillion-roofed houses by the river, though Henri hadn't any
sense of their whereabouts. He tripped a few times and begged
Margaux to go more slowly, but she refused.

"Everyone's waiting," she said.

Her voice took up all the space in his head. *Everyone* who? A
few minutes later, they paused. Margaux's hand pressed the top
of Henri's head down, so he bent, feeling branches catch his curls.
Navigating a thicket? But where? Then she stopped and Henri
crashed into her back. Giggles and whispers greeted him.

"Aimée?" he called.

"Hold on a moment," Margaux said.

She untied the sash, now damp with his sweat. Behold, a
clearing! Someone—Aimée, probably—had trained willows to
bend and grow into an arch overhead. The girls sat in a circle,
as if waiting for him. A few of them had their lace pillows out—
probably catching up from the week before. Odil Michaute, the
only other boy here, sat cross-legged, rocking to a 4/4 rhythm, his
preference.

"Where's Aimée?" Henri asked.

Most of the girls looked away. Margaux shrugged. Henri
didn't know whose property they trespassed on or whether they
had permission. The girls didn't seem worried, though, and the
shade from the willow branches was refreshing.

"Oh, you hurt yourself!" Margaux pointed out his bloodied
trousers, the new hole in the knee. "I'm sorry."

"I fell—not you." He would have to beg his mother to repair
them. He touched the wrecked fabric, then sat down and rubbed
the blood off onto the grass. Then he worried maybe he should
have wiped it on his shirt instead; this was their place, not his,
although feeling the cool air waft through the branches, he
wished desperately to belong. To be invited here again and again.

Someone had strung ribbons through the branches that intersected overhead like a roof. The girls whispered to each other. Odil kept up his rhythm. Henri began to wonder whether he had been tricked.

Suddenly, a rustle. He whirled around but couldn't see anything. An animal? The property owner? This secret enclosure wasn't in the forest on the outskirts of town; he'd have found it on one of his walks if it were. His heart pounded with Odil's motions—boom-BOOM, boom-BOOM—agreeably in 4/4 time. Just as he felt his chest might explode from worry, Aimée parted the brush on the far side of the dome, her head popping into view, followed by her shoulders, then the rest of her. He was so relieved to see her.

"You're mad, aren't you? Poor, bewildered Henri!" She kissed his cheeks with lips so dry they chafed his skin a bit. Aimée and Margaux and the other girls began laughing, and Henri joined them, because it was funny, being trussed up and marched to the meeting space. Besides, he knew everyone there. Bernadine DeBourgignon had a brother a few years younger than him. Yvette Rappatout, his cousin on his mother's side, sat on a log with her legs splayed out, knee knobs making bumps in the fabric of her long dress. Anne-Jeanée Picoult, the daughter of his father's serinette salesman, propped a thick book on her knees, its binding partly cracked. Her father knew English better than his father.

"We have gathered The Shadow Council of Apprentice Lacemakers today—" Aimée began.

"To solve a mystery!" interrupted Margaux. Then she nudged Henri.

He lifted the letters out of his waistband and handed them to Aimée, who turned them over to Odil. Odil had rounded shoulders and a shock of brown hair that reminded Henri of roof thatching. Henri felt a sudden rush of affection for the other boy. Neither fit their father's mold; neither belonged here in the girls' clearing, but Odil looked as comfortable as Henri felt now that Aimée had arrived. Henri reached down and touched the place where he had smeared his knee blood. *Please let me come back*, he thought.

"Odil reads English," Aimée explained to the group, "and he was kind enough to volunteer his services."

The boy began to read, moving his lips silently around unfamiliar consonants, until he gasped. His rocking ceased and he fixed his eyes on the ground.

"What do they say?" Henri wanted to know. He felt, suddenly, as if he had sprung a trap. Odil and the girls knew more than he did. The letters: bait. Not a game, as he suspected when Margaux untied the sash and let him look around. Aimée had tricked him. To entertain her friends? If he had wanted all the girls in the village to know his private business, he could have told them himself.

"Must I tell him?" Odil asked Aimée.

"*Mais oui!*" Anne-Jeanée and Yvette said at once.

Aimée nodded her encouragement.

Henri had two choices: to ask Odil not to tell or to go along with the girls, add his voice to theirs. And he *did* want to know.

"Please," Henri said.

Odil stared up at the sky, wincing at the brightness, his unruly hair a peaked meringue. Henri wanted to lick his palm, lean over, and flatten it into place the way his mother often attempted to tame his curls. A wave of impatience crashed over him. Henri—future master craftsman, a much more essential societal position than Odil's—needed this information. Odil owed it to him to speak. But instead he kept staring upward, as if something up there had changed, when really it was the same old sky: too bright.

"Go *on*, then," Henri said. "I don't have all day!"

Odil clenched his fists, then opened his mouth. The words unfurled like buds turning to blossoms. Delicate. "You are not—" and here Odil paused, seeking the right words. The girls urged him gently.

"Oh continue!"

"Tell us."

"Not what?"

Odil gave a polite, parlor-sized cough before finishing his sentence. "Not your father's firstborn son."

The words slammed into Henri's chest, each one a fist. Not a firstborn son.

C'est impossible.

Odil had said it sweetly. With kindness. With an apologetic cough. But Henri wanted to punch his mouth, jam his fingers into Odil's teeth to make him take the words back. Everyone knew Henri as the firstborn—the only son—of the Sun-Bringer. If he wasn't that, he wasn't *anything*. He leaned forward and Yvette and Bernadine grabbed his elbows to hold him back. Henri didn't struggle. He didn't want to hit Odil. It wasn't anyone's fault but his father's.

"If I have a brother, then where is he?"

Aimée whispered the question to Odil and he nodded.

"An older brother," Odil elaborated. "*Roh-bair.* He lives with his mother in a place called New York."

Only firstborn sons could inherit their fathers' workshops. That meant *Roh-bair.* Henri would always be inferior: second born. No wonder Papa criticized him all the time. Not because he wanted Henri to learn, but because Henri would never matter

as much as *Roh-bair*. He shut his eyes and leaned backwards. His
ringlets splayed along the hem of Bernadine's dress. She reached
for his head and stroked it. He remembered climbing into his
father's lap as a tot, grabbing onto the rims of his ears, Papa pretending to be a steamer floating across the ocean. Henri would
steer and beg for more. They loved that game, both of them,
only Papa had really wanted to steer his way back. Away from
Henri, toward the boy he left behind. His whole life, he had
been a substitute. Second born. Second best. Which isn't best
at all.

Henri's voice rose to a high-register wail—not a word so
much as an outpouring of sound. His cheeks turned wet from
rivulets of tears.

"I broke him," Odil said, wrapping his arms around his knees
and rocking in 3/2 rather than 4/4.

The girls begged Henri to hush, and when that didn't work,
one of them used the blindfold as a gag. He sputtered and tried
to shake it off, the sound quieting in his throat, the tears dripping down his cheeks and making dark marks on the fabric.
Bernadine scooted in front of him, kneeling face to face, and
made him promise: stop crying, no noise. His cries of despair
would surely bring an adult and they would be found out. The
Shadow Council of Apprentice Lacemakers would be banned
from congregating.

"And if that happens," Aimée added, "we'll tell about your
dad."

Henri could not let that happen. His mother would be dev-
astated. Would the other master craftsmen reject Henri as one of
them? Would they call for this Roh-bair to be sent to Mireville to
take over the workshop, once they knew Henri did not have this
birthright claim? After a few more subdued wails, Henri agreed

with an up-and-down snap of his head. He had to calm down; he had no other choice. He slumped and breathed and within a minute, Bernadine unbound him.

Odil continued his agitated rocking through this scene, not meeting anyone's eyes.

"Thank you for telling me," Henri told him. "You did the right thing. I wanted to know."

Aimée snapped a thorn off a wild bush and pricked the girls' index fingers one at a time, making them swear never to tell anyone the Blanchard family secret. This reassured Henri slightly. If nobody found out—except for these girls—he could go on being his father's firstborn son to the people who would count his true birth status against him: the music-makers. These girls' fathers.

Bernadine leaned forward to detangle his ringlets, keeping her one bloody finger out of the way.

"*Roh-bair* may be musically gifted," Anne-Jeanée said, "but he is unfit to be a master craftsman."

"How do *you* know?" Henri asked.

"Because he's not here and you are."

Nobody tried to prick Henri; it was his secret because it was his father's. As they sucked their fingers, the girls speculated about the giant storks that brought babies—and how one of those ungainly creatures could be so misguided as to bring a Frenchman's baby to a rich New Yorker. Did the bird fly all the way across the ocean? Where did it sleep when it got tired? Odil kept rocking and mumbling, his fingers twined around a locket that had come loose from inside his shirt.

"What if it's a mistake?" Yvette said, piping up to be loyal to family. She had smudges for eyebrows, and she raised them hopefully.

Henri, fed up with Bernadine's grooming, sat up and moved to the other side of the clearing. Papa had played that game of steamer to America. He kept all those letters in his trousers. It was not a mistake.

The girls all agreed: they preferred Henri to the boy in the letters.

"You are more interesting," Anne-Jeanée told him.

"How do you know?" he insisted.

"You are far more handsome," Yvette added.

"HOW DO YOU KNOW?"

Shh, Aimée mouthed, her finger against her lips. "We cannot let anyone find us here."

Henri, despite wanting to remain undetected, let out a sob and then could not put it back inside. He cried harder.

"I broke him," Odil said again. He ducked under the brambles and fled.

Henri stood up and, ignoring the girls' protests, bolted in the direction Odil had gone. His place in the world had shifted. He needed to get home before his father got back from church and decided to change out of his Sunday clothes.

Home.

The word pounded in his ears as he ran.

He had three things to do, the first two easier than the third.

Get home.

Return the letters.

Pretend nothing had changed.

II.

A Pin on the
Cylinder of Industry

Chapter Nine
Henri discovers a talent.

Curiosity soon overcame Henri's misgivings. The girls knew his secret and didn't treat him differently; this gave him courage to ask them for more translations. Over the next few months, he kept meeting Aimée after church to exchange new clutches of letters for knowledge of the contents. Odil Michaute agreed to stay in the Shadow Council and translate the missives only if he didn't have to interact with Henri directly. No matter how often Henri swore he'd remain calm this time, Odil wouldn't change his mind. Which meant that Henri found himself exiled from the willow-branch camp. That breathy, shady place of beauty. Part of him had known, when he planted his bloody palm on the grass, that he would not be allowed back.

Still, learning more about his half-brother was worth it. Aimée memorized Odil's translations, best she could, and repeated them back to her friend. It was little different than learning a hymn or the order of ingredients to add to a soup.

Aimée appreciated Odil's honesty; a more eager-to-please boy would have said *oui* without setting conditions. Aimée, moreover, appreciated having an ongoing reason to include him in the council. Odil had good ideas and often could articulate both sides of an argument without having a stake in either one.

Aimée suspected herself of a temper; as a leader, she often sided with one girl over another without examining the full situation, and when she changed her mind mid-course, she feared speaking up and being unmasked as inconstant. She quickly learned to ask Odil what he thought before deciding her feelings on a matter.

Soon all the girls in the village—even the meanest ones—acknowledged Odil with nods and smiles and *ça vas*. Their parents quickly followed this example, not wanting their daughters to think them unkind.

By September 1847, Odil was no longer invisible. He couldn't walk a meter by himself without being greeted. The boys his own age ignored him, but nobody expected those boys to change, and besides, Odil had real friends now. Nobody seemed to think him daft anymore. It became a commonplace sight for the girls' parents to go out of their way after church to tip their hats to him. If he had already started rocking, Odil didn't stop to acknowledge them, but occasionally a few fingers rose in greeting or a quick nod affirmed the interaction had been welcomed.

Henri tried interacting with Odil, pulling him aside to chat in the doorway of a closed shop like the girls did, but the boy rebuffed his attempts, running away or pulling his fringe low over his eyes in an attempt to disappear. Henri knew the other boys could be cruel; he too had earned their wrath and this, he felt, should be a bond between them.

"Just leave him alone," Aimée counseled Henri.

Henri agreed, not wanting to upset the source of the information he needed. Still, it made him feel a little lonely, cast out of the center of the circle by a boy nobody had paid any mind to before. Henri liked that Odil had friends. He just wished he could be one of them. Gathered together inside that pretty space, instead of being left outside like a dropped petal.

Through the course of the painstaking translation process—from his father's drawer to the Shadow Council, then delivered back in whispers from Aimée—Henri grew to understand that his half-brother was made not of flesh but of ink on paper: a story that populated his father's heart. Robert would never get paste in his hair or forget to carry his dishes to the wash-basin.

About two months after they read the first letter, Henri and Aimée held a short conference in one of the alleys between *violon* shops.

"Your father still hasn't found a new hiding spot?" she asked.

Henri shook his head *non*. "Do you think he loved Mme. Stanton?"

Aimée shrugged. "He'd hide them better if he really cared about her, because he wouldn't want you to find out. Besides, she's across the ocean."

"Still, though."

"Your father trussed up your mother, not some American, for keeps."

Henri remembered when he and Aimée had made that thread web in the trees. Had his father trapped his mother like that? He envisioned Aimée inside a birdcage, her pert mouth turned into a beak, spilling forth her husband's words instead of her own. The cruelty astonished him. His lower lip began to tremble. Was that what Aimée thought of him? Just because he was born a boy? He burst into tears, too worried to ask.

Aimée, wanting to soothe him, added, "Love can be good too. Like with your parents. Even though your father—" and here she let her voice drop off for a moment. "Your parents are happy, *n'est-ce pas?*"

Henri wiped his eyes and nodded. *Happier than yours*, he thought. Madame Maullian walked behind her husband and never spoke. The whole village knew that M. Maullian drank too much wine and, when he could afford it, chartreuse, a bright-green liquor made by monks. Henri swiped a tear away with a finger and then licked it, savoring the salty, familiar tang. At least the earliest letter from Delia was dated before Papa and Maman got married. Henri felt certain Papa had not gone farther than the walnut grove in years. Henri had been alive nearly a whole decade by now. And in all that time, his father had sent serinettes across the ocean without going himself.

"Do you think Robert will come visit us?" Henri asked.

Aimée didn't think so, because of the long trip and how much more likely Monsieur Blanchard's secret would be found out if a young stranger who resembled him arrived in Mireville.

"Maybe he's cross-eyed," Henri suggested, "and his mother won't send him because she doesn't want Papa to find out."

She squeezed his shoulders with delight. A new game! "*Roh-bair* uses too much pomade," she suggested.

"His feet are so big he goes shoeless."

"He keeps losing his baby teeth but the adult ones aren't growing in. His whole mouth is a pianoforte with missing keys."

"He's unlovable," Henri said, and that was the end of the game, for his father loved that boy. It was there—love *and* loyalty—in the worn creases of each and every precious letter.

In December, the schoolmaster released the class early due to a rare blizzard.

Henri imagined that if all the lacemakers in town snipped their work free from its bobbins and threw the whole white lot out their windows, perhaps it would be as beautiful. He headed down toward the river, his eyelashes frosty. Snow glazed the houses as if an exceptional varnish had been applied. Henri thought of puffy white birds in cages—cold snowbirds. Perhaps Papa would agree to pin new songs for a snow-themed serinette. "Neige, Neige Blanche" could be one of the selections, and "Alouette" too, because even though that tune didn't include snow, a song about a lark being plucked might make the canaries learn extra fast.

The river usually flowed slowly past the vermillion roofs, tucking itself in close to the banks to avoid making an undue ruckus as it passed the holy convent, where nuns ticked in and out of doors with the steadiness of minutes. On this particular snowy day, though, the river rushed by, taking bits of its banks to Ambaville. Henri followed its course to Le Vieux Pont, the oldest bridge in the village, *sans* railing. On the hottest days, the girls of Mireville congregated there—Aimée and Bernadine and Yvette and Anne-Jeanée and all their sisters. These girls' great-grandmothers, when they were young, used to stand on the bridge, gossiping about what it might feel like to plunge in. Their grandmothers took this indulgence a step further. They dared to sit, throwing their legs over each other, reaching out to put their arms around each other, a hot and giggling mass of girls who preferred each other's sweaty company to being alone in their parents' houses. The next generation of girls not only sat and giggled and mused about swimming but unlaced their shoes to feel the breeze through the stitches of their stockings. And now, this present gaggle had progressed to taking off not only their shoes but their stockings. Oh, the joy of baring one's feet in public! This—right this very moment, in a village that rarely allowed change, let alone frivolity—was modern life.

Today, though, the bridge was midwinter deserted, save a lone gray cat huddled in the middle. There were plenty of strays like this one in town, since the cat-gut strings of the violins were not real feline innards but sheep's intestines. This cat, however, looked scared or stuck. A ferocious gust could blow it over the edge, and it would drown. Or it might freeze, unprotected from the elements.

Someone should help it, but Henri feared being blown over the side himself. He believed himself a better type of boy than his taunting classmates. But here, on the banks of the river, his fingers numb despite his heavy wool mittens, he realized the horrible truth about himself. He would rather go home and get warm than rescue a living creature. Perhaps it'd be a relief if his half-brother came to Mireville and took over the workshop.

As Henri considered his options, Aimée Maullian was creeping quietly downstairs in her stockings, tiptoeing past her father, asleep—or more likely still soused—in his favorite chaise in the parlor. She donned her green wool cape in the slush room. Her own shoes, with crimped points for toes, would take much too long to lace, so she shoved on her father's boots. One had a length of white lace for tying the top together, as the upper clasp hinge had broken. Her sister Émilie had made the strand; she was the best at threadwork besides their mother. Way better than Aimée. Who would get in terrible trouble if Papa discovered she had stolen his boots. If she put the boots close to the fire upon her return, though, they would dry before Papa woke.

She avoided the creakiest floorboards, not wanting to turn around and find her brother Guillaume there, watching her. So what if he was? She could go out in the storm. Their six sisters had gone out to play an hour ago. It felt like a holiday, this kind of cold. Besides, if Guillaume told on her for abandoning house-work to play in the snow, Aimée could threaten to tell Papa about Guillaume's late-night adventures. Her brother would take that bargain—he'd have to if he wanted Papa not to lock him in his room at night. Aimée had tried staying up past bedtime, wanting to catch her brother sneaking out, but she always fell asleep too soon. Proof discolored his body on the mornings after his mysterious sojourns, though. That's how she knew she was right: a bruise on his cheekbone, splashes of mud on the backs of his trousers, a deep cut along his forearm. She didn't know where he went—someplace with rain—or why their father didn't wait up to stop him.

Aimée skated her father's heavy boots across the frozen ground, sliding one foot, then the other. The wind pushed her wool hood off and she did not bother to fix it. Tiny dots of cold landed on her cheeks and ears and hair. She liked this—improvising. She also liked the attention that came with being tsked over and cleaned afterward, except for when Guillaume did it, as he always insisted on reaching up her chemise to scrub out her armpits.

Henri spotted his friend just as she saw him too: a relief. Aimée would know what to do about the cat. Snowflakes landed in her hair like sparkly *bijoux*—diamonds, perhaps, or filigreed silver. He moved closer and pulled her wool hood back on, because kind people made sure their friends didn't freeze. Aimée pushed the hood off again and grinned.

"Let me have your boots," she said.

"For what?"

"I'll go out there and get the cat."

"What's wrong with your boots?" Henri asked.

"They're too big. Trade with me."

Aimée could convince Henri of anything, and he knew she knew it, and there they were exchanging boots, leaning on each other for support. She bent down and laced his boots onto her

feet. Henri had discovered his grandmother's British novels earlier that year, and Aimée wore the very sort of cloak someone
would put in a frontispiece illustration. *It would be nice to live in a
book*, he thought, *pressed safe between the pages.*

Aimée marched out onto the bridge. She scooped the cat
up and carried it back to land, whereupon Henri sat back down
on the frozen ground and took off his wool mittens so he could
receive and relace his boots.

"It froze to death," she said. "We're too late."

Aimée dropped the stiff animal onto Henri's lap. The cat
leaned against his chest. A common-looking one, gray and striped
and skinny. Henri ran his fingers over its ribs, playing them by
feel like pins on a serinette barrel. He wanted it—her—to be all
right.

His fingers began to buzz. He imagined bubbles of whole
notes, round ones, blown out of nothing and into being, the
new sounds pushing under the animal's ribs, slow and lovely
and unafraid to sustain themselves. He held on, letting the song
vibrate through his body, down his arms, and through his fingers, ignoring Aimée and the snow.

Henri understood, suddenly, how this cat sounded to herself without other cats nearby. As he worried this thought in
his brain—how could he be so certain it was a *she*?—there came
a gasp, and another gasp, followed by a yawn-like gulp of air.
Her ribs began to mark out whole notes. The tempo acceler-
ated, from *adagio* to *andante*, those ribs and their music moving
beneath Henri's palms. Boy and cat shivered against one another,
vibrating in equal measure from joy and chill.

"She's not dead," Henri said. "Look."

Aimée crouched down beside him, her hair wild and dotted
with snow. Her eyes flashed with dots of reflected sunlight. "What

did you *do*, Henri?" She said the words to his nose, his eyes, his wind-numbed cheeks.

"Nothing," Henri said.

"The cat didn't move, not once, when I carried it," she insisted. "What did you do, Henri?"

"Your hands were cold. You just couldn't feel her breathing."

He kept petting the animal. A masterful vibrato began on his lap, deepening the rib song, as if it resonated not just through the cat's bones but through both of them. Aimée grabbed one of Henri's legs, gently tugging off her father's boot. His toes, and the blue lines inside his skin, felt heavy and slow, the purring vibrato on his lap a strange, warm hammer, chipping away at the ice spreading through his body. He let his friend tie his boots back on. He knew the impossibility of petting a cat back to life but was pleased by the attention. Aimée finished lacing his boots onto his feet. He stood up, dislodging the feline, and the vibrato stopped. This made him feel better and worse, and he had no words for either, so he turned and started picking his way across the slippery road. The cat followed.

"I promise I won't tell," Aimée called.

"About the letters? I know! You took a blood oath."

"About the cat."

"Nothing happened!" He turned toward home. If he didn't keep going, his toes would freeze, and the pressure of walking all that distance would make each toe drop off the stem of his foot, ten round grapes rolling around inside his boots.

When he burst in the kitchen door, Henri asked Maman for an old bedsheet and a saucer of milk for his new companion. Nathalie, he'd call her. Madame Rigoniet, the mother of three similarly aged daughters, had been by with a custard. Once he settled the cat into the workshop, in a nest he made for her beneath the hayloft, Henri ate a bowl of custard and soaked his toes in a footbath until they returned to a reassuring shade of pink.

Maybe he had healed that cat, restarted her heart, just like Aimée thought. Hadn't he? Doesn't the word of a witness count as proof? He'd rubbed his own sadness, and perhaps some of his mother's, into Nathalie's fur, and her breath came back. Robert Dumphries Stanton, for all his musical precocity, couldn't revive the dead. Perhaps this was Henri's true talent, what made him extraordinary. Perhaps this would make Papa proud.

The next morning, Henri fussed with his bread and *beurre*. He pulled a piece of round meat off the platter and folded it in half and lodged it under his tongue. If it unfolded, he would tell his parents about the cat. It did not. This disappointed him. Which meant, of course, that he *should* tell, now that he knew he wanted to. He pushed his chair away from the table and stood up to address his parents.

"I have something to tell you."

His mother looked over with fixed interest, while his father tore off a hunk of bread and began to chew it.

"It's that I am special. Like you, Papa."

Maman sighed. "Of course you are special, darling." Her approval landed sweet and soft, more fit for a lamb than a growing boy with powers. Henri suspected she was humoring him.

"It's true!" he insisted.

Papa continued chewing far longer than Henri wanted to wait. Eventually he swallowed with gusto. "You think you've made the sun shine brighter?" An eight-note laugh followed, quick and mirthless.

"No. My gift is different." Henri took a deep breath. "I can heal the dead."

Papa's lips puckered like pieces of leather sewn by a new apprentice. Maman arranged a clump of her hair, fingering through two wavy sections that had knotted together.

"The dead," Maman mused. "Was it M. Fiboneaux, poor soul?"

"Not a person, a cat," Henri said. "The one from yesterday. Nathalie."

"That's nice," Maman said.

"*Mon fils*," Papa warned, his shoulders tensing under his shirt.

"Ask Aimée Maullian," Henri said. "She saw it happen."

Maman's gaze bounced between Henri and Papa. "Aimée is a very nice girl," she finally said. She nodded, as if the conversation had ended, then shoved the meat platter in front of her husband. "More?"

"Just because I am extraordinary—" his father continued.

"Don't, Georges," Maman interrupted.

Henri gripped the top rung of his chair and squeezed. "If you don't believe me, then I'll quit believing you moved the clouds."

Maman flashed a patient grin. "But your grandmother Cérine witnessed it. The paper ran an article."

"How is that any different than Aimée watching me yesterday?"

"As the lacemakers say, cut it out," his father said. "Nobody will listen to you."

Henri wished Papa had the guts to add, "because you're a second-born son," but he didn't.

"YOU DON'T EVEN LIKE THE SUN!" Henri shouted, then bolted from the kitchen.

Geneviève would have loved to share this gossip with her mother-in-law. Henri had a point about Georges, though; he

claimed to hate the heat and brightness. Could it have been
Cérine who moved the clouds? At four months old, Georges
wouldn't have known what he wanted. And a new mother would
have yearned for the world to be more hospitable, *n'est-ce pas?* Love
like that could crack open the sky and let the brightness through.
Besides, everyone knew the sun made babies cry. And all women
knew how often men took credit for what women accomplished.

Georges stuck a piece of meat in his mouth and chewed it.
He didn't ruminate on his cloud-moving feat or Henri's outra-
geous claims but on his firstborn, Robert, the musical prodigy.
Robert wouldn't have made such a scene at mealtime. He had
better manners. And he didn't need to get attention with fits and
falsehoods. His skills earned him plenty.

Georges felt sorry for Henri more than annoyed with him;
this son would never equal the other in talent.

Chapter Ten
Modern life.

The following Sunday, after church, Henri hovered around Aimée's family until she broke away from her sisters and followed him to a quiet spot in front of the *boulangerie*. She wore a new dress, brown and poorly altered. Henri guessed it had been her mother's, and that it would be passed down to her next-oldest sister when she had outgrown it. Unless her father found a job. The last "new" dress of hers had been a hand-me-down too.

Henri leaned his shoulders against the sun-warmed stone wall and marveled at his frosty breath fogging the window. Soon it would be Papa's birthday. And then a new year. And then his birthday. Aimée's shoulder-length hair flew into her face until she traded places with Henri, and then it fluttered mostly over her shoulder, only occasionally tangling against her cheek or falling into his mouth. She would pin those tresses up when she turned sixteen, signifying she had come of age.

"I told my parents about Nathalie. That's what I named the cat." Henri's cheeks radiated a furious blush. "They don't believe me, though."

"I can't believe you told them!"

Henri paused. "But it really happened."

"I know it did. But parents are too sure of the world. Especially master craftsmen. I'll bet your father believes everything he says is the truth."

Henri considered this.

"It doesn't matter what they think, anyway. I was there. I saw you."

"My father won't care what you think any more than he cares what I think."

"*Pourquoi pas?* Because I'm a girl?" Aimée arched her tiny eyebrows. They were the daintiest thing about her face, which was mostly square, with a broad forehead that her mother made her hide beneath bangs, and with an equally strong jaw.

"I didn't mean it like that."

"There's no other way to mean it," she said. "Besides, you know I'm right. You wouldn't have gone looking for his opinion if mine was enough for you."

Henri felt a hot flush creep up his neck. If he had been content to share this secret with his best friend, who just happened to be a girl, he could have avoided the whole breakfast scene with his father. Just then, Odil Michaute wandered by. When he spied Henri, he pointed his index finger at him.

"Hello, Odil," Aimée called.

"I'M FINE," Henri said, same as always, a pre-emptive strike against the boy's usual litany. "You can join us if you'd like."

Odil shook his head no, then mumbled his usual—*I broke him, he's broken*—and wandered off still chanting.

"Can you please convince him I'm fine?" Henri asked Aimée. "I hate it when he does that."

"He's reading your heart," she said. "It's supposed to be uncomfortable."

❋ ❋ ❋

According to Delia's letters, by ten years of age, Robert Stanton had mastered the violin, cello, flute, pianoforte, and the unlikely ophicleide—a large-keyed bugle. How Georges wished he could hear the boy play! He had stuck Robert's portrait on the underside of his chiffonier with a daub of paste intended for securing tune sheets to the inside lids of serinettes. Occasionally he knelt and reached down to touch the boy's face. Better to touch the portrait than to gaze at it, elongating the boy's toddler face, widening the space between the eyes, styling the hair in his mind to guess at current appearance.

Delia had given him the perfect Mireville son: a prodigy. His French son could not compare. Henri had no musical gifts and hadn't even bothered to crank the parlor serinette in months. And now that cat! Surely it couldn't have been dead in the first place. One night, when Geneviève sat on the edge of the bed unpinning her hair, he tried to draw her into conversation about Henri's delusion.

"Shouldn't we treat this new mania of his?" he said. "A few months in a Swiss sanitarium would straighten him out."

Geneviève pulled the last pin out and set them one at a time in a dish on the vanity table, *ping ping ping.* "He needs your attention, not a doctor."

"We can afford it," Georges said. "If that's what you're worried about. There's a clinic over in Lucerne that deals with delusions—"

"He's only a little boy!" she said. "He looks up to you."

"Little? He turns ten in May. Kids know when one of their own doesn't fit in—and they are unforgiving. I just want him to be *normal*."

"What if Henri doesn't want to be normal?" Geneviève's shoulders rose, then fell, and rose again. She imagined her body hitched to the crank that turned the cylinder of their days. She hoped her husband would interrupt so she didn't have to complete her thought, but he didn't, so she added what they both knew: "He wants to be like you. Worthy of you."

Georges rubbed his eyes, as if the words were a physical irritant. "What's special about me—"

"I know," she interrupted. "It's a myth, not a talent; you don't even remember moving the clouds." Perhaps she had fallen in love with this man not because of the story surrounding him, or his personality, but because she admired his mother. Perhaps Georges had been turning back into his father ever since Cérine died. All this talk of *normal*. Of *cures*.

"You're upset with me." Georges used his fingers to apologize, wiggling her arms out of the white sleeves, stroking the skin of each arm as one would test a new fingerboard.

Ah. Her husband's touch asked a question—always his way, to inquire by feel, as if she were another one of his serinettes, pitched to his liking. But Geneviève could decide how to answer, because this—here—was modern life.

"We are not done talking about Henri," Geneviève said.

"Tomorrow," Georges said and blew out the candle.

She couldn't help thinking about it these days—*a baby*. Henri would start apprenticing soon, and she would be left alone in the kitchen. Maybe she had been hasty in her decision—all those years ago. Her husband didn't have enough imagination to suspect her of deviousness; she never left her herbs in obvious spots, and if he found them, he would think she had them for cooking.

Moonlight played a long cadenza against her husband's neck. Geneviève remembered how she used to stay awake to watch the moon move over his body, how sometimes his lips puckered and yet he never made a sound besides the sticky pop of his mouth opening and closing. She used to love the light on his skin. Maybe her marriage did need a baby.

Georges Blanchard heated his workshop with a woodstove so the materials wouldn't warp and the apprentices could bunk comfortably overnight on their pallets in the back room. Nathalie enjoyed her status as the only feline allowed to partake in these luxurious conditions. Georges didn't mind her, because he hated mice and sometimes dreamed of the scritching of their tiny claws against the floorboards. In his dreams, he tried to step on their tails.

In February, Henri discovered a dead orange cat in one of the violin alleys. He wanted Nathalie to have a companion. And he still wanted his family to believe in him, the way Aimée did. He carried the cat up the hill and burst into the workshop, running past the apprentices, most of whom didn't look up from their workbenches.

Papa took one look at Henri's offering and said, "Toss it in the woodstove."

Henri had to show his father what he could do. Perhaps then Papa would treat him as a real firstborn son. He leaned close so the other apprentices wouldn't hear. "No—come outside."

Georges set down the courbette; he had been straightening bent pins. Returning metal into its intended shape satisfied him. A surge of anger flashed through his veins, the way he imagined it might feel to be struck by lightning. *Not this delusion again.*

He blamed Henri for being so impressionable. He blamed his wife for not disciplining the boy enough. Perhaps Georges himself had contributed, too—all those evenings sitting on the floor, letting Henri crawl all over him. He had wanted the boy to love him.

"Just come outside," Henri insisted.

"I have work to do."

Henri didn't want to threaten his father, but what choice did he have? "Come, or I'll tell Maman about *Roh-bair*."

Georges had been practicing saying his son's name the American way, with that hard *T. Rah-burt*. It sounded like a cheer that way. The French sounds didn't parse for him right away, those syllables from his son's mouth. It took a moment for Georges to understand the implications.

The boy knew about his half-brother. Georges's most dangerous (and most beloved) secret. A wave of dizziness, of terror, surged through his body. He grabbed the lip of his workbench to steady himself. "Come with me," he hissed, then proceeded to march out the back of the workshop, only pausing to hold the door for his son. The boy still cradled the dead animal.

"Put that down." Georges shut the door and gripped the boy's shoulder. "You can't tell your mother. Or anyone! Do you understand? Only firstborns can inherit workshops. You will lose your place in the world. You will lose everything."

Henri sighed. Papa didn't understand at all. "I don't care about the *workshop*. You are the Sun-Bringer. Why shouldn't I have magic too?"

Georges sighed and gestured at the cat, thinking this might be an efficient way to change the subject. "If nothing happens, you won't talk about it again?"

By *it*, at first Henri thought he meant resurrection. But maybe he meant Robert. Either way, he promised.

Henri led Papa behind the ice house, then sat down and made a nest of his lap. The cat needed a bath. He laid his hands on the orange, matted fur, stroking the powdery white whiskers. He tried thinking of bubbles, but nothing happened. He tried thinking of rib songs, but nothing happened. He channeled whole notes, then buoyant arpeggios, and finally the joy Nathalie brought him—the gray-and-white fishbone patterns on her fur moving up and down with each breath.

"Please," he whispered into the cat's ear. "Let this be something I can do."

Henri pulled his fingers through knots in the fur. He sang songs—not out loud, but in his mind, songs his grandmother used to sing—to refill the cat's body with warmth.

After a while, his back began to cramp and his fingers grew cold. He lifted his head. Papa had left. Henri stood up and rubbed his neck. The goats' water trough stood nearby. With his hand, he broke through a thin crystalline layer of ice on the surface, then plunged the cat in. He pushed its body up and down in the water, hoping such vigorous dunking would wake it back up. That didn't work either—*zut*. Lacking a better plan, Henri left the cat submerged in the trough.

Shame stuffed his throat like pollen. He wasn't extraordinary. Or even special. He had believed in himself for no reason. Moreover, he had proved his plainness to Papa in trying to argue the opposite.

Henri didn't want to be around his father. Or to explain to Maman how his heart had broken, cracked open like an egg, and now the viscous mess was filling his belly with dread, making him not want dinner. If he told her what happened, Maman would claim Papa didn't care whether or not he cured that cat. But she didn't understand. She didn't know about Robert. Or how every single day when Henri woke up and pretended to be the firstborn son of a master craftsman, he was lying to her. He and Papa both.

❋ ❋ ❋

As the only child of a wealthy family, Robert Dumphries Stanton expected to be doted on—and he was, he *was!*—by his mother and the women she hired as nursemaids, cooks, maids, and playmates. Even his male teachers constantly swore his smarts surpassed every one of their previous charges'.

His father loved him and said yes to all of his demands, but occasionally added, "If only you looked more like me..." before going back to his newspaper.

An odd complaint, but it was true. Robert's ears stuck out and he had a medium-sized nose set in a heart-shaped face, plus those loopy curls. His father had diminutive ears, an impressive schnoz, and a square chin that balanced his wide forehead and slack bangs. So what if they didn't look alike? Robert began slipping compositions into his father's reading pile, just to court his attention, whereupon Alastair would return them with corrections.

To commemorate his eleventh birthday, in October 1848, Robert convinced his mother to hire two live-in musicians to help further his gifts. They schooled the boy in harmony, counterpoint, and the differences between European and New World music. As his music lessons increased in complexity, Robert began composing furiously—not to impress his father, but for himself. Soon his originality blossomed.

Delia scoured the countryside until she found and purchased an old, high-pitched flageolet that he could use to train her canaries how to sing his compositions. Long before serinettes, musicians had used these high-pitched, clarinet-like instruments to train birds. The cocks that Robert trained with his own compositions sold quickly to women who had tired of "For He's a Jolly Good Fellow." Variety kept Delia's customers happy.

And what wonderful afternoons they had, Robert and his mother, locked in the majestic glass aviary, the keys dangling from her neck, both of them breathing in the wet and musty stench of seeds dunked in water to soften them. He played for them too—the hens—knowing they wouldn't memorize the music, just for their enjoyment. The birds twittered back at him, as if in conversation, inspiring new compositions.

Robert imagined he could be happy at home forever, playing his flageolet, blowing so hard his notes lifted the crocheted greenery away from the fake branches. Wings ruffling his hair and eyebrows. His mother clapping for him, not her birds.

Chapter Eleven
Geneviève acknowledges her loneliness.

Usually, only gifted boys stayed in school past age twelve. Guillaume Maullian, now thirteen and a half, had no special traits or intelligence; he merely had nowhere else to go during the daytime. Nobody wanted him as an apprentice because nobody wanted his father, a former lace designer who had made one poor pattern. Many women had spent many days ruining their eyes turning M. Maullian's pattern into lace. The resulting trousseau had been hand-carried to a princess in a very fine country, and the princess grew so sick of looking at its ugliness that she died. The other pattern designers refused to train Guillaume; the master craftsmen running the music workshops didn't want him, either. So Guillaume stayed in school, kept an eye on his sister, and teased the younger boys.

At night, usually about once a month or whenever he couldn't take the sameness of his life anymore, he sneaked out to an abandoned farmhouse across the German border. There, a rowdy group of young men congregated to drink and pummel each other. Guillaume had to risk stealing the admission fee from his mother's coin purse—that was the only reason he didn't go every night. That and the long uphill walk—two miles past the Blanchard place, then off the road and into the woods. Yet he desperately needed the physical release. Hitting another man, applause ringing in his ears like a punch, kept his anger sharp, focused in the right place. Otherwise he might hurt one of his classmates. Then there'd be even less of a chance anyone would give him an apprenticeship.

In recent weeks, his mother had been hiding her purse—had she discovered his habit?—which meant he hadn't been out at night in forever. One spring afternoon, after school, he considered his alternatives. If he chose well, he could fight one of his classmates and make it seem like the other boy's fault. Most of them were circled around the biggest, flattest stump in the schoolyard, involved in a game with stones. Guillaume was bigger than all of them but knew better than to attack a group. Then he spotted that measly Blanchard boy, the one who had everything handed to him by his father. A plan formed.

Guillaume called to him with a friendly voice.

Henri trotted over, half certain this was a trap, but he so rarely received an invitation from the other boys. "What do you want?" he said.

A bit of boldness to him after all. Guillaume said, "Ready to see something neat?" and Henri said, "*Mais bien sûr*," and then, with a quick flick, Guillaume speared a worm with the tip of his fountain pen. He had been practicing his aim using water pipes or trees as victims. The worm-and-pen trick required more delicate aim. Guillaume laughed in jubilation when the worm juices splattered out of the hole he had made.

Henri screamed. "You are horrible!"

"You watched," Guillaume said. "That makes you horrible too."

He expected a punch in return—or a slap at the least—but instead of retaliating, Henri ran to his favorite oak. At the base, he spotted a fledgling bird that had fallen out of its nest. Maybe his scream had startled it. Another thing to feel awful about. Poor worm. Poor bird! Henri began to climb, wanting to get farther away from Guillaume. Once hidden in the branches, he cried at the unjustness of the world until the leaves blurred. If he had known the older boy's plan, he could have stopped him. Punched him in the stomach or yelled in his ear to give him a headache. Henri wiped his snot and tears with his cuffs. He needed to go home before his mother began to worry, but he didn't want to walk by his classmates in this sorry condition.

When the other boys' voices eventually trailed away, he let himself down, scraping a knee against the bark, and then ran over to the worm. Both halves still rested close by each other. Henri nudged them back together with an expert flick of his fingers, glad the cut had not gone through its heart. The worm shuddered. Its ooze congealed like paste. Then it wiggled off, whole.

Charles DeBourgignon, the smallest boy in school, appeared from behind a different oak. He had straight dark hair, which the sun had done little to lighten, and it stuck out on all sides like poorly tied fringe.

"Are you all right?" Charles asked in a hopeful voice.

Henri said *oui* without looking at the boy, then asked if he had seen Guillaume anywhere.

"No?" All of Charles's sentences ended with an upward lilt that made them sound like questions. "They're all gone now?"

Henri usually tried to avoid Charles, but this was a useful piece of information. He breathed a sigh of relief. Charles liked complimenting Henri, probably in the hopes of being friends, but Henri didn't like being praised; it felt so unfamiliar. Like putting on someone else's trousers.

"How did you do that?" Charles asked. "*C'est magnifique.*"

Henri had the sudden impulse to show off. "That was no big deal," he said, "but wait until you see this."

Even as he approached the dead bird, he knew he shouldn't. He would fail—again—and Charles would no longer have that admiring look on his face. Henri had promised he wouldn't try again. He was not God. He did not change the sky. He was nothing like his father. The worm, well, surely anyone could glue one of them back together with a touch. Like two pieces of a cream pastry. Henri had done it without even thinking about it. He stopped himself.

"Never mind," he said.

"I can keep a secret," Charles said, this time without a questioning lilt at the end. "I swear on my sister."

"I bet you can," Henri said. But suddenly it occurred to him: *of course—birds.* He knew their songs from the woods, and from the workshop, where men put measures together one pin at a time. Henri was fluent in tweets and trills, the warning calls, the gorgeous pomposity of good singing. He couldn't fail if he tried healing a bird! Henri approached the tiny feathered being and bent down; Charles followed suit, then poked at it with a finger.

"It's still warm," Charles pointed out.

Henri pushed the younger boy's hand away, then touched the bird's chest. The new feathers felt like dry straw, its tiny claws brittle like discarded wood shavings. Henri whistled the melody to "Neige, Neige Blanc," for he had been thinking about that song on the day at the bridge with Nathalie. He reached out with his mind to what had once sung beneath those hollow bird-ribs— sixteenth notes, *allegro* tempo, perhaps. He wished so hard, he promised he would never wish for anything else if he could just make this one thing happen, for he sensed the younger boy's admiration, warm and true, and it flooded him with the longing to prove himself.

The *oiseau*'s tiny head swiveled. Henri stroked the dear little feathers until the beak opened and a thin trill came out. He cupped the baby in his hands, then set it upright on its fragile stick-legs. The bird struggled against his hands, wanting to move, and Henri let it go. One wing had bent in the fall. It stretched its good wing, then hobbled away into the bushes, emitting a wavery trill. Probably calling for its *maman*.

"It's alive," Charles said. "You unkilled it. Oh Henri!"

He *could* heal the dead. He had proof now—and a witness his father would approve of: a boy. Henri had surpassed the Sun-Bringer's feat! His miracle of reviving dead things was repeatable. At least sometimes.

"I can't always do it, though," he admitted. "Charles, please don't tell the other boys."

Charles sprang out of his crouch. "If you'll be my friend, I won't tell."

Henri had never tried having a boy for a friend, but it was a small price for silence. He walked Charles home, two lots away from the convent, and they paused a moment to listen to the nuns shake their sheets and blankets out. The flapping of cloth sounded like adventure, like flight, although both boys knew the nuns never left the convent, where they belonged.

Charles told his sister Bernadine—not about the bird resuscitation, because he had sworn, but about Henri's hands. Their fluency. How he calligraphed better than their teacher, and how he tied knots faster and more securely than Thomas Rigoniet, whose uncle captained a ship in Le Havre.

"You've been watching him?"

Charles's face turned pink. Bernadine felt sorry she had asked. She had warned him that spying on other children wouldn't help him make friends, but Charles kept doing it.

"If Henri's hands are so great," she said, "perhaps he can help me with my lacework."

"He cannot," Charles said. "Do not bother him."

Despite her brother's pleas, she ambushed Henri after school the next day with an incomplete doily pinned to a cylindrical lace pillow, along with a tangle of bobbins and her sharpest needle to pick apart the mess. After all, she knew his secret and had taken a blood oath to protect it. Surely that made them friends on their own terms, regardless of Charles.

Bernadine thrust the pillow in Henri's face. "I hear your hands are *magnifique*."

"Charles," Henri said. "I told you not to tell."

"She's a girl," Charles said. "You said nothing about girls. And I said nothing about the bird. *Zut!*"

Charles's embarrassment made him look like a red-throated thrush with its mouth full of seed. Henri patted him on the back for reassurance.

"It's fine," Henri said. *That's what friends do*, he thought. *Forgive each other's missteps.*

Bernadine ignored them both and pulled her bobbins out of the fabric strip holding them in place to avoid tangles. She held the lace pillow out to Henri, then lifted her finger—the one Aimée had pricked that day among the brambles—and said, "Please?"

"Just this once," he agreed. He sat down on the biggest stump and opened his legs to place the heavy pillow between his knees. He didn't think Bernadine would really tell—she had sworn. But he had always liked thread. And he remembered what Aimée had taught him that day when they played in the woods with her mother's linen. A bit of concentration was all it took to coax threads where you wanted them.

On this particular cloudless day, there were five hundred and fifty-nine lacemakers in Mireville, including the young sons of farmers, who learned the craft when they were still too small to till, plant, and plow. Some became lace pattern-makers, earning more money than the girls who carried out the designs. Music-makers' sons never learned lace, though, especially not sons of master craftsmen. Except here perched the Sun-Bringer's son with a pillow between his knees—an anxious, odd boy once startled in church by a hat with an unconscionably large feather (in truth it was not the feather itself so much as the woman's audacity that upset him, how wronged the people in the row behind her must feel)—a boy fiddling after school with *la dentelle* and bobbins and the wrong kind of pins.

Guillaume Maullian noticed the spectacle and called his classmates over. "Look at the Sun-Bringer's useless son! He's making lace!"

Shocked gasps from the boys, who hurried over, jostling and laughing.

"Cloud off," Henri said to the lot of them, but mostly to Guillaume. "I am *not* useless."

"Because you've been taking lace classes?" Guillaume asked. "Your father must be so proud."

"Bernadine needs a boy's help," René Lupot taunted.

Henri's cheeks flushed—embarrassment always made him think of sunburns, and therefore Papa—but he didn't respond. He kept his focus on the work. Bernadine's bobbins were all of equal length, a little longer than his index finger, skinny on top, with round little hats and white thread faces, and plump on the bottom. Henri pushed forty-two of them to the side so he could concentrate on the twelve that had tangled. His classmates made a ring around the stump as he studied the weave of threads.

"*La dentelle, la dentelle*, Henri's hands are *belle*," Guillaume chanted. The other boys joined in.

Henri had made a terrible mistake. He'd let himself be seen. All because a girl had asked a favor. He could not react, though, or the boys would do worse. He fed one of the strands under the next, untwisted, and uncrossed until he reached the knot itself, which he nursed apart with the needle. When he finished, he wished it had been a bigger knot. He would have liked to spend an hour sliding those bobbins. If it had taken an hour, the boys might have gotten bored and left.

"Girl hands."

"Doily maker!"

"Thank you, Henri," Bernadine said. "May I have my pillow back?"

He unclenched his knees, stood up, and dropped the lace pillow on the stump, his cheeks stinging with equal parts shame and pride. Then he ran to his favorite oak and climbed it. Safe— up there, close to where he imagined the cloud bank used to be. The boys headed to the river, or home, or wherever they liked to go when feeling superior. Henri felt a small stab of delight when he spotted Guillaume heading the other way. The other boys hadn't invited him to tag along. Down below, Bernadine wound the extra thread back onto her bobbins. When she finished, she and Charles came over to say goodbye, but despite their pleas, Henri stayed in the tree until they left, and then he stayed there longer, until his hips started hurting from the branch cradling them. When he finally made it home, his mother seemed glad to see him—and not at all worried. In fact, she didn't even seem to notice he was late.

Bernadine told her lacemaking friends about Henri's hands, and they showed up the next afternoon with their projects, and the next, and the afternoon after that, begging him for help. After a few afternoons, Aimée appeared, her latest work a tangled mess under her arm. Henri raised his eyebrows at her and grinned.

"Let me guess, you need my help," he said.

She shrugged and grinned. "I suppose I have time for you today, if you have time for me."

Henri nodded and said, "I do," and Aimée nodded and said, "I do too," and Bernadine said, "Aimée, quit flirting and get to the back of the line!"

What shame for these girls' brothers—to have a boy from a music-making family hold their sisters' lace pillows between his knees. The boys took to insulting Henri after school before moving on with their usual games.

"*Bonjour*, Pin-Head."

"Don't you mean Bobbin-Head?"

"Lace Boy, we're in stitches."

One by one, the girls left their places in line to admonish their brothers or threaten to reveal their secrets. The brothers wandered off eventually, to throw rocks at each other, or carve their initials into trees, or whatever boys of that sort do to impress each other.

The cold stabbed into Guillaume's lungs and made his chest ache. His sister laughing at him by the stump after school felt worse than his weather-numbed hands. She and her lacemaker friends should all listen to him. Henri Blanchard was acting unworthy of the apprenticeship reserved for him since birth. *C'est injuste.*

Guillaume had been handed nothing; creating his own good fortune would make everyone respect him. Sometimes, when Guillaume couldn't bear the thought of Henri's privileged hands on his sister's work, he commanded Aimée out of line, led her by the hand behind a tree, and pushed her spine against the bark so she couldn't escape, one palm against her collarbone, another on her stomach. He'd pin her there, like a butterfly, while she whispered "please" and "let me go," but of course he never listened until she came up with a good-enough bribe. The cookie she had been saving in her dresser. Chopping wood so Guillaume wouldn't have to do it. Telling one of her pretty friends that he would make a good catch. Sometimes Aimée pretended to laugh in case a friend came running. They never did, those parlor girls, because they didn't want to lose their place in line. They only cared about themselves.

At home, when Aimée misbehaved, Guillaume raised her skirts and pinched her thighs. He never wanted to see her legs, or her *putain* part, but sometimes—when he needed to feel better about his station in life—he made a show of lifting the layers above the knee where her stockings ended, to investigate the damage his fingers had done: that rosy bloom a measure of his only authority.

It had been eleven years since Geneviève went to the midwife and begged for herbs, carrying newborn Henri in her arms. She remembered his suckling sounds, the bouts of wind that made her laugh, his tiny fists flailing in discomfort, how easily she could soothe him with her voice.

Now the house, at last, was quiet. Henri would join his father in the workshop next May, and he had been staying in the village for hours after school; perhaps he had made a friend. A daughter would remain by the hearth instead of growing up and leaving for the workshop. They could whisper about metal spoons the way she and Cérine once did. Besides, Henri would make a good big brother. Having someone small to worry about might help him feel useful.

Geneviève quit taking the midwife's herbs in the first month of spring 1849 and began advancing on Georges each month, hoping to become *enceinte*. Georges's pleasure at her brashness helped the process along. But she was not used to doing things that earned no results. Six months later, without a belly to show for her efforts, she went down the hill to consult with Sibylle.

"I am afraid I am too old," she confessed.

"How long between births?"

Geneviève admitted that her youngest would turn twelve in the spring. He had begun to develop spots on his face, little white protuberances, but hadn't yet complained to her of them. She suspected he was nearing that invisible line at which point he would no longer confide in her.

"If your body has decided not to bear more fruit," Sibylle said, "then I cannot help you. However—" She thrummed her fingers on her chin and ahemmed politely. "Georges could be the problem."

Her husband, clever in the workshop, and clever enough in bed, surely would have produced a baby if left to his own devices. Built it from myrtlewood, with springs for hair, if he had to. And he wanted more babies, or at least he used to.

Sibylle opened her bag, pulled a pair of forceps out, and dug below the rags for a scrap of paper, a pen, and a stoppered bottle of ink. She wrote down an address on the other side of the bridge. "Go on a Tuesday, at the noon hour, when you believe yourself fertile."

Geneviève's fingers fluttered to her throat.

"It's medicinal," Sibylle added.

This reassurance cheered Geneviève during the week before her next fertile time, which occurred during one of her husband's trips to the walnut grove, where he marked trees he wanted cut and delivered to his workshop for serinette cases. She memorized the address, then walked down the hill, past the workshops, enjoying the tremolos and scales floating out of windows and feeling glad that Henri had grown out of his *violon* fear. At the correct location, she found a dull-witted little house. Geneviève knocked and a tall young man opened the door, stooping a bit to stick his head out in greeting.

"Is Sibylle here?" she asked.

He waved her in, leaning past her to lock the door. The musty cool air gave her goosebumps. The young man ushered her into a room furnished only with a bed. He explained that certain men had trouble fathering children. "In such cases, the sowing of extra seeds can give the crop a better chance of success."

A farmer's son, obviously. She crossed her arms and rubbed them with the opposite hands. "What are you proposing?"

"Extra sowing," he said. "Should we produce the intended results, you will have your baby, and your husband will be a proud *papa*. And if your womb has dried out, then at least you will have given it a good try."

Geneviève considered. Henri needed a little brother or sister, didn't he? Only children spoiled fast. Like cheese left unattended in the sun. And without a baby in the house, she would be left to tend the table, the broom, the mantle.

"All right," she said. "One sowing, please."

The farm boy helped unbutton her clothing and remove her corset; tight lacing could interfere with the procedure's intended results. He kept asking, "Is this all right?" button by button, until she pulled her chemise off with an eagerness she never suspected, baring her breasts in the dim room to a stranger, this man who kept his eyes on her instead of focusing on the wall above her the way Georges did. The farm boy's equipment reminded her of a corncob. No wonder Sibylle trusted his fertility. Perhaps all tall men had big corncobs in their pants. She decided to look around church on Sunday for the tall men, and this silly thought thinned her fear. She could barely feel it coursing through her body, and soon it gave way to a more insistent, delicious sort of thrumming. She leaned back on the bed, opening herself to this boy. He began to plow. Improper sounds escaped from her throat, and the sounds urged the boy on in his duties, until they had been completed to both parties' satisfaction. She gave him some money, hoping it was enough.

"Can you return next month?" the boy asked.

Geneviève pressed a cluster of fingers to her lips. They smelled like his body, salt and earth and turnips mixed with a satisfying whiff of perspiration. He had worked hard to pleasure her. Did he want her to return because he enjoyed her body? Or because she had overpaid him? She could not imagine being spotted crossing the river by a woman who might guess her secret.

She told him she'd think about it, then packed her embarrassment beneath her coat and went home.

✳ ✳ ✳

The farm boy! He riled Geneviève with desire, riddled her with want, filled her with an intoxicating mix of gratitude and shame. That night she burned supper. She forgot to clean the bristles of the broom the next morning. By midday, she couldn't do anything but sit for an hour eyeing the wallpaper in the parlor, letting her mind rub over the memories of his hands on her.

Henri noticed the change and called it *happiness*. Geneviève flashed him a questioning look, as if she had no idea what he had seen in her.

"Something delightful has happened! What is it?" Henri asked. "Oh, do tell me."

"It's a secret," his mother said.

"Please, Maman?"

"If something comes of it," she said, "I will."

The following month, she scraped together money from the savings hole Georges had cut in the settee: raiding her husband's secret place to pleasure her own.

She grew bolder during her third and fourth visits, touching the farm boy's face where his eyebrows arched like the bridge she took to visit him, the arch like her back when he dipped his fingers into her, then painted the wetness against her bare breasts. Her body belonged to him in some fundamental way, a gift she could give him. Georges didn't notice anything different, but he hadn't threatened to send Henri for a cure in Switzerland in many months, so perhaps he sensed her new contentment.

Geneviève liked seeing her ring finger touch the farm boy's skin, the simple gold band where it didn't belong. She counted the nights Georges failed to reach for her and came to prefer them, because in falling asleep alone, she could better imagine waking in that squatty little house on the wrong side of the river, shuttling her fingers through the hairs on the boy's chest, matching her breath to his—her cheek pressed against his shoulder, her leg thrown over his in sleepy possession.

The midwife's prescription eventually did its job, either due to the foreign seed or her husband's, grown virulent through competition. In March 1850, Sibylle confirmed Geneviève's pregnancy. She was due in October.

Georges had no idea how resourceful his wife could be. This thought consoled her. When Geneviève told him the news, he lunged for her body, wrapping his hands around her back, kissing her neck, her cheekbones, the tip of her nose.

"I thought you couldn't have any more children," he said. "We've certainly tried."

She had decided on crediting the giant stork nest on the neighbors' roof for this surprise. "Monsieur Rigoniet is terribly upset. It's blocking the chimney."

"It would follow that Mme. Rigoniet should be pregnant," Georges said. "Not you."

Geneviève, her cheeks already a little rounder than usual, pointed out that the birds' noisy bill-clattering could be heard from the Blanchard kitchen, so surely their fertility powers extended to anyone within earshot. Georges didn't quite believe this, but the news pleased him. Having a happy wife pleased him even more. Georges had long suspected a skittishness in her around the subject of fertility. When he plunged his seed into her dark cave, he imagined being the light—not just the Sun-Bringer but the sun itself—while she turned her head at the moment of release, grimacing, as if resisting his power. Now that she had succumbed, he wanted to carry her upstairs, throw her down on the bed, and ravish her, but he was too polite to voice the request—they never spoke of intimacy—and besides, he wouldn't want to do anything that would damage the baby. Instead he took her hands and squeezed them in congratulations.

When Geneviève fell asleep that night, Georges stayed up late in the parlor, writing a letter to Delia about his wife's welcome news.

Henri, as soon as his mother told him, asked, "Is this what has been making you so gleeful?"

It seemed close enough to the truth, so she said *oui*, and Henri hugged her with gusto.

Spring precipitation plus bright skies caused a daily crop of rainbows. How Geneviève longed to return to the farm boy's arms, though she no longer had an excuse. She missed how he bit his own fingers to prolong their mutual pleasure. Georges would never go to such lengths.

Henri was excited—though wary—about his mother's pregnancy. Would this birth lead to more babies? Madame Maullian—with her seven daughters and one son—didn't even have a personality. Henri did not want that to happen to his mother.

But he *did* like the idea of a younger sibling. A baby would make him an older brother. He could teach it things. He attuned himself to the village women, learning to identify the pregnant ones in the earliest stages. He noted many new mothers pausing to remove bonnets to press their noses against the tops of their babies' heads.

"I sniffed you all the time," Maman told him when he inquired. "You smelled like warm nut butter."

"May I smell our baby?"

"*Bien sûr*," Maman said, thrilled he had said *our baby*.

✳ ✳ ✳

On May 3, 1850, his twelfth birthday—on his way to being a middle child by way of his mother's burgeoning belly—Henri became at last a pin on the cylinder of industry alongside his father.

During his first official lesson, Henri took a pin, positioned it in the pliers, and drove it into the wood with fluidity, whereupon Papa did a funny little waltz around his workbench. Heads sneaked up to watch. A ripple surged through the room: the master, *dancing*. Let them watch. Henri extracted another slippery pin from the cup on the workbench and banged it into its rightful hole. Forget unpredictable, slippery magic; his hands had an important job to do. Practice would increase his skill and speed. He had arrived at his one and only future. Robert couldn't compete with this. He might be a prodigy, but Henri had their father's attention.

"Quit smiling," Papa said.

"But you are smiling."

"Hush and set another pin."

Nathalie rubbed against Henri's leg with her usual appreciative purrings. He did not break his concentration to pet her. Soon he had planted a small brassy forest of pins and staple-like bridges in the barrel. Papa had told him stories about the aviary Delia built for her winged menagerie. Henri imagined those canaries as distant extensions of the pins his fingers planted on the barrels, metallic beaked chirpers with gear-wings, eating worm gears *snap-snap-snap*, their songs a product of his father's workshop, of his own fingers. Those beak-gears biting Robert's fingers for getting in the way. Someday Henri wanted to see a canary for himself, though he suspected the truth might be duller than his father's stories.

Each morning thereafter, Henri sat up in bed and wiggled his fingers. If one seemed a bit stiff, he rubbed cooking oil on it until he was satisfied. This paid off in his father's praise, earned daily. At first he missed being surrounded by girls at the tree stump. Every afternoon, Henri looked up from his workbench and thought about how those girls used to thank him. Bernadine kissing him on the cheek. Françoise Abelard bringing him fresh baguettes and tartelettes. The time Aimée grasped both his hands and squeezed them, drawing so close that he could smell her unbrushed hair, which always reminded him of beechwood's brazen and unpredictable cross-graining—squeezing him until Marie-Marie Ouchard complained that his hands had more important things to do than be held, and *oh!* how he had wished that moment could last.

Geneviève's belly grew pleasingly round over the summer. The new baby pushed the knots of its bones against her, kicking and elbowing to the rhythm of her interior song—*je suis là*, I am yours. Geneviève had come to think of this one as having sprung from her own hair, her own eyes, her own streak of disobedience. She wouldn't let her husband or son touch the taut skin, despite Henri's begging, because their fingers might make the baby grow a fickle limb, and she did not want another boy. When she craved a food she did not have in the kitchen, she sent one of the servant girls down to the village to bring it back, lest the baby die from unfulfilled desires. She did not ask her husband to get the old cradle out of the root cellar, for fear someone might rock it when empty and curse them all.

Chapter Twelve
A trio of incidents.

On a chilly Saturday in September, Henri entered the workshop and touched the canary illustration that had hung on the wall since his grandfather's time. He loved Saturdays: most of the apprentices went home, and those without families slept late on their pallets in the back room. Saturdays meant working together, him and his father, without interruption.

As usual, Henri settled into the rhythm of dots and dashes—pins and bridges—eighth notes and quarter notes and whole notes—each with its own tonal identity, just like Maman's lace patterns. As he worked, Nathalie the cat rubbed against his trousers. Henri leaned down to pat her, but she slid right by, tracking a field mouse.

Georges thrust a bent pin into the courbette with a snick. He enjoyed the act of insertion. Perhaps that was why he loved using the courbette. His wife hadn't opened her thighs to him since the baby made itself known, not that he'd dared to ask. The straightened pin dropped on the tray. He thought of Delia's thighs. Robert's sonata had earned first prize in a contest, as noted in the latest letter, which meant it could have happened a few weeks ago, or perhaps a few months ago. Georges didn't have any close friends; he blamed his Sun-Bringer nickname and did not criticize himself for failing to cultivate such relationships. Still, he wished he could boast about this to someone. Henri, perhaps, would appreciate the news, but he hadn't mentioned the letters since that first time. Georges decided he'd better not bring it up again. And besides, anything he said about his firstborn would invite a comparison. And why should it not? Henri had not written any sonatas at all, let alone a prize-winner!

The field mouse clambered onto Georges's thick leather work boot as he turned the courbette around to check whether its pointy snoot needed oiling. He lined the tool up directly with his eye as the rodent nosed under the hem of his trousers and wiggled through the dark tunnel between boot and pant.

His son's resurrected cat pounced on the trapped bulge in his trousers. Georges startled at the sudden prick of scrabby claws and poked the sharp end of the courbette into his eye. He dropped the tool. He became aware of a loudness coming from his knee. No, not his knee. An ache in his open jaw. Not a word but a lamentation—the outcry of a pin being bent in half. He put his elbows on his workbench and pressed his palm against his eye—a reflex. He shut his mouth. The sound stopped. His head hurt like a headache. Yes, that was it, a headache. He lifted his palm away. Blood—why? His red hand shook.

Mon globe oculair, Georges wanted to explain. *My eyeball is hurt.* But that could not be—he preached carefulness, gave his apprentices lessons on avoiding accidents. He had never had an injury before. His mouth worked like a crank attached to faulty bellows, the sound missing. He wrapped and rewrapped his arms around his head like bandages.

"Papa?" Henri asked. "What—"

Georges folded himself like a handkerchief, tucking his legs up to meet his elbows. He growled and dug his fingernails into his skin to keep his body closed in on itself. If he didn't let Henri see, his eye would be all right.

"Papa? TALK TO ME!"

Georges wanted Henri to leave him alone and find the courbette. It felt like yet another ache, having a tool out of place. His leg stung where the cat had scratched him, and there was a wet spot of blood on his upper thigh—but the mouse had been trapped at his knee—if Henri would pick the courbette off the floor, everything would make sense. Georges felt certain his American son would understand this without being told.

Lacemaking filled the parlor with a softer kind of music than the flittery birdcalls of the serinette. Geneviève's fingers sang lullabies to each other, crossing and twisting the linen thread pinned to the pillow she held between her knees. She had completed tiny cuffs and a collar for the baby and begun an intricate tablecloth. Her back ached from leaning over her belly. The lace progressed twist by cross by twist by cross, a rhythm she knew by heart. The house: quiet. It would get loud soon with the sounds of birth, then hunger. The baby (a girl, she hoped) would need her the way her son now cleaved to his father. If it turned out to be a girl, she would teach her—Cérine—lace. Henri would no longer be her youngest.

She rocked to the *andante* tempo of the bobbins. The baby had not been kicking much this morning. Henri had moved all the time, even in labor. He arrived that way, too, a squall needing to be fed, then calmed, then fed. And here came the squall now.

"PAPA IS INJURED!" Henri shouted.

He could be so dramatic. Geneviève rubbed her eyes and smiled at him. Georges took great care in the workshop. Other master craftsmen had lost fingers; never her husband. She placed the bobbins on the sawdust-filled lace pillow and gave her son a reassuring smile. "Take a deep breath, dearest," she said, knowing she would have to quit calling him that when the baby came. When she had two dearests.

Henri shook his head, his curls bobbing with insistence. "He's really hurt, Maman. His eye."

She hoisted herself up, Henri frantic at her elbow, his shoulders shaking, his cheeks too pale.

"Papa will be fine," she told him. "Get some ice and follow me."

Geneviève held her husband's hands down by sitting on them, straddling his lap. She pulled at the slippery membrane, taking stock of the damage, unwilling to wait for the doctor. Henri sniffled behind her. Her belly pressed her fervent wish into her husband's shirt buttons: *let him be all right.* The courbette had punctured the lid; she could not tell about the eyeball. A rivulet of blood mixed with the clear tears running down his cheek. Geneviève wiped it with her thumb, transferring the fluids to her bodice. Then she wiggled herself backwards, until the toes of her shoes touched the sawdust floor. She eased her extra weight onto them, rolling back onto her arches and extricating herself from her husband's lap.

She grabbed the cloth-wrapped ice from her husband's workbench and pressed the bundle to the injury. Too soon it melted, the liquid trickling down her arm, under the band of her cuff, down her sleeve, beneath her chemise and down beneath her waistband until it dribbled down her leg, like a slow leak in the water barrel. Not ice—warm. Urine. Probably the baby had kicked her bladder, or it was fear, or both. Her right shoe grew mushy, for the stream headed inexplicably to the right. The first few pulses of her belly, no more than the wind tugging at a puddle, brought her back to her body.

Not ice. Not urine. The child coming too soon.

"Maman?" Henri asked.

The next wave of contractions took her breath and kept it. When the release arrived, she gasped, then thrust the ice into Georges's lap, praying the baby would look like her. She went to Henri's workbench, grabbed a blank tunesheet, and jotted a few words, dotting the paper with excess ink in her haste and folding it before it dried.

"Get Docteur Nanin," she told Henri. "And give Sibylle this letter."

When he reached the main road, Henri began to run. His toes jammed into the toes of his boots. His too-big black coat—originally his father's—flew behind him. He should have buttoned it. He couldn't stop now to correct it. Papa could die! His brain might squeeze out of his eye socket and roll down his vest. It would be all his fault. *Your cat*, Papa had said. Henri skidded on loose soil, lost his footing, and fell. His palms dragged along the gravel. Skin flecked up, opening smooth, stinging pink fields dotted with dirt. His trousers were ripped. He cried out but forced himself to stand, brush off his knees, and keep going.

The doctor lived in a vermillion-roofed home with canary-yellow lace trim on the curtains—Docteur Nanin's wife, introduced too late to lacemaking, hid her lack of skill with dye. The Maullians lived next door. Aimée happened to be gazing out the parlor window as Henri raced by.

"*Ça va?*" she called.

He ignored her as he ran past and then pounded on the doctor's door until Sibylle the midwife unlocked it.

"My father. His eye! He needs the doctor!"

Henri threw himself upon the midwife, holding tight to her neck. His heart beat *vivacissimo*. His breath hurt in his throat. The world loosened as he clung to her—he had to give her the letter, then run back home—not only loosened but unplied, like string knotted and unknotted too many times to keep its shape. The doctor's voice loomed, shuttling questions into Henri's ears, but he could not make sense of them. The morning light thinned to the single white thread of Sibylle's apron. That strand of light narrowed itself into a speck, and Henri disappeared in the dark.

Henri found himself on his stomach in the doctor's front hallway. He rolled over on his back. Dirt and pebbles tracked in by patients stabbed at his skin. Sibylle put her hand on Henri's chest until the pace of his heart settled into a less agitated rhythm. She went to the kitchen for a glass of water and helped him sit up to have a sip.

"Papa?" The word tasted like wood shavings, dry and loose in his throat.

"The doctor has gone to him. You fainted." Sibylle held her hands out. "Can you stand?"

Henri grabbed hold of her forearms for balance and lifted himself. He felt achy: his knees, his rib bones, the front of his skull, having met that hard-crack floor—was that a thing—hard-crack floor?

"Do you lose consciousness often?" she asked.

He shook his head *non* and let go of Sibylle's arms. Then he pulled at his ringlets, his heart pounding like it wanted to escape. Sibylle opened her mouth too wide, and he wanted to stopper that hole, so he pulled at his ringlets some more, but her words swallowed him the way a forest closes around a single bird.

An *épisode*, she explained, when he quit panicking and his breathing slowed back down. He opened his eyes and blinked; Sibylle hadn't swallowed him.

She went to get him some more water, glad that the boy had come to his senses. He had suffered a shock and would recover with a bit of quiet.

Sibylle led him upstairs to a guest room with one bed and an old gold-rimmed wardrobe. Docteur Nanin's mother had lived there before she died. The sheets still smelled of old skin though they had been washed countless times. Sibylle loosened the bed-covers and motioned for Henri to remove his boots.

"Climb into bed and rest."

"I must get home," Henri said. "Papa—"

"You cannot do any more for him today."

"My knees. They are bloody. I shall mess the sheets."

Sibylle told him she'd be right back. Henri sat on the edge of the bed and let the boots drop off. His heels ached from pounding against the cold hard dirt. His toes hurt from jamming into the rags. Had he been fast enough? Surely the doctor knew something by now. He tried to fly home, a piece of his mind surging upward, only to be caught by the roof, its eaves like hands, pressing him back down into his sore body. He inspected the rips in his trousers. Maman would be furious. But what about his poor father—all that dripping blood—and here he was thinking about his knees. And Maman—she had sent a letter.

Sibylle returned with a white nightshirt and a glass bottle of clear liquid, which she set on the table beside the bed. At her instructions, Henri removed the old black coat and then his white tunic and then the shirt underneath. He crossed his arms over his bare chest.

"I will get blood on this," he said.

"The doctor does not like me using his bandages when he's not here," Sibylle said.

"I can get blood on it?" Henri asked.

"It's fine. If you ruin it, perhaps the doctor will be less miserly with his supplies."

Henri scrambled into the nightshirt, which hung down to his ankles, for he was not particularly tall. Then he peeled his trousers away from the cuts and stepped out of them. She held the covers back. The sheets were cold on the backs of his bare legs.

She retrieved the bottle and offered him a glass dropper. "This will help."

Henri did not respond, so she used a finger like a crook to pull open the side of his mouth. The dropper slid in, cold against his gums, and she squirted the medicine into the back of his throat. It tasted strong. Lemon and sugar and unpleasant sourness. His throat burned.

"I have a note for you," Henri said.

"Shh." Sibylle drew the covers up to his chin.

"From my mother," he insisted. "In my coat pocket."

The midwife promised to read it. Soon the room softened. The pattern on the bedcovers twisted into a tangle as the drug licked the inside of his skin. Sibylle's voice, a voice that had none of the high-pitched urgency of manufactured birdsong, grew feathers at its edges. For an uncertain while, he floated like a grace note from measure to measure. He didn't mind this sensation. Sibylle breezed in to check his pulse and put a hand on his forehead, then took the note and wafted back out the door, leaving him suspended, alone, in this unreality.

Geneviève pushed bedding into her mouth, not for silence, but for comfort. Nobody would hear her all the way in the workshop, even if she did cry out. Sibylle would arrive soon with her stool. Or perhaps Henri, good boy, would run home and hold her hand through the worst of it. She whispered their names into the wool. Henri's a sigh, Sibylle's an urgent bite as the pains increased, until the urge to push increased, until she could do nothing but push, push out, push away from her own body, though she knew she should hold on until help arrived.

But nobody came.

Not her son. Not the midwife.

Nobody except the baby.

Swift and tiny. Her mouth open in protest of the noose around her neck. Geneviève eased herself into a sitting posture. A perfect girl. Conjured by desire. She muddled a breast out of her maternity corset, untying the ribbon with shaky fingers to reveal her nipple, and when the baby did not take it, she removed the other one. Perhaps she would like that one better.

"You must wake up and eat," Geneviève said.

She paused her efforts to unwrap the cord before prodding her baby again. If her husband had come into the world loud, then it was equally possible for this newborn daughter to arrive silent. The first taste of milk would loosen her voice. Surely it would.

Sibylle read the note, then locked Henri into the guest bedroom so he couldn't get into the doctor's supplies or try to go home when he woke. She rushed up the hill, unlatched the Blanchard kitchen door, and found the place deserted. The others were probably in the workshop tending the father. Sibylle wished the boy had given her the note before fainting. She took the back stairs to the bedchamber, calling out softly that she had arrived. Instead of finding the mother in mid-labor, she found it over. Geneviève smushed her baby to a nipple, sticking a finger in its cooling mouth, trying for a latch.

"She's hungry," Geneviève said.

Sibylle perched upon her birthing stool and drew scissors and twine from her pack and cleaved the cord from the placenta. She tied off a generous stub to avoid spraying, the same way she would for a live birth, before handing the baby back, grief a smudge across the mother's forehead, not yet true. Mothers and their capacity for hope.

"I am sorry," she said. "If I had arrived earlier—"

Only Geneviève knew otherwise.

She had wrought this.

Women were meant to give pleasure, not take it for themselves.

Chapter Thirteen
Grief sets in.

Women lost babies all the time, even in Mireville, but Georges never expected it of Geneviève. He had married a strong woman who took precautions. When a rabbit wandered across her path during her pregnancy, she made three small rips in her petticoat to ward off a harelip. She kept the cradle tucked away in the root cellar and didn't buy cloth for nine months, lest hopeful preparations attract misfortune. Geneviève even insisted the servant girl bring thank-you fish to the storks on the neighbors' roof, though Georges complained of the expense.

At first, when Sibylle told him the news, he didn't understand. Her frown seemed a strange after-effect of anesthesia.

"She's all right?" he asked Sibylle.

"Geneviève is fine. She's sleeping."

"Not my wife—the baby."

Sibylle explained how the cord of life had transformed into a noose. Georges shook his head, as if he had just returned from Ambaville with rainwater in his ears. She told him again, this time using the word *morte*. When the truth pestered its way into Georges's ear—*a stillborn daughter*—he sat up and pulled on his ringlets.

Not with grief, Sibylle thought, *but with a sudden desperation to punish himself.* "It's not your fault. Or your wife's," she added. "The cord was wrapped."

Georges was at a loss. He had not yet had time to adjust to the knowledge that one of his eyes was gone forever. And now? There was a smear of blood on Sibylle's cheek. He wished she would wipe it off. He shut his eyes—the good eye and the lid that now protected an empty hole, concealed beneath a wrapped cloth—and waited for the midwife to leave.

A few hours later, Georges requested to return to the house so he could comfort his wife. Two apprentices helped keep him balanced on the short journey. Once tucked into bed, he contemplated the mound of Geneviève's stomach under the covers. He wanted her to say something, or at least roll over on her side, so he could see her face. A spell seemed to have frozen them both here. Apart in the same room. Both of them suffering.

Could grief kill a person? He loved Geneviève. He appreciated her honesty, her sturdiness. How she never complained that his once-bounteous ringlets had flattened and gotten oily with age. Or that the skin beneath his eyes—rather, beneath his remaining eye and the now-empty socket—peeled and flaked. Years of excessive sun had left scorched splotches on both their cheeks and shoulders. All the villagers had such marks and paid them no mind, but Georges—knowing himself to be as culpable as the sun—hated them more than any of his other faults and foibles. Another wife might not be as forgiving. He figured if he didn't want her to die of sadness, he'd better make her laugh.

"You're not practicing for your casket, are you?" he asked, winking his good eye. *Quel horreur*—without another eye for comparison, the gesture could not be distinguished from a blink.

"Don't make jokes." She pressed her hands against her belly. "It hurts."

The strip of cloth around his head itched and made a lump when he leaned back. Had his wife rolled on her side, he would turn too, and they might commune like that, breaching the space between their bellies where their baby girl should have been opening her tiny fish mouth in search of that great milky lure: a mother.

"What did Docteur Nanin say?" Geneviève asked. "About Henri."

Georges twitched at the sting of this. "He'll be fine. He fainted."

"He's coming back later today, *n'est-ce pas?*" Geneviève said. "It will be such a comfort to have him here when we are both bedridden."

Georges had not expected this sentiment; he had begged the doctor to keep the boy for as long as possible. If Henri were around, he'd interrupt their healing with his worries, needs, and tears. They would have to console him, promise him that life would go on—even though it felt like the opposite.

"I asked for him," Georges lied, "but the doctor wants to keep him under observation."

After seeing her husband's eye pinched out of its socket and the pink tendons snipped away, Geneviève didn't feel obligated to travel all the way down to the outhouse to take care of her private needs. She waited for him to nap, then relieved herself in the chamber pot and wiped her sore, sorry, bloody parts with a cloth she tossed in the corner.

The servant girl brought both patients ice, tied with twine inside cuttings from old flour sacks. She took Geneviève's used cloths downstairs and scrubbed the now-brown blood from them best she could before hanging them on the line to dry. She replaced the strip of cloth binding Georges's eye socket with a fresh one, burning the used strips to ward off additional afflictions. Geneviève kept wishing for Henri to walk in the kitchen door and holler up the stairs at them, but he did not appear.

The apprentices—*sans* supervision from either Blanchard—filtered down to the village in search of sweets and mischief. The boys drank and smoked and peered in the windows of the head lacemakers' parlors, trying to earn the girls' attention.

Henri quit crashing his shoulder against the locked bedroom door when he realized no one would let him out. Had Mlle. Sibylle abandoned him? Why hadn't Docteur Nanin checked on him? Would they forget him, let him starve? At last the doctor unlocked the door and brought him a cold biscuit, which Henri wolfed down. Docteur Nanin proceeded to check his heart, tonsils, and temperature, finding nothing amiss.

Henri sat up in bed. "Then I can go home!"

"Your father has requested we keep you under observation until he recovers."

"My mother can take care of me."

"She cannot," the doctor said, but he would not explain why.

A few hours later, Sibylle unlocked the door to check on Henri and he begged her to release him.

"In a few more days."

"But what about Maman? What did her note say?"

The midwife did not meet his eyes. "She's taking care of your *papa*."

Sometimes Henri thrashed around in the middle of the night, wishing the midwife would run up the stairs to reassure him, although she had probably gone home or to a birth. During the day, he craved being out in the weather—the sun, the wind that loosed branches, the occasional moisture that tricked the sky into generating rainbows. Crying, complaining, and banging on the window didn't do much, although once Aimée wandered into the street, spotted Henri making a ruckus, and waved at him. Then she went back inside. Did she understand he was trapped? Would she alert his mother?

On the fourth day of his confinement, Sibylle explained that Maman's baby had died, and *oui* it had been a girl, and *non*, she didn't know its name. Henri suffered such a crying jag that the doctor carried him downstairs to the parlor, hoping a change of scene would pacify him.

"How dare you keep this a secret from me?" Henri shouted at the doctor.

Dr. Nanin spoke fondly of bed rest and avoiding agitation, but Henri clung to him, wrapping his legs and arms around his torso. Surely the baby had been buried in the cemetery by now. He sobbed and hiccupped, muttering *four days* and making a terrible wet mess of the doctor's shirt and his own, until Docteur Nanin leaned forward to deposit him on the settee. Henri begged to know where the baby's body was. Neither the doctor nor the midwife would tell him, though surely it had been buried already in the cemetery near Charles's house. Henri reluctantly let go and wrapped his arms around his chest, folding his knees together and apart and together again, like butterfly wings, to the tempo of a slow waltz.

"I could have saved her," he whispered.

The doctor twirled his muttonchops. "What do you mean?"

"Your sister is dead," Sibylle reminded him. "I couldn't find a pulse."

Henri nodded, impatient. "But she *wouldn't* be if you had brought her to me."

Docteur Nanin, hands clasped behind his back, peered at his young patient with new interest. "What do you mean?"

"Don't you understand? I can revive the dead."

Henri spent the next few hours locked into his room, pacing. They didn't believe him. They thought he was crazy. They wouldn't bring the baby, and therefore she'd stay dead. Forever. Although if they listened and brought her, would his magic work anymore? (*Four days!*) Oh, how he wished he had Aimée's spunk and insight. She would have suspected what was wrong right away. She would have fought the doctor until he let her go free.

A few hours later, Sibylle unlocked the door and invited him to return to the parlor. Henri felt a wild surge of hope: the baby! He bounded down the stairs ahead of the midwife and his hand flew to his mouth. Not the baby. Docteur Nanin had procured a dead goat from M. Abelard's farm. It smelled sour and wild, with a denser, headier odor than horses. He didn't want to touch it, get that smell on him. He wanted to touch his sister. Cradle her small head in his hands. Find out if she smelled like nut butter or toasted bread.

"Try to bring this goat back, and you can go home today," the doctor said.

Henri didn't want to show off. It seemed a cheap trick to comply. He'd be no better than the Pignons. The family who gave up serinette-making in favor of barrel organs meant to be played on the street. For onlookers. The Pignons' customers sent their monkeys around for coins. All show. No talent.

"When did it die?"

Dr. Nanin looked puzzled. "I have no idea."

This didn't sound promising. But home! He wanted to be with his mother. *She must be so sad*, he thought. And he had a talent, didn't he? Perhaps if he could revive the goat, the doctor would believe him. Give a name to his gift. It wouldn't hurt to see what he could do. He placed his hands on the animal's belly (not warm, not promising), then listened, trying to inflate its lungs, to wish it back to life.

"Please," he whispered. "Come back into your body, goat. Make milk again. Chase your friends again." Nothing happened. Henri hummed a waltz to the animal. Then he tugged the goat onto his lap, thinking if he could hold it in a different position, it might begin to breathe. He no longer worried about the smell and instead imagined tail flicks like sixteenth notes, and hoofs pounding chords into the dust.

"That's enough, Henri," Docteur Nanin said. "We're done here."

"May I go home now?"

"In a few days."

"You said I could if I tried!"

"I meant if you succeeded," the doctor said.

Chapter Fourteen
Henri has an affliction of his own.

Eight days after he lost his eye, Georges cast his singular gaze about the parlor that had been his father's parlor and his father's father's parlor, first settling on the doctor's muttonchops, then the side table and the serinette resting atop it, then the hem of his wife's dress—anywhere but Henri's face.

"Your son suffers from a terrible delusion," Docteur Nanin said.

Henri sat on his hands, crossing his ankles, next to his mother on the settee. He studied the floorboards.

"I told you we should have him examined," Geneviève told Georges. She turned to address the doctor. "But my husband didn't listen to me. He never does. I had concerns about—"

"I listen," Georges said, "when you're making sense."

"Papa never listens to me, either," Henri told his mother.

The doctor brushed his arm through the air, dismissing the family's squabbling. "Henri has grown up in your shadow," he said to Georges, "and he's jealous. He has invented a special talent of his own by way of a delusion."

Georges waved a hand in front of his face, which was decorated with one of six beige patches his wife had sown once she recovered enough from her ordeal to work on them. "Bah. The villagers don't even like the sun."

"A delusion?" Geneviève pressed.

"After consulting with Sibylle and reviewing my medical journals and finding no precedents," the doctor said, "I have decided to call this condition Son of the Sun-Bringer Syndrome."

Henri groaned. Those words took his father's myth and flipped it into a weakness. To punish him for being born to a legend. For not being a legend himself. Only he *had* saved that cat. And a worm. And a bird.

"That's ridiculous," Georges said.

Throughout his lifetime, Georges had been blamed for peeling noses and the high price of vegetables, and now this? Infecting his child? Ruining his son with thoughts of grandeur? It didn't seem fair to consider this his fault, too.

"Are you sure, Docteur?" Geneviève leaned over to pat her husband's wrist but straightened back up, as the pressure of bending so far forward hurt her belly, which hadn't yet collapsed to its usual size.

"I am not saying Georges caused it," the doctor continued. "It's a mania that could have erupted in any number of less-outrageous ways, and probably would have, if this boy had different parents. But given the irrefutable cause—Henri wanting to prove himself worthy of his legendary *papa*—and the extraordinary proportions of his delusion—"

"Son of the Sun-Bringer Syndrome," Geneviève repeated. "He believes too much in himself?"

"Exactly," the doctor said.

"He can't really heal the dead," Georges interrupted.

"Indubitably he can't," Docteur Nanin said. "Hence the delusion."

"I can," Henri interrupted. "Sometimes. If the conditions are right. That goat—"

"Was too long dead, you told me," Dr. Nanin interrupted him. "Or perhaps had died of the wrong ailment, or was unlucky."

Geneviève scooched over on the settee to drape her arm over Henri's shoulders. "Georges, if you had paid more attention to Henri before he started his apprenticeship—"

"I DID PAY ATTENTION TO HIM!" He used to let the boy crawl all over his lap, didn't he? What else could his wife have expected of him? Besides, Henri had always been fragile and too easily startled, preferring the safety of the parlor to adventures with his peers. Maybe his weakness of spirit was Geneviève's influence. It couldn't all be Georges's fault, could it?

Or perhaps it was. Maybe Georges's best work had been completed at four months of age, when colic loosened its grip and the sun reappeared. Ever since then, he had been undoing his goodness, one mistake at a time. How else to explain fathering a child on another continent with a married woman? Perhaps if he had sat Henri down on his lap as a tot and told him how wrecked he felt every time he looked at the sky, every time he saw a villager squint, Henri wouldn't have grown up wanting to be special.

"Henri can still work?" Geneviève asked. "My husband needs all the help he can get."

"Geneviève—" Georges said, a warning. The headaches would go away, the doctor believed, but they hadn't yet. Maybe in a few months.

Geneviève gripped their son's shoulder with her fingers. "With all your fears about *excessive self-worth*, you ignored your children, Georges. And now it's turned into a syndrome. I'm glad the good doctor is naming it after you."

"*Ça suffit*," Georges growled.

Henri wanted to put his hands on his mother's belly, to feel where the baby had been. It looked like she was still in there. He marveled that this had nothing to do with him: their anger at each other.

"Now as to the prognosis," Docteur Nanin continued, "the more stimulated your son becomes, the more likely an episode. Your role will be to keep him rested, fed, and cajoled."

"What do you mean, *cajoled*?" Georges asked.

"What do you mean, *rested*?" Geneviève asked.

"Your son may work once you re-open the workshop," the doctor said. "Although I recommend daily constitutionals and a two-hour break in the middle of each day. Nature and naps combined should help him stave off any delusions. Plus it wouldn't hurt Henri to spend some time away from his father."

"Because it's my fault," Georges said. "That's what you're saying?"

"You are but a contributing factor," Docteur Nanin said.

Georges leaned forward, furious. He—not the doctor—had a son with a disordered mind. "I have injured myself, and my infant daughter has died, and now you claim I have ruined my son?"

"Papa—" Henri began. He meant to take issue with the word *ruined*, because he did not feel any different.

"YOU HAVE TAKEN EVERYTHING AWAY FROM ME!" Georges shouted at the doctor. "EVERYTHING."

Henri kept silent, though he wanted to say: *Aren't I something to you?*

"Come along, Docteur," Geneviève said, "and I'll collect your fee and some tinned plums."

Georges imagined himself kneeling beside Delia, birdsong all around, the heavy smell of brick-heated air and indoor vegetation, white and black dots of excrement on their shoulders, marking them as companionable members of the same tribe. He'd had so many decisions ahead of him back then. To change any one of them might, even now, if he wished hard enough, cause him to wake up in some other situation than this, which was—*sans doubte*, when he dared open his good eye and look around—his life, his one and only life.

Maman entered Henri's room. A groove carved her forehead in half horizontally. It wasn't a wrinkle so much as a crease in the fabric of her skin, as if she had put herself away in a drawer for a while and only just now decided to take herself out for an airing.

Henri sat up in bed and ran a hand through his matted ringlets. She sat down on the edge of the bed.

"I ruined our family," Henri said. "I fainted before I delivered the letter to Mlle. Sibylle. That's why she didn't come when you needed her."

"Dearest," she said, "it's not your fault. I delivered too early."

Maman's lips had become chapped from too much sun or the grueling labor or both. Henri wanted to smear bacon fat on them so they would heal faster.

"But I failed you."

Maman scrunched closer. "You would have liked being a big brother." She wrapped her arms around him and leaned back on his pillow. Her wavy hair fell over his curls.

Henri still smelled like goat, but that could not be helped. He needed his mother's arms. He burrowed against her, face pressed to her middle. "Did the baby float off and become a cloud?"

Maman gave a slight grin. "*Ça va*. She and Grand-Maman are up there, swirling storms around with metal spoons. Whenever

there's lightning in Ambaville, that's your sister and your grandmother dancing."

"Where is she *really*?"

"Her body?" Maman sighed like a bellows being slowly
squeezed until it had no more air in it. "You have a syndrome.
It's not real."

He pulled his head away from her side. "Ask Charles
DeBourgignon. Or Aimée. If you had brought the baby to me—"

"Go to bed, Henri. If he heard you, your father would—"

"But Maman—"

"Your father loves you. You don't need to prove anything to
him."

"BUT MAMAN—"

"*Ça suffit.* I am tired."

Geneviève wandered downstairs, feeling her way in the dark
by touch. She had been pleased with that vision of storm-stirring,
her daughter and her mother-in-law mid-ruckus, their playfulness thundering above Ambaville; but Henri was growing up. At
twelve, he didn't believe in stories as easily as he used to.

The family serinette sat in its plain walnut box on the side
table in the parlor. She opened the lid and smelled: home. The
serinette had always promised this. The songs went around on
the barrel, metal stubs triggering the keys on the wooden bar to
open passages to the ten tin pipes, every measure ornamented
exactly as Georges intended, each swell of mechanical breath
exactly the same as the one that came before. Her husband considered this art, but it was no different than building a barn or
assembling the pieces of a carriage.

She pinched one of the small brass pins between her fingers,
pulling and nudging it. Her husband and sons would be able
to identify the note with a glance, but she did not want their

explanations, not today or tomorrow or the next tomorrow. When she couldn't get the pin to wiggle free, she lifted the limewood barrel out of its walnut fixture and applied her teeth, the metal sour in her mouth, other pins tickling her lips, pressuring her gums. She pulled, and the barrel released its hold on two pins. They stuck out of her lips, notes erased.

She had only meant to take one. For her baby, Cérine.

III.

Variations on a Syndrome

Chapter Fifteen
The Blanchards adjust to the circumstances.

The doctor's recommendation of rest breaks and daily constitutionals didn't disrupt Henri's life too much. He liked having a few hours unsnapped from the harness of routine and particularly enjoyed the gentle, quiet walks. The sun on the back of his neck. Making conversation with the girls out on errands. He even came to enjoy the strange sounds from the *violon* workshops, which had frightened him as a boy. Now he wound through the alleys on purpose to listen to the tunings, tremolos, and scales. When he had the time, he zigzagged from one alley into the next, making a maze for himself, letting the sounds haunt his consciousness on the way home, lending a sense of occasion to the experience, which was not an experience at all but a prescription. And it was working: he had quit obsessing about resurrection.

Straighten a pin, sand a barrel, sweep the floor. Walk.

Straighten a pin, calligraph a tune sheet, check each new serinette with the pitch pipe. Go back to the house, take off his trousers so workshop dirt would not get on the bed, feel the cold sheets warming beneath his bare legs, then get up after a sufficient period of time, put his trousers back on.

Straighten a pin, sew a bellows. Walk.

Straighten a pin, attach the padding to a key, knock in a staple. Rest.

The other apprentices teased him for his lax schedule, but he ignored the taunts and kept to his regimen. It was the least Henri could do for his parents, who worried about him.

Docteur Nanin usually kept his patients' cases confidential, but if word of Son of the Sun-Bringer Syndrome spread outside Mireville, perhaps doctors in other villages would begin using it, and credit him, and perhaps he would be invited to speak in Paris. Or Parisian doctors would come to the village for research. Docteur Nanin could become famous not for a myth—as the boy's father had—but for doing his job.

To the tavern keeper: "It's a shame about the youngest Blanchard boy," Docteur Nanin said, leaning over the bar. "I've never come across such a debilitating delusion in all my years of practice."

To three patients in a row: "Have you heard about Henri Blanchard?" The news would certainly make them feel better about their own conditions.

"A strange, bedeviling case, that one," Docteur Nanin muttered, leaning close to M. Rigoniet after church, whereupon M. Rigoniet said, "Who?" and the doctor had no choice but to name Henri Blanchard. "Imagine believing yourself capable of miracles!"

Soon music-making men approached Georges, asking for confirmation of these rumors, which he reluctantly offered. The men told their wives. The wives passed the news back and forth in their lacemaking circles like hand-carved bobbins. The grand-mothers remembered Georges's colic and recounted where they were when the sky brightened. How dreary life was before the Sun-Bringer's miracle.

"Henri wants to be as important as his father," the women mused to themselves.

"It's sweet, really."

"I wonder what Cérine would say. I dearly miss her."

The mothers of similarly aged daughters had no patience for such empathy. They preferred to complain about Henri no longer being a suitable match for their daughters.

When Aimée heard about the syndrome from her mother, she raced up the hill to the Blanchard workshop, flung open the door, and touched the canary for luck. Monsieur Blanchard came reeling toward her as if walking on the deck of a ship, angry lines forming around his mouth.

"It's bad luck if a woman touches the canary," he said.

Her beech-colored hair hung like poorly sewn drapes all around her face. If his daughter had lived, Georges would never have let her wear a dress that plain.

"Where's Henri?"

"In the house. Resting."

"Can I see him?"

Georges mustered his sternest expression. This was Henri's first caller since his diagnosis, but he didn't want to encourage other girls to come up the hill and thoughtlessly step into the workshop like this impertinent one did. "He doesn't want to see anyone."

Aimée said *oui, M. Blanchard, merci, M. Blanchard*, and reassured Henri's father that she would not bother him again. Her mother had resigned herself to being invisible, a lacemaker and the wife of a drink-addled man, but Aimée had other models. Madame Oeuvriot, her bobbin lace teacher, sang with her pupils several times a day, precisely because their fathers and brothers forbade such frivolities. Sibylle the midwife often sneaked alternate instructions to women who came to see the doctor, and they listened to her advice and recovered. Aimée did not want to be invisible. She had important things to say. And one of them she needed to say to Henri. But not here—not anywhere near his father. She wouldn't disobey M. Blanchard today; she could wait.

Henri turned fourteen in May of 1852. Robert must also be growing tall, his voice deepening with the passing seasons, but Delia had not sent a letter in months. Had some harm come to Georges's firstborn? He catalogued the possibilities: a popped eardrum from repeating the flageolet's highest note, broken elbows from tripping on crocheted greenery, an eye poked out by an angry beak. Georges hoped nothing had happened, but terrible luck befalling them both would confirm the tether between father and son.

Losing his eye—and the resulting headaches—caused Georges to form himself more in his father's boxwood mold than ever. Out of spite, he buried his wife's metal spoons in the yard and didn't tell her where, nor give her money to buy new wooden ones. She resorted to stirring stews and soups with a whittled branch. He quit letting the servant girl buy vegetables from Ambaville farmers, claiming expense as an excuse. With the savings, he purchased a prosthetic cryolite eyeball, which arrived at the Blanchard home packed in a tiny, string-tied parcel.

"To be stored in a solution of saltwater when not in use," warned a slip of paper that accompanied the parcel. "If there is erosion of the orb's surface over time, please discard and purchase a replacement. Beware abrupt changes of temperature, as artificial eyes have been known to explode in extreme climates."

After numerous attempts, Georges learned to tilt his head back and hold his forefinger over the pupil to orient the eye properly. With his other hand, he peeled back the upper lid. Then he worked the eyeball into the cavity. After he released the upper lid he went to work rolling the lower lid over the orb, pushing his forefinger against the eye to be sure it was snugged in place. He then picked up his wife's hand mirror, adjusted the location of the pupil, and admired the results.

Georges's new eye irritated his socket the way grit stings a skinned knee. It was quite handsome, though he had forgotten to specify *blue* when he wrote to Germany for the latest in cosmetic optometry—a hollow orb, made of arsenic oxide and cyolite. The sclera had been painted a realistically pale, reflective gray, with delicate red veins around a brown pupil and unmoving brown iris. Georges took to popping his faux eyeball out after church to show the villagers. He had corrected his misfortune with money, and this pleased him.

"Here—touch it," he commanded after church.

The baker held out his hand. The eyeball was lukewarm and sticky in his palm.

"Yes, yes," Georges plucked his eye from the baker. "Who else wants to hold it?"

"Give it here."

"*Moi aussi.*"

"How is Henri, Georges?"

"How do you think?" he replied.

The men in the crowd laughed, and Georges joined in their merriment. Because otherwise they would be laughing *at* him.

"Has he tried Magnalle's Sedative Solution?"

"Or strong coffee?"

The false eyeball traveled from palm to palm as Georges reassured them all that Henri only imagined he could heal the dead, and no, the syndrome could not be caught—after all, it only affected Sun-Bringers' sons. He did not add: of which there were precisely two, and one was perfectly normal, everyone could see that.

When the men passed his eye back, Georges spat on his palm, rubbed the sphere around, and then popped it back in the open cavity. Working without the aid of a mirror, he absently pointed the pupil upward. It made sense to the other music-makers that he would look at the sky, just checking to see whether anything had changed.

Aimée disbanded the Shadow Council of Apprentice Lacemakers when she and the other girls grew too big to comfortably slouch through the opening of their lair. They remained friends, though, and the council girls were the first ones she told when her father announced he planned to move to New York City. He wanted to go as soon as his bedridden mother, Aimée's Grand-Maman, died, which could be any time now. His sister—Tante Pierrette—already lived there and had promised accommodations and steamer fare for the whole family, if the Maullian girls would work in her seamstress shop for three years.

"Can't you change his mind?" Yvette asked.

"Papa thinks there will be better opportunities for him and Guillaume in New York," Aimée said. She didn't need to tell her friends they had few opportunities here.

Everyone knew of M. Maullian's failed pattern. There was

no future for him or Guillaume in France. The girls understood this, though they cried and wrapped their arms around their friend.

In America, there would be work building instruments, or wooden crates for transporting goods by train, or whatever was needed.

When Aimée told Henri, though, he refused to believe it. He blinked silent tears away.

"What if you moved in with us? You could stay and work with Mme. Oeuvriot and help Maman in the kitchen."

Aimée said, "Papa would never allow it. He needs me to take care of my younger sisters. Besides," she added, "your parents don't have an extra bedroom."

"Perhaps we could share mine," he said, blushing wildly.

"And your bed?" Aimée elaborated, whereupon they both crumpled into giggling fits.

Aimée didn't tease him like the boys nor treat him as a curiosity like the other girls did. Not that he hadn't fantasized about some of them: Anne-Jeanée Picoult, for instance, with her feet that stuck out at an angle, as if she might dance away at any second. And Bernadine with her bossiness, what she might ask him to do—where she might want to be touched—if they married. But Aimée was his friend. His best friend, in childhood and now. Grand-Maman would have to stay alive or he'd lose Aimée forever.

Panic crested in Henri's body. He imagined it like the river rising, the blue of his eyes replaced by a glossy, mercurial flood of fear. "You have to change your father's mind!"

"I'm not going yet, silly," she said. "Breathe."

❄ ❄ ❄

The tendrils of Henri's adolescence sprouted in late summer. Maman reassured him about the breaks in his voice and his addled complexion. This happened to all children and was not—as he feared—another delusion. If Georges had grown sturdy like his father (like boxwood), then Henri grew like the wood of a plum tree, swirled with streaks of olive, orange, pink, and purple, smelling a bit like cooked squash. He could hear his ligaments stretching at night, offering the possibility of a stronger, more handsome Henri emerging.

On the other side of the ocean, Robert had very different growing conditions: sun and rain and leisure time. He had his own servants. His servants had servants. He could use as much paper and ink as he wanted without ever having to ask permission. Someone was always waiting in the corner of whatever room he occupied, ready to hand him supplies. Not boxwood at all, nor plum wood—Robert was more like exotic pernambuco, often used for violin bows: fiery orange when exposed to the elements.

Delia had quit sending letters to France because Georges kept asking for a visit from Robert. She did not want her son trained to the sound of someone else's voice, especially that of a serinetter who left without saying goodbye. Let her once-lover stew in the hot muck of transcontinental jealousy. Alastair agreed that it would be all right to stop informing the father. Georges had a teenage son of his own. Surely he understood that Robert had what he needed: absolutely everything he asked for.

The tempo of Geneviève's days soon evened out. She took her herbs and did not get pregnant again. She was not happy, but neither was she as unhappy as in the years after her mother-in-law's death.

Mothers of eligible daughters quit visiting her kitchen after word spread about Henri's syndrome. She missed their gifts of soft cheeses and windfall apples, but she appreciated not having to entertain unexpected guests. Or any guests at all.

Plum wood had its own appeal, though, especially in proximity to such an excessive supply of boxwood. The local girls found Henri kind and pleasant. Instead of talking about himself, he made delicate and honest inquiries about the girls' lives. (So unlike Georges, who at that age had leaned against buildings and fiddled with the crank in his pocket.) Henri truly wanted to know: What pattern were the girls working on? When was the lace cutter due next? What would they make for themselves if someone supplied them with time and good thread? The girls, fueled by his interest, popped onto the path of his daily constitutional like corn kernels thrown into the fire. Others tossed handkerchiefs at his feet so they could watch his golden curls bounce as he performed the expected gallantry.

Henri's heart was a fragile thing. The girls waited with their pins to tack its pattern down and make it theirs. They liked that he made them feel strong, and good, listening closely as if they— each girl, every single one of them—mattered. And they did: to Henri, at least, who had the temperament to appreciate them.

Georges hired an English tutor to help Henri become a better businessman.

"But Papa," Henri argued. "I am already required to leave the workshop for my rest and my daily constitutional."

"You will leave three times now."

"You only want me to learn English because of *Roh-bair*."

Georges's ears and neck grew hot. Was that a threat? What else could it be? Georges slapped his son across the cheek. His fingers vibrated the way sound shakes itself through wood.

Henri, too startled to cry, said, "You hit me?" A question, just how Charles would have said it.

Shame bloomed in Georges's stinging hand, racing up his arm and into his spine. He slouched with the weight of what he had done but could not let himself apologize. Instead he stared at his hand, the reddened palm, and before Henri could say another word, Georges turned his back and left. Neither brought the matter up again, and thereafter on Mondays, the English teacher trudged up the hill to meet with Henri.

Despite resenting Papa for this new interruption of his daily schedule, Henri liked the lessons. He could now read all of Delia Dumphries Stanton's letters and understand them as braggery. The clever cinquains! A sonata! Who *cared* about the ophicleide? Or the flageolet? He and Aimée must have been correct when they joked about Robert having something wrong with him, or Mme. Stanton would not feel obligated to list his achievements in such exaggerated detail.

A few years passed like this, with Henri perfecting his serinette-building skills in between English lessons. Grand-Maman, though still bedridden, continued to take meals and make conversation, and after a while, Henri forgot to worry about Aimée moving away. Occasionally, during his daily constitutionals, Henri spotted a flutter of movement behind a tree or around an alley, as if an animal had crept close. Or someone was spying on him. *Odil?* Henri wondered. Although Odil always ran away when Henri tried to say hello. If the feeling persisted, and he couldn't rub away the prickles on the back of his neck, he climbed trees to conjugate verbs in the branches until it went away.

After he lost interest in the American letters—so obviously full of bunk—he carried one of his grandmother's British novels down to the village, where he sat beneath a tree reading and giggling to himself. This spectacle encouraged passing girls to inquire about the plot, which he gladly described, mindful not to detain them too long from their chores. Sharing his pleasure with the girls deepened it. Inside the pages, Henri and the girls tarried in gardens alongside sweet-cheeked damsels.

Once, when she happened to pass by at the right time, he asked Anne-Jeanée to define *cuckoldry*, since her salesman father had taught her some words of English, and when he used it in context, her mouth rounded into an O and she toppled over in a dramatic faint. Whereupon Henri fainted. Their friends roused them and sent them back to their own houses to recover, blushes on everyone's cheeks.

Chapter Sixteen

Whereupon Aimée requests a favor.

By sixteen, Aimée filled out the tops of her gowns in a way that made the farmers' sons take notice. In truth, Henri noticed too, though he pretended nothing had changed so she wouldn't feel embarrassed. He visited with Aimée at least once a week, more frequently if he timed his constitutionals to match her midday trips home to fix *déjuner* for her sisters. She often stood so close to Henri that their arms brushed, though neither spoke of courtship. Their teasing took on an intensity that it had previously lacked.

Late one night in March of 1855, though, between Aimée's sixteenth birthday and Henri's seventeenth, she sneaked into the Blanchard house. Nobody locked their doors; the villagers trusted each other. Aimée tiptoed up the back stairs with a lantern and found Henri asleep in his bed. "Get up," she whispered, flipping down the sheet and tugging at his shoulders. "I need your help."

Henri rubbed his eyes—Aimée? She touched a finger to her lips and then pantomimed a cranking motion—*hurry, hurry.* Henri roused himself and dressed while she waited downstairs. He would have borrowed his father's razor yesterday had he known she was coming. Aimée must have put that ribbon in her hair because of him; there was no one else awake to admire it.

"What's going on?"

"You'll see."

He laced his boots in the kitchen, and they held hands down the hill, Aimée swinging her lantern. When Henri tripped, she held on; he avoided a knee skinning. Henri wanted to walk all night with her, safe beside her, and never get anywhere. Soon, though, they arrived at the Maullian house. He followed her through the foyer and then the parlor, where M. Maullian drooped on the settee, stomach rising and falling, socks puckering where they had been mended too many times.

"He drank at home tonight," she whispered, "instead of going out."

In the former servant quarters off the kitchen, Aimée pointed to a lumpy, sheet-covered mound on the bed. She peeled the sheet back and revealed her grandmother, mouth fixed open as if still trying to suck in one last breath. Her skin stripped of pink.

"You must bring Grand-Maman back to life." Aimée mustered the commanding tone she used with the Shadow Council.

"*C'est impossible.*" Henri's voice slid into its highest, most desperate register before he cleared his throat and tried again. "I cannot—not a person! I haven't even tried it with animals in years, because—"

"Shh—or you'll wake Papa. You revived that cat. And Charles told me about the worm and the bird."

Henri cut her off. "It's a delusion. A syndrome. The doctor's right. I can't revive anything."

"With the cat," Aimée pressed, "you felt something change, didn't you? When you touched her?"

"I felt sorry for her."

"Then feel sorry for me," she said, leaning in, barely brushing the longest of his curls, pushing her hot breath into his ear. "You don't want me to move to New York, do you?"

If he tried and failed, Aimée would leave. If he didn't try, she would leave and be mad at him, too.

He leaned over the bed and put his hands on the old woman's dressing gown, distressed from years of aggressive washings. The seams pulled tight around her bent elbow, exposing brighter-white threads. The fabric over her stomach pooched like risen bread dough. His hands were warmer than her body, but not by much. He closed his eyes and palpated her midsection, squeezing handfuls of loose flesh.

"That's it," Aimée whispered.

Nothing happened. It occurred to him Grand-Maman might be coaxed back with food; he pictured a link of sausage with a good burnt crust and an ooze of juice. No—that's what *he* wanted. His mother hadn't made sausage in years. Not since she lost the baby. What did *she*—Grand-Maman—want?

His fingers chanced upon a lower rib; was it vibrating? No, not vibrating, but there was a beat to it, a steady stair-climbing progression of quarter notes, as if Grand-Maman wanted to find an apple tree, pull herself over to the trunk, and begin to climb.

"I'm right here," Aimée whispered.

Not stairs at all, or an apple tree, but scales, Henri decided. Yes, scales. First A, then B-flat, then C—a path of notes leading up to the clouds, each scale a half-step higher than the last, Grand-Maman tugging her own self upward on these stairs with some of the notes missing. He began to hum up the scale with her, filling in the blank spots, feeling the vibrato of her ribs—stronger now that both his hands were on her ribcage—only she shouldn't be going that high, she should come back, settle down into her body. She wanted the scales to descend, not to keep climbing! He took the notes by the hand and led them down, starting each new octave a half-step lower than the last, until he approached middle C and then kept going lower and lower, humming in his mind to keep her from floating away.

Grand-Maman's dreary middle age had sagged her mouth. Her husband's death: three straight lines across the forehead. Being truly old and bedridden had caused the rest of her, even her proud nose, to shrink, and she wished she hadn't spent those early years thinking she was old. Because now—truly—she was.

She soothed herself with the remembered sound of her husband practicing his violin. That's all life is, *n'est-ce pas*? The practice of going up and coming back down, just like scales. The tempo didn't matter, nor the key, for now, at the end of the ballad, no one was listening. Except someone was.

She felt a thrill beneath her ribs, a sudden brightening of an E-flat run, a sharpening of the sounds, sharpening so much there came F, both major and minor variants, rubbing against the fingerboard of her remembering, until she opened her eyes to find a strange young man with his hands pressed to her chest.

"Get! Your! Hands! Off! Me!" she shrilled.

Henri took off running, all the way back home, not caring that Docteur Nanin would scold him for the exertion. He couldn't risk Grand-Maman telling anyone that he had performed a miracle on her. The next day Henri went about his workshop duties and his daily constitutional as if nothing had changed, though there was a subtle swagger to his loose-limbed walk.

His father's son after all.

Perhaps not boxwood, but an orchardist capable of coaxing a drought-ruined tree to leaf once more, capable of bending the nature of existence. Best of all, Aimée would stay in Mireville. Her father would not dare leave his bedridden mother behind, and Grand-Maman showed no signs of deterioration after the unusual process of her reconstitution. In fact, she now smelled like lavender.

Grand-Maman told Aimée that her first suitor had brought her a box of lavender pastilles all the way from Paris. "They're still my favorite. Isn't it odd that I now smell them all the time? As if they were in the same room with me?"

Aimée agreed: quite odd.

Even on cold days, Grand-Maman's scent seeped its way into the Maullian parlor. Guests remarked on its delightful freshness. (If only they knew the source!) Grand-Maman now had an unusually restless leg on the side where Henri had ministered to her, she could go days without eating, and she had developed a habit of singing the chromatic scale in a quavery alto. Henri liked stopping by on his daily constitutionals to check on her. The sun made her lavender emanations stronger, so Aimée kept the curtains closed during the day and opened them at night.

The whole village was abuzz with the gossip: M. Maullian had tried to have the gravediggers bury his mother while she was still alive.

"He must have gotten tired of feeding her."

"This is why they invented coffin bells—for sweet ladies like Mme. Maullian when their sons decide to bury them alive."

"Who's he going to try to get rid of next—his wife?"

The gossip didn't bother Aimée, who knew the truth. But her father and Guillaume were furious about it. They assumed

Grand-Maman had tricked them somehow, out of spite, perhaps. The two men refused to visit her bedroom at all, even just to bring her food and water, leaving the sisters to take turns caring for her. When Henri found this out, he vowed to visit Grand-Maman every day so she wouldn't feel lonely or abandoned.

"Have we done the right thing?" Aimée whispered to Henri a few days after the reviving, her mouth against Henri's ringlets. They were conferring in the hall after visiting Grand-Maman, who was as cheerful as ever—still bedridden but singing.

"We can't very well *undo* it," he said. "Besides, she's in such a good mood."

Aimée held her hands out to him, and he took them.

"You are so much more confident now," she told Henri. "I like it."

He squeezed Aimée's hands hard, as if he could pour his miracle into her body and share it with her. They seemed two parts of the same whole, like peach and pit, or bean and vine. She leaned over and gave him a swift dry kiss on his startled lips.

April began exactly the same as March: bone dry and bright. One afternoon, about a week after Grand-Maman's miraculous recovery, Henri felt he was being spied upon while walking through one of the long, skinny *violon* alleys. He didn't have many options. Backward or forward? The only other possibility, knocking on a workshop door, would disturb the apprentices and probably earn him a scolding from their master. Before he could decide, Aimée's brother appeared at the end of the alley. The skin beneath Guillaume's eye had a yellow-green cast to it, as if someone had punched him.

"My grandmother doesn't eat much now," the older boy said.

"That's strange," Henri mused. "Why don't you buy her some Ambaville vegetables? Surely a winter squash would tempt her. Or a potato."

The whole village knew the Maullians couldn't afford prized vegetables—not with so many daughters to feed. Guillaume ignored the obvious jab. "Why do you visit her every day? She's not your family."

Henri did his best to appear nonplussed. "I have more free time than most apprentices, as you probably know. She's lonely. And I didn't have time to see her yesterday, so it's not every day."

Guillaume placed his hands on Henri's shoulders but resisted sliding them to his neck in a move one of the boys at the abandoned farmhouse had taught him. If you did it right, the other person didn't even struggle when the pressure came. Once they realized the threat, they were halfway to passing out.

Henri stepped back, cautious. Guillaume decided to push with words instead of his body. See what Henri would do next.

"You know she died, don't you? My grandmother?"

Henri lifted his eyebrows in surprise. "I'm so sorry to hear this sad news! I wish I had come by yesterday to say farewell."

Guillaume barked a cough-like laugh. "Before, I mean."

Henri raised his eyebrows as if he had no idea what *before* meant.

"Surely you've heard the rumors. Everyone's talking about how my father paid to have his mother's grave dug," Guillaume continued. "When she was still breathing."

Henri nodded and acknowledged that yes, he had heard this, and the mix-up must have been inconvenient and confusing, not to mention costly.

"Moreover," Guillaume continued, "last night Grand-Maman and I had a very interesting conversation. She remembers you visiting her the night she died."

Henri took another step back, panic coursing through his body. "Oh, cloud off," he said. "I can't actually heal anyone."

"You brought Grand-Maman back from the dead. I'm going to prove it," Guillaume said. "Then everyone will quit taunting my father. And they'll cast *you* out. I don't know how you did it, but—"

Henri, feeling like he might faint, interrupted to insist he was due back at the workshop right away. "I seem to have lost track of time." The words came out a little high, almost serinette-pitched. Henri meandered through town, taking long strides to resist the urge to run. He turned down the main street to pause in the baker's doorway and press his hands to his chest. Make it quit hammering. If Guillaume pursued him, he could go inside. The mothers buying bread would protect him.

Henri waited there a few minutes—no Guillaume. Then he proceeded back to the workshop, where he discovered another order had arrived that morning from Mrs. Delia Dumphries Stanton of Pleasant Valley, New York, this one for a dozen instruments. As he settled into work, Henri mentioned his syndrome to a few of the apprentices, just to make sure they still believed the old story about him.

Chapter Seventeen
A dreadful misunderstanding.

As a sixteen-year-old boy who rested during the day, Henri often had difficulty sleeping. He kicked at his sheets. Pulled at his pillow. Ran his fingers along his ribs as if they were keys on an instrument. Sometimes he worried about what Guillaume meant by *proving it*. Would he pop out of the shadows with a dead goat and insist Henri revive it? Aimée swore to him that Guillaume was just mad about the villagers' teasing and wouldn't actually do anything. "Nothing to worry about," she said. "My brother is trying to get a *violon* apprenticeship. He's much too busy to plot." Still, the idea kept Henri awake.

When he wanted to calm himself, he reminisced about the girls at the stump, the hems of gowns lifted by the wind, the feeling of belonging beside those girls, although now that he was nearly a man, he embroidered his wistfulness with girls' mouths brushing his ears, a bit of Margaux's hair falling out of its cap, or Yvette's hair snagging on his short crop of whiskers. Aimée's hands grazing his lap when she reached for her lace pillow.

On some of the nights he couldn't sleep, Henri lit a candle and sneaked downstairs to visit his mother's old lace kit. He liked wrapping the thread around his fingers. The bobbins fit in the palms of his hands. He practiced what his grandmother had taught him: identifying wood types by touch.

Henri's seventeenth birthday arrived in May: the cusp of adulthood. Papa said nothing about the special occasion at breakfast, not even when Maman gifted Henri a razor. Had he remembered Robert's birthday in October and now forgotten Henri's? Perhaps Papa had another headache. Once the pain subsided, he would remember.

What Henri wanted most for his birthday, besides Papa's acknowledgment, was time with his best friend. So he complained of being tired, and when Maman agreed to let him go back to bed and skip work, just this once, he calligraphed a letter asking Aimée to visit.

"I need to see you immediately!" he wrote.

The servant girl who carried his letter down the hill returned an hour later with a favorable reply. Henri begged his mother to let him receive Aimée in his room.

"I can't possibly say *oui*," Maman said. "What would her mother think?"

Henri placed the back of his palm against his forehead, then fell back onto his hard pillow. He waited a few moments before releasing a dramatic sigh.

"Oh!" his mother gasped. "Are you feeling all right?"

"Terribly weak." Henri let his eyes close as if it were too much trouble to keep them open. "Do I have a fever, Maman?"

She confirmed he didn't. "Shall I fix you a crock of broth or a spoonful of Magnalle's Sedative Solution?"

"Broth, please," Henri said, opening his eyes and smiling weakly at her. "Although—" Here he coughed quite convincingly.

"What?" she asked.

"Seeing Aimée would really cheer me up. More than broth."

His mother sighed, longer and deeper than he had. "I'll let her decide," she said finally. "If she agrees, I'll permit it. Just this one time."

"I won't ask again, Maman. Only once. For my birthday."

"You mean because you're feeling so poorly?"

He nodded, suppressing his grin. When she left, Henri changed into his best shirt. He wandered from window to door until he heard footsteps on the stairs, whereupon he lunged for the bed and propped himself up as if he had been there all along. He feigned a cough for his mother's sake.

"I'll leave you two," Maman said. "Call me if you need anything, Aimée, and do not tell your parents of my leniency."

Aimée promised and Maman went back downstairs.

His best friend wore a formal golden traveling cloak over a dress the very color of *l'herbe*. Grass, he thought, remembering his English lessons. Aimee tossed her cap off and went about unpinning her beech hair, shaking it loose. It seemed to Henri that glorious spring had cracked open its fragile chrysalis heart right there upon his winter-dulled floor.

"Your mother said you were ill."

"An excuse." Henri grinned. "It's my birthday. I wanted to see you."

"Seventeen," Aimée mused. "Almost a man." She admired the leather-bound British novels on the side table, the light dipping through the curtains and illuming a swath of hand-knotted rug.

He would never be able to bear her going home every day to a man who wasn't him. But with her father not being a music-maker, she would be betrothed to a builder, a farmer, or a butcher. If a man in one of those physical professions suspected someone of spying, he'd never climb a tree to hide. He'd tear through the bushes until he found the source of the noise.

Henri sighed, this time a real one. "I wish I were more like the other boys."

"I am quite glad that you are not." Aimée shut the door, promising that she would take the blame if his mother came upstairs. She tossed her glorious cape onto the ground and hopped onto the bed beside him, her many green layers falling like leaves on his blanket.

"I'm not scared of you," she added, touching her finger to the side of his jaw.

Henri didn't know how to interpret this. Her lips, so close, a tiny mole beside her nose that he hadn't noticed, the buzzing from her touch even more insistent than a rib song.

"You proved yourself to me," Aimée said, "saving me from a life in New York."

She leaned close and opened her mouth onto his. Their teeth banged together, sending an unpleasant shiver down the back of his neck, but Aimée, resolute, continued to plunge her tongue into his mouth. Henri sucked back at her lips and tongue with equal fervor. He wrapped one of his hands in her hair, and in reply she twisted one of his curls around her finger. Between kisses, he told her, "I forgot what you're proving."

"Me too," she whispered.

Every bit of him against every bit of her, with layers of corset and chemise and underthings between them. He relished the press of her tiny muffin breasts. Henri's flagpole protruded with fervor into a fold of her dress. He found himself devouring the sides of her mouth as if she were one of the baker's sweets. She broke from him when she lost patience with the licking and picked up her cape to fasten it back on.

Henri spent the rest of the afternoon staring out the window at the little cottage he could see in the distance, imagining smoke rising from the chimney, a clothesline with dresses and trousers fluttering in the sun, and Aimée in his arms in the bedroom.

Ever since Guillaume had accosted him, Henri had been changing his daily walking path. Sometimes he had that old feeling of being followed, but he never spotted anyone. Until one day in early June, when he ventured through the town square first, crossing Le Vieux Ponte and turning around midway. At one point Henri thought he heard footsteps, but when he called hello, nobody answered. He ducked into the first *violon* alley, bits of sawdust sticking to the bottoms of his shoes.

The tremolos and tunings reassured him. When he turned into the next alley, though, he was startled to see a man's boot kicked up against the wall: the ankle still in it, the boot laced the way he or a servant had laced it that morning, the toe a little scuffed. What he recognized next was the rest of the body: Odil Michaute, lying on the rutted mud, sawdust in his hair, mouth open, purple-red marks like a necklace around his throat. Henri watched his chest for a while, the way he used to watch his mother sleep, hoping to spot a heave of breath; none came. Dead! Around the red marks, his skin had been leached of color.

Oh no. Oh no. He's broken, Henri thought. *But I can fix him.*

Henri plunked down on the ground and pulled Odil's body onto his lap. The older boy was much heavier than he expected; he let the weight comfort him. *Some* of Odil was still here. As he positioned the body to lean against his chest, a dark shadow moved over the buildings on either side of the alley. When Henri looked up, he gasped. Clouds blocked out the sun.

He opened Odil's heavy coat and ran his hands around,

feeling for ribs. How had it gotten so dark midday? A gathering storm? That made little sense. Mireville did not have storms, only occasional, fleeting sun showers. Perhaps his agitation had caused the narrowing of the world; perhaps in the next few seconds, he would faint. But no—he had to try reviving Odil. The boy's parents—not to mention Aimée and the other Shadow Council girls—would be heartbroken if he failed. Henri leaned over the body, touching the purple marks that circled Odil's throat. They had a raised texture to them, as if they had been scraped into his skin by a coarse rope or a handful of violin strings.

Violin and cello apprentices leaned out of the windows of their workshops, shouting that the clouds had returned. Right away they spotted Henri, his hands circling Odil's neck.

"Murder in the alley!" one shouted.

"HELP ME!" Henri shouted to them.

The apprentices flocked outdoors, forming a ring around him and Odil. At first Henri mistook their presence for assistance, but then one of the Vuillaume boys grabbed Odil's wrist, feeling for a pulse.

"He's dead!"

The news spread through the crowd.

"The Blanchard boy strangled him!"

"Murder!"

"It's Odil! Poor Mme. Michaute!"

Henri ignored their misplaced outrage; he had work to do. He laid his palms against Odil's chest and closed his eyes. Whole notes—breaths—bubbles. Should he sing? Henri flipped through the litany of what had worked before, all the while thinking of what Odil wanted most. *Friends.* He had them—people who cared about him—which meant he had to come back into his body. He *had* to live.

"Look!" Guillaume called from someplace in the crowd. "Henri Blanchard can heal the dead. He's doing it right now!"

Henri felt his palms begin to buzz just as the Vuillaume boy pulled the body off his lap. Henri screamed and struggled and tried to clutch Odil's coat. But arms grabbed him from behind and feet kicked at his legs until he fell to the ground. First his knees hit the hard-packed dirt, then chest, then face, as if he were a wooden doll. A boot heel dug into his back, pinning him down.

"Let him go!" Guillaume shouted. "It's Henri Blanchard. Don't you recognize him? He'll fix this. Just let him do whatever it is he does. LET HIM GO!"

Guillaume kept yelling, trying to sway the crowd, but nobody released Henri. It began to rain. Fat drops landed on the dirt path, raising tiny dust puffs with each impact. It had been so dry for so long. Henri's cheek hurt from the rocks beneath him. A hand held the side of his head so he couldn't move. He wished whoever was holding him would help him up so he could explain. He had *found* the body. That's all.

"They've caught Henri Blanchard!" came a cry from above. "*Assassine!*"

"He can prove it!" Guillaume shouted. Henri's lone defender.

Prove it. The menacing words stuck in his head. Henri wished more than anything to turn onto his back, feel the rain on his eyelids, his nose, his cheeks. He felt like things would make more sense if he could only turn around and see everyone. But everyone was busy screaming at each other. A boot stopped within Henri's line of sight and he recognized it as Aimée's father's. A white piece of lace held the top closed where a fastener ought to be. Was M. Maullian here too? Or just Guillaume, borrowing his father's boots?

"Guillaume?" Henri called, desperate. "Tell them. Please! I can save Odil!"

No response; the boot moved away. Water dropped in Henri's left eye, making it sting. When he tried to rub it, someone grabbed his hands and bound them behind his back. His fingers started tingling the way they did when he touched a bobbin with his eyes closed, practicing to tell the wood kinds apart. Mud puddles formed by his cheek. Some of the liquid muck splashed into his mouth. This was a mistake—these *violon* apprentices believing what they thought they saw. His hands on Odil's neck. But Papa—the most famous man in town—would sort it out. Fix the tangle. Set Henri free.

The heel pressure on Henri's back eased. Someone rolled him over. Monsieur Cocteau, the newspaper editor, helped Henri sit up. His wrists stayed bound behind him. Rain dropped onto the apprentices as they quieted, waiting for M. Cocteau to speak.

"Henri," he said. "Did you harm Odil?"

Henri shook his head. "No—I swear. He was lying in the alley. I wanted to help."

"The apprentices saw your hands around his neck."

Henri had never thought much about how the other adults in town viewed him, because his father mattered most of all. But now he wished he had made an effort to be friendly with the newspaperman. If M. Cocteau believed him innocent, everyone else would too.

Docteur Nanin shouldered his way through the crowd and Henri felt a rush of relief. The villagers would listen to the doctor. Monsieur Cocteau held the group's attention, congratulating the apprentices who'd brought rope to secure the assassin's hands. There was a coil left over—*enough for a hanging*, a voice called. Then some of the apprentices began to move back inside the workshops, away from the rain, but from their shelters they tilted toward the scene, holding onto the moldings of doors by the top joint of each finger or leaning out windows. Henri scanned the remaining crowd for Guillaume but couldn't find him. Or M. Maullian either.

"I found Odil's body," Henri told the doctor. "I can save him. I know I can."

Docteur Nanin held up a hand. The crowd quieted, just as it had for M. Cocteau. "I can vouch for this boy and his family. He is not cruel enough to commit this kind of crime. He must have been trying to revive M. Michaute. He has an excessive belief in his own power."

Monsieur Cocteau waved his hand through the rain, as if conducting it, but it didn't yield. "He's delusional! And we are to take this as a *defense*?" The spattering drops gave the proceedings a wet drumbeat that Mireville hadn't experienced in decades.

"Delusional, perhaps, but not dangerous," Docteur Nanin clarified. "It makes perfect sense that, as someone who believes he can bring the dead back to life, he would want to help this unfortunate boy. I assure you he did Odil no harm."

"You weren't here!" a voice shouted.

The words formed a rising tide: "You weren't here, you weren't here," all directed at the doctor.

"True," Docteur Nanin said, loud enough to quiet the crowd. "I am not a witness, while some of you are. As an impartial party, therefore, I will take Henri to jail myself, and leave it to the jailer to contact the constable for further instructions."

The crowd fed off its own energy, hissing, theorizing, catching plinks of rain on their noses and upturned palms. A scholarly man had spoken up for Henri, and still the violin apprentices didn't seem to care. The doctor grabbed hold of his elbow and pulled him up.

"We'll get this cleared up quickly," Docteur Nanin told Henri. "Just as soon the constable arrives from wherever he's stationed right now. We'll explain that you have a syndrome."

But the crowd didn't disperse. Henri found himself pushed, prodded, and—when he stopped to catch his breath—kicked through the alley, past the old bridge, and toward the jail behind the newspaper office. The jailer locked him in the single cell, then unbound his hands through the bars before leaving him alone with dirt for a floor and a chamber pot that had not been properly scoured.

The jailer and the doctor held a whispered conference of their own. Docteur Nanin raised his voice a few times—"release him to his parents," Henri overheard—but the apprentices were shouting "murderer" and "fiend" from outside the walls.

"The constable wants me to keep anyone turned in on suspicion of a crime," the jailer finally said, loud enough for Henri to hear. "Until he can interview the suspect and decide whether there's enough evidence for a trial. Or a hanging."

"How long will it take to get the constable here?" Docteur Nanin asked.

"A week, usually," the jailer said. "Depending on which jail he's visiting currently and how fast my letter finds him."

Chapter Eighteen
Henri befriends the night jailer.

The jail was, like everything in Mireville, a bit more special than any of its kind in the world. Its best feature: sweet water that coursed from ceiling to stone floor. Before the rain came, it had been a scant trickle—allowing a few swallows to be captured in a stoneware dish every hour or so—but now it flowed with such ample enthusiasm that Henri sat on the opposite side of his cell unless he was thirsty.

The day jailer admitted Docteur Nanin to Henri's cell later that afternoon. The doctor admired the waterfall, how it promoted good hygiene, helping to prevent the disease outbreaks that plagued other towns' prisons. He proceeded to look in the accused's nose, eyes, and throat, and to push at his abdomen.

"You are feeling all right?"

Henri shrugged. "I want to go home."

"The jailer hasn't hurt you?"

Henri told him no.

"Has he fed you?"

Henri said yes—some bread and cheese. "Can you ask my parents to visit?"

Docteur Nanin assured him he would try. "They are worried about you."

After the doctor left, Henri realized he should have said thank you. He should have asked after the doctor's health—had he ever?—or asked about the rain and if anyone's root cellars had flooded, if any stores of wood and thread had been ruined.

Perhaps this was the true Son of the Sun-Bringer Syndrome: believing oneself to be in the center of everything.

Geneviève woke, gasping, from another drowning. In the dream, the river Madon rose to her ankles, then her knees. It swallowed her waist, her dress billowing along the surface as if a gust of wind had been trapped underneath the fabric. How lovely, for that suspended moment, to be wanted with such force, though her ankles were cold and her knees were cold, the warm place between her legs stabbed by coldness that reached up under her ribs and slowed her heart, and at the very moment this slowness felt good, comforting, compared to the grind of daily life, and the lovely skirt rose up and engulfed her, stuffing her mouth and nose with fabric, then with a terrible whooshing sound the dress dragged her down to the silty bottom.

Georges slept on his back, hands folded. With his eyes closed, he seemed the same familiar husband she used to have, before the accident. Monsieur Cocteau had warned Georges that visiting Henri could make things worse for their whole family. That the town might turn against them for raising a murderer. So Georges had forbidden her to go.

But this was her kind and gentle son. Her sweet Henri. If Georges wouldn't fight to save him from the noose, then she would.

Geneviève fumbled for a match and the oil lantern. She put on her gray wool slippers, then tiptoed past Henri's empty room, down the back stairs to the kitchen, and through the kitchen to the parlor. She grabbed a basket for her lace kit and pillow, then swaddled the magnifying flask in a blanket and placed it on top.

"Let me into his cell!" she commanded the night jailer, who pulled the key from his pocket and obliged, noting the wool slippers still on her feet and her dressing gown muddied from the wet late-night journey. He wondered if Henri and his mother shared a streak of madness, each one holding an end of it.

Henri roused himself from the cot. His curls had grown matted; one slung itself over his eye. He hugged his mother. One efficient squeeze before letting go.

"Maman! Did you bring me food? I am so hungry!"

"I will tomorrow night," Genéviève assured him. "I came in a hurry. But look."

She pulled the magnifying flask out of the basket, a round glass orb with a hole on the top and a flat bottom. She trickled water from the waterfall into the glass, then she floated a candle in it to throw the light out. It was as bright as day in the cell now, the oldest trick lacemakers had for meeting their cutoff dates: working through the darkness, huddled together around one of these devices. Genéviève set her lace pillow between his knees and began to teach her son what she hoped might comfort him, or at least pass the time: how to make bobbin lace. He took to it with ease, learning quickly.

"Will Papa come?" Henri asked. "I very much want to see him."

"He has a headache," she replied. "But he will. In a day or so. Certainly before the constable gets here."

At sunrise, she took the empty basket but left the supplies so Henri could keep himself occupied. The day jailer complained that the prisoner had been given tools without authorization, but watching him practice with threads was vastly superior to hearing him sniffle and sob. Geneviève returned the next night to criticize Henri's tension, explain the prickings, and educate him on the use of the gimp, that thick thread prevalent in local designs.

Henri fussed over his work and marveled at his progress. He had always suspected he would have made a fine lacemaker, if born into a different family, and this small solace kept him company.

Monsieur Cocteau reported on the murder in the next edition of the newspaper. He did not record Docteur Nanin having sworn to Henri's innocence because there were no other obvious suspects, and he didn't want the villagers to panic about a loose killer. When the constable came to town, if he agreed with public opinion and sentenced Henri to death—or at least a trial—then the villagers would be relieved. If the constable decided something *else* had caused the unfortunate death, well, there would be mayhem, but it would be the constable's problem to address. Not the newspaper's.

Charles DeBourgignon appeared as soon as he read this headline, hair lying flat on his head for once on account of the rain. He looked half drowned. The day jailer wouldn't let him into Henri's cell because he wasn't family, so they had a quiet conversation with the bars between them.

After Henri reassured him of his general well-being, Charles asked, "Do you want me to bring the body to you?"

Henri raised his eyebrows. "You would do that?"

Charles nodded, though glumly, not meeting Henri's eyes. "It would mean stealing him from his parents. He's in their front parlor till the burial."

Henri imagined Charles trying to lug the bigger boy's corpse through the village without anyone noticing. Even late at night, it sounded too risky. Surely Charles would get caught and thrown into the cell too.

"He died yesterday," Henri said. "It might already be too late. Besides, I can't see how you could bring him here safely."

Charles looked visibly cheered. "Well," he said, "that's probably true. But do keep my offer in mind. As a backup plan."

Henri said yes, of course. Charles stuck a few fingers through the bars and Henri gripped them in a goodbye handshake. It felt good to have that momentary contact.

Aimée appeared about an hour later, wearing her fine spring cloak. She passed through the entryway, said hello to the day jailer, then curtseyed to Henri with a surprising formality that seemed, at first, a tease. She had appropriate shoes on, though the tips were muddy. He launched himself toward the bars, wanting to reach through and touch her. It seemed everything would be all right if they could hold hands. But she shied away from his touch.

"Tell everyone I'm not delusional," Henri begged. "Tell them about Grand-Maman. Your brother suspects the truth. He knows she was dead before I visited. He said—"

Aimée didn't meet his eyes. She folded her arms and the cape closed around her body like curtains being drawn. She hadn't bothered to bun her hair, even though she had been doing it every day since she turned sixteen. Her cap sat askew on her head. Beech-colored strands matted around her face, the ends dripping. Her eyes blinked big and wet. Tears or rain? Henri couldn't tell.

"Did you?" she asked.

At first he thought she wanted him to talk about Grand-Maman.

But she knew, of course she knew, that he had saved her. She had been there. Henri leaned his whole body against the bars, trying to stretch a bit closer to her. One touch, just her fingers against his, and he would feel bolstered against whatever the constable judged, whenever he finally got there.

"Did I what?"

Aimée rubbed a fist over one of her eyes. "Strangle Odil?"

Henri reflected on the necklace pattern around the boy's neck. *Strangled.* He glanced down at his own wrists, now chafed by the binding rope.

"You have to ask?" They had done what they had done with their lips and tongues and teeth—Aimée had filled him with her own spit and courage—and she had to ask. He felt as if she had stuck rocks in his pockets and pushed him off the old bridge.

"Why would I hurt him?" Henri asked in a dull voice.

Aimée shrugged, staring at the floor. "People are saying you... well, that you wanted to prove you could revive a person."

So this was the rumor: pride had turned him into a killer. And Aimée worried it might be true? Henri turned away, dropping his body onto the damp floor of his cell, his heart lower and lower, not hitting the bottom of his chest but filling with algae and fish and whatever lives beneath the coldest rocks, and even though she called his name—called it and called it and called it— he did not sit up or twist his neck to meet her gaze. If that's what she thought. If that's what everyone thought.

"At least—" Aimée said, and her voice trailed off.

Her bracelet banged against the bars of his cage. He could stand up and touch her now, if he wanted, if she kept her hand there, but he belonged with the silt at the bottom of the river, his best friend unsure, having to ask.

"He was dead when I found him," he said to the wall.

Aimée sighed and brusqued her tone—all business. "All right, I believe you. Now will you turn around and talk to me?"

Henri shut his eyes. He didn't want to give her the satisfaction. He breathed; she breathed. The day jailer rustled papers and ate something that he had stored in crinkly paper. Maybe a fresh biscuit from home. Aimée's knees cracked. Or maybe it was her elbows, readjusting to his silence. Her ring rubbed against the bars when she adjusted positions. The sound made him think of his mother's metal spoons. He remembered Maman and his grandmother dancing around the kitchen, banging spoons against metal pots. If he ever got out of jail, he would buy his mother new metal spoons.

"I can't make you talk to me," Aimée said. "But please—just say something."

Henri sat there, stubborn as his father and grandfather, not ready to forgive her the question. Or the *if*.

Aimée thanked the day jailer with a wobble in her voice and left.

❊ ❊ ❊

The day jailer and the night jailer, their shoulders damp, glided in and out of the cell, offering food and taking empty plates, as if they were pins on each side of a cylinder. Both men had sent letters to the other local jails, urging the constable to attend to their young prisoner as soon as possible. But there was no sign of him. Their letters went unanswered. Aimée did not return.

"The wheel of justice is slow," the night jailer assured the prisoner.

"So I just have to sit here and wait? Even though I didn't do anything wrong?"

The night jailer nodded. "The constable is probably over-seeing a trial. He'll be on his way when he can. If you're innocent, he'll let you go."

Henri worked the thread and bobbins the way his mother had taught him. He wished he could stand beneath the gray sky for himself—the very thing his father had spent his life longing for. *Rain.* Now it was here, and Henri couldn't experience it. He wondered if his grandmother was up in the sky someplace, dancing in a pair of silk stockings her friends had woven from rainbows.

Again he thought of his syndrome, his self-centeredness. Aimée had not come to the jail for him; he knew this now. If she had, she would have tried to cheer him with a sweet or a song. Something had changed for her, something he didn't understand, and he had wasted the chance to ask because he was wallowing in his predicament.

Charles stopped by again, this time with news. "There's been a robbery!"

Henri appreciated his effort but did not have the energy to talk. Despite his waterfall rinsings, a distasteful ripeness rose from Henri's armpits when he reached out to shake his friend's hand through the bars. Charles prattled on about the break-ins: at the baker's and the cheese shop and the newspaper office. All in the heart of the village, all the tills cleaned out. Henri settled back on the ground and pressed his arms across his belly, hoping to keep his odor to himself.

"Cheer up," Charles said. "The whole village is discussing who the thief could be, and of course it can't be you. Maybe when the constable gets here he'll focus on—"

"A thief? Instead of a murderer? Unlikely." Henri slumped against the wall of his cell. "If they even catch the thief."

"I've been telling everyone maybe they're the same person," Charles told him. "I believe you. I know you'd never do anything like that."

Henri heard the words like tiny drums beating against the clouds: *it's not enough, not enough, not enough.*

Maman returned, as she did most nights, after dark. The orb-like magnifying flask cast a warm flickering light around the cell. It comforted Henri. He turned his hands in the light, creating fluttery shadows on the back wall.

"Let me see your progress," she said.

Henri held out the swath of unfinished lace, pinned to the pillow. "Papa still won't come to see me?"

Genéviève didn't have the gumption to lie to their son. To mention headaches again.

"He thinks if he is seen coming here—" She did not know what her husband feared most: M. Cocteau's scorn or the loss of his leadership role in the community. But the village couldn't turn against them, could it? The Blanchards had been contributing to the local economy and donating to the church for generations. They were good people. The last serinetters in a town that revered the craft, or used to. It had been the Blanchards and the Pignons, until the Pignons started making regular barrel organs, leaving only the Blanchard workshop to carry on the local tradition.

Maman wore an old dress, refashioned with gussets to make it fit. Her waist had lost its definition since the baby. Why had Henri taken his father's side when he found the letters? Papa didn't even care about him enough to visit.

"Perhaps if I were his firstborn, I would matter more."

Maman merely nodded. Deep lines cupped either side of her mouth like parentheses.

"You *knew*?" Henri said. "About *Roh-bair*?" This felt like a betrayal as deep as his father's continued absence. All this time he had been guarding the secret, afraid to hurt her feelings.

"Your older brother," Maman said. "*Oui.*"

"Half-brother," Henri corrected. "Did Papa tell you?"

Maman put her hands on his cheeks, framing his face with her fingers, and pushed the question back to him. "Did he tell *you*?"

Henri admitted he hadn't. He explained about finding the letters and the girls' council and Odil offering to translate. He wished he had corrected Odil's litany when he had the chance. Odil hadn't broken him; his father had.

Maman had found the letters too, plus a small portrait of the boy stuck with paste to the bottom of the dresser. She hadn't translated as many of them as Henri had done through Odil, because she had rudimentary English skills and did not want to confide in anyone. When she found the portrait and compared the features to her husband's, she understood enough.

Henri filled her in on what he knew of *Roh-bair*, how Delia Dumphries of Pleasant Hill, New York, filled her letters with blustery exaggerations and compliments.

"He is not a real son to Papa," Henri added. "They haven't even met!"

"Another firstborn son will be little comfort if you hang," Maman said, whereupon she burst into tears.

Henri nestled his mother's head on his shoulder. He was a pin's length taller, and he wrapped his arms around her and let her sob until he felt he couldn't hold his own grief any longer. "The night jailer thinks I'll be set free," he said.

"Not if the constable refuses to give you a trial."

"Can he do that?"

Maman shrugged. "There hasn't been a murder here in my lifetime. I would expect a trial. I'll insist on one, but—"

"Men of power can be unpredictable," Henri finished.

She nodded. "He can decide whatever he wants."

He squeezed her, then let go. "Back to work, Maman," he said. "I want to finish this piece of lace, if I can."

Neither of them had to say *before*. The word crawled up their arms, made their hearts thump.

The day jailer assumed Henri was guilty of murder. The world was a little safer because the cell key was in his pocket. It fell, therefore, to the night jailer, to share the news.

"Your friend Aimée left for America," he told Henri, "with her family."

"That's not possible," Henri said. "Monsieur Maullian wouldn't have left his mother behind. She's bedridden."

The night jailer placed a palm on the back of his neck, fingering the shaved hairs out of habit. "They paid someone to take care of her."

"Are you sure?"

"That's the gossip."

"Who said?" Henri wanted to know.

"The Niçoises, and the Rigoniets, and the DeBourgignons."

All families he knew and trusted. Especially Charles's. The night jailer handed him a piece of paper with a New York address on it and a request for him to write.

"I'm sorry I could not visit again," Aimée had added in tiny print at the very bottom of the note. "Papa forbade it."

It made no sense. Grand-Maman being alive meant America couldn't happen. Aimée promised! He had done something that terrified him, something that felt more wrong than right, just to keep Aimée around. And it hadn't worked after all. Henri banged his hands against the cell bars. He gulped for breath and couldn't find it. He wanted to reach the air with his tongue, the way he'd reached for Aimée's tongue, only nothing was there—no girl, no air, no clothesline with dresses and trousers fluttering in the sun. Henri pushed his fingernails into his wrists and cried out. There were so many things he had never asked her. The night jailer kept saying things like *shush, quiet now, you'll only make it worse for yourself, what if someone hears you carrying on like this, you seem like a rational young man, I don't want to have to report this outburst.* Henri wanted to be quiet. But there was loudness coming from his throat, raw and harsh, like his mother hitting a slab of meat with a mallet to make it cook evenly.

In the morning he was sore and quiet, and he did not eat the mush served for *petit déjeuner.* What the night jailer told him made no sense. What would have made M. Maullian abandon his mother and travel to a far-off land?

"Shall I be hanged?"

"Probably, unless the constable finds another suspect," the day jailer said.

Henri imagined his father's remaining eye scanning the villagers, hunting for the true killer.

Children began playing in the side yards of their houses, not in the fields, so their parents could keep their eyes on them. If Odil could die, then their children could die. Of course they had lost sickly infants, but they had no reference for this kind of loss.

The littlest village children, too young for school, played murder, killing their friends with mean touches. Between the murder and the thievery, fear and suspicion clouded friendships and neighborly relations. The adults began building locks to secure their doors and windows. Someone—or several someones—in their community couldn't be trusted. And not everyone believed Henri capable of murder.

"That weak young man couldn't possibly have hurt the Michaute boy."

"*C'est impossible.*"

"If it wasn't Henri, who?" the women wondered.

"Have mercy," the nuns of the Convent of Notre Dame prayed.

Clouds huddled over the village as if they had been bottled all these decades somewhere offstage, and now they found themselves uncorked. For the first time in several decades, greens grew without charring. Tomatoes stayed green, apples took their time. Sunburns peeled and then disappeared. There was a sudden, distressing ebb of even the cutest freckles. The villagers reminisced about their former bronzings, how sun-flushed skin could hide wrinkles and pimples; the locals with naturally dark skin became revered, symbols of the healthy color the rest of them had lost.

Gray days made for quiet conversations. For coughs. For unexpected aches. Rainbows disappeared, for the sun had gone into hiding. No one blamed or credited Georges; they pointed fingers at his son. Who else could have returned the clouds and made it rain? The villagers had asked Georges to do so over the years, and he never could.

Henri passed his days in jail practicing his lace work and licking the waterfall. Aimée was the one who could have straightened the whole misunderstanding out—well, Aimée and Charles, but Charles did not know about Grand-Maman, just the animals, and he lacked the brazen quality that would make adults listen. Still, he was there. So was Henri's mother, who continued to pass the nights working side by side with him, practicing the town's other art in the bright glow of the magnifying flask, as carefree as if it were midday in their own parlor. Georges had made her promise not to visit; she kept that promise only during his waking hours.

It felt good to work with each other, to create for the sake of beauty. Their pieces wouldn't fetch much money, if any, but having something to show for his time kept Henri from being submerged in endless despair. He focused on his technique, picked apart bad stitches, tried again. The rhythm of his days, naps and lace in alternating segments, led him to the evenings, when Maman would take his project and critique it, adjust it, tell him how to do it better.

At last, sixteen days since his imprisonment, a letter arrived from the constable. The day jailer waved the letter in front of Henri, who hopped up with great anticipation, not even bothering to dust his trousers off.

"What does it say?"

The day jailer grinned. "He's arriving in three days to proceed with the hanging."

"The hanging?" Henri gasped the question. He gripped the bars as his knees went weak. *The hanging, the hanging.* The words devolved into syllables without meaning. *The hanging.* It felt separate from him, from everything about him.

"He hasn't interviewed me yet!" Henri protested. "He hasn't even met me. How could he decide?"

The day jailer shrugged. "Since no other suspects have been brought forward, and the constable has another pressing matter in Baudricourt, he has decided to proceed without a trial."

"That's not fair! What about the thief?"

"The thief doesn't concern you."

"But what if they're the same person? The thief and the murderer? Wouldn't finding the thief possibly clear my—"

"The constable has decided, and I report to him."

Henri's fingers burned from how tight he was gripping the bars. "Odil was my friend. I never hurt him."

"Odil ran away whenever he saw you," the day jailer pointed out. "We have numerous eyewitness accounts of this. Monsieur Cocteau has been doing the interviews. Evidence enough, the constable thinks."

"So he's deciding based on M. Cocteau's opinion?"

"His is the word of truth in this village," the day jailer said. "Why shouldn't the constable believe the local newspaperman?"

"Because it's not true!"

Henri reached out to grasp at the man's shirt sleeve, trying to get him to listen, but the day jailer nimbly stepped back, laughed, and returned to his post in the other room, guarding the door.

Chapter Nineteen
Charles and his friends try for a miracle.

The night before the constable was due to arrive, Henri told his mother, "If you really want to help me, you'll bring my friend here."

"You have a friend!" She patted his wrist as if this were even more wonderful than his lace-making progress. "Who is it?"

Half an hour later, Maman returned with Charles DeBourgignon. His hair stuck out from rolling around on his pillow. Henri begged his mother to give them some privacy. She seemed disappointed but agreed to go home and get some rest.

"Are you all right in there? It looks awfully damp."

"It is damp," Henri agreed. "But clean."

"Perhaps not quite as damp as out there." Charles gestured toward the outside world.

"Can you stop talking about whether I am more or less damp?" Henri said.

Charles reddened. "Maman has not taught me what is appropriate to say to a man in jail. It's a rather delicate situation, *n'est-ce pas?*"

"Remember your idea? About Odil?" Henri gave a half-smile to hearten Charles. "The day jailer thinks the constable will hang me tomorrow, unless the real murderer is found."

"The family buried him two days ago. I could, though, if you—"

"You would do that for me?" Henri reached out to grasp Charles's hands through the bars. "Dig up a body?"

Charles sighed. His hands were cold and uncomfortably moist.

Henri let go and added, "I don't want to die for a crime I didn't commit."

"Then I have to try," Charles said. "Most of the village thinks you did it. Monsieur Cocteau has convinced them."

"He's convinced the constable, too," Henri said. "But if you don't want to—"

"I do." Charles grinned at his friend. "I mean I don't—not truly—but I will."

❋ ❋ ❋

Charles needed help. As soon as he agreed to the plan, he realized he couldn't possibly follow through on his own. He raced home and turned the doorknob to the bedroom his sister Bernadine shared with their other sisters. No one had ever trusted Charles with a more important task. If he woke the wrong sister, or all of them, he would fail.

Heel-to-toe steps lessened the squeaking of the floorboards. Bernadine slept beneath the window, for she was the oldest and could withstand a breeze better than the younger two. A breeze had killed their great-grandmother and, three years later, their grandmother. Their parents had boarded up all the house windows, so it was not so much a window Bernadine slept under as a former window, but it was still drafty. Charles had his own room, a former closet, because it had no windows and his *papa* refused to take chances with his one male heir.

But now—he had a friend to save. Heel to toe, he stepped one creak closer to Bernadine's mattress. When he bent down to rouse her, his hair fell forward into his eyes and tickled her cheek. She opened her eyes and peered toward the boarded-up window. Still dark outside. Charles put one finger to his lips and motioned her to follow him outside.

She approved of the plan, as bizarre as it was. "But it can't just be the two of us. We'll have to dig in shifts."

Charles suggested a few of his fellow apprentices, ones who worked hard and didn't complain, but Bernadine insisted on recruiting the Shadow Council of Apprentice Lacemakers.

Their leader had left the country, but Bernadine trusted them.

Besides, the girls knew Odil as well as anyone in the village. They'd want to help find his true killer. Clear Henri's name.

Charles let his sister organize the grave-robbing party, for she had a festive spirit, even in her nightclothes, and did not worry as much as he did. One might think, in spotting her knocking on friends' windows in the middle of the night, her bedcap askew and driblets of rain rolling down her cheeks, that she had some grand adventure in mind for them all. And perhaps this was an adventure. Yvette, Margaux, and Anne-Jeanée agreed to help, also in their nightclothes, for there could be no delay and no noise, lest the adults wake and condemn them to staying home.

"Can Henri really revive the dead?" Margaux asked.

Charles swore it was so. Despite the macabre nature of this excursion, he couldn't help but marvel at the unusual conditions. He would never again be in the company of this many young women so inappropriately attired in the middle of the night. He wondered if this was what Odil felt when Aimée let him join the council. Included. Welcomed. Like one of them.

Charles carried a lantern and the two shovels he'd procured from his father's toolshed. Anne-Jeanée pushed a wheelbarrow from her yard.

Yvette held a lantern in each hand and couldn't wrap her arms around herself to ward off the chill. "I wish I had my coat," she said.

"Think of poor Henri," Charles said. "What is a little dampness compared to the noose? Or to poor Odil rotting underground?"

Bernadine turned around and smacked Charles on the shoulder. "Yvette's allowed to be cold—and say as much—without you making her feel bad about it."

Charles, chastened, offered his apologies, and then Yvette admitted her thoughtlessness in complaining of a small discomfort at a time like this, and then Margaux lamented that she did not want to see Odil in whatever condition he might be in, and Charles regretted saying Odil might be rotting because of course he had only just been buried, and they should expect no change whatsoever to his condition, at least until Henri had laid hands on the body. In which case, any change would be welcome.

"So if you don't want to try—"

"*Mais oui*, I do," Margaux said.

"Me too," said Yvette.

"You do have a backup plan, don't you?" Bernadine asked.

Charles confessed that this *was* the backup plan.

"We'll need to do some more thinking, then." Bernadine proceeded to lead the bedraggled, bed-clothed band to their destination, while deep in quiet conversation with Anne-Jeanée. Charles felt relieved. His sister would know what to do if this plan failed. She always had good ideas.

Bernadine led her friends and brother up the steps, through the unlocked gate, and into the cemetery, where they spread out in search of upturned dirt. Charles wandered farther south than the others, swinging his lantern past rows of Vuillaumes and then pausing at the name Blanchard. M. and Cérine—Henri's grandparents. Beside them, a small mound, also labeled Cérine. Chills ran up Charles's arms. *Madame Blanchard's dead baby.* He didn't want Henri hanged and buried here too. If they would even allow a supposed murderer to be interred alongside the good people of Mireville. Maybe they'd just throw his body into the woods.

"Over here!" Yvette called. "I think I found him."

No headstone marked her find, but no one else had died in the past week. Bernadine decided it must be Odil's grave. If Henri could perform his miracle, Charles thought, the family would be out a lot of money for the stone—but they would have their son back.

Charles offered the extra shovel to Margaux, who handled it like an enormous bobbin: with equal parts yearning and frustration. To set a good example, he bent his elbows to the task, slopping a heavy hunk of the mud over to the side.

"I'll be right back," Bernadine said after watching for a while.

"Where are you going?" Charles had been counting on her strength and optimism.

"I have to get supplies for the backup-backup plan." Bernadine flashed him a grin, then promised she was only running home for a few minutes. "I'll return before you miss me."

Margaux passed her shovel to Yvette, and she and Charles dug together, alternating strikes, *un-deux, un-deux, un-deux*. His forearms began to ache from hefting the rain-saturated earth out of the way. Charles allowed a minuet to sashay through his head as a distraction: *un-deux, un-deux, un-deux*. He hoped Odil's parents had paid for a casket, for if not, their spades would snag on the body.

Soon Margaux changed places with Yvette again; Charles refused to cede his shovel. Then Bernadine returned and spelled Margaux, and still Charles kept digging. He could do this one thing for his friend. He could almost hear his shoulders screaming, the bones moving apart to let a flood of anguish flow out between the ligaments.

"I hit something solid!" Yvette whispered with excitement. The girls clustered around with their lanterns but Charles kept digging, digging, digging.

"It's pine." Anne-Jeanée was excellent at identifying bobbin woods.

"A casket!" Margaux said. "Thank goodness."

It had a bell and a string rigged through the top, a safeguard against live burial. This, somehow, reassured Charles. He opened the lid and unwound the string from Odil's finger before helping Bernadine hoist the body into the wheelbarrow. Charles had completed his part of the miracle. He collapsed on his knees and heaved a breath of relief.

"Get up," his sister said. "You can rest later."

Bernadine, Yvette, Margaux, and Anne-Jeanée took turns wrangling the wheelbarrow. Poor Charles had dug so much that angry red blisters had formed on both his hands, then erupted into white bubbles, which were now seeping fluid. He followed along, wincing every so often, pressing his palms together to see if that made them feel any better.

In the wheelbarrow, by the light of their lanterns, Odil appeared disheveled, the backs of his sleeves streaked with dirt, his face set like one of the baker's sugar baubles. His neck seemed swollen. The necklace of marks had turned blue-black. The girls kept peering at him as they trundled him over the threshold of the cemetery gate and then onto the street, half-expecting him to sit up and indulge in his usual rocking. It seemed strange to see him without motion of his own.

As they walked, Bernadine explained the secondary plan to everyone, Anne-Jeanée interjecting here and there. Charles agreed to his part—should this revivery business not work as intended. He was much cheered that his sister had come up with such a smart ruse.

The night jailer refused to admit the ragtag bunch of children. They had pale faces and streaks of dirt on their cheeks. Moreover, they had the deceased in a cart: Odil Michaute, legs akimbo, his skin gray and swollen from the rain or death or both. The only dead people the night jailer had ever seen lived and died in the sun. Some of them were swollen from their ailments, but none was as bloated as this. Then again, he had never before seen a body that had been buried, then unburied. He liked the prisoner, but this seemed like an extraordinary turn of events—one that would lead to no good.

"What do you think you're doing?" he asked.

"We are here on important business," Bernadine said. "We must see your prisoner."

Henri called from the cell behind the wall, "Hello, Bernadine," though without much enthusiasm. Had he already lost faith in the project?

The night jailer prided himself on being a permissive man, and yet he could not condone grave-robbing. Not even of a murder victim. Though he had, it must be admitted, a certain insistent curiosity.

"If you agree to our plan," Bernadine told him, "we will prove Henri is not the murderer, and he will be set free, and you will be lauded by the constable when he arrives tomorrow for preventing an unnecessary execution and making his job simple."

"It is quite expensive to bring in the hangman from Baudricourt," the night jailer mused. "And it would be a relief to the constable if he arrived and found the situation resolved."

Charles stepped forward to explain Henri's gift was a true one—not a syndrome. "He can heal the dead."

"I don't believe in fairy tales," the night jailer said. "I've grown fond of the young man, but—"

"Oh good," Bernadine interrupted. "Then you have nothing to risk by letting him see the body. He'll try and fail, and you'll send us back home, and none of us will speak a word of this tomorrow. And we will be grateful you gave us the opportunity. Perhaps I will even bake you a plate of cookies."

"But if he should succeed—" the night jailer couldn't help adding.

Yvette piped up, "Then that would be something, wouldn't it?"

"Please?" Charles begged.

The night jailer loved his mother and wife, and he liked these spunky girls who talked to him as if they were adults, and he did have a sweet tooth, but it was the boy speaking up for his friend that convinced him. The night jailer was the son of a day jailer, and the grandson of a constable from Baudricourt. He had been born to listen to men.

"Go on then, through the doorway there," the night jailer said. "But I can't open the cell for you, since you're not family."

"I'm his cousin," Yvette said. "On his mother's side, the Rappatouts."

Anne-Jeanée said, "Please? I'm his cousin too, same as Yvette."

Yvette eyeballed Margaux until she admitted that she, too, was his cousin.

"Us too," added Charles and Bernadine.

"Seeing as you're all family..." The jailer shrugged.

The girls parted to let him through. He unlocked the door, then retreated to his post in the front room. Charles pushed the cart into the cell, Bernadine following. She adjusted Henri's mother's magnifying orb to project light on the body.

Henri nearly applauded with joy. His friends had done it! Odil's skin was cool. He smelled a little like that dead goat, but at least his hair hadn't been eaten by worms yet.

Odil had been buried without the wool coat Henri had stripped off him in the alley. If Henri could do his part, Odil would wake up with metal marks where his legs were supported by the lip of the wheelbarrow. And he would be able to go outside and know the scent of damp earth for himself. To know life in this village with rain.

Henri touched the spots on Odil's neck. Cold. And rubbery. A little like Mme. Rigoniet's custard, but with the color of poached chicken. He was glad his mother had agreed not to return tonight; he wouldn't have wanted her here. Her presence would have distracted him—made him even more worried about failing.

Bernadine and Yvette and Margaux and Anne-Jeanée and Charles made a ring around Henri.

What would Odil want? What would he wish for? Not scales, not sausage. Henri put his hands over the boy's heart, thinking about the song he had felt escaping from his ribcage before the apprentices started shouting. That was it—now he knew what would entice him back to them, to this room, this cell. He closed his eyes and imagined Odil waking, surrounded by friends.

Nothing happened.

"Come on, Henri," Bernadine said. "You can do it."

"I believe in you," Yvette added.

Henri didn't want to let them down. *Try harder*, he told himself. The body felt heavy and clammy on his lap. Like a giant fish pulled from the icehouse to thaw. Henri shuddered. He didn't want to be here. He wanted to go home. His cell smelled like the dirt around the goat trough when water spilled out of it from overzealous slurping. Wet and fertile. He didn't mind the reek, not anymore. But he would have preferred the smell of his pillow.

What does Odil want? People who cared about him, who wanted to help him, but what else? Friends to dig up his body in the middle of the night? A best friend, someone who would love Odil for his oddness, not in spite of it?

"Your friends are here waiting for you," Henri said. "Come back, please."

Still nothing.

Henri grasped at images that might entice this particular soul home—the empty fountain in the center of the village; Odil's grandmother's hat; a broken necklace sparkling in the dirt, waiting for Odil to find it; carrots, chard, parsnips. Rose pastilles from Paris. The small bulbs of new apples, before the sun cooked them all the way to mush.

Nothing.

"Odil!" Henri grabbed the boy's shoulders and shook them. "Wake up!"

A gentle touch on his shoulder startled him, but he didn't turn around. It didn't matter who wanted to offer reassurance; the constable would arrive tomorrow and M. Cocteau would convince him to proceed with the hanging and Henri would die for a false reason, and there was nobody who would be stupid enough to dig *him* up in the middle of the night.

Henri had failed. He had believed himself greater than he could possibly be, and now he would hang for it. His tears came swiftly.

"It's okay," Charles said, giving him an awkward pat on the back. "It might be too late. I mean, he was buried already."

How could Charles think this was okay? A wail escaped Henri's lips. It didn't matter if the girls thought less of him for crying.

"Shh. We have an alternative, *tu comprends*?" whispered Bernadine.

Henri leaned away from her, pretending he didn't hear; after all, what kind of backup plan could you try *after* grave robbery? He stayed crouched over the body in an awkward hug, his curls brushing Odil's forehead. His tears fell, silently now, on the older boy's face.

Yvette summoned the night jailer to help Charles bring the body back out of the jail. "Can't you see it's distressing your prisoner?"

Charles nodded. "Perhaps you would help me wheel the body back to the cemetery," he added. "The girls are tired from the walk over, and my blisters are terrible. It's either that or leave him here overnight. The day jailer—"

"—would look askance at a dead body in the foyer," Bernadine said.

The night jailor paused, uncertain. "I can't very well leave you all here alone."

"Lock us in the cell with Henri," Yvette said. "The cemetery is not far. You'll be back soon enough to let us out. Tomorrow Henri will be at the mercy of the constable! Even if he decides to hold a trial, it will not be a fair one. You know that as well as I do."

"Do you want to deprive him of a few last minutes with his friends?" Margaux added. "That would be cruel."

Charles took a handle of the wheelbarrow, winced from the contact with his blisters, then quickly let go. He raised his eyebrows at the night jailer, who nodded with a sigh, stepped into the cell, and took both handles. Charles walked ahead, helping the night jailer navigate the body-laden cart out of the cell and through the narrow doorway into the main room. Then the jailer came back to lock the girls and Henri in.

"Quick," Bernadine said to Henri when those two had left, "change clothes with me."

"What—strip?" He intended to refuse, but she began unfastening her gown with no thought to modesty.

Such a ruse wouldn't fool anyone! Absurd. They would all get arrested. And yet, the night jailer couldn't arrest him again. And there was Bernadine in her underthings and wool socks, handing her nightdress over. Henri blushed and tried not to look. He had never seen a girl undressed before, only read about their many layers of clothing in his grandmother's British novels. And he'd felt a bit of the boning from Aimée's corset when she pressed against him while kissing. Bernadine's attire looked quite a bit more comfortable than what he had been picturing. Girls must not wear their corsets to bed. By the light of the magnifying flask he noted how the soft cotton clung to Bernadine's body like a second skin. What he could see of her breasts created a frisson of eagerness in him. No—he wasn't supposed to be looking. He had this one chance to escape.

He wiggled out of his trousers and shirt, keeping his back to the girls, glad his undergarments didn't have holes in them.

He wished he had wider hips to fill out the bell shape of the nightgown, but the weight of the fabric felt good. It smelled like Bernadine too—sweat and kitchen oils. Yvette began fussing with the bodice, pulling the ribbons tight and tying them in a bow. She retrieved cold, damp potatoes from her own pockets and arranged them inside like breasts. Henri shivered.

"That's tomorrow's dinner you're wearing," Bernadine said. "Don't smush them and you won't go hungry."

Henri realized that as much as his friends had wanted to believe in his ability to heal the dead, they hadn't wanted to let his safety depend on it.

"You planned all this for me?" he asked them.

In response, Bernadine twisted her hair into two plaits. From her waistband, she withdrew a concealed pair of scissors, then hacked the braids off close to the neck. Anne-Jeanée pulled hairpins out of the back of her head and went about attaching the braids to Henri's loose curls.

"Quick, Margaux, your cap!" she called.

Margaux stuffed it on top of his head, then giggled. "Fetching."

"This won't work!" Henri rubbed his jaw, feeling the hairs that had sprouted during his imprisonment.

Yvette took the scissors from Bernadine, let the waterfall run over her hand, then splashed the liquid onto each of Henri's cheeks. "Hold still," she said. She opened the scissors wide as they could go and used one side like a straight edge. Henri felt an immediate bite.

"Oops," she said. But she kept going anyway, until he was as clean-shaven as she could manage under the conditions. At which point Anne-Jeanée blew out the candle in the magnifying glass and the room went dark. A lantern hanging over the night jailer's desk projected more shadows than solace.

"Perfect," whispered Bernadine.

When Charles and the night jailer returned, the girls seemed terribly mournful—sniffling and crying, each leaning over to kiss or whisper to the prisoner, who had his face turned to the wall. The night jailer unlocked the cell and used the waterfall to clean the dirt off his hands from smoothing out the top of the grave. The guests filed out to rejoin Charles in the main room.

The night jailer had expected some words of thanks from the prisoner, perhaps even a smile, for it was no small feat to re-bury a body. But, he supposed, with the constable due in morning, better Henri rest than wail about his fate.

The constable arrived to find an innocent girl imprisoned. No sign of the intended prisoner. The day jailer
apologized; he hadn't noticed anything amiss when he began his
shift, and for this inattention, the constable fired him.

The constable let Bernadine out of the cell, then summoned
M. Cocteau, who rang the bell in the town square to call for
everyone's attention. Villagers amassed, despite the drizzle. The
constable reported the news of the prisoner's disappearance to
the gathering crowd. Those who felt sure of his innocence now
doubted it. Why would he have escaped, if not guilty?

Spurred on by the newspaper headlines and the constable's
speech about lawlessness, a tide of angry, frightened villagers
surged uphill, past the Cocteau farm and the Rigoniet cottage.
The music-makers had brought their wives and children along,
for this concerned all of them. The families lined the front loop,
which was big enough for a horse and cart to turn around, as well
as both sides of the path that led back down to the village.

Once the crowd settled, as much as a crowd can with all its
murmurs and shiftings, Monsieur Cocteau knocked on the door
of the serinette workshop and called for Georges. A few minutes

later, the master serinetter ducked out of the workshop, coatless and ill attired for the rainy damp. Monsieur Papineau appeared at the kitchen door, shepherding Geneviève, likewise uncloaked, to join her husband outside.

"If you have something to say to me, say it in the town square when the constable arrives," Georges bellowed to the lot of them. "This is my home and my place of business."

"That's why we're here!" a voice shouted from the back of the crowd. Georges didn't recognize it. Had the constable already pronounced their son guilty? Without a visit to the parents, let alone a trial? Georges felt a pang of guilt for not visiting his son. For taking M. Cocteau's advice.

The villagers shifted the brims of their finest hats, which they had worn for today's proceedings in order to reassure themselves of their own prominence. They did not meet Georges's gaze or answer his questions. Their wives and children had a reckless air of holiday about them: hat brims soggy, pretty boots spattered with mud and coming unlaced from the steep trek. A few children tamped down the wet ground—still a novelty—to make a flat course for their marbles. Some of the men carried lanterns, for it was a dark morning, as they had been lately, despite the days growing longer.

Docteur Nanin had also made the trek—and pushed his way to the front of the crowd. Georges nodded, appreciating this show of support. The doctor nodded back and did not fiddle with his muttonchops.

"We've come for Henri," M. Cocteau said—not loud enough for the men and women lining the hill to hear, but they already knew why they had been summoned. Not to participate, but to watch what happened next.

"He's in jail," Geneviève said. "Is this some sort of trick?"

Georges noted the presence of the man whose workshop made the C-shaped cranks—a hallmark of French instruments—and the butcher and his eldest son, and the dairyman, plus the Rigoniets and the Niçoises, neighbors whose parents had been his parents' neighbors. These were men he trusted.

"Here, in my pocket." Monsieur Cocteau pointed to the exact spot where the papers were buttoned away from the rain. "I have a signed petition, authorized by the constable, giving us all rights herein to apprehend your son with force if necessary. He is a known murderer and a danger to our community."

At this, the crowd nodded and murmured.

Georges grabbed Geneviève's hand. Whatever happened, it would happen to both of them. She pressed her thumb hard into the back of his hand as if she were making a thumbprint cookie.

"Georges," Geneviève whispered. "Say something."

"I told you, he's not here." Georges tried to make his one eye look pleading as he gazed at the men he knew: boxwood, boxwood, boxwood. The men nodded back with stiff necks, *sans* encouragement.

Geneviève twisted out of her husband's grip and rushed to the house, her dress flapping around her ankles. She threw the door open, raced past the hearth, took the stairs two at a time, and burst into Henri's bedroom. She had been keeping it tidy, dusting each day, but now the covers had been messed and clothes thrown on the floor in haste, which made her think someone had been here last night. But how? If Henri had somehow gotten free and returned home, why didn't he pause to wake her? Geneviève's legs buckled and she fell beside the bed to pray, kneeling on her dress so that it pulled uncomfortably on her shoulders.

Outside, Georges nodded to the people who'd raised their kids the same way he raised his, all these fathers and mothers and sisters and brothers. It didn't matter that he had one eye. He could see them turning on him. His apprentices wandered out to observe the proceedings. He lodged them and fed them and taught them and presided over their occasional squabbles with fairness. They would take his side, wouldn't they? After all, they thought Henri was a firstborn. A future master craftsman.

Geneviève reappeared, her face ashen, the rain mingling with tears. "Someone has been in his room," she said simply.

"We need to search," the husbands said.

"She could be hiding him."

"It's our duty to be sure."

Monsieur Cocteau ordered four men into the house and another four into the serinette workshop. Clapping began. Those who chose not to clap pressed their palms against their trousers or reached for their children's shoulders. A few men volunteered to check the root cellar. More followed the first cluster into the workshop. Some of the non-clappers looked at the other non-clappers; wasn't a search of the Blanchards' property going too far? Georges shouldered blame for sunburns and drought, but he was not a liar. The non-clappers suspected themselves of a fundamental goodness that would allow them to stand up for the Blanchards, helping to rally the rest to halt the search, if only someone else would speak up.

The searchers returned to the circle, resuming their places next to their wives. They could not find Henri. Georges stayed where he was, facing the crowd, hatless, water streaming down his face, his cryolite eye tilted skyward because he'd rubbed it too fiercely. A master craftsman outside his workshop is just a man like anybody else. He was not better than the luthiers, than the tailor, than the man who made C-shaped cranks.

The music-makers grumbled to each other about losing time at their workbenches. Children tugged on their mothers' dresses, wanting to return home.

Charles caught his friends' eyes, and they nodded at each other. Then he cleared his throat and said, "You won't find Henri. He's gone. Or at least that's what I heard."

The men in the crowd murmured and shuffled their feet at this report.

Margaux stepped forward, away from the rest of the Rigoniets, her hands on her hips. "I have heard the same rumor!"

"Me too!" piped Anne-Jeanée.

"A very pervasive rumor," added Yvette Rappatout, "for I have come across it as well." Her father—Geneviève's brother—put his hands on her shoulders in support and nodded.

Bernadine said nothing; she had been inside the cell when the rest fetched gifts from their houses and said their good-byes. During the bell-ringing ruckus and the constable's speech, Bernadine ran home and changed, borrowing an old-fashioned sun bonnet from her mother to hide her shorn head. Then she followed the assembled crowd of villagers uphill, leaving Geneviève's lace pillow and magnifying glass at home so she could return them safely later. Henri had kept the thread and bobbins.

Yvette and her father went to stand beside the Blanchards. Georges nodded his thanks. Geneviève reached for her brother's hand. Hurt broke open in her chest, tempered by gratitude. Henri hadn't asked her for help, hadn't woken her to say goodbye, hadn't needed her, because his friends stepped up—not just Charles but the children of several families. Henri couldn't come home, at least not now, but he would be okay—wherever he was. His friends had made sure of that.

The lacemakers wanted to hand Geneviève a dry bonnet. They wanted to wrap her in blankets and set her beside their hearth, stick a lace pillow between her legs so she could twist and cross her favorite bobbins instead of thinking, instead of standing here in front of everyone, humiliated. The children dipped their trouser and dress hems into mud puddles, tugging on their parents' hands, ready to go home and dry off.

Monsieur Cocteau had anticipated a triumphant parade surging down the hill, Henri slung like a lion in the arms of the strongest men. He stood, unsure what to do next. The musicmakers checked their pocket watches and shifted from foot to foot, expecting him to issue another order.

"Let's go," a few of the wives said to their husbands.

"*Allons-y!*" the children echoed.

The women led the way downhill, back to the village, back to their lives. The men appeared reluctant to abandon this quest, to leave without anything to show for their efforts, but the children grabbed their fathers' hands and swung them, chattering merrily now that the occasion had turned less somber, and led the men on.

Georges and Geneviève watched them go, holding onto each other for support. He kissed her cheek, then tilted his face toward the sky. Thick raindrops fell in his good eye and the cryolite one, but he didn't rub them away or shield his face from the deluge. His shoulders shook silently. Geneviève realized her husband was crying.

"Henri will be all right," she said.

"You don't know that."

"Not for sure," Geneviève said, "but I think he'll make his way."

IV.
Concerto in the
Key of New York

Chapter Twenty-One
Henri runs away.

Henri took off into the night with a lantern in one hand, a suitcase in the other, and the family serinette stashed awkwardly under his arm.

A scant hour ago, his friends had linked elbows with him and sashayed out of the jail, calling their farewells back to the prone figure locked within. If the jailers didn't figure it out in the daylight, Bernadine would reveal herself to the constable.

The girls led Henri and Charles to the secret willow enclosure, now overgrown but a safer place to wait than a doorway or one of their houses. One by one, the girls returned with supplies. Margaux climbed through the kitchen window at the Blanchards' to fill her father's suitcase with Henri's clothes. She also took the serinette from the parlor. The others brought back food and coins—a heavy sackful—and a few small lace pieces that he could sell or barter, as well as a plain feminine traveling cloak and hat.

After crawling out of the hidden sanctuary, Henri felt for Bernadine's braids still pinned in place beneath the hat. An ingenious touch! He liked feeling them bob against his ears when he turned his head. Kind of like having foliage. It would take years for Bernadine to grow all that hair back, though. He began to unclip them so Charles could give them back to her in the morning.

"Keep the disguise on until you get out of Mireville," Charles said, "and my sister and I will come up with a good story for my parents."

"You could tell them the truth," Margaux added, beaming at him. "You've been very heroic tonight, and surely your parents like Henri. They're so nice. They'd understand."

Charles blushed.

Henri didn't want to leave his friends, let alone the village, but he knew the longer he stayed, the higher the risk of discovery.

"Go on," Yvette insisted, "or we shall push and pummel you until you run away."

He grasped the folds of the cloak and curtseyed, whereupon his friends laughed and each gave him a quick hug goodbye. His steps scattered pebbles as he headed toward the road to Ambaville. His friends called out whispered farewells.

"Shh!"

"Write to us!"

"Travel with care."

Henri had been cooped up in a jail cell for days, and the gentle daily constitutionals prescribed by Docteur Nanin hadn't prepared him to cover any sort of distance. But he had to get farther than the next town. If the constable sent out a patrol to look for him, they'd surely search in Ambaville first.

He switched the serinette from one arm to the other as he walked. When he tired, he kept going. Farther, farther. Both arms grew weary and reddened from the instrument chafing his skin, the left arm less willing to continue to hold the weight because it had been unaccustomed to this much work. He kept going until his legs ached enough to distract him from his sore arms and the blisters erupting where the suitcase handle rubbed. On the far side of Ambaville, he paused to change into his clothes—back to a man—in some underbrush. He folded Bernadine's glossy braids with care inside his extra shirt.

The sun came up as Henri stumbled into the village of Baudricourt. He used some of the girls' coins to pay for a room, assuring the innkeeper that he was not drunk, merely tired from walking all night. He caught a glimpse of his visage in the mirror over the washbasin—*haunted* came to mind. His curls a frenetic, matted mess. He would have done better to leave the hat on. The dark circles under his eyes looked like fistfight bruises.

The pillow had too many feathers for his liking, and the bedcovers did not cover his ankles, and the water basin had not been cleaned in recent days. Despite these discomforts, Henri napped and woke midday, refreshed. He opened the parcels of lace his friends had given him. Two handkerchiefs, one pair of curtains, and a table runner. They didn't have names on them but Henri recognized each girl's style. Margaux never pulled her stitches tight enough. Bernadine often twisted when she should be crossing. Yvette, when she thought she could get away with it, improvised. If she had been born a boy, Henri felt certain she would have been elevated to pattern-maker.

He rewrapped each piece and only then did he fall back on his bed and sob. Already he missed his parents. The certainty of Maman's breakfasts. The smell of wood mingling with cat and old newspaper in the workshop. He had never been offered a future outside the one his village expected of him—and now he could have anything *but* serinettes. At least until the outrage died down over the allegations. Perhaps, in a few months, he could return. But what would occupy him in the meantime? He had neither friends nor an occupation save the one he had been born to carry out. Who is a serinetter, away from his workshop? He cried until he didn't have the energy to continue.

Could a person just *decide* not to be sad? Henri figured it might be worth trying. He sniffed a few more times, wiped his eyes, and plastered a grin on his face. He sat up and bounced on the bed a few times, whereupon a flash of an idea stilled him. An irresponsible *ah-ha* of a *what-if.* One that would turn this debacle into an adventure. Henri conjured a romantic, mist-imbued image of himself in a sharp sailor's cap, staring ahead without fear, dots of water along his smooth jawline. Being on the water would bring out the blue in his eyes, he felt certain. Other passengers would stroll by and murmur, *What a dashing figure!* Upon disembarking, he would set himself to finding his beloved friend Aimée and his half-brother.

It cheered him, the idea of going to New York and finding both of them. Asking questions, or—if he felt brave enough by then—demanding answers. Besides, he had spent much of his youth studying English. He would be able to ask directions and find his way. Surely the murder charges would be dropped in his absence and he could return bristling with news from across the ocean.

Now that he had a plan, he could tackle the tasks that would allow him to achieve it. Henri bargained for a length of rope from a street peddler. He traded Bernadine's fine braids for a razor and soap in a drawstring bag. He procured a handful of loose flour from the back door of a bakery to pour in his socks so his feet would not get so sweaty. He borrowed a map to copy from the innkeeper and added the cost of the ink and paper to

his supper bill. His map did not look much like the innkeeper's—
the proportions were all off—but at least now he knew where to go.

Le Havre. The famous port. And from there to New York.

Life moved faster when adventuring. Henri didn't have the luxury
of deep, uninterrupted contemplation. He had another kilometer
to hike, another blister to wrap, another meal to procure. For
the rest of June and part of July, he trekked toward Le Havre,
gaping with awe like a fish intent on swallowing every hook. So
much to see! One long song of newness. At home, he appreciated
lace and music as functional crafts. He rarely had time for their
beauty. But travel activated all his senses. He nibbled light, but-
tery pastries that his mother would consider a waste of dough.
He pressed his fingers against cool marble statues. He rested in
the elegant shade of cathedrals, admiring spires, flying buttresses,
and gargoyles that made the real world seem like something out
of a book.

On the road, men and women—of different shapes, sizes,
colors, hemlines, hats, silhouettes, riding jackets, canes, capes,
and noses—carried themselves forward with an agenda that had
nothing to do with Henri. He felt small beside them, in personality as well as in height. Being a pin's-length taller than Maman,
at home, was enough for him. But out in the world, he had to look
up at some of the women. They smiled down at him as if they
had spotted a doll or a particularly appealing tea set. These daily
measurements—bigger than, or mostly smaller than—kept him
anchored in his body. As did the discomforts. His back throbbed
on nights he slept on bare ground. His jawbones ached by the
middle of each day from responding to each passing traveler with
a grin or a few words of greeting.

He wore the serinette strung around his neck with the rope he had purchased in Baudricourt. This allowed him to rotate which hand carried the suitcase. Both of his palms developed *ampoules* that filled with liquid and popped, then turned into calluses. Soon it became routine: to wake someplace unfamiliar and move on. The strain of keeping moving felt like fire in his body, good and hot, and he slept well each night. Only occasionally did he wake in an unfamiliar bed, sweaty and agitated from a nightmare about the constable.

As he traveled, Mireville shrank in his mind. Or more accurately, its specialness shrank in proximity to the novelties of other places. Every village offered something interesting. Here, craftsmen made carriages. Here, utensils. Here, fine furniture that would look even better draped with a stretch of Mireville lace. The weather proved an extraordinary distraction as well. A downpour that began at two o'clock might well last until the next day—or cease by the time he reached the stakes that identified the next farmer's land. He bought himself a new shirt and admired the meticulous pleats around the cuffs. He traded one of the lace handkerchiefs for a pair of supple boots that fit much more comfortably than his stiff ones from home.

After buying the shirt and boots, he grew anxious about saving money, so he began bartering serinette music for lodging and supper. At inns, he acted as the evening entertainment. At farmhouses, he played so families could dance. Most of the strangers he played for had never heard birdsong coming from a box. While listeners could identify the air whooshing in and out of the bellows and the click-click sound of the cylinder turning, it did truly sound like birds had roosted inside the plain wooden contraption—although he detected two notes missing from his father's favorite waltz. *Odd*, he thought, but none of his audience members noticed. Over and over, Henri pulled the C-shaped crank out, lifted the lid, and showed gawkers the bellows, pipes, and pinned cylinder inside.

During these weeks, Henri learned he could rely on himself if he didn't overdo it and get heat exhaustion; he had a knack for bargaining, and serinette music was well received this far from Mireville. And so he continued east, checking the map and adjusting his course as needed. He didn't rush or fret. He stopped whenever he fancied a rest. On the occasional nights when he lucked into a private room, or a barn to his own, he pulled his mother's thread and bobbins out to practice twisting and crossing. He found the rhythm soothing.

When he arrived in Le Havre, about three weeks later, he found an open steamer ticketing station that boasted *Amérique!* He joined a short line and waited for his turn. An attendant was standing behind a tall desk, wearing the same loose white shirt as the sailors.

"One round-trip ticket, please."

"*Monsieur, écoutez.* The Mercury is an immigration ship. We provide one-way tickets. Going the other way, we fill our ship with parcels and mail."

Henri thought for a moment. "A one-way ticket, *s'il vous plaît.*" He would find a different ship to carry him back. Although Henri rather liked the idea of sitting upon a pile of letters, staring out to sea, no other people around except Aimée, clasping his hand. If she wanted to return with him.

The attendant handed over a fare list fingerprinted with travelers' indecision. "First class? Second class? Steerage?"

Better to be frugal. He had done well with his friends' savings, but he would continue having expenses until he made it to New York, then all the way back home, which seemed awfully far away now. "Steerage, please." Henri took his pouch out of his trouser pocket and counted out the fare.

The man handed him a yellow ticket, stamped *London, Liverpool, Glasgow, Havre, Hamburg, Bremen*, and *Southampton*, with pictures of ships illustrated in fine detail. "Where passages can at all times be engaged on reasonable terms, either to or from the above ports, in Sailing Packets or Steamships. This Entitles the Bearer, to a safe passage, this present voyage, (the dangers of the seas excepted), to New York Harbor in the Steamship Mercury."

"Write your name here," the man said, and Henri obliged.

He was given two tickets, one with the number of his bunk and another with a different number, and told to keep them both safe.

"In two days, we leave. Eight o'clock in the morning."

Henri ate corn out of paper cones sold by street vendors and traded music for sips of ale, which helped him sleep better in the cheap rooming house, where fights were apt to break out at late hours.

On the morning of departure, Henri gave too much money to one of the street hawkers for a canvas bag of utensils and a cooking pot that he could sling over his shoulder. From another, he bought a bedroll and a blanket knotted together into a crude rucksack. Then he joined the throngs of passengers staring up at the enormous gray steamer.

Henri missed his grandmother Cérine. The ship was the color of her hair, the color of the sky over Ambaville on days it stormed. As the crowd amassed, he used his elbows as shields, protecting his torso. Soon everyone settled, parents building blockades for their children with suitcases. Three hundred passengers, fifty of them with reserved first- and second-class cabins, the rest crammed into steerage with him.

"Find your room and stay there until we disembark," called the sailor who checked Henri's ticket. "No drunkenness, no dice or cards, no visiting the women's quarters, no fires except in the galley tent on the deck, no visiting other decks besides your own."

It was not a stairwell but a ladder that brought the steerage ticket-holders to their bunks stuffed between the better decks. Henri dropped his suitcase to the person beneath him, then shifted the serinette to his back before climbing down so it would not bang tunelessly on the rungs. Once on the ground, he waited to catch the next person's baggage. The slender passage reeked of refuse and debris. Perhaps it was not too late to request an upgrade. A sailor pointed him down the hall toward the men's quarters.

"Excuse me, sir? I must purchase a different room. I did not understand how—"

The sailor paid him no mind, so Henri turned around and tried to forge a path back to the ladder. Women pushed at him, and men cursed, and no one let him through, so he turned around again and headed the way he had been directed. If that was his choice—to take what he had chosen or be trampled and risk not getting to America—better to locate his quarters.

Neither on the surface of the world nor beneath it, Henri elbowed his way through a hallway streaked with dirty hand-prints and the scuffs of old boots; this was presumably better than a packet ship, where the passengers had to stay in their own quarters for forty days. Here, at least, on the wall was a sign pointing to the saloon, the galleys, and the grand room. Plus the Mercury boasted about its speed: twelve days and he'd be in New York. He paused to close his eyes and steady his nerves.

"You are blocking the way," the man behind him said.

Henri moved deeper into the ship, not stopping again until he found his room. A bunk bed was bolted to the right-hand wall; there was barely enough space to walk in alongside it. On the lower bunk, a slight young man with a wisp of a mustache sat scraping dirt off the soles of his shoes with a bent fork. Above the door, shelves had ropes running like Xs across them. Sacks of food had been strung in tightly. Oatmeal, dried peas, barley flour, and some sort of meat wrapped in white paper that had already begun to smell, all labeled in English. Henri suddenly wished for fresh air.

His roommate didn't want to converse, so Henri spent the journey sitting on his bunk, walking the cramped halls, and fighting for a cooking fire in the galley, which was a big smoky tent on the port-side deck. There was sun and wind and salt and the smells of other people's cooking on the decks above them. And real light, shining hot and bright, the blistering kind of sun bouncing off the water, brightness drawn through the clouds by a pushy wind. Henri burned all his food but no matter; it was something to do.

Waiting in line for his turn to cook *déjeuner* on the third day, he thought of Aimée. Where she was, what she might be doing. He couldn't let himself imagine her when in his quarters. With the claustrophobic press of the walls, the rolling of the ship, and the sullen bunkmate—there was already too much energy in there.

At the jail, Aimée had asked: "Did you? Strangle him?" It seemed obvious to him now; the conversation wasn't about accusing Henri. He had put the pieces together during his long weeks of walking. She had wanted to corroborate someone else's guilt by confirming Henri's innocence. Guillaume *had* been following him. *He* had killed Odil. For entertainment, or to pin blame on Henri, or perhaps Odil had caught Guillaume spying. The Maullians wouldn't have left town quickly for no reason, especially with Grand-Maman still alive. Henri should have realized all of this during his days in jail. And now what? He and Aimée had done what they had done with their lips and bodies, and she had decided her brother was the one worth saving. Henri had been so stupid, following her to New York. Stranding himself in the middle of the ocean with three hundred people he didn't know, heading toward her (and Guillaume). He couldn't change his mind, turn around, go home. He had made a terrible mistake.

A family took advantage of his reverie, pushing in front of him in the cook tent line. Henri snapped back to attention, said *pardon, pardon*, he was next; they didn't understand his language or chose not to listen. He took one more deep breath of salt air, then ducked around the line-cutters and into the back of the tent, where he found a place behind a Frenchwoman. The woman liked his curly hair—or maybe she just felt sorry for him—so she gave him her long-handled spoon, which made it a triumphant thing to stir the oats. If only Aimée knew how self-sufficient he was now—how alive, how powerful—she'd regret her choice.

Chapter Twenty-Two
New York, at last.

In a parlor in the Garment District, where young women turned supplies into finished goods, a drop of blood fell onto the rose-colored gown in Aimée's lap. Her thumb had betrayed her. Her pay would be docked. Again.

Aimée stuck her thumb in her mouth to keep the prick isolated while she blotted the incriminating splotch with her other hand. The stain spread in diameter but shrank in saturation. Perhaps Tante Pierrette would not notice.

Bien sûr, she would notice.

Aimée was no better with a needle now than she had been when the family arrived a few weeks ago—minus her father. Tante Pierrette had given the Maullians black dye for their clothing so they could mourn their patriarch properly. She then unlocked the dusty attic and introduced it as their sleeping quarters; Aimée's mother had little choice but to accept the accommodations from her shrewd, widowed sister-in-law.

Tante Pierrette ran a bustling bridal wear business, specializing in puffed sleeves that she hoped would come into fashion. Pale lavender, oyster gray, rosebud pink, the yellow of earliest morning. Aimée might as well have been working with white, as blood showed on all of them. Every day, she woke up, ate whatever her aunt had set out before locking the pantry, and shared a few bites of her portion with whichever sister seemed the hungriest. Then they clustered in the parlor with the other hired girls, the ones who arrived at daybreak. They spent their hours elbowing one another for the scissors or a certain shade of thread. Each evening, they waited for the light to fade so they could quit work for the day. Aimée looked forward to fall, when darkness would arrive earlier, although lying awake on her upstairs pallet, it would be harder to ignore an empty belly. Evening meals were only slightly more filling than the morning ones. Tante Pierrette never ate better than they did at mealtime, but her ample figure made Aimée imagine she kept a secret stash of food just for herself. This didn't look anything like the New York Aimée had imagined. The one her father had promised.

Late at night, when she most needed to distract herself from hunger, Aimée let her mind rub over the memory of Henri's teeth bumping like chalk against her own; she would allow herself that much, nothing more, certainly not his name, just the gap in between his two front teeth, a space she could squeeze her heart inside. She knew she must not think of him, she had no right to miss him. Tugging on the string of Henri's memory tightened the noose around his neck. If she didn't use his name— she had no right—perhaps he would be spared. How, she couldn't imagine, with the true murderer hiding in an attic here in a faraway city.

Her brother earned sporadic wages sweeping the front sidewalks outside of theaters, or so he claimed. He brought coins home to their mother, who hid a few at a time in the lining of her travel cloak and gave the rest to her sister-in-law for food. Here in New York: Papa dead, the family upside down, their ankles caught in Tante's net. Her father had committed the family to three years of this servitude, but Aimée felt certain: her mother and sisters would never escape. She might, but not by choice. The day after she arrived, before the black dye had dried on their clothes, Tante Pierrette had announced a courtship arranged in advance for her with a local shopkeeper's son. Thereupon she paraded the young man into the parlor like one of her fabric finds. He was plain-faced and gawky, neither offensive nor particularly interesting.

After he left, her aunt explained the plan. Once an appropriate mourning period ended, Aimée would be traded out of the family in exchange for weekly deliveries of produce—terms her aunt had found favorable during negotiations that took place before the two had even met. This—right here—was modern life! Aimée didn't want anything to do with it. Still, it might be better than sewing in her aunt's parlor for the next three years. Or more. Her father had somehow amassed enough funds to pay for carriages to speed their way across France and to afford ocean passage for the whole family, but if he had anything left after those expenditures, it went overboard with him. Somewhere in the ocean, fish feasted on their only hope. Guillaume had stormed up to the deck above theirs, demanding to see the captain, but a team of sailors blocked him. The ship couldn't turn around. Not if it wanted to make the crossing in twelve days.

Papa would never have agreed to any of this. Not if he knew about the sleeping quarters, or the long hours, or how Tante Pierrette refused to pay them wages. He might have urged the courtship—after all, a grocer's son would provide a comfortable living for his wife and their children—but he would never have insisted on it. He would have let her choose. Tante Pierrette seemed to think only her opinion mattered, even though she'd immigrated to this place twenty years ago, before Aimée was even born. She half suspected her uncle had died just to get relief from Tante's brusque sourness.

Mais non—better to think about brides than feel sorry for herself. She had cried a few times already, during working hours, and it only made her sisters cry. The brides who came to the door shared exultant stories about their beloveds that made Aimée's belly warm—to have a beau like that! Even Maman, who was struggling to bear up under these new conditions, smiled on dress-fitting days. Trails of loveliness ribboned out of everyone's mouths on these occasions. Being in proximity to happiness, Aimée had decided, was as close as she'd get for a while. Perhaps forever.

Her shopkeeper came to visit every few days. *Smitten*, perhaps, but more likely doing his duty to his father. The young man courted her with practicality: he spoke of how she would spend their years together dusting off cans, unpacking boxes in the back room, and bearing children. The very things her aunt seemed to appreciate about this particular match. But that matter-of-fact approach left Aimée's heart throbbing beneath a dry husk of *yes* and *that would be nice*. Her shopkeeper did not whisper lovely compliments. He did not try to touch her knee. He did not even get close enough to kiss her cheek.

The one time she tried to complain, it did not go at all as she had planned. She'd waited until her sisters were washing up after dinner and she was alone with her mother in the attic, just the two of them. Guillaume had gone out on his rounds an hour or so before.

"I don't even know the grocer's son!" she cried.

"Don't be selfish," Maman said. "Marry for your sisters' sake. You will have your own quarters—a real bed! And think of all the food he would share with us. All those damaged fruits and vegetables that he can't sell."

"Guillaume's the eldest," Aimée protested. "When he gets a steady job—"

"He'll find one," Maman said, "and it still won't be enough to support us all without your father here."

"Papa didn't make any money at home!" Aimée said. "Why would it have been any different here?"

Her mother slapped her. Pain flared through her cheek and into her jawline. Aimée opened her mouth but then closed it again. Whatever she said wouldn't make any difference. Even if she wanted to change the situation, her mother had no power in New York.

"You need to do your part," Maman added.

As the second oldest, she meant.

Tante Pierrette decreed the mourning period for their father over at the two-week mark. The shopkeeper's son arrived the following afternoon with his mother, bearing an official proposal. It sounded clunky, but then English was often clunky. Under the stern gaze of her aunt, Aimée said *oui*.

This cinched her future—there would be no refusal now, no more arguing with her mother to step in and save her. After the groom's mother shook hands with Tante Pierrette, the adults retreated to the kitchen, leaving the couple alone (but within listening range, as was proper). Aimée sank into her customary work chair. The shopkeeper opened a jar of peaches to celebrate. He leaned over to feed her a piece of sugary, succulent fruit from a spoon he had tucked in his breast pocket. It was a kind thing—the can, the spoon, the cloth he had brought so she could wipe the stickiness from her lips—but she still wished he did not cut his hair quite so short. When he set the spoon on the napkin on the table, she admitted she wanted to earn the money to buy the dress fabric from her aunt at full price.

"If you are amenable to waiting," she added, blinking her lashes at him. "It'll be just a few months."

The shopkeeper fidgeted in his chair. Did he worry, too, about how little they knew of each other? "No need to rush," he agreed. "You have just finished mourning your father."

"Do you really think I have finished?" she retorted. "Do you think two weeks of black sufficient?"

The young man reddened. "Take as long as you want. In the interim, we shall become better acquainted."

That had been about a week ago. She expected him again this afternoon—a welcome, Tante-approved break from stitching. And today's mistake would cut back on Aimée's earnings. Again. She would tell him, apologize if she had the energy, so he knew of it. As long as she made honest mistakes, nobody could accuse her of postponing the wedding on purpose. Although of course that was exactly what she was doing.

Tante Pierrette appeared from nowhere and shook her by the shoulders. "Are you dozing, girl?"

Aimée pulled her thumb from her mouth and squeezed it. A neat drop of blood fell on the exact spot she had been scrubbing. "Don't sneak up on me. Look what you did!"

Tante Pierrette snatched the dress and bolted toward the washroom. Aimée was left with an empty lap and a shiver of glee. Her pay would still be docked, but at least her aunt would be busy for a few minutes. When she stood up to stretch, her littlest sister Clémence begged for help in meeting her quota. Aimée sat back down, checked that her thumb had quit its dripping, and took the start of a lemon-colored sleeve puff from the pile. Soon her aunt returned the gown she had bled on, the area around the spot damp and distressed.

"Finish the stitching before supper," Tante said. "If there's a spot left once it dries, I'll sell it to you on layaway at a discount. Then you can get married."

Aimée opened her mouth to argue that she wanted to earn a full-price dress, but at a glare from her mother, she merely nodded. It would be a relief to live someplace else, even if that meant committing her life to a man she didn't love. And the arrangement would ensure her sisters would be well-fed.

An officer in a uniform thrust a lantern up toward Henri's bunk.

"This one's alive," he shouted into the passageway.

Henri scrambled to the ground, then rubbed his eyes in the sudden brightness. His sullen roommate's things were gone. Henri must have slept through the docking.

"Go up to the promenade deck for inspection."

"We're here?" Henri asked.

"Six miles south of the New York harbor," the man said. "I am an officer of the Boarding Department, and the ship is currently under quarantine. Once our work has been accomplished, the Landing Department will come with tugs to escort you into America. You were given a piece of paper when you boarded. That's your number for the line in Castle Garden."

Castle Garden—Henri hadn't heard of it. The official explained that a few weeks prior, it had opened as an immigration station to cut down on the crimps and riffraff preying on newcomers.

Here, here, here, here, Henri thought to himself, each word a quarter-note in 4/4 time and the key of self-reliance. He had come five hundred kilometers on foot, and then who knows how far by ship, all alone, without anyone telling him what to do or how. He had spent his whole life listening for instructions, obeying his father and mother, and yet without that guidance, he had done quite well for himself.

Henri climbed the narrow stairs to the promenade deck, and oh—air! Land! Above him he heard the footsteps of other passengers with better-class berths waiting their turns, scuffling or maybe even dancing. From where the steamer had anchored in the harbor, he could see the ragged edge of the New World: docks and their ships, so many manmade protuberances cluttering the clean face of the city. He had survived the passage. He had earned this next step of his adventure.

In the harbor, a tug puffed its way toward shore. Henri could see passengers huddled on its deck.

"Have I missed it?" he asked the man next to him. "Are we quarantined now?"

"Another tug," the man said. "Another *kommen.*"

After twelve days at sea, it seemed not as though solid land were greeting his feet but the lurching deck of another vessel. Henri tilted against swells that weren't there. He braced against his suitcase, the serinette dangling from his neck on a piece of rope, grateful for his good footwear and the potential to walk anywhere, just as soon as he got through the disembarkation lines. When the dizziness lessened, he stood and stretched. All around him, passengers swayed, weathering the same imaginary surges after days adrift like a cork.

Castle Garden, a former military fort, squatted on a manmade island like a rotund maiden, perhaps preparing to unbend her legs to dip her toe into the bay. Inside, the walls crumbled from being rubbed by bodies, weapons, and whatever pointed objects the children could use to carve their initials in the softer spots. There was a small brass plaque on the wall near the door, telling a foreshortened version of the building's history and remarking on Jenny Lind's performances five years earlier, during its concert hall years.

A man stationed a few paces north of the entrance pointed Henri and the others toward a row of benches. He queued up. The numbers—printed on his *billet*—were called in six languages, each with its own cadence. His spot on the bench was close enough to hear the French desk. Everybody's money was counted and the same questions were asked: Name, occupation, age, gender, literacy, ship, arrival date, country, port of departure, place of last residence, destination, life plan, passage details, relatives left behind, who paid for the ship ticket, whether someone was expecting said individual's arrival.

When it was Henri's turn, he rose, *derrière* sore from the wooden bench but not so sore that he stood hop-footing like some of the others. The official pushed a pen across the desk. Henri dipped it into the ink and signed all the papers—without reading them, for he wasn't really immigrating—with his best calligraphy. Henri chose *unknown* for whether or not someone was expecting him.

"Do you need a bed? You may stay at Castle Garden for a small fee."

"I can afford accommodations," Henri said.

"How about a job? Food? Money exchange?"

"I do need local currency," he said.

When he had replaced the French funds in his pouch with an unfamiliar kind, Henri was directed toward the medical examination line, which looped back outside. After a half-hour wait, a staff member called Henri to approach for his screening. He gathered his things and followed the man toward a makeshift canvas room propped up by poles.

"The doctor will be with you in a minute," the man said.

There was no ceiling, only sky. Inside was as full of day and sound as outside. The medicinal tang in the air made him think of the licorice sweets he had tasted in one of the cities he'd passed through. The tools on the table included a saw for amputation, a tourniquet with brass fittings, a spool of wire, a wicked-looking miniature saw, two packets of needles, four leather restraining straps, a spool of white silk thread, and a pincushion. He had heard another family whispering in line about how failing the examination meant being sent to a nearby hospital, mostly likely to die.

Finally the canvas flap opened and with it came a small burst of air. Then it was lowered, the makeshift room corked. Stale with others' breath. The physician tugged at his shirt with an urgent nod. The language of Mireville: hands doing work. Henri understood and shed his waistcoat and shirt. His underarms were soaked.

"I do speak English, sir," Henri said, "and I am very healthy, I assure you."

The doctor didn't acknowledge this statement as he set about his task. Henri dared a glimpse at his own body, taking stock of his chest and its smatterings of hair, freckles, and angry blemishes—some of these due to oily seventeen-year-old skin, others due to the mites in his bedroll. He had grown skinnier on the ship but retained most of the muscle definition earned by the kilometers he'd covered on the way to Le Havre.

"Looks like you're one of the lucky ones," the doctor said. "Many of your fellow passengers came down with dysentery."

"Dysentery?"

The man pantomimed a vomitous spit. Henri cringed at the specificity of this response. He didn't consider himself to have a weak stomach, but between the mimicry of illness and the ill-tempered swaying of the land beneath his feet, Henri felt as if he might retch for real.

"Many dead," the doctor added.

Henri took a deep, steadying breath. He could not let his stomach turn sour, or faint, or do anything that might get him quarantined. The doctor turned Henri's wrists from one side to the other and checked the reflexes in his knees. Henri tried to keep his breathing steady, although he wanted to run out of the tent. The doctor prodded a bruise along the ridge of Henri's ribs, where he had slammed into the shelving in his quarters when trying to dislodge a packet of beans. The injury had morphed from a bloody purple into an ugly green.

The doctor pointed to the slit of light that marked the door flap.

"Go. *Allez*."

Henri had passed the exam. Just like that, the nausea—probably caused by nerves—cleared. He dressed and, with a grateful glance at the instruments on the table, all of which he'd been spared, hoisted his luggage and walked outside. He found himself back inside in a moment, directed next to the bathhouse line. When Castle Garden was a fortress, the bathhouse had served as a strategy room for patriots to discuss tactics for attacking the British. Or so it said on another plaque. When it was his turn to enter, Henri stacked the serinette on top of his suitcase on a bench and began to disrobe. It seemed a waste to have gotten dressed again only to strip back down a few minutes later.

He left his underclothes on, after darting glances at the men who had chosen to disrobe entirely. They had lax hanging parts, flabby buttocks, salubrious bellies. Henri couldn't understand why these older men didn't care to preserve their modesty. Maybe they were too glad to be in New York to care about anything else. Henri approached the trough of circulating water and stuck his hand in it. So cold! He gritted his teeth and began sloshing water out of the trough and applying it under his shirt to freshen his torso. Cotton towels hung on poles for communal use and an abundance of soap encouraged the most laborious applications. It was excellent water—flowing into the pipes straight from the Croton River. Clean and cold and a little grassy. It reminded him of the jail waterfall back home. A kind of magic, this. Engineered by learned men. He cupped his hands beneath the hole in the pipe closest to him and shoveled the liquid up to his face.

After soaping and rinsing, Henri went to the dry side of the room to find his canteen. He poured out the oily ship water and filled it to the brim with fresh river water. As he dressed, he noted other immigrants fetching their canteens. Copying him. He didn't know anything about New York, but he had figured this one thing out.

When Henri emerged from the bathhouse, his damp curls a darker shade of gold, he finally joined the line approaching the exit. Or rather, the entrance. To New York! He dropped off his serinette and suitcase for safekeeping in the storage room. His waistcoat pocket bulged with good fortune, the pouch of unfamiliar money inside. Henri held out his paperwork once more, but the uniformed guard waved him through without reading it.

A short bridge connected Castle Garden's tiny island to the tip of Manhattan. Henri took the last few steps across the little bridge and onto land: the Battery. He didn't fall to his knees. He didn't recite something beautiful. There was no moment of grace with so many people behind him, waiting to cross.

The smell of salt and wet paper wafted from the docks, along with the unmistakable scent of meat frying: a street hawker. Henri launched himself into the parade of strolling couples. Listening to New Yorkers converse with each other was like walking in the *violon* alleys in Mireville, each instrument played at full-blast, without regard for the new, tight-lipped French horn, who didn't yet know his part.

Chapter Twenty-Three

An unexpected reunion.

Men's knocks demanded entry, hard smacks of hand against wood. The brides knocked with shy certainty, as if even their knuckles were blushing at the thought of gowns being purchased for the purpose of being unlaced, unclasped, and undone by a groom. If none of the seamstresses answered straightaway—for there were pins to scoop out of their skirts before standing up—only some of the brides would bravely knock a second time. The men always knocked for as long as it took.

This knock was a woman's knock—tentative, polite—and late, much later in the day than they usually took appointments.

Aimée, closest to the door, dipped her needle into the fabric to secure it. She pulled the gown she was working on over one arm so it would not drag, then stuck the spool of thread between her thumb and forefinger, lest it fall and get tangled.

When she opened the door, to her surprise, it was not a bride at all—but Henri Blanchard, looking pale but well-dressed, his shirt collar neat, his outlandish curls tucked beneath the brim of a nondescript hat. All the unbidden dread she'd felt over his fate came out in a terrible gasp. She stepped into his arms, crushing the bodice of the unfinished dress between them. His arms pinned hers to her sides in a warm squeeze, and for the first time in their friendship, she realized he was holding her together, and not the other way around.

"How did you get here?" she asked. What a silly question—by ship, of course. She had wanted to write him, but she had feared a black-edged envelope might return with news of his hanging. She'd written instead to Grand-Maman, describing the shop windows, the men selling fruit, the museums of beautiful things, as if she could afford the entrance fees, or even the leisure time to explore the city.

Here, in her aunt's parlor, she could not hide the truth of what she had become, what her sisters and mother had become because Papa had chosen it for them. She deserved this for protecting Guillaume, for telling her father her suspicions, but her sisters were innocent.

Henri kept hugging her. Her body pressed the unfinished dress into his chest. He'd arrived with nothing—no supplies, no boxes or cases—as if he had magicked himself to her. All the way here: New York.

"Who came with you?" she asked.

"Nobody."

Henri who, as a boy, couldn't walk around the village by himself without getting scared of violins or crying over a skinned knee. He had not only escaped but crossed the ocean alone. *For me? Oh*—then she realized the truth. *He's not here for me. Not after I accused him of murder.*

"You came to meet your brother?"

"*Oui.*" Henri whispered the word into her hair, setting it there like a fancy comb.

She wished she could explain, how she'd had to be sure about Guillaume, how she always knew Henri couldn't have committed such a terrible act. But she couldn't, not within earshot of the parlor and with her brother napping upstairs like he did most afternoons. She needed to stay strong. To push Henri away. Let him go on with his life. But what harm would another moment in his arms do?

Aimée tilted her chin, letting her nose rub against Henri's neck, remembering the way they used to speak into each other's mouths as if they had ears behind their teeth—did he remember? She blushed to think of how she appeared: hungry, waiflike. Caught unawares—or she would have brushed her hair.

"The Shadow Council sprang me from jail," he said, squeezing her tighter. "Thank you."

"I didn't do anything." If she had spoken up, told the truth about her brother, Henri wouldn't have been imprisoned. The top of her head fit right beneath his chin and nestled in against his neck. Aimée knew they wouldn't have long; any minute Tante Pierrette would pop in to check on her seamstresses and send Henri away.

"Papa died on the crossing." She directed the words to his ear, hidden among his ebullient ringlets, each drooping like a grape on a well-watered vine. He smelled fresh and clean. She had not washed recently. She wanted to tell him about her life now, without Papa there to negotiate with his sister for higher wages or longer breaks. They didn't have wealth and freedom, as Papa had promised; they had less of everything.

"I'm so sorry to hear that," Henri said.

"Just four weeks ago. And it's horrible here," Aimée whispered. "My aunt treats us like factory workers and doesn't give us wages. She claims the money only covers room and board and our mistakes."

Henri's muscles went taut. "That's not fair!" he said.

She stepped back, let go. Her hands held the air for a moment, as if unwilling to break away from him, but she had to, she really did. *Ça suffit.* Enough indulgence. The girls in the parlor had quit talking. They must have heard Henri's words. *That's not fair.* Well, it wasn't. Clémence whispered something to their mother. Émilie pressed a finger into her mouth.

Tante Pierrette, who had been mulling over a new pattern for even-puffier sleeves, appeared from the back room. "Who is this?"

Aimée's mother stood to speak, but at Tante's glare, she sat back down and continued to work. Aimée took another half-step back from Henri, not wanting to further irritate her aunt. At least they hadn't been hugging when she appeared.

"A friend from home," Aimée said.

"Send your brother down, then," Tante said, "and get back to work. I'm not paying you to socialize with grooms."

Henri looked offended. "But you're *not* paying her."

Tante Pierrette gaped. How dare a foreigner question her in front of her employees? What had the girl said to him? No matter; Guillaume would chase him off with a threat or two. It was handy having a scallywag on the premises, even though he didn't work nearly as hard as his sisters.

"*Au revoir*, Henri—you'd better go." Aimée held the gown close to her chest.

"I'll call him myself," Tante Pierrette said. "Billy! BILLY!"

"Go," Aimée said. *Please*, she urged him with her eyebrows, the hair on the backs of her arms. "Before my brother sees you."

"I'm not afraid of Guillaume," Henri said. "What could he do to me in your aunt's parlor?"

"Anything he wants," Aimée hissed.

"It's not like we're in a *violon* alley," Henri said. "There are witnesses."

The truth seeped into her heart. Her knees buckled. Henri knew what her brother had done. What he might do again. Then why wasn't he running away? Why would he risk visiting her at all? Especially after she protected her brother instead of him?

"*Vas-tu!*" she urged him.

Henri crossed his arms. He seemed stronger, more confident than she recalled. Guillaume held on to the banister as he descended from the attic, the reek of the streets on him. He had tied his hair back with an ostentatious length of green satin ribbon and he wore white stripes on his pants symbolizing membership in a street gang. Which one, she had no idea. His eyes had red, flaky patches of skin beneath them. A fresh pink scar marred the skin above his lip. He went out at night and came back early in the morning smelling of other men, sometimes of perfume.

"The son of the Sun-Bringer," Guillaume said.

"I have come to see to your sister," Henri said. "She is much better looking than you, *Billy*."

The girls tittered. One of Aimée's little sisters said, "Oh!"

"I bet your mother celebrated when you left home." Guillaume gave Henri an exaggerated wink, as if the joke belonged to both of them.

Aimée braced herself through a wave of anger. She wanted to hit Guillaume, to pinch and punish him for their family's change in fortune. Papa, though useless compared to her friends' fathers, would have at least taken charge of the situation. Insisted on wages and warmer blankets. It wouldn't do any good to yell at her brother, though. Not in front of Tante Pierrette, who always took his side. Tante claimed it made her feel safe to have a man in the house, and every time, Aimée had to bite back the same reply. *Not this one.*

"Guillaume—" she pleaded.

"I left under unfortunate circumstances," Henri said. "As you might imagine."

Guillaume raised his eyebrows in mock surprise. "Did you not get to say goodbye to your *maman?*"

The room seemed to pause with them. Fingers halting with needles mid-stitch. Breaths being held. Tension permeated the air—that and the clean smell of Henri still on her clothes, competing with Guillaume's overnight funk. Henri rolled up his sleeves. Preparing to fight? He'd never win. Guillaume was too strong. Too practiced.

"Henri, I beg you to leave!" Aimée reached out and gave his shoulder a shove. Henri stepped back, his mouth open in surprise. The dress fabric rustled in her arms. He would only make things worse if he tried to stand up for himself. "Don't listen to my brother."

"You heard her," Guillaume said. "She doesn't want you here."

"She didn't say that," Henri said. "Aimée? Do you want me to stay?"

Aimée smiled hard, so she wouldn't cry, and said in as cool a tone as she could manage, "Things are different now. I met a shopkeeper. We are engaged to be married."

"But you just got here yourself!" Henri protested. "How could—"

"You must leave me alone, or you'll ruin it." She held her breath, willing herself not to cry. Henri needed to walk away for his own safety. He had nobody to vouch for him here. If he upset Guillaume, well, she didn't even want to consider the possibilities.

She had put Henri in danger once, by letting Papa hustle Guillaume and the rest of them out of the village. She didn't want to provoke chance a second time.

Henri turned his back on her and hugged himself. *Good,* Aimée thought. *Get away from my brother. Even though it means getting away from me.*

Henri opened the front door to let himself out. Guillaume itched his nose, then grinned, which made his pink mustache-like scar wriggle. He followed Henri outside. Aimée rushed to close the door, leaving a small crack so she could eavesdrop.

"You murdered Odil," Henri said to Guillaume in an unafraid, matter-of-fact tone. "So everyone would see me healing him."

No! Aimée covered her mouth with the gown still in her hands. They mustn't suspect her presence or Guillaume would only get more upset.

Her brother took a moment to speak. "Aimée told you that?"

"I figured it out. It wasn't hard."

Aimée pulled away from the crack in time to see Tante Pierrette throw the sash up on the parlor window to listen.

"*You* killed Odil Michaute," Guillaume said to Henri. Now that he had an audience, he raised his voice. Everyone inside could hear him. Her mother, her little sisters, Tante. "YOU KILLED HIM!"

The girls made frightened noises from their perches in the parlor. Little bird squeaks from one of them. Clémence, probably.

"GO!" Aimée shouted through the door to Henri. "Get out of here."

"Come with me," he called. "You don't have to stay here. I have enough money."

She couldn't possibly leave her sisters. Even if she could dodge Guillaume and run fast enough to get away.

A small blessing, not being able to see Henri's face at this moment. "I'm engaged," she said firmly. Strands of hair, fallen out of a messy bun, stuck to her mouth and wet cheeks. She flipped her loose hair behind her ears, first one side and then the other. She bit down hard, bracing her jaw. She needed him to believe her.

"My fiancé can provide for my sisters and mother and me," she added. "You must never come back here. You are not welcome."

Tante Pierrette, eager to participate in this family drama, shouted, "Murderer! Murderer!" and soon all the girls were shouting it, even Aimée's little sisters, even sweet Clémence, to whom Henri had given all his marbles when he outgrew them.

Hearing Clémence chime in made Aimée change her mind. She dropped the gown, flung the door open, and stepped onto the porch just in time to see Henri flee the scene: his fine hat flying into the street, his curls bouncing atop his head. Her brother whooped his delight.

"Guillaume." She let her exasperation and sadness flow into the syllables. She wanted to yell at him but she could see her aunt's head poking out the parlor window, cheeks flushed. Tante would turn this against her if she lost her self-control.

"That should do it," he said. "He won't be back."

Aimée bit down hard on her finger, trying to distract herself from the real pain. She had done the right thing, but what she wanted most was to throw her arms around Henri and beg his forgiveness. Guillaume was right, but not because of his threats or swagger; Henri would listen to her because he *always* listened to her.

"That cad isn't worth it." Guillaume pressed her back into the house, a gentle palm resting on her shoulder. She knew this side of him too, the protective big brother. She couldn't help but think if their father had been more responsible—and by that she meant *less drunk*—Guillaume could have turned out as well as any other young man. She still hoped that could happen for him here, with this fresh start, even though she knew his anger, his capacity for violence.

"Back to work!" her aunt commanded. She punctuated her decree by slamming the window sash down.

Chapter Twenty-Four
Henri meets his first canaries.

Henri charged past startled city dwellers, some of them calling after him in annoyance. He felt his head pound to the tempo of his feet. He didn't pause to look back in case Guillaume had followed him. It was cruel, for Aimée to hurl the finality of her engagement out the door like a river stone. She hadn't even been in New York all that long—a month, if that! Certainly not enough days to develop affection for someone else. And yet her words—*never come back*—reverberated in his ears. As if Henri was still the naïve boy whose mouth she covered so furiously with her own desire. As if he didn't realize their lives had changed and he needed her to make it clear to him. He felt a rush of resentment. Did she think him a child? He had come all this way without anyone's help.

Anything could happen in New York. Even, apparently, his best friend marrying someone else. This foreign city was teeming with romantic possibility. Why did the shopkeeper swipe *his* best friend when there were so many other options? He passed all sorts of women and girls, any one of whom might be a better match for the grocer's son. It didn't seem fair.

When he became too short of breath, Henri slowed to a swift walk, too busy thinking to consider where he might end up.

Aimée had been glad to see him. He felt certain of this. She'd pressed herself against him so hard her corset stays dug into his ribcage. She'd breathed against his neck, inhaling his scent.

Nobody embraced someone like that unless they cared. And until her brother came downstairs, she'd spoken to Henri with such tenderness. Confided how miserable her life had become. She had wanted him there. Wanted him to stay. To talk. Didn't she? Henri recalled the young women in his grandmother's British novels, always talking to each other on the surface while meaning something else underneath. Had she tried to send him a secret message?

Pas du tout, he decided. "You are not welcome" left no room for interpretation. He should have understood when she abandoned him to the hangman.

He dodged young streetwalkers and reeking fishmongers and women selling hot corn, feeling sorry for himself. Newspaper boys approached, waving afternoon editions like batons.

"*Post!*"

"*Evening Journal!*"

Henri ignored them along with the men selling wood for burning and the rag pickers and the corner carts of the fruit vendors, bright with ripe berries.

He kept trying to sift through these two opposites to discover a true answer. *This*—Aimée's dismissal—and *that*—how she cinched herself against him, whispering, her whole body pressed into him. Maybe she really did want to marry the shopkeeper. And where did that leave him? Walking through an unfamiliar, crowded city, that's where. Despite so many turnings of streets and alleys, he felt pinned down. Stuck. He passed groggeries, groceries, and an oyster bar tucked into the ground like a root cellar. The smell of other lives assailed him.

Eventually he found himself in a neighborhood where small wooden shacks appeared to be sinking into the ground one joist at a time. Bigger brick buildings, jammed between the dilapidated ones, were two or three stories tall. Women hung their arms out of the upstairs windows offering half-hearted shimmies of their bare shoulders. Garbage festered outside these establishments, piled like someone else's problems.

"Hello, fellow!" the women called down to him.

"Fellow, fellow, fellow, here!"

"Want a slambang?"

Henri did not, in fact, want a *slambang*. And the neighborhood stench—sewer-like and chemical with the overlay of rotting oysters and fruit peels—was getting to him. Festering in his brain, rotting his confidence. He needed to get out of here, wherever *here* was, exactly. Find a place to sleep, a haven where he could figure out his next steps without dodging peddlers or fearing he might get robbed. Castle Garden, perhaps. It seemed as safe a spot as any. Better than this neighborhood, certainly.

Henri approached a cart selling hot nuts. He ordered one paper cone full, handed over what was probably too many coins, then asked for directions back to the port. Heat curled through the newspaper, stinging his fingers, but it smelled like a miniature bakery, waftings of molasses and cinnamon disguising the street's filth. Castle Garden would be an hour's walk, the nut seller guessed. Henri nearly sat down right there and cried. But he took off in the direction the man pointed, in search of the Hudson; once he found the river, the mighty fortress would be visible to the south.

Henri popped one nut at a time into his mouth, relishing each sweet crunch. He hadn't realized how hungry he was. Soon the air smelled better—fishy, still, but not as much like sewage. As he walked, a plan formed, as obvious as the blister now rubbing against his big toe. He would go find his brother next, giving Aimée a day or two to adjust to the idea of his presence. Then he'd return to have a real conversation. Him and her. He'd figure out how to see her alone, without her brother. She'd have to tell him the truth then. And if she still chose the shopkeeper, when it was just the two of them, he would respect that decision. He had always followed her lead back home. It would be just like that, only terribly sad.

When the nuts were nearly gone, Henri found the river and headed south, making a game out of savoring the last few. Thirty steps before the next nut. Then fifty. *Almost-there*, his footsteps pounded. *Almost-there.* The treats were all gone by the time he arrived at Castle Garden. Before crossing the bridge, he licked the still-sticky insides of the paper cone, not caring if newsprint inked his tongue, before folding it flat and packing it in his bag in case he needed it later.

Henri explained to the guard about arriving on an earlier ship and needing a bed for the night. The man let him through and pointed to the lodgings desk. Henri handed over some foreign coins for a cot. He would never have thought to go to bed during daylight back home, but he felt like he had lived two days in a matter of hours. The room was mostly empty, although a few cots had coats draped over them; fewer still held men already asleep. He chose a bed in the corner, farthest from the door, so that when later guests arrived, he wouldn't be interrupted. The mattress was hard, with a thin sheet, but Henri was too tired to care. He pulled his shoes off, then his stockings. A stink rose up from his sore feet, unused to so much walking after two weeks on the ship. The new toe blister had popped and begun to ooze. Henri slipped quickly under the blankets, hoping to suffocate the stink.

Tomorrow he would find his half-brother and see for himself whether he had giant feet or crossed eyes. And then he would return to the city. To Aimée. He could use the information about Robert as an excuse. Claim he had returned to tell her about his brother. Maybe that's how he'd ask for privacy. *A family secret.* His mood lifted just as he closed his eyes.

Robert wore his ringlets long to hide his huge-rimmed ears. He had been a rather fair brunette as a child, but now that he spent so much time composing indoors, the color had mellowed to a darker brown. The color of a cared-for cello. He found the effect dashing. He didn't spend enough time around girls his age to find out if they did as well, so he succored himself on self-appreciation.

The affection that had rekindled between Delia and Alastair upon the boy's birth dimmed a bit over the following years but did not extinguish itself. Delia poured over the coal reports like she did in the early days of their marriage; Alastair began visiting the aviary once a week—and occasionally, his wife's bed. This was not the relationship they had promised each other on their wedding day, but it would do. Robert didn't suspect the truth of his birth, and they decided not to tell him. Delia devoted herself to his upbringing with as much gumption as she had in training her birds for the outside world. Alastair focused on his mining business but took all his meals with his family.

Alas, one tragic day in September 1854, a servant entered the men's smoking parlor to stoke the fire and found Alastair bent over in his chair, expired. He was only fifty-two years old, still hale despite the occasional backache from studying charts and papers for too many hours.

The men's smoking parlor had been built directly beneath the aviary; its fireplace heated the brick wall that kept the canaries from freezing. But the parlor's wallpaper, which Delia had picked out for its robust cheerfulness, was dyed with Scheele's green, a color made with arsenic. The constant drip of the aviary's water system down the walls of the parlor hastened the growth of fungi that bred on the paste holding the wallpaper up. Alastair didn't mind the dampness, and neither of them realized the danger. As the mold feasted on paste, it released poisonous fumes, which built up in Alastair's system over years. He'd marinated himself in arsenic, poring over his reports, and then died from the exposure.

A few birds had died before Alastair did, but Delia hadn't understood why until Mrs. Hamden—the same woman who long ago accused her of ruining her family's Gilbert Stuart portrait—read Alastair's obituary and thought to bring over an article about Scheele's green. The doctor confirmed Mrs. Hamden's theory. Delia had her husband's study stripped of its wallpaper. She did not want to pick a new color. It had been her fault. Her insistence on that toxic wallpaper when she could have chosen so many others. The article made that clear. At least, now, she could make sure her son stayed safe and had everything, absolutely everything.

Delia grieved by taking an even more aggressive interest in Robert's career. She procured commissions for him. She transcribed his latest compositions and buried these secondary copies in a metal tin behind the garden shed in case of fire.

Robert missed his father. The gentle bulk of him at the dinner table, the rustle of his papers, how sometimes he overlooked a patch of whiskers while shaving and wore the mistake all day like a proud badge. Alastair didn't care what others thought of him; his mother only claimed not to care. His father worked hard and read voraciously and parlayed these habits into a fortune. Mr. Alastair Stanton, unbudged by others' opinions. A thinking man, that's what his father was, quiet and reserved in company. Perhaps, Robert thought, it was this evenness of temper that kept the household in balance.

Everyone liked Robert's father, though few knew him well.

In Alastair's absence, Delia's attention had only one focal point: Robert. It had quickly become tiresome. Nearly eighteen years old—a man!—and he didn't go anywhere without his mother, who dressed in black long after the mourning period ended. He begged her to commission some fashionable outfits, just for their city trips. For his sake. But she couldn't see the worth in it. Young men on the street grimaced in sympathy when Mother paraded him down the sidewalk, clutching his arm. He knew she was older than their mothers; she had birthed him in her thirties. *A very nice surprise*, she had called him.

Robert began composing more elaborate works with the idea that more fame might get him invited to live in the city, an hour's carriage ride away from his mother, perhaps in a lavish flat near the concert hall. Hard work would surely open the very door his mother wanted to keep closed: the one that led *away*.

Upon awakening on his cot in a dormitory-style room, with only his coat for a pillow, Henri sat upright, checked that he still had his billfold, and slipped away barefoot to relieve himself without waking his fellow travelers, as it was still very early. The Croton water felt especially fresh after sleeping hot and restless, waking every hour or so to the sound of other fellows' breaths. He filled his canteen, then paid the storage fee to retrieve his suitcase and the Blanchard serinette before setting off to hire a carriage. It'd be worth the expense. He knew from Mrs. Stanton's letters that the New York of his half-brother's life was a place north of the city, though how far, he didn't know. (Certainly too far to walk comfortably with his new toe blister.)

Henri crossed the bridge to the main island again, brushing past the offers of lodging and jobs and the church pamphlets. He carried his suitcase and serinette a few blocks away from Castle Garden, the bag of cookery banging against his back. His post-disembarkation dizziness had returned. The port doctor had mentioned dysentery; Henri shivered. He didn't want to be sick in a foreign land. Probably his nerves were jostled, that's all.

He soon found a driver feeding and watering his horse outside a pub. The man agreed to convey him to Pleasant Hill, New York, if Henri paid him in advance, which he did. It would take an hour and a half, or thereabouts.

Henri leaned back on the bench seat as the carriage bounced away from the curb. His stomach jolted. Nerves: about meeting the prodigy, the oh-so-special *Roh-bair* who penned cinquains while Henri sat on his grandmother's lap. The boy in the letters existed in the real world, not that far from here. Of course that would make his stomach lurch and wriggle. It wasn't necessarily dysentery. (Although it could be.)

The morning air through the window smelled like the beginnings of fall, fragile and cool, though it was still August. Henri preferred September of all the months. Its gentle in-betweenness. He supposed he could look at any month like that, as a bridge, but only September felt like one. Maybe because of the village school schedule.

A half-hour into the journey, his canteen already drained, Henri's headache increased its pounding. The road, fiendishly full of bumps, didn't help his spirits. With every minute, the carriage took him farther from Aimée. What if a servant turned him away at the door? Or, worse, what if Henri and Robert didn't like each other? He shouldn't have let Guillaume or the talk of a fiancé frighten him off. Aimée's eagerness to hug him spoke louder than her voice.

Henri pulled the curtains closed to keep the sun out, for the day was properly beginning, and it felt more like summer now. He dozed through the Hudson Valley, occasionally waking to thoughts about his father, who had traveled this road twenty years ago. Papa had lost both his sons to the New World. One he had never met. The other fled a baseless rumor and would return when it was safe. Henri closed his eyes and held the family serinette on his lap like ballast. Weighing his body down against the next inevitable rut that would send the seat of his trousers straight up in the air and then back down. He thought of his old marbles, how if he flicked one with enough technique, he could make it fly over the others. Aimée always used to beat him at that game. At everything they played, really.

He missed her already. He felt an urgent desperation to ask the driver to change course and return him to the Garment District.

Henri opened the drapes and called through the window. "Excuse me. Is it possible to turn around?"

The coachman barked a command at the horse, and the carriage slowed. In a moment, he opened the passenger door and peered in at Henri, a map in one hand.

"Have you forgotten a bag?"

"I have...misgivings," Henri admitted.

The man unfolded the map and pointed to the address Henri had given him. Then he pointed to an unmarked spot of road, a finger's width away.

"We're that close?"

The driver nodded in agreement. "Fifteen minutes, maybe less, depending on the roads."

What would Aimée do? Give up and turn around? Or keep going, since he had come all this way? An ocean and beyond to get to this spot on the side of a dirt road in the middle of a New York that looked nothing like the one he imagined. All trees and the occasional farm. Aimée had a flair for adventure, a yearning to tilt against anything that might be boring. Which would she pick? Both of Henri's options felt like adventures. Well then, he would go ahead with both. He could spend the night at Robert's, have a meal or two and sleep in a real bed, hopefully in his own room without the snores of others, and then make the trek back to the city tomorrow. Robert might even have his own coachman on staff—or he'd know where to find one.

"Let's proceed," Henri said. "Thank you."

The coachman tipped his cap, pushed the door closed, and hopped back on the front bench. The carriage jolted forward, slow at first, then at the same jaunty pace as before. Henri opened both window curtains and eyed the trees and farms, which soon gave way to palatial estates, monuments to wealth. He knew the Stantons had money, but he hadn't expected a neighborhood meant for royalty.

When the carriage stopped at his destination, Henri lunged out of his seat, swung open the door, tilted his head up, and gasped. Stories often outshine reality, and Henri had prepared for disappointment. But here was the aviary, just as Papa described it. The structure jutted out above the porte cochère, much as a pair of spectacles balances atop a protuberous nose. Did this mean his brother would be the actual boy in the letters—the magnificent prodigy—and not some flatter, plainer thing?

Henri dismissed his driver, grasped a tarnished lion-shaped knocker, and rapped at the door. When he told the doorman he needed to see M. Robert Dumphries Stanton, he expected to be turned away. But no! The doorman guided him into a parlor to wait. Henri considered his seating options and chose a walnut chair with no padding that seemed the least expensive one in the room.

He stacked his suitcase, serinette, and bag of cookery on his lap, taking up as little space as possible. He wondered if his father had once waited in this very parlor, and if so, which chair he had chosen. The leather one, perhaps. Henri had particularly avoided that one because he didn't want to stab the smooth surface with a cooking utensil by accident. Georges Blanchard had probably never worried about such things. He was born knowing his worth. The Sun-Bringer—and the firstborn son of a master craftsman.

Henri took note of the wainscoting and the wallpaper, counting golden stripes to keep himself occupied and to stifle his lingering worries. He had never been anyplace this fancy. He should have sent a letter first. His back began to feel tight from his careful posture, but he didn't dare slump, not when Robert could walk in at any minute.

Robert might argue with him. Claim his mother to be faithful. What kind of person made an accusation like this right in the lady-in-question's parlor?

Henri moved the luggage to the floor and stood up, feeling increasingly agitated. Maybe he should leave before anyone came to receive him. He had accomplished the physical part: getting there. Maybe that was enough. He didn't really have to know how special *Roh-bair* was, did he?

He had already taken a step toward the doorway when, out of sight in the hallway, an authoritative voice asked who had come calling. Henri sat down and assumed appropriate posture once again. Footsteps. *Should* he be standing?

Before he could change his mind again, Robert appeared. He was a cheerful-faced sort, with round cheeks and a pleasant chin. He had lush curls like Henri's. One flopped out of place on his forehead. Henri had expected a fussy man—every aspect of his self in order—and this small unexpected detail made him smile. Perhaps the encounter would go all right.

"Ah," Henri managed to say.

"You are not John," Robert said. "I was expecting a violinist client of mine. Are you looking for an audition piece too?"

Henri opened his mouth, and it stayed open. Whatever he said next would change everything. His life, and this stranger's as well. Would they accept each other as family?

Robert looked concerned. "Did you swallow wrong?"

Henri shook his head, trying to rid himself of the rising dread. "I'm your half-brother," he managed.

The words didn't make sense to Robert, but here was this stranger. Eager. Waiting for a reply. In his mother's parlor!

"What?" Robert managed.

Henri repeated himself. Twice. Robert still didn't understand. He felt like he had fallen asleep to a cantata and woke up mid-fugue. The same refrain, over and over, and it still didn't parse.

Half.

Brother.

Half of what? Which half?

He needed to say something, didn't he? It was rude to just stand here. Robert pulled at his earlobe, as if trying to discern a tone beneath a clamor of more-insistent instruments. This went on for some time.

Henri took the opportunity to stand, so at least he didn't feel quite as minor to this person's major.

"I have no brother," Robert said finally. "At least none that I know of. What's your name, fellow?"

"Henri Blanchard of Mireville, France."

Robert did not appear offended, much to Henri's relief, but he did seem rather uncertain. "My mother has never been to France. Nor my father."

Oh! This Henri could answer easily. He pointed to his lavish curls, which matched Robert's in temperament though not in color. "My father—*our* father, a Frenchman—lived here for several months before I was born," he said. "He's a serinette builder."

Robert knew the best compositions came together in phrases. One note at a time led him in the wrong direction. So he stayed patient, holding this new information in his mind, weighing the possibilities. His father; not his father. This man; his brother? If this were the beginning of a refrain, what would come next? How would he proceed? Robert truly had no idea. But he did know music. And in his compositions, after the volume swelled, he often proceeded into a quieter passage. All loud and showy was the famous conductor Jullien's forte, not his. Having both—more and then less, loud and then soft—gave a piece the texture it needed to delight the listener.

That still didn't solve the issue: what words come after such a shock?

His actual father, or at least Alastair Stanton, the man he had grown up knowing as Father, had been devoted to him, a fan of his music, always delighted at his precocity, but he always ceded punishments to Mother. As if Father had no backbone, Robert had always thought. But maybe that was because of this invisible line of belonging? This Henri Blanchard looked like him. He couldn't deny that. They had the same ears.

"Say something," Henri said. "Please, I beg of you. Are you angry?"

Robert shook his head to reassure him. "Befuddled, most of all. This comes as quite a shock."

"I'm sorry," Henri said. "I'm so sorry! I wasn't thinking—"

Robert brushed his concerns away with the back of his hand. He tried to rewind the thread of the story to a time before either of them existed. If this set of events were an overture, would he understand? A Frenchman coming to see his mother. That phrase held together. Made sense. Mother had always loved serinettes—and insisted on buying the best, which were Blanchard-made. As a boy he accused her of loving her instruments more than him.

And then—well, he knew enough about the ways of men and women to understand what, exactly, had happened next. (Thanks to Gretchen.)

Robert studied Henri. "*Our* father. And my mother. Did they love each other?"

Henri admitted he had no idea. "I found letters she sent him. But those were about your growth and development. Not romantic feelings. You are quite accomplished."

Half-brother, Robert thought to himself. He was quite a bit taller than his French counterpart, which pleased him. And he lived in this magnificent house. Why, Henri had already called him *accomplished* and he hadn't even sight-read any of his études or sonatas! "And what do *you* do?" he asked.

Henri felt a wave of heat flame into his cheeks. "I make serinettes." What else made Henri special? He could pin a *danse* onto a cylinder. He could revive the recent dead. He took long walks and knew the rudiments of bobbin lace. He liked reading British novels. He had grown up in the shadow of Robert's achievements as much as his father's, and now found he was not only younger and less accomplished, but shorter.

Robert was clearly the son the Sun-Bringer deserved. Henri thought with a pang of Odil. The boy could have been a translator in a big city—maybe even Paris—if fortune had favored him the way it had Robert, who was made golden not only by his talents but by his parents' wealth.

"A serinetter. I see."

Henri agreed: this was his occupation.

"You're not a thief?"

The question stung. "Of course not!"

"You wouldn't tell me if you were," Robert said. "I suppose."

Henri wished to reach over and adjust his half-brother's waggling forehead curl. Put it back with the rest of them. In its rightful place. Instead he said, "I came to meet you, that's all. And your mother, too, if she's here."

Robert leaned into the foyer and called, "Mother, a surprise has arrived! Shall I gift-wrap it for you?"

The faint sound of footsteps on wood. Coming closer.

Henri raised his eyebrows; Robert grinned and put his finger to his lips. "Don't say anything," he whispered.

Henri liked him right then. He could imagine the mischievous little boy Robert had been, even while dazzling the maestros and his tutors. The kind of boy who hid in closets when he didn't want to practice. Imperfect. Maybe even a scamp.

"Do not shout in this house," a voice admonished from around the corner. Mrs. Delia Dumphries Stanton swished into the room, a floating barge of layers with clicking heels hidden underneath. She took up space in a way that Henri's mother did not. Large, not in size so much as in presence.

When she saw him, she gasped and fanned herself.

"Why—" she said. "Why!"

Henri didn't know what to make of this. If he was supposed to answer these *whys*. They didn't sound like questions. More like exclamations. Was this one of America's customs? To ask without asking?

"Why—" she said once more.

"Mother!" Robert cried. "Are you suffering a bout of indigestion?"

She ignored him and proceeded to take Henri's hands in her own. The enormous diamond on her wedding ring had tilted sideways enough to bite into his finger, but he didn't pull away. Did she recognize him from his father's letters? She had warm, soft hands. Not like Maman's chapped ones, which he loved, of course, but these were special too. If only because Mme. Stanton had reached for him.

"Why, Henri Blanchard, you found us," she said, a slight vibrato in the words.

Henri's smile grew so wide he felt his cheeks might split like a vine-cooked tomato. "Did you expect me, Mme. Stanton?"

"For many years," she said. "Call me Delia."

At this point, Robert interjected, "So it's true? Mother?"

She gave a single, slow nod to her son. "Can't you tell? Just by looking at him?"

Robert squinted at Henri, as if trying to make his face resolve into focus. "I suppose we have some qualities in common."

"I have so hoped your father would send you," Delia continued, addressing Henri. "All these years, I've waited. Did you know that your father's father sent him to me? To learn the canary-training business?"

"I didn't." Henri squared his shoulders and straightened his spine. "And my father didn't send me."

She looked puzzled but still pleased. He hoped she would like him beyond this awkward introduction. For who he was, not just his parentage. Mothers usually did. He recalled the ones who used to trudge up the hill to give his *maman* gifts, hoping to pair him with their daughters. Newfound confidence bolted through him.

"Madame Stanton." He pronounced her name the French way—without a garish N at the end. "I should like to stay the night. If that's possible. Unless you would rather I not, and then—"

"Delia," she insisted. "While my haughty neighbors disagree with me, I find titles to be obstructions to good conversation. And of course you must stay."

She swept him into a lavender-scented hug, enveloping him with her layers before letting him go and patting him on the head. Robert seemed ill at ease now. His hands moved from his sides to his hair. Had he been hoping for Henri to be turned away? Or did he disapprove of the attention being given to someone else for a change? It's one thing to share a father, Henri suspected, but perhaps Robert did not want to share his mother.

"I know my arrival must be quite a shock to you," Henri said.

Delia asked her son, "Haven't you always yearned for a brother?"

Robert did not meet his mother's gaze. Nor did he reply.

"You're the oldest," she added.

Robert appeared slightly mollified by this news. Before he could think of what to say next, Henri's stomach made a rolling gurgle. He stuck his hands against his shirt, hoping to quiet it, feeling a flush of shame heat his cheeks.

Delia laughed and said, "Growing boys," and "You must be starving," and "Come along," then put her arm in his and led him toward the kitchen. Robert made an exasperated noise and didn't follow them. Henri glanced back, thinking about the small pile of belongings he was leaving behind, but Delia misunderstood.

"Never mind him. He's waiting for a persnickety violinist. I don't know why he keeps agreeing to work for this one client. It's not as if he needs the money."

The kitchen had windows in the back and over the washbasin, but the room had also been fitted with electric lights. Probably for evening meals, he suspected, and short winter days. Delia pulled a turkey carcass from the icebox while Henri admired the slapdash heap of carrots by the washboard. They were enormous—easily the largest he had ever seen. His mouth flooded with saliva. He hadn't had a fresh carrot in more than a year, although he supposed with the rain now in Mireville, crops might begin growing again.

"May I have one of those?" He pointed to the pile.

"A carrot?" Her voice lilted upward. Quizzical. Had nobody ever come into her kitchen excited about a vegetable? Henri suspected as much from her reaction.

"Yes, s'il-vous plaît."

"Uncooked, or shall I put a pot of water on?"

"Raw is fine."

His mother used to cut winter squash into long sticks, then roast the pieces and call them cooked carrots; one squash could feed all four of them, which made it an occasionally affordable luxury. But nothing compared to the sweet crunch of a fresh carrot. Delia handed him one with a paring knife. She bade him sit at the servants' table in the corner; it was mid-morning, and nobody would need the space for another hour or so.

A surge of joy flowed through Henri's body. His mother never let him peel carrots himself, afraid he might damage the vegetable or cut himself with the blade. Delia not only welcomed him, she trusted him with a knife. Just as quickly, though, a twinge of homesickness seized him. He wished he could see how rain was changing the landscape in Mireville. If apples were ripening. Maybe next spring, his mother could go out back, to her garden, and pull up carrots of her own.

Stripping the tough outer skin of the vegetable was smoother than gutting a fish, easier than splicing a wire. Precision didn't matter. He worked his way around the bulky head and down to the spindly, ugly tip. Peeling off the dirty parts a small swathe at a time. Only when he finished the task did he indulge in a taste. The first bite filled his mouth with fresh, earthy flavor. Once he swallowed, Delia asked his opinion, and he said, "the best I've ever tasted," which made her laugh and fix a plate with a turkey leg for him.

He spoke of the drought in his hometown, how heat burned plants before they could turn into decent crops. Delia disappeared out the back door for a moment and reappeared with a handful of lettuce, which she rinsed and dried for him. When both carrot and turkey were gone, he started in on the lettuce. It tasted of summer, like how he imagined well-watered grass might taste. When he finished that, he began gnawing on the discarded carrot peels, savoring them despite the soil pressed into their wrinkles. Whereupon Delia presented him with a slice of thigh meat and two more carrots; these he didn't bother peeling.

After he had completed the repast, Henri sighed with contentment. *Ah-ha*—now that his belly was full, the dizziness and nausea had disappeared. He didn't feel the slightest bit ill! Relief poured through him and for a moment he forwent his perfect posture in favor of a happy slump.

"There," Delia said. "You feel better."

"Much revived." He felt as satisfied as he could imagine feeling. He had made it all the way here, to the house of his father's stories, and as a prize, he had been given three whole carrots, all to himself. Plus the turkey, which was delicious. But there was one more thing he had come here to experience. He said, "Now—if you wouldn't mind—I would love to meet your canaries."

Delia's grin turned her face from motherly to girlish. Her elation sparkled, giving Henri a wave of joy nearly equal to his appreciation of garden-fresh treats. She stood, swishing her layers—burnt umber and cream, swirling around her—and held out a hand to him. "Nobody ever comes to look at my birds anymore."

"They don't?"

She shook her head sadly.

Henri decided not to pry. "Shall I bring my serinette?"

"Not to meet the hens," she said. "Just come along."

Henri accepted her hand and stood, then inquired about where to place his dirtied plate. He had piled the turkey bone, carrot tassels, and the few peelings he didn't eat on it.

"Leave it there," Delia said. "Gretchen will take care of it when she begins lunch."

Then Delia led him back through the main hall, past the parlor where Robert was deep in conversation with the violinist, and up the front stairs. In a moment, he would see the birds of his destiny. The ones he had imagined from childhood, the ones whose voices his father and the apprentices boxed in the work-shop. Henri wanted to pinch himself. He followed Delia down the hall, up another set of stairs, then down another corridor.

As they walked, Delia explained how she had lost some of her flock due to arsenic poisoning; the wallpaper fumes had risen from the men's smoking parlor. *Scheele's green*, she called it. "It took my husband too."

"I'm sorry," Henri said.

"So am I," Delia said. "Alastair and I got along well. Most of the time."

They stopped in front of a leaded-glass wall, just as Henri's father had described it. Inside, peppery dots of color flitted around in the air, as if the layers of rainbows had peeled apart from each other. Delia unlocked the aviary and beckoned him inside. It smelled like the root cellar back home. The birds flapped their wings and called to each other. Delia recited their names—she had fourteen left now, in brilliant hues of yellow, green, white, and flabbergasting orange.

They weren't singing any songs he knew. Not even measures of songs he knew. The cacophony had a sumptuous, irreverent humor.

"Ha!" he exulted. "They are exquisite! Every one of them. I can hardly figure out where to look. Which ones are trained?"

"None of these," Delia said. "They're all hens."

Henri didn't understand. "I didn't think they could sing at all."

Delia said, "They sing their own way—however they want, depending on how they're feeling. They can't memorize whole songs like the cocks."

He had gone his whole life thinking the wrong thing about girl canaries. *Hens.* Because of what his father told him. And his father had been here! In this very aviary! How could a piece of valuable information like this get lost? "But they *can* sing," he said.

She swept a hand around the aviary. "What do you think?"

Henri decided he preferred this wild, imprecise musicianship to any waltz or *danse* he and his father pinned on barrels. These hens reminded him of the lacemakers back home, when the girls each had something to say and talked over each other with zeal. "I love them," he said.

He found himself particularly mesmerized by a small bird of brilliant yellow hue with an irrepressibly twittery voice, only to shift his focus onto an orange one, and then a white, and then another yellow, or perhaps it was the same as the first. He compared these brilliant birds with the solitary illustration from the workshop—same beak, same wings, same funny little feet— but the drawing had been gray and dulled by fingerprints. He remembered, suddenly, how Aimée had waltzed in and touched the canary like it belonged to her. How Papa, that night in the parlor, had lectured him about luck.

Aimée at her aunt's looked more like that image of a canary than her real, rambunctious self. Delia's canaries, on the other hand, reminded him of Mireville on its very brightest day, and also of clouds and sunset and sunrise and the spun sugar a traveling magician once brought through town. The way these birds sang whatever they wanted made him giddy. His father and grandfather and great-grandfather had spent their lives forcing études and sonatas over natural, ebullient trills. Now that he'd heard the birds' voices himself, he could not imagine the business of changing them. He thought suddenly of his grandmother Cérine. Somehow, without ever having left France, she had suspected this: how human music couldn't possibly be better than the bird kind. It was just different.

An orange hen flew to Henri, tightened its claws around his pointer finger, and gave a dulcet *chuwheet chuweet* greeting. The little bird cocked her head at Delia before flitting to the brim of Henri's hat. Thereupon she tested several of his other fingers and, eventually, both shoulders. The bird's feet pricked at the skin in a gentle way—a hello of a grab. It danced from one foot to the other as it sang its native song.

What a marvelous place, New York!

Henri stayed as still as he could, not wanting to disrupt his companion. In another minute, though, Robert let himself in to join them and the bird took off, whirling into the colorful chaos.

"John left," he told his mother.

"Did he like your composition?"

Robert shrugged. "I think so. He paid me and commissioned another." He sat down a few paces away, never-minding the moss and the frosted dots of excrement.

Henri took his lead and sat, too. The damp sponge of the ground cover turned his trousers into a wick. He could feel the saturation, the cool ache of nature soaking into the cloth. Nature—or rather a clever imitation of it. Fabricated, replicated. Not the real thing. But close enough to make these birds happy. Henri crossed his legs, breathed the musty smell, and admired the canaries just the way his father had on his one and only trip to the United States. The trip that gave Henri a half-brother. One he hadn't thought he wanted, based on Delia's braggadocious letters—but here they were together, while soaring birds called to each other overhead.

"So what do you think of my mother's aviary?" Robert asked him.

"*Magnifique*," Henri said. "Better than I imagined."

"You two," Delia said. "You are both *magnifique*."

＊ ＊ ＊

Delia had a servant set up a guest room for Henri. He took a several-hour nap in the comfortable bed, aided by his full stomach, and awoke to join his hosts for dinner. Delia insisted Henri sit right beside her, while Robert settled himself at the head of the table and pulled out a steaming roll from a covered basket.

"The house is too quiet these days," Delia said. "Robert gets musicians coming by, but none of the local women call anymore."

"Why is that?" Henri inquired, to be polite. He thought of asking Robert to pass the rolls, but whatever was cooking in the kitchen smelled even more delicious. And besides, he was still a little full from his afternoon snack.

"My compositions are in much demand." Robert stared at Henri as he said it.

"I meant the question for your mother."

"Since her breeding program ended," Robert said, "they don't need her."

Delia flashed her son a look. Henri felt certain he'd misheard. His focus on the bread basket evaporated like one of Mireville's fleeting bouts of fog.

"What?" he said.

The canary training couldn't have ended; Delia was his father's best customer! She had requested a dozen new serinettes in May, a scant three months ago.

Just as he pondered this, Gretchen, a very pregnant member of the household staff, stepped in between Henri and Robert with a platter of thin-sliced, steaming meat. And another, heaped with cooked squash, blanched green beans, thin-sliced tomatoes, and ruffly piles of lettuce. Gretchen set the meat in front of Robert and the fresh garden delicacies next to Henri. He thanked the woman profusely, then paused, torn between culinary delights and his craving for new information.

"Go on," Delia said. "Whether you eat or not won't change the state of my business."

He obliged, forking heaps of goodness onto his plate, making sure to leave enough for the other two before passing the platters. Gretchen filled their glasses with wine, from a bottle she retrieved at a side table, then retreated into the kitchen. Henri tucked into his food, sighing with pleasure at each bite, before setting his fork down and continuing the conversation.

"Your breeding program," Henri reminded Delia. "I didn't quite catch what you said."

"It's over, unfortunately," Delia said. "Canary contests have gone out of fashion."

"What?" Henri gasped. The tart-sweet flavor of the tomatoes lingered in his mouth. "After all your work?" *After all of ours?* he wanted to add.

"The women lost interest once they realized there wasn't anything to win anymore," Robert said. "Just like everyone else in this town. So fickle."

"What about the canaries, though?"

Robert rolled his eyes. At the women? Or at Henri for not knowing the answer? "They let them go free. A lot of my mother's best birds have been eaten by hawks. But others are adapting. Building nests. Doing the usual, just differently."

"The ladies of Pleasant Hill have determined kite flying to be the best sport," Delia added. "They hire servants to handle the strings and take their tea on the cliffs, watching the spectacle instead of participating."

It didn't make sense to Henri. "The instruments you ordered in June—why? If you don't breed canaries anymore."

Delia blushed. "Let's not spoil our meal. I'll show you after." Then she motioned to Robert to pass her the sliced meat. "A good roast will make us all cheer up a bit."

When Gretchen came to clear the plates, Henri observed a strange sort of friction between her and Robert. Gretchen had pleasingly sharp cheekbones and small damp wisps of hair peeking out of her cap. The sort of buxom young woman a man like Robert might find attractive. Henri was fluent in the language of gazes, having learned it from his grandmother's British novels and by tarrying with the young lacemakers whenever they could spare a few minutes. The young man kept his eyes on his plate, except when Gretchen leaned toward the center of the table; then they darted toward her belly. Robert's fixation on Gretchen was no idle or absent-minded thing. Henri decided he would ask about her at his next opportunity. It seemed like the sort of thing brothers might talk about with each other.

"Shall we adjourn upstairs while Gretchen washes up?" Delia gave a sad smile. "I will show you my serinette collection."

Henri nodded agreeably, feeling grateful that in this mansion in a foreign land, there was a room that would remind him of home. Delia led him to the third-best guest room, which, instead of furniture, held piles of serinettes, some set precariously on top of others.

Years of work. His father's work. His own. All those apprentices. They had been churning out boxes, perfecting the pin placements, adjusting the angle of each staple and pulling out any bent ones, making sure each F-sharp lent itself to being sharp enough, and for what? Tears sprang to his eyes.

"They're still beautiful instruments," Delia said, probably to reassure him. "And we still play them for our own enjoyment."

This didn't make him feel any better. Henri opened several walnut lids with care, checking the tune sheets, pointing out to Delia which ones he had calligraphed. Next he inspected the cylinders, touching a few of the pins to make sure none wobbled. Each C-shaped crank was secured inside the box, as was proper for serinettes that were not in the midst of being played. If Delia left the cranks in the slots, they could bend the metal that connected to the crankshaft. He would have thought less of her if she had done that.

But this space, these piles. It didn't feel like a room meant for jolly entertainment so much as a cemetery for good craftsmanship. Where his father's work—and his own—had come to rest in peace. When he closed each lid, he noted his fingerprints in the dust. What a waste! Each box had been put together with love and exacting specificity. Each was supposed to have a destiny: teaching canaries. Being appreciated by the purchaser, too.

To find out that the work to which he'd once pledged his future was no longer necessary or wanted made his heart sink. By showing him, Delia didn't have to say the words. This room, these piles, the dust told the story. Or most of it, anyway.

"You kept buying all these?" Henri couldn't understand. "When you didn't need more?"

Delia picked up one of the untouched boxes and opened the lid, as Henri had. She plucked the crank out and inserted it into the proper place on the back of the box.

"I wanted to support your family." Delia admitted that she had sent more purchase orders than necessary over the years, even at the height of the canary fashion. She had learned to bypass the city importer to make sure as much of the profit as possible went straight to Henri's father. "Each Blanchard serinette lasts a long time. We've only had to retire a few of them—when the bellows started to leak or if one of my men dropped a box. I was pretty sure your father had figured it out—that my supply exceeded the demand for trained canaries."

"No, he hasn't! And I don't want to tell him."

"We are in agreement there," Delia said. "I have the money to keep purchasing new serinettes, and the space to store them, so it's a simple enough matter to continue. I've filled two rooms already and have plans to use my husband's former study next."

Henri's stomach turned over. He wished he hadn't eaten so much at dinner. He didn't like the idea of birds being trained, especially now that he had heard the hens' natural voices, but neither did he like the idea of his fellow apprentices dedicating their lives to boxes that would go straight into storage. Barrel organs were meant to be heard, not hidden.

Had he escaped a useless future by tracking down Delia? Seeing the true fate of his family's work? Hearing these birds in an unnatural habitat, but in their natural state of singing? Now he could never go back and toil in the workshop along with the others, touching the canary illustration every morning and pretending nothing had changed.

Delia held the serinette steady on top of the stack with her left hand and began to crank with her right. An eerie, mournful version of "Le Violette," the beloved Alessandro Scarlatti piece, floated out of the pipes.

"*Plus vite*," Henri said, turning his wrist in a pantomime of *faster*. "Otherwise it sounds out of tune."

Delia obliged, and the music quickened its pace.

"Better," he said. When she got to the end, Henri clapped.

If tastes had changed in New York, they had likely changed in Massachusetts and Vermont, probably everywhere. It was only a matter of time before the workshop had to close, and then what would the apprentices do? Go to Switzerland, maybe.

After she secured the crank back in the box, Delia bustled over to Henri and hugged him. Again, the warm layered lavender scent suffused him. He wanted to bury his head in her neck and cry, but she had intended to show him a kindness. Without her support, the family would have lost its income years ago. His body began to tremble, tears dropping out of his eyes and onto her shoulder.

Delia could sense the grief in him. "I am sorry."

Henri nodded and let himself cry on her. He wanted to lift his head, to say, "It's all for the best," because it was, truly. Canaries didn't need lessons to be stylish; they had it inside them all along. He thought he might tell her this, but Delia kept holding onto him, and he realized he didn't need to say anything at all.

Chapter Twenty-Five
The brothers plot a rescue.

After Henri had gone to bed, Robert's mother showed him some of the letters from M. Blanchard. Reports on the serinette workshop interspersed with questions about Robert and occasional phrases about Henri, all in rather decent English.

"...a kind boy..."

"...his apprenticeship is coming along..."

"The doctor has prescribed daily constitutionals."

Robert, whose first impression of this young man had been *foppish*, now considered him a gentle soul with fragile health. It didn't hurt to see all Georges Blanchard's questions about himself. How his appetite was after an extended bout of fussiness. Whether he had learned a new instrument since the last letter.

After his mother went up to bed, he fixed himself a drink, then sat in his father's smoking parlor considering this news in relation to his own situation. Robert didn't want to believe Gretchen regarding the paternity of her offspring, but as the well-to-do part of the equation (one plus one on the cusp of equaling three), he felt like he ought to give her some money anyway. Also a referral to another grand house, if she didn't want to live here anymore. She was competent—and even thinking this made him blush, considering how *more than competent* she had been when they were alone together. Plenty of grand homes hired new staff before the first frost. She'd be fine. So would the baby.

Moreover, Robert had plenty of income from his composition sales, so Mother would never know he was providing financial help, and he did like Gretchen. Very much. Their dalliance had started about a year ago, when he had visited the kitchen for a late-evening snack and offered to share a bottle of wine with her. They discovered an unexpected hunger for each other that night, then proceeded to explore it further over the coming months. When Gretchen discovered her condition, she called off their liaison, and no amount of persuasion on Robert's part would make her reconsider. He liked that about her: how firm she was with him. She had decided to give up the baby, a decision Robert appreciated as well. He didn't have any interest in being a father under his mother's roof.

The timing—with Gretchen being due in September—matched the era of their dalliance. Was it true? Was the child really his? He fell asleep in his father's chair, waking only long enough to take the last few swallows of his drink before heading back to his room.

Henri came looking for him the next morning, wanting to talk about a situation he had gotten himself into with a lace-maker. They met in the hall, just to the side of the main staircase. Robert decided his limited experience with Gretchen qualified him to claim a certain wisdom regarding women.

"Let me guess," Robert said. "It's someone back home."

No, Henri told him, she lived in New York. "I'm thinking of sending her a letter."

Robert clapped him on the back. "Wow! You've been here what—two days? Three?"

"She's *from* home."

Robert felt a zing of connection; he always had wanted a friend to talk about escapades with. Henri seemed a little more like family this morning. Especially since Robert had considered his own situation. Fathering a baby—how easy (*how amusing!*) it could be. To make that kind of mistake with another person.

Not that *he* was a mistake. Not that Gretchen's baby would be one, either.

"Have you kissed your girl?" Robert asked.

Henri's blue eyes widened and he laughed. "But of course! Have you kissed Gretchen?"

The topic's turning took Robert by surprise. He feigned outrage. "She's not my girl!"

Henri only stared at him, still smiling.

How did he know? "All right. Yes, we've kissed," Robert said. "Let's adjourn to my father's smoking parlor to continue this. Mother hates it in there."

Henri, still the agreeable boy Robert had read about in the letters, followed him without hesitation. Wallpaper paste hung in unattractive clumps around the room. Robert offered Henri his father's armchair and took the settee for himself. He and Gretchen had used this room more often than any other, because it had a lock.

"I'll tell you about Gretchen," Robert volunteered, "but first let's talk about your situation."

"She's my best friend," Henri began. "Aimée Maullian. She's a lacemaker like most of the other girls in my village, only now she's making dresses for her aunt."

"In New York," Robert filled in.

Henri nodded. "Exactly."

Suddenly Robert frowned. "Friends, though—"

"What about friends?"

Didn't this Frenchman know anything about girls? "That's what they say when they don't like you," Robert explained.

"But it's what I say about her, and I like her very much!" Color rose in Henri's cheeks and Robert felt a bit guilty. Maybe it was different in France.

"Her family had to move here because her brother did something terrible at home," Henri continued. "And now she's living with her brother and her sisters, up in an attic at her aunt's, and I think she's miserable. But also she's engaged?"

He said it like a question, giving Robert a hint on how to reply, for he was not used to speaking of the heart with other young men. "Wait—what? Engaged? Are you sure?"

Henri's curls drooped as he tilted his chin down. "Aimée told me so herself."

"But you didn't believe her?" Robert pressed.

Henri admitted that she had only been in the country for a few weeks. "Can it be serious?"

"What exactly did she say?"

Henri thought for a moment. "That he'd provide for her family."

"Ah ha! Now it's making more sense." Henri stared, seemingly baffled. Robert felt a flush of superiority. How could this young man be so out of tune when he came from a family of music-makers? "Just because they're engaged doesn't mean she cares for him," Robert said. "When I was younger, my mother took me to all the grand houses, and none of the wives seemed to like their husbands very much. But they all married into money."

"Into? Like a river?"

Sort of, Robert conceded. "Men with money can provide a level of comfort to their families that less well-to-do men can't."

Henri sighed. "I know that. I'm not an idiot."

"Some women like the luxury, that's all I'm saying." Robert gestured around him, not meaning this ill-kempt room but incorporating the aviary above and the whole grand house. In such a context, his mother having an affair, even briefly, didn't surprise him as much as it might have. His mother had married a much-older, wealthy man. Maybe she didn't have those kinds of feelings for him.

"Tell me exactly what Aimée said to you," Robert demanded.

"Never to come back."

Robert admitted this didn't sound good. "But what about this brother of hers? Was he there?"

Henri thought for a second, then gave an affirmative nod. "He's...not very nice. You might even say *murderish*."

The word didn't quite translate, but the point was clear enough. Suddenly Robert snapped his fingers. "I bet she was protecting you."

Henri considered this. "She was?"

"Think about it," Robert let go of his knees, then stood with excitement. "It makes absolute sense. Aimée is in a bad way, see, and she doesn't want you to risk your life help her, because she knows what her brother could do to you."

"He's strong," Henri added. "Much stronger than me."

A perfect plan formed, a picture in Robert's mind. "But that's exactly what you should do!"

"Be strong?" Henri's lips adjusted into a mystified expression.

"Go to her!"

Henri shook his head no. "If I send a letter—"

"What if she doesn't respond? You'll have wasted time, and you still won't know her true feelings."

Henri said he felt certain she'd respond. "She owes me that much."

"That is, if her aunt gives her the letter. Or her mother. Or her brother. Any one of them could decide to read it and destroy it before she even saw it. And then you'd—"

"Be heartbroken," Henri filled in. "Do you really think she wants to see me?"

Robert nodded. "Definitely. She only said what she did to scare you off. To keep you safe from her brother. If he really is *murderish.* Why, I'll bet her brother is pushing the engagement and she doesn't want you to get on the wrong side of his opinions."

"Or his fists." Henri fidgeted with his hands, thinking. "I don't know. What if she really does want to marry someone else?"

"Then I'll take you to one of my favorite bars for a few drinks. Where's her place again?"

"The Garment District." Henri raised his eyebrows. "You mean you'll accompany me?"

"Do you want me to?"

Henri said he would appreciate that. "Especially if Guillaume is there, it would be good to have two of us, in case—"

"Enough said." Robert cut him off. "And I'll bring my pistol, *in case.* We're brothers, aren't we?"

Henri grinned and nodded. He decided not to worry too much about the unexpected mention of a weapon. It would be good to have a way of scaring Guillaume off. Just in case.

"There's an excellent oyster bar just to the south of the Croton Reservoir," Robert continued. "We'll go there if Aimée turns you down."

They basked for a moment in their new plan.

"What about Gretchen?" Henri asked. "You said you'd tell me."

"Fine. If you truly wish to know, the baby's mine," Robert said. "But Gretchen doesn't want to keep it."

"Do you?" Henri asked with a slight hitch in his voice. True concern, or at least that's what it sounded like.

Robert liked him much more this morning than he had last night. "Mother would kill me if she found out. Gretchen told her it was an itinerant salesman."

"Oh," Henri said. "I guess that makes it easy for you, then."

"Probably easier than I deserve," Robert said. "But come on—let's go find your girl."

"Now?" Henri asked. "Are you sure a letter wouldn't be easier?"

"She's really going to have to choose between you and her fiancé if you're standing in front of her."

With that, Robert turned his back, opened the study door, and headed for the staff quarters to rouse the coachman.

The carriage waited for them beneath the porte cochère. A finer one than Henri had ever seen, with gilt trim and a coachman in a starched uniform. Henri ducked inside the compartment first, scooting over on the bench to make room for Robert.

"You travel in style," he said.

"It's the best way. You'll see."

Henri took issue with this, regaling Robert with his adventures crossing France on foot, begging farmers for a place to sleep, buying favors with serinette music. "I went where I pleased and stopped whenever I wanted to."

"Didn't you get scared?" Robert asked. "I mean—not that *I* would be fearful on such a trip, but you—"

Henri admitted that he worried about finding a place to sleep each night, and about the ever-changing weather and getting robbed. But on nights he couldn't find a hotel or a farmer willing to rent his barn, he slept under the stars. And when it rained, Henri kept going. "What other choice did I have?"

"To stop, of course!" Robert said.

Henri understood this response. Before he'd left home, he couldn't imagine the widening of his world without a frisson of fear. Why would he want to leave a place where he knew everyone and the expectations they had of him? Better to be known than invisible, he had thought. "There's a wonderful quality to being alone," he told his half-brother. "Until my travels, I had never thought much about my preferences. I got to choose everything—how far I walked each day, which inn I visited. Nobody has ever cared about what I liked before. Not even me!"

"And what did you decide?"

Henri reported that he preferred two pillows to one, and using his suitcase as a pillow beneath the stars to sleeping in a hay barn, because of the ticklish allergies that plagued him. He preferred afternoon snacks from food vendors to sit-down meals in more official establishments.

"Have you ever done as you wished?" Henri asked. "Day after day?"

"My mother is much too domineering for that," Robert said with a rueful twist of his lips.

"You're a grown-up," Henri pointed out. "Maybe it's time to test yourself a bit. Figure out what *you* want, not just what makes her happy."

"Are you saying this carriage is another one of my mother's cages?"

Henri laughed. "She does like to keep her prized possessions where she can see them."

"And she loves to feed them." Robert sighed. "At least this cage comes with an excellent picnic." He proceeded to pull out the basket his mother had packed: cheese, freshly baked bread (one of Gretchen's specialties), jam from last year's plum crop, and a type of round meat that Henri found too salty.

They finished the food quickly, all except the round meat, then Robert occupied the opposite bench for a nap. Henri sat up straight, wide awake, thinking how impressed Aimée would be when he pulled up at the curb. Although wouldn't such a vehicle attract Guillaume's attention? He considered waking Robert to explain the situation more fully, but he supposed *murderish* had given enough context. It's not like they could prepare a battle plan or train themselves in the art of wrestling between now and their arrival in the Garment District. Henri put to use the skill he had learned on the road: moving forward into the unknown. Soon the clopping of hooves and the juddering of wheels lulled him to sleep too.

The young men both awoke to a flurry of whistles—they were in the city already. Police were busy apprehending someone. Fabric peddlers called out prices; oyster cellar pitchmen sang of shucking. Newsboys sat on stoops, blandly waving their papers. Henri asked his half-brother why the newsboys weren't yelling like everyone else. Because they were too young to care?

Robert stretched and sat upright. "It's after the morning papers and before the evening ones come out," he said. "They won't sell many until the fresh edition prints."

"Why don't they just go home and wait?"

Robert shrugged. He hadn't thought about it. "Maybe they don't like their homes?"

They passed another fabric seller and then another, and he realized they must be in the Garment District already. They really needed a plan.

"Do you know how to fight?" Henri asked.

Robert tilted his head, curious. "Yes, of course I do. I had my share of fisticuffs as a boy. *And* I took fencing lessons. Are you still worried about Aimée's brother?"

Henri didn't know if the sort of experience Robert could have gotten in Pleasant Hill would do any good against Guillaume, who did not fight fair, but it seemed auspicious. "I just wanted to remind you, that's all."

"I've *got* it," Robert said. "He's killed someone, you don't want him to kill us, et cetera. Am I correct?"

Henri stared at his nonplussed half-brother. "You don't sound worried."

"What did you say about traveling—keep moving? Get through what you can't control?"

Henri nodded; he had said something like that. But Guillaume was dangerous.

"Remember," Robert added, "I brought my father's pistol."

Ah, Henri thought. *Well, that does change things. But not in a way that makes me feel more comfortable.*

The carriage slowed. The coachman stopped the rig one doorway beyond Aimée's aunt's house. Henri's heart pounded.

"Well, come on." Robert hopped down and shook out his trousers. "Let's see what happens."

❋ ❋ ❋

This knock was a man's knock. No blush in it at all. Aimée gathered up her work, dropping a few loose pins onto the sideboard, and went to open the door. A delivery or a groom. Possibly the shopkeeper. But Henri Blanchard was standing there instead, next to a taller stranger with a dash of roguishness to his smile.

"Henri!" She felt like her whole face had dazzled itself into a rainbow. "And—"

"Robert Dumphries Stanton," the stranger said.

A surge of gladness and surprise rose in Aimée. She knew this man by his mother's words, by way of Odil's translations.

"You found him!" She reached for Henri and wrapped her arms around his neck, holding tight, for this might be the last time.

"Come away with us," Henri said. "We have a carriage waiting."

Aimée clung tighter to him. "What? You mean it? We could just—go?" she whispered in French.

"Right now," Henri affirmed.

Aimée paused. "What about my sisters?"

Henri pressed his face against her head, relieved. She'd mentioned her sisters, not her fiancé. Robert was right: this was no love match. "We'll figure that out together."

"What's happening out there?" Aimée's mother called from the parlor in heavily accented English. "Is it a customer?"

"I'm afraid we knocked on the wrong door, ma'am," Robert called. "We'll leave in just a minute."

Henri ignored both of them. He gripped Aimée's face in his hands, desperate to kiss her but not wanting to take advantage of the situation. "With all my heart, I mean it. Join me."

"Hurry," Robert hissed.

Henri said, "Please, Aimée."

Her whispered response flooded him with dread. "But how can I walk away from my family? My mother? She has lost so much already."

"I swear to you." Henri let go of her face to touch her forearms gently. "We'll make arrangements for your sisters once we get you out of here. Your mother too. Robert's family has connections. And money. They'll help us."

Aimée bit her lip. Thinking. Henri had said *us*. When the shopkeeper spoke of *us*, he meant his family. His father's grocery. Not her. An *us* that she would join. But from Henri, *us* sounded more like two threads that had come apart for a while now being twisted back together, reincorporated into one whole design. She wanted to be part of that *us*.

"Before your brother interrupts us again," Henri added. "Unless you really want to marry—"

"The shopkeeper?" Aimée said. "But my aunt—"

"—does not seem to care much about you," Robert interrupted.

Henri saw Aimée's answer before she spoke it. Her face, a pale smudge of worry, eased into a tentative smile. She had considered—and decided. She'd go with them.

"I just need a moment to tell Maman," Aimée said. "Otherwise she'll worry."

"You can send her a letter from Robert's house," Henri said.

"I have a minute. It's all right. Tante Pierrette is taking a nap and Guillaume's out getting eggs," Aimée said.

She slipped through the doorway to the right before Robert or Henri could insist otherwise. In her absence, they didn't know what to do with their bodies. Should they step all the way inside and close the door behind them, or move back to the stoop and close the door because Robert had claimed they were lost? Voices and quiet sobs came from the parlor.

"Just her mother?" Robert whispered.

"She's telling her sisters too."

"Go get her," Robert said. "We can't risk waiting any longer."

Henri could see the bulge of Robert's pistol beneath his vest. He moved into the doorway of the parlor. Aimée knelt on the ground, her arms around two of her sisters. Fabric piles overflowed on a central table. Sobs and sniffles came from most of the girls. Madame Maullian gazed at Henri, not with anger but with worry.

"Come on, Aimée," Henri said.

"You can't leave!" Madame Maullian said. "You're engaged. Henri—Aimée. Be reasonable. Both of you! She can't disappoint her fiancé, not now."

"Can't or ought not to?" Henri said.

"Aren't I worth more to you than groceries?" Aimée added.

"We need that food. Your sisters need it."

"I promise I'll find a good job and send money back. Enough for you all. I'll be safe with Henri. Don't you trust us?"

"If your father hadn't—"

"He died, Maman. He's not here to help us!" Aimée said. "Things would be different if he were."

Madame Maullian gave an anguished cry.

"Shh." Aimée went to hug her mother. "I'll be okay." Then she reached for another sister, and another, cycling through one set of arms after the other, whispering their names into their hair, telling them to be good and stay safe and that she'd figure out how to help them escape this horrible place too.

"Come on!" Robert said from the doorway.

Aimée rushed from the room, tears streaming down her face, and Henri grabbed her hand to hasten her along to the carriage. They joined Robert at the threshold and bounded down the porch stairs.

"I thought you'd never get her to leave," Robert said.

Aimée opened her mouth to offer a retort when a shout interrupted her.

"Hey! You!"

"Oh, no," Aimée said.

Guillaume. Henri felt his knees buckle. He grabbed his brother's arm for support.

Guillaume waved a hand in the air, hailing them from a block away. He had white stripes on the outer hems of his pants and a basket cradled in his other arm. Henri let go of Robert and pointed at the Stanton carriage.

"Scramble in and draw the curtains," he told Aimée.

"I'm not leaving you out here with him," she said. "He'll listen to me."

Robert and Henri exchanged glances. *Murderish* passed between them. Now what? If only Aimée could have said goodbye faster. But that was Aimée, Henri realized. She needed to leave on her own terms. Not be rushed.

Robert pulled back his coat, revealing his pistol. "Stay back!" he shouted.

Aimée issued a frightened squeal when she spotted the weapon. "Don't," she cautioned Robert. "Please don't hurt him."

Guillaume paused with a frown, enough paces away to make Henri feel safe. Like he couldn't possibly want to fight. Not with his sister right there on the street. Still, there was a tense, invisible line drawn between the parties. Henri recalled Aimée's thread maze in the forest back home. How she pulled each piece taut before wrapping the next length around another trunk. He felt like that. Tight enough to break.

"Come on, Robert. I don't think there's any need for that. Let her talk to him." Henri tugged on his half-brother's sleeve.

Guillaume pulled a revolver out of a holster at his waist. "How's your aim, stranger? I've been training. Took third place in a contest last week. Next time I'll earn the grand prize."

Robert kept his hand on his weapon. He didn't speak French, so the taunt didn't register.

"Control yourself," Aimée said to her brother. "Don't be rash."

Guillaume spun the barrel of his revolver and lifted it, aiming first at Henri, then at Robert. In turn they each forgot to breathe. He lowered it again and said, "She told you not to come back."

Henri examined both sides of the street; his friends and Guillaume were standing four whole buildings apart. Far enough to make an accurate shot improbable, weren't they? Although what did Henri know about firearms? Monsieur Cocteau had one, and of course the farmers did, and the butcher. Not any of the master craftsmen.

It was much too late for him to ask Robert whether he had ever fired his father's pistol.

"*She* didn't mean it," Aimée said, still clutching Henri's hand.

"What are they saying?" Robert whispered to Henri.

Henri ignored him—there wasn't time to translate. Guillaume set his basket of eggs in the gutter, careful not to break any—a small gesture that seemed to slow time. Then he straightened up and pointed the revolver again, this time at his sister.

"Get back in the house, *ma soeur*," he said. "You don't even have shoes on."

Aimée lifted her skirts and jigged. "Tante has locked them up again."

"What did you do this time?"

Two pedestrians hastened to cross the street away from the man with the gun. Henri grasped Aimée's hand and pulled her behind him.

"Help!" Robert screamed. "Help! Someone help us."

A garment shop door swung open, but when the woman saw two armed men, she hurried back inside.

"Help!" Robert called again. "Anyone!"

Tante Pierrette's door opened and Mme. Maullian stepped out. She gasped at the spectacle. Her son—pointing a revolver at her daughter.

"Guillaume!" she said. "Get back in the house."

He turned to answer his mother, and Robert seized the opportunity. He lifted his pistol and fired into the air. Madame Maullian screamed. Henri pushed Robert and Aimée toward the carriage. Another shot rang out just as Robert and Aimée tumbled into the back seat, shouting, "Henri! *Vite!*"

Henri leaned into the lavish compartment as the carriage began to move, but another shot sounded, and this time, a bolt of pain flashed through his leg. Robert and Aimée hauled him the rest of the way inside as the carriage gained speed, the open door swinging wildly.

"You've been hit!" Aimée said.

Henri heard her voice, wobbly and distant, as if she were submerged in the river. The words didn't connect to his body right away. It seemed as if she were talking about another Henri. He sat on the bench seat beside her, perfectly fine, wasn't he? The expression on her face, the raised eyebrows and purse-string mouth, told him otherwise. Robert blanched. Stared out the window like he might become vomitous. At that point, Henri's leg—the stinging—ricocheted through his shock-addled brain. He bent to check the wound. Red drenched his trouser cuff. Liquid pouring out of him, not sticky like a minor cut. So much red. Dizziness overtook him.

"Catch him!" Aimée cried to Robert, a few beats too late.

❅ ❅ ❅

With Henri sprawled on the floor, Aimée managed to tuck his undamaged leg inside the coach and secure the banging door. A few more shots sounded as they raced away. Robert, at Aimée's direction, pulled off his shirt and then ripped it into strips, which she applied to Henri's leg. The bullet had sliced clean through his calf and exited on the other side.

Their ministrations in the back of the carriage slowed the bleeding, though when Henri woke up, his rising panic overtook them all. His anguished howls made Robert feel as if he had been hit in the heart. If only he was a better shot, he might have saved his brother this pain. Even Aimée, who had remained calm while fashioning the tourniquet, began to shake furiously when Henri's lament reached a crescendo. Robert moved over to sit beside her, wrapping his arms around her until she trembled only a little. She then grasped onto Henri, holding him as tight as she could, trying to slow his fear. He struggled for a moment, then relaxed into her.

To help him get his mind off his plight, Aimée said, "Tell him a story!"

Robert launched into an account of the time his father, furious at something his mother had said, opened the aviary door to let all the hens out. But the canaries liked their quarters quite a lot and refused to budge.

"Did your father have a terrible temper?" Aimée asked him.

"Not much of one," Robert said.

Henri listened to this story with attentiveness, but when it ended abruptly, his sense of alarm crested again.

"Sing to me?" he asked Aimée.

She began with "Neige, Neige Blanc," one of his favorite children's songs. Robert tried repeating it in French, which made them all laugh, even Henri. But then he gave up and concocted some silly English lyrics. It went this way through the whole carriage ride—Henri conversing, even laughing and answering questions, and then becoming nearly insensate from pain and franticness.

They made it all the way to the Pleasant Hill doctor in this manner—Robert's idea, because he didn't like city doctors. He had heard rumors of perfectly healthy patients being poisoned in slow increments by doses of unpredictable substances. After his father's untimely demise, such stories made him especially edgy. Aimée agreed with the plan, wanting the best for Henri.

"I trust you," she told Robert. "But will you really help me get my mother and sisters out of my aunt's house?"

"Did I say that?"

"You did," she confirmed.

He looked at her then, really looked at her, and saw a half-starved thing, shoeless yet smiling. He didn't find her pretty, but he liked her spunk and thought she'd make a good match for Henri. "Fine," he said. "I happen to know my mother will be looking for a new cook and housekeeper soon."

"You want my sisters to come work for your mother?" Aimée asked. "As servants? Isn't that—"

"Nice of me?" Robert asked. "I suppose not."

Henri had fallen into a light slumber, resting his head against her shoulder. Aimée sat for a moment, listening to his breath. She softened then. "Your mother pays well enough, though, n'est-ce pas? That would be better than our family's current arrangement."

"I can do more," Robert said. "Between my mother and me, I'm sure we can come up with something. She doesn't have anything else to do right now and she knows all the women in town. Tell me: what are your sisters' skills?"

By the time they arrived at the doctor's house, Robert knew each sister's name and temperament. His mother might not welcome them all to come live with her, but perhaps she could invest in renting the empty storefront on the town square. The Maullians could set up shop there—Aimée's mother making hats, for her grandfather was a milliner, and she had a knack for proper fitting. The other girls could make lace, bridal gowns, and whatever else they wished. Aimée played along, singing the praises of Émilie, who loved braiding ribbons, and Marie-Jean, who had taken to seamstress work better than any of them. Clémence enjoyed drawing; perhaps she could bring pictures of their clothing to women's houses and invite them to visit for a fitting.

The more Robert talked of a little shop, the more the idea seemed a castle built on air, a tale worthy of a place where it never rained, not a real possibility. And yet. He kept talking as if he might truly be able to offer such a thing to her mother and sisters.

"Do you think they'll agree?" Robert asked.

Aimée laughed. "Of course they would. The question is whether your mother will finance this scheme of yours. Because we have no money, so—"

"They're stuck at your aunt's, I know." Robert smiled kindly at her. "I think she will, though. She loves a new project. Besides, if Mother refuses, I have my own earnings. And very few expenses."

"Right," Aimée said.

"I mean it!" Robert objected.

She turned to him, a curious expression on her face. "No, you can't possibly. It's just a line, isn't it? To make me feel better about having run away?"

Robert shrugged. What could he tell her? That he didn't have much in his life besides his mother and music? And an illegitimate, secret baby on the way? He'd make sure Gretchen, if she did go ahead with leaving, had some money too. But the

Philharmonic had paid him handsomely for his last symphony, and commissions kept rolling in.

"I'd like to help, that's all."

Henri woke again when they arrived at the doctor's house. Dr. Manion—who had delivered Robert as a baby and confirmed Alastair's cause of death—dosed him with laudanum. Once it took effect, he stitched the entry and exit holes from the bullet with his wife acting as his assistant.

"Let him sleep for as long as he will," Dr. Manion told Aimée and Robert. "He'll be sore when he wakes, so best postpone that as long as you can."

Chapter Twenty-Six
Recovery.

Delia raised her eyebrows at the French girl's scrawny waist, sallow complexion, and lack of shoes, but she didn't ask questions. The girl would trust her, or not. Aimée was safe here, whether or not she believed it. At least she had a healthy appetite. Robert, Aimée, and Delia sat at the small table in the kitchen, Aimée chewing carrots with enthusiasm.

When they'd arrived not that many minutes ago, Robert and the coachman hoisting an unconscious Henri, Delia whisper-yelled at her son for not telling her where he had gone.

"You could have been hurt!"

Robert ignored her until Henri was settled into his bedroom. Then he returned to the first floor, looking for her and their petite guest. His answer—*to assist Henri's friend*—helped her forgive him. Delia had always worried that she and Alastair had pampered and coddled Robert too much over the years. Parented the fellow-feeling right out of him. An only child with his own musicians on staff. A bit much, anyone would agree. He preferred minor chords to the wails of other children! But hearing about this trip into the city and the plan he laid out for this girl's family made Delia miss her husband. They hadn't done so poorly after all. For their boy to want to help.

Granted, they were related, Robert and Henri, and this proposition was a favor to Henri, which meant the act of charity had a personal dimension. Still. It sounded as if this girl and her sisters had been conned by an unscrupulous relation. Three years of servitude? After that, they still wouldn't have any money saved up to move out, so they would likely take another equally poor deal from the aunt. Delia had read about such situations in the paper—Alastair had shown her a few of those articles—but had never known anyone affected personally.

"You think a shop would help them?" Delia asked.

"I'll put in some of the money to start the enterprise—or all of it. Whichever you prefer, Mother!" Robert said. "If you can only agree to house the Maullians for a few months while they build their clientele. Then they'll be able to afford to rent a place of their own."

He *had* thought about the difficulty of this. Six sisters. Plus Aimée. And the mother. Eight more mouths to feed. Good thing Delia had an ample garden and a storeroom full of preserves, cured meat, and flour—plus plenty of money to buy more.

Delia turned to the girl. "Is this an arrangement your family might like?" she asked. "Or is my son meddling where he's not wanted?"

Aimée finished chewing. "You are really considering this? Helping us? Bringing us to this nice town?"

Delia waved a hand around the kitchen. "I have far more space than I need."

"Well, then, I think Maman and the girls would be thrilled." Aimée looked suddenly much younger, more like a sprite than a refugee. "And we would work hard for you!"

"You mean for yourselves," Delia said.

Aimée faltered. "I don't understand. We would work to pay you back."

"Over a period of time," Delia said. "Not all at once. It would be your family business. You and your sisters would form better ties with the local ladies, I'd hope, than I ever have around here. The clientele, the shop—all that would be yours to keep."

Aimée said she suspected that was the kind of arrangement her father had hoped to find for them in New York.

"Well, now you are making it for yourselves," Delia said. "I'll fetch a pen and inkwell. You can write to your mother and we'll send an official business proposal out with the morning mail."

"That way she won't worry about you," Robert said.

"What if my brother takes the letter, though?" she asked.

"Then we'll deliver another one in person," Delia said. "You, me, Robert, Henri—all of us."

Aimée hopped up to hug them both with gusto. Much to her surprise, Delia found tears had formed in the corners of her eyes.

Following through with this arrangement would be an adjustment, especially at first. But she had plenty of bedrooms and she quite liked the idea of having more young people around.

The darkness heaved and ached. Henri rolled on the bed, the ship plowing through the waves beneath him. He dreamed of fish attacking his leg with razor teeth. He woke, just enough to scratch the surface of reality—what ocean?—then fell back to sleep.

He woke again, hours later. His eyes felt rough in their sockets, as if someone had painted them with salt. His tongue unstuck itself from the roof of his mouth. The room was well-furnished, his suitcase in the corner. Back at Delia's? He didn't remember returning. The last thing he—oh.

The city.

Blood.

He threw the covers off and found his left calf bandaged in thick white cloth.

"Aimée?" he called.

She didn't appear. Henri swung his legs over the edge of the bed, the injured one less cooperative. It took a few tries to stand, and then he could only hobble to the doorway of his room and call, "Hello? Anyone?"

Gretchen heard him hollering and came to tell him to get back into bed. "Doctor's orders."

"Shouldn't you be in bed too?" Henri asked.

"The midwife believes in exercise," Gretchen said. "If I laid down and stayed there, the baby might be born breathless."

Henri wondered if his mother had rested too much during her pregnancy. He didn't know Gretchen, not really, but he didn't want that to happen to her. "How are you feeling?"

She thought for a moment. "Like I devoured all the canaries in the aviary. Stuffed full of poking feathers. But how are you?"

"My leg throbs."

"Of course it does," Gretchen said.

"You heard, then. About my ordeal."

"The shooting? Why yes—it's all anyone is talking about. Robert and the young lady saved your life. That's what Dr. Manion told them. Would you like me to go tell them you've awoken?"

"Please," Henri said.

Gretchen found them in the kitchen, Delia writing a letter.

"Don't get ink on my table," she warned.

Delia raised a guilty eyebrow. "About that," she said. "We can get you another table?"

Gretchen shook her head, trying to stifle a smile, then let them know that Henri had woken up. "He's in pain, but he's all right."

"*Bien sûr!*" Aimée spoke around a mouthful of greens, then blushed at her lack of manners.

"Let's go!" Robert said.

Delia tugged her son's arm. "Let Aimée visit first. We wouldn't want to overwhelm our patient."

Robert agreed and Aimée darted away; she knew where to find the room, having peeked in on him a few times already. The cold marble floor in the foyer gave way to the soft, well-worn wooden tread of the stairs.

"Aimée?" Henri called.

She counted three bedrooms to the left, then opened the door. There he was—her Mireville friend. Her Henri. He sat up and invited her to sit on the bed beside him. She didn't hesitate. "I have the best news!" she exulted. "Wait until you hear!"

When he opened his mouth to respond, Aimée opened hers at the same time, and she leaned over and pressed her lips against his. They avoided banging teeth, and Aimée made sure to not bump his injured leg.

After a few gentle kisses, Henri's fingers grew fidgety, and the buzzy feeling inside his throat spread deep into his belly. He wanted the world to end at her shoulders.

"You look pale. Go back to sleep," Aimée said. "I'll tell you everything later."

"Will you stay with me?"

She helped him get comfortable, then nuzzled in beside him, tucking one of her legs over his good one.

Here in Pleasant Hill, this room, on this absurdly pleasant day, in this full-bellied quiet moment, Aimée relaxed enough to close her eyes and nap: here, nowhere else but here.

Henri and Aimée sat on the floor of the aviary gazing at the flock of hens. He had propped his cane against the brick wall. Dots of color swirled. *Suwheets* and *chirrups* permeated the air, like an aural moisture that blended seamlessly with the warm, damp conditions. Henri's good leg leaned against one of Aimée's, their knees pressed together. These small, constant touches drove him wild with desire. Henri's calf still throbbed, but with help he could get down on the floor and back up—progress from a few days ago, when walking down the hallway exhausted him and Robert had to support most of his weight when he climbed up or down the stairs. Henri had waited to invite Aimée to meet the birds until he could sit down with her in the aviary.

"They're beautiful," she said. "But quite smelly."

Henri inhaled the odors of excrement and damp moss. The humidity, while overwhelming at first, now smelled to him of comfort. He had the same surge of joy letting himself inside the glass room as he used to when walking into the workshop at home. Like the space held its arms out to him. But the workshop in Mireville was all brown and gray; entering the aviary felt like stepping inside a kaleidoscope.

"You'll get used to it," he told her.

Aimée spoke of the gray drawing in the workshop. "Somehow, I thought canaries were colorless. I never imagined—"

"This shade of yellow?"

"Or orange."

"Or green."

"Or peach."

They smiled at each other.

"They are lovely," Henri added, "though not nearly as lovely as you."

Aimée swatted his arm. "I smell better, even at my dirtiest."

She had gathered her skirt layers beneath her bottom so the moisture wouldn't reach all the way to her skin. Delia had given her the garment, since she hadn't had time to pack any of her things, and three pairs of shoes as well—more than she ever had at home.

Henri had gotten used to the wicking; damp trousers meant he had spent time in his favorite place in Delia's house: with the birds.

They spent the next few weeks living the charmed existence Henri's half-brother had always known. They woke on their own time, usually in Henri's room, though Aimée mussed her bedcovers each morning for propriety's sake. She helped Henri get downstairs, now that he had more strength in the wounded leg, then they ate a leisurely breakfast set out by Gretchen or another one of the servants.

During this spell, several letters passed between Mme. Maullian and Delia. A storefront had been rented on the Maullians' behalf. A sign fabricated: *The Ladies' Store*. Not particularly inventive but forthright. Madame Maullian had requested everything be readied before she moved her family north, perhaps not quite trusting the extravagance of the gesture from strangers.

Aimée had sent her mother private letters, too, confirming that the bedrooms were being readied, that there would be enough to eat. That there would be enough of *everything* for all of them here.

Except Guillaume, of course, who was not to know until they were gone. Let him and Tante Pierrette deal with each other. That was the rule Aimée set for her mother.

Robert was too busy to join Henri and Aimée in planning the store. His *Concerto for Harp in D Minor* was slated to premiere in November during the New York Philharmonic's second concert of the fourteenth season, which meant he needed to turn in a finished draft, all the parts penciled out, as soon as possible. He kept making small changes, rewriting a few measures, and then changing his mind. He needed it to be perfect. Unlike other contemporary composers—many of whom used sound effects, odd instruments, and flashy stunts like fireworks to charm the common man—Robert held that the dignity of European compositions should be replicated here in the New World. The Philharmonic liked him because of this. His peers called him stuffy, and the press came back mixed. His old-world style made more sense now, knowing his father was a Frenchman.

Henri's recovery meant slow, stamina-building walks around the property and time admiring the garden. According to Dr. Manion, his wound was healing but the muscles would need to be retrained to function in spite of the injury. He might always need a cane. In between conversations about Aimée's weeks in New York and Henri's solo travels, they plucked leaves of lettuce and pushed them into each other's mouths. They nibbled long beans, starting at opposite ends.

On dry days, Henri sat on the garden bench, propping his sore leg up while Aimée carried buckets of water from the well to keep the garden growing through the late-season hot spell.

He thought of asking her if she wanted to return to Mireville but feared her joy, her *oui*. He couldn't imagine harnessing himself to the cylinder of industry back home, not after this grand adventure. Not that there was an industry left. Henri sent a letter to his father, explaining the situation with canary contests falling out of fashion. Surely Papa would come up with a way to adjust to this news. It was better than the workshop continuing to churn out instruments that nobody wanted.

Henri spent most afternoons in the aviary with his wounded leg propped up, while Aimée explored the house, helped Gretchen with mending, or borrowed Henri's mother's lace bobbins to try designing her own patterns for the family store. She didn't take well to idleness. Delia chided her whenever she caught her doing chores, but Aimée kept watering the garden and washing the silverware nonetheless. These were hard tasks for Gretchen, now that her belly had grown so huge.

Gretchen often brought Henri his afternoon tea in the aviary to save him the trip downstairs. She loved the colors and flutters nearly as much as he did, now that she had grown accustomed to the odor. Besides, they had excellent conversations there, where nobody else bothered them. While she told the missus *fine! perfectly fine!* in answer to any questions about her health, in the aviary Gretchen was free to complain to Henri about her aching hips. How the baby's well-timed kicks could rouse her from the deepest sleep and how, these days, she couldn't complete the smallest task without having a chamber pot nearby. She even told him why she didn't want to keep the baby. She did not love Robert, nor have any interest in tying herself to him permanently, even if it were possible. But neither did she wish to suffer the daily indignity of working for Robert's mother while secretly raising the woman's grandson.

Then again, Gretchen didn't expect she could find a position in another house with a fatherless newborn babe on her breast.

"An orphanage is the best option," she said. At nineteen, sending money home to her parents, she needed to keep working. A baby would get in the way.

"Delia would give you money if you told her," he said. "Look at how generous she's being with Aimée's family. Or—" and here he brightened. "Why don't you just give Delia the baby? She'd raise her well."

"Have you *met* her son?" Gretchen gave a short, bitter laugh.

Henri didn't understand. "Of course. We are half-brothers."

She shook her head from side to side, signaling he had missed something in translation. "Henri, that boy hasn't ever had to do anything for himself. He's a nice person, but I bet he can't even prepare his own bath."

Gretchen had a point. Delia—strong-willed, wealthy, independent Delia. From reading those old letters, Henri knew his father had stayed for a long time—much longer than he had intended—because that's what Delia had wanted. He understood, suddenly. If Delia knew her son was the baby's father, Gretchen would be hers in a more permanent way than employment. And the baby would grow up sheltered from everything—life skills, experiences, friends. Anything that might hurt.

Besides, Henri knew what it was like to grow up in someone's shadow. "You don't have to decide yet," he said.

Gretchen told him this didn't make her feel better. "None of my options are good ones. Unless I can find a really nice orphanage."

To distract her, Henri offered to crank a few songs on the serinette. Not to train the canaries: to accompany them. In this green and fluttering context, he found a new appreciation for

even the most tired of songs: "Marlbrough S'en-Va-t-en Guerre."
Today Gretchen joined him, providing the English lyrics.

For he's a jolly good fellow!
For he's a jolly good fellow!

She grinned between verses, as if Henri were the jolly one of
the song.

About three weeks into Henri's recovery, Gretchen set the serving
tray on the floor, nested in a springy pile of moss. Tea and toast
with some of last fall's apple butter, his favorite. Henri attempted
to rise to his feet to thank her—he felt uncomfortable sitting
while she stood—but stumbled when reaching for his cane.

"You don't have to get up for me," Gretchen said.

"Of course I do. You're my friend," Henri said.

Gretchen studied him for a moment. "You really mean that?"

Of course he did; their conversations had a happy ease to
them. Henri had more in common with her than with his half-
brother. Henri and Gretchen spoke of the weather, the birds,
Robert's occasional temper, and the small moments of their days.
With Aimée, questions about their future thrummed like an
insistent bassline anytime they were alone. How soon would her
mother be ready for the carriage to arrive. Whether the coat of
paint Delia's man applied to the interior of the new shop was the
right shade of yellow. (Perhaps it was too lemony.) What position
Aimée might fill in the family shop. Certainly not seamstress or
lacemaker; she had enough experience with both to know she
would only make mistakes.

"I'd rather eat a sleeve than sew one at this point," Aimée had
said yesterday when the topic came up, as it did just about every
day.

As Henri reassured Gretchen—yes, *friends*—her legs buckled. She slid to her knees with a deep groan. The birds called out *suwheet-suwheet* from their perches. Gretchen gasped back at them, collapsing her knees so she could set all her weight on the ground.

"Oh no!" Henri said.

Gretchen gave him a glare. "That's not helpful."

"I'm sorry. Are you all right?"

Gretchen responded with a small wrenching cry, whereupon Henri asked if he could go get someone.

"Don't leave!" she said through gritted teeth. "Promise me you'll stay."

He did, without hesitation. When his mother labored alone, it had cost his sister's life. Besides, any moment another servant would walk by, or Delia herself, and then he would be relieved of this duty. Sent away from the birthing room like menfolk always were.

Another contraction came. The birds kept up their reassuring chorus—*suwheet, suwheet!* When a dropping landed on Gretchen's arm, Henri plucked it off. Another rest; another wave. He tried calling for help but the glass of the aviary kept the sound perfectly enclosed.

"Sit on me," she begged.

Henri caught the desperation in her voice, so he did as she asked. He extended his legs over hers, her belly bumping against his stomach. When each new wave came, he pushed down with his forearms and legs on her upper thighs. The pressure seemed to calm her. He didn't cry out when she dug her fingernails into his forearms. To ease her mind between contractions, he told her stories of the serinette workshop and how he learned to pin barrels—the day he impressed his father so much that his father danced in front of all the apprentices!—but Gretchen did not say much, only nodded to keep him going and parted her lips to moan when the next undulation shuddered through her body. Henri had no idea how long this would go on. Would a baby just pop out at any minute? Or was it only the beginning?

Being sat upon stopped feeling good to her. Henri gingerly moved his wounded leg off her, then the other, and sat behind her to act as a backrest, squeezing her shoulders whenever she told him to.

He asked again, then pleaded, for Gretchen to let him go find Delia or Aimée. "I'll come right back. They'll know how to help."

She shook her head and bared her teeth at him—begging *stay!* in a hoarse and desperate voice. Henri was exhausted already—and it wasn't his body doing the work. *How do women bear this?* She didn't have a choice, he decided, so he would proceed like he didn't, either.

Maybe she was thirsty. Henri lifted his teacup and pressed it against her lips. She drank it dry. He told more stories—about the Shadow Council of Apprentice Lacemakers, the legend of the Sun-Bringer, and what it was like to bite into a hot mushy apple right off the tree, then pick the sun-brittled skin out of his teeth with a twig. After more minutes—an hour? several hours?—Aimée pressed her nose to the glass, looking for Henri. He waved at her in desperation.

Aimée opened the door, wriggling her nose at the humid, avian atmosphere. She knew about labor from helping her mother and guessed it was too warm for Gretchen's liking. "Let's see how far along you are," she said. "If it's still early, and you feel like you can walk, we'll move you to a bedroom."

Aimée helped Gretchen wriggle out of her underclothes and spread her legs. She stuck her head and arms beneath Gretchen's skirts and announced that it would be a few hours yet. Gretchen groaned at this, while the birds chirruped and swirled in the air at this news like living confetti. Aimée sent Henri hobbling downstairs to tell Delia to boil some water for clean, sterilized towels. As soon as Delia put the kettle on, she rushed upstairs to help move Gretchen into one of the bedrooms set up for Aimée's sisters. Henri went to inform Robert, who received the news with a panicky expression. "What can I do? Should I go up there?"

"She hasn't asked for you," Henri said. "Besides, wouldn't your mother suspect something if you visited her now?"

Robert considered this. "I want to help, though."

"Aimée has experience, but if it's a difficult birth—"

"Right!" Robert said. "The midwife. I'll take the carriage."

Henri returned upstairs to discover Gretchen's distress had increased. The women had moved her into a bedroom close to his. She took one look at him and screamed.

"I'll—ah," he began.

"Don't take it personally," Delia said. "She's close now."

"Stay," Gretchen added between gritted teeth.

Rivulets of sweat and tears turned into rivers on her cheeks. Delia left and reappeared with some steaming hot towels in a large mixing bowl and a few dry ones looped over her arm. As Gretchen panted and groaned and her body seized, fear bright on her face, Aimée offered reassuring coos and upbeat comments. Henri held her hand and sang children's songs, "Neige, Neige Blanc" and "Au Claire de la Lune." Delia took a turn cradling Gretchen so the girl could push against her.

"Where is Robert?" Henri asked. "He should be back by now. Why don't I go find him?"

Gretchen didn't seem to hear. She gripped Henri's hand harder. He tried not to think about her nails jabbing into his skin and instead prattled on about how traveling to America was the bravest thing he would ever do, and how he had no desire to cross the ocean a second time, though if he ever wanted to see his mother again, he would have to find the courage. He said this last bit mostly for Aimée's benefit, but she kept her focus on Gretchen.

"I see the head!" Aimée said. "There's hair!"

Gretchen pushed, bracing her back against Delia, and after a few more pushes, the baby came.

"It's a girl," Aimée said. Gretchen gasped ragged sobs of relief and held her arms out.

Aimée wiped the baby with one of the damp towels, then dried it, taking care with the tiny armpits and earlobes. Then she gentled the baby into Gretchen's arms, keeping hold under its torso just in case the new mother was too weak to support the weight.

Henri stared at this new, very small person. She had a sticky, tousled mat of fuzz on her head, wide blue eyes the color of Le Madon in summer, and rosebud lips. Creases on her cheeks and on both wrists made it look like she had been folded up in an envelope, then mailed into the world. *Family*, he thought. He had never seen anything so beautiful.

A thick cord ran into Gretchen still, and she pushed a few more times until the placenta appeared. Aimée dragged it out from beneath Gretchen's skirts, using both hands. Delia tied the cord with a bit of twine, then cut it close to the baby's stomach. Then she leaned over and hugged Gretchen, not caring about the blood or whether they belonged in each other's arms, the mistress of the house and her servant, while in the aviary at the far end of the hall, the birds offered their usual blessing: *suwheet.*

❊ ❊ ❊

The midwife had arrived after the baby. Robert brought his old cradle upstairs to the guest room. Gretchen was too weak to make it downstairs to her regular quarters, and besides, this way Aimée and Henri could visit anytime she called for them.

The three of them spent hours in the room, marveling at the baby's tiny toes and soft mews of hunger. Henri thought his heart might crack in two like a walnut when it was time to say goodbye to her. It was no small thing to know a person for her entire life. Even if that span had only been a few hours so far.

Two days after the birth, a letter arrived from Aimée's mother:

> *Dearest Aimée,*
>
> *I suspect this news will come as a disappointment, but I hope you will grow to understand my decision. I am very grateful for the plans you and Mme. Stanton have been forming for us, but your brother has found out, and he is desolate about being left in the city alone. He needs us here. We cannot just pack up our lives, simple though they are, and go on without him.*
>
> *Yesterday I made mention to your aunt of finding other housing, and she made it clear that Guillaume would not be allowed to remain in residence here if we were to leave—not even if he could contribute to rent.*
>
> *Moreover, as you know, Guillaume relies on your sisters and me to wash his clothes and prepare his meals on the days Tante doesn't provide them. He will never advance in this city if we don't support his efforts. He has a lead on a theater job that sounds promising. Clémence is excited to see a free show or two if he gets the position. Send him all your luck!*

> *I am sorry not to tell you this in person. Visit us*
> *soon? Tante Pierrette doesn't mind that you've left; she*
> *doesn't insist on you returning. So that is my good*
> *news. You are free to come to us anytime you wish.*
> *Much love,*
> *Maman*

Aimée showed the note to Delia, then translated it for her.

"I am so sorry," Aimée said. "You have gone to so much expense for us."

"Some mothers are like that," Delia said. "Sacrificing the whole family for the benefit of one."

She did not have to say *the male one*. It was how things went, in this country and back in France. Delia told Aimée about growing up in a coal-mining town and how if she hadn't met Alastair, she would have spent her life cleaning up after her brothers and then—if she were lucky—her husband. Aimée let herself cry. She didn't want that life for her sisters! Her mother had struggled with much work and little joy for all her years; this ladies' shop was supposed to change her story. As she cried, Delia held her and stroked her back. *How could her mother choose Guillaume?* It wasn't fair to her sisters. It wasn't fair to Delia or Aimée, either, not after how hard they had worked to procure a location.

"I bought the building and the lot," Delia said, "as an investment. So now I'll just rent it out to someone else. With the fresh paint and the tables we ordered, I'll get a good price. Unless you want it?"

Aimée had no interest in seamstress work, or lace, or millinery. Could Henri start a business there? Not without learning a new trade. And who would teach him? Who might want a serinetter as an apprentice?

"I don't know," she said. "Maybe."

"You don't have to decide anything today," Delia said.

At home in Mireville, Henri knew the rules and expectations. He would follow the expected path from boyhood to workshop to grave, the crank of years turning, turning. Only now, like a canary that had escaped training, Henri and Aimée could play any song they wanted.

After Aimée handed him the disappointing letter and he absorbed its contents, the two of them decided to sit in the garden. October. The lettuce was gone, its seeds picked and set in Delia's wooden box so she could grow more the following year. The remaining beans had hardened. Their seeds would be dried and preserved for winter soups.

"I don't want to stay here through the winter," Aimée said. "Not when my sisters and mother aren't coming to join us."

"Do you want to go home?" Henri felt very brave asking this question, after they had been avoiding it for so long.

Aimée thought for a moment. "I miss Grand-Maman, but no, I do not wish to go home."

Relief flooded through Henri. "Neither do I."

"I figured as much from what you told Gretchen," she said.

"You can't go back to the city," Henri said. "Even though your mother says it's safe to visit—"

"Anyplace else," Aimée agreed. "I'll find work. As a seamstress if I must. I can send money to Maman."

"She'll only spend it on Guillaume," Henri said.

"I don't care!" Aimée said. "I need to do something to help them!"

Henri put his arm around her, pulling her close. "I know,"

he said. "We'll find jobs and earn enough to give plenty to your family. And to mine too."

They sat in silence for a few minutes.

"If your father stops making serinettes," Aimée finally said, "then what will he make instead?"

Henri only hugged her tighter. He had no idea. He didn't want to think about the workshop emptying out. Parts abandoned at dusty workbenches. Nor did he want to imagine the apprentices being trained to make instruments that had stopped selling.

And what could Henri do in this country to earn a living? Physical labor seemed a stretch, with his injured leg, but he could work with his hands. A clock shop might have him. Perhaps he could learn the art of the daguerrotype. Or find work as a calligrapher. His tunesheet labels were the neatest of anyone's.

"We'll come up with something," he reassured Aimée.

Gretchen moved back into her regular living quarters, but she refused to name her daughter; that would make the baby hers in a way that felt like *forever*. Although each day, she came up with a new excuse not to drop her off at the orphanage just yet. The one time Robert offered to do it for her, she summoned a fierce glare and then shouted at him until he backed out of the room and ran to hide in his father's former smoking parlor.

"Today?" Henri asked.

"She's still so little," Gretchen said.

"Today?" Aimée asked.

"Not today."

"I want her to gain some more weight first," she told Delia, who had offered to help raise the girl—a generous offer that made Aimée and Henri suspect she knew the truth of her parentage.

Robert had turned in the final draft of his composition for the symphony and was now working on a trio of viola sonatas for a pianist in Massachusetts. He continued to side with Gretchen, insisting his mother couldn't—and shouldn't ever—know the baby's true origin. Delia would surely invent excuses to keep Gretchen there—and Robert too—both of them, and the child, forever part of her flock.

How could they not want the baby? was a question nobody asked.

Do we want the baby? was a question Henri and Aimée asked each other. Their families were locked into their own futures—in Mireville and New York—freeing Henri and Aimée to imagine what a life together could look like. Whether such an existence might have room for a new, small person in it. They had let go of so many others that maybe...possibly...could there be space in their lives for one more?

As they considered this, Aimée carried the girl around the grounds, identifying objects in French, then repeating the words in English. Clouds, grass, birds. Henri took turns rocking her to sleep and burping her after meals. The more time they spent with the baby, the more certain they became. After dinner one night, they met with Robert and Gretchen in the men's smoking parlor, Gretchen rocking the baby in Alastair's favorite chair.

"We love your mother, but—" Aimée said.

"We can't stay here," Henri continued. Already they felt the presence of a debt they couldn't repay.

"You can," Robert insisted. "As long as you want. She loves you. She'll take good care of you. If you want to start a business, her storefront—"

"We don't want to stay," Henri clarified, and this Robert understood. He admitted to considering an apartment in the city, one close to the symphony hall—another reason not to accept the role of father at this time in his life.

Aimée took a deep breath and told Gretchen and Robert their idea. "We would call her Cérine," she said. "If you like that."

"Serene," Robert said. "That's beautiful."

Gretchen spoke the syllables to the bundle in her arms, those rosebud lips parted slightly, the girl mid-bliss of milk-breath sleep. "Serene. It suits her."

"We could send you letters," Aimée added. "If you'd like."

Robert thought of the letters his mother had written to M. Blanchard and what it must have been like for Henri to find them in his father's possession. If he had children someday, he would tell them about Serene—not keep her a secret.

"She's already family to us," Henri added.

Gretchen didn't answer in words. She stood and passed the baby to Aimée, who began a rhythmic swaying, just as she had soothed her baby sisters over the years. Gretchen's tears fell silently. Henri suggested they leave tomorrow morning; it would only get harder, the longer they stayed, and it was too late to walk very far tonight.

Aimée felt a wrenching grief, handing Cérine back to her mother for one final night—as Gretchen had the cradle in her room, and nobody wanted Delia to suspect their plan.

Later, maybe, if Robert and Gretchen agreed, they could bring Cérine back to visit, maybe even tell Delia the whole story, but they needed to be on their own for a while first. Make their own way.

Henri and Aimée packed their things as quietly as they could, then slept poorly. At dawn, they picked up Cérine from the cradle in Gretchen's room, then proceeded out the door of the servants' quarters without saying goodbye to Delia. Robert and Gretchen were waiting for them outside. Robert held a suitcase with Aimée's few belongings, the old baby clothes Delia had unpacked from a trunk in the attic, and some money to get them established. He handed Aimée his grandmother's wedding ring, in case the couple had trouble renting a place without proof of being a family. Which they were—no matter the absence of a ceremony or official paperwork. Gretchen handed Aimée a basket of food, which included a glass jar of fresh pap and four table napkins to serve as diapers.

The four of them stood on the stone path behind the house, the baby in Henri's arms, Aimée clutching Gretchen's basket.

"This is it," Gretchen said. "I want to say goodbye, but—" Tears welled in her eyes.

Robert met Gretchen's gaze and then, with the permission he saw there, pulled her into a hug. She sobbed on his shoulder, which made Robert cry too.

"The right decision isn't always easy," he whispered to her.

She pulled back and grinned through her tears. "How did a pompous prodigy like you get so wise?"

This made Robert cry harder, which started Gretchen off again.

Henri and Aimée couldn't stand to watch them sobbing, so they waved goodbye, then followed the dirt path to the edge of Delia's property. Two escaped canaries—one green, one vermillion—watched them from branches overhead, singing what Henri would have recognized as an improvised version of his father's favorite waltz if he hadn't been so focused on Cérine's every coo.

First Aimée, then Henri and the baby, stepped off the Stanton estate and onto a common road.

"Which direction?" Henri asked Aimée.

"North," she said. "Don't you think?"

"Yes. I have never been north of here."

Arm in arm, they walked into the village proper, past a fruit seller with a cart full of new apples, past fishmongers and newspaper boys. Aimée found a quilt shop and ducked in, leaving Henri and the baby outside. She bargained for a long dark strip of cloth, unhemmed. After knotting the ends together, she twisted it around her body, making crosses in the front and back, until she had secured it fully.

Henri kissed Cérine's squishy little nose, then handed her to Aimée, who settled her into the fabric pouch for a long journey.

On a road like any other road headed north, there walked two people, the dirt kicked up by their shoes dirtying the hems of their clothes. It hadn't rained in days, but the gray clouds overhead made them suspect it might soon. October had half passed. The couple held hands and swung them, making shadows fly over the carriage ruts. Odd, dark bands crisscrossed the back of the woman's dress, as if she had gone into partial mourning, but no, there came laughter, followed by a tiny cry, which made the travelers pause, peel back the cloth to assess its contents, and, thus reassured, begin to walk again.

Down this particular road, in about twenty minutes' time, save the time it would take to unbundle the baby and spoon some fresh pap into her wanting mouth, this pair with dusty hems would come upon a village, each lot a perfect square, as if the yards had been stitched together with fence posts by someone with a steady hand, each white house trimmed with sober taupe or perhaps hearty beige.

Upon approaching this village, the travelers would step to the side of the road and confer, the grass brushing their ankles. The baby would stir at the sudden change in pace. They could rent one of the white houses and pretend to be the same as their neighbors: a proper family. They could find a wet nurse, string up a clothesline, and keep their secrets to themselves.

Or they could keep searching for a place that suited them better, a village full of canary-green houses with a river coursing through it and secrets the locals had spun into fairytales, where anything could happen, a place with muddy-footed children jumping on the banks, waving and hollering to Henri and Aimée and Cérine: *Come and join us. You are welcome here.*

THE END

Research Notes

I am grateful to the following individuals and resources, all of which added to my understanding of serinettes, the mechanical music industry, 1850s France and New York City, and the craft of bobbin lace. Any errors are my own.

I discovered the word *bird organ* in the Musical Box Society International glossary, which led me to the synonym that ended up singing at the heart of this novel: serinette.

In 2010, Jean-Michel Roudier, *conservateur* of the Varzy Musée Auguste Grasset in Nevers, France, answered my questions about the serinette the museum has in its collection. He sent me notes on what it was like to crank the instrument for a CD the Varzy produced a decade earlier. Those emails, the recording, and several accompanying photographs became the prototype for the Blanchard family's serinettes. Without his time and expertise, this whole project would have fallen apart.

Also in 2010, at my request, Sarah Cypher and Erin Lopez toured the now-shuttered Musical Wonder House in Wiscasset, Maine, to hear the serinette in that collection. They sent me invaluable videos and notes.

Though I never managed to get my hands on a complete copy, I learned about the art of setting pins on a barrel by translating some publicly available pieces of *La Tonotechnie* by Marie-Dominique-Joseph Engramelle, first published in 1775. A few serinette-specific pages from *Barrel Organ* by Arthur W.J.G. Ord-Hume added to my technical knowledge of the instrument.

I studied barrel organs—and how their construction differentiates them from music boxes—by reading books in my parents' personal library, including *From Music Boxes to Street Organs* by Mr. R. deWaard, translated from the Dutch by Wade Jenkins and published by The Vestal Press, and *Musical Boxes and Other Musical Marvels: A Decade of Enjoyment*, edited by Angelo Rulli and published by the Musical Box Society International. The Vestal Press was founded and run by Harvey and Marion Roehl for many years; anyone seeking to learn more about mechanical music will find gems in their backlist, which is now distributed by National Book Network. Harvey and Marion used to pull into our driveway wearing white straw boater hats with red ribbons, pulling a calliope on a trailer behind their truck. Their zest for mechanical music and their contagious delight made its way into these pages.

Mireville is based on the real village of Mirecourt, home of the serinette; a distinctive type of bobbin lace; and much lutherie. While I didn't have the opportunity to visit in person, I spent weeks of my childhood traveling around small villages in Germany, attending outdoor street organ festivals, and I used those experiences combined with Google Maps to create Mireville, which like its inspiration sits close to the French-German border. A conversation over dinner during a Women in Portland Publishing meeting shaped my decision to further fictionalize the real Mirecourt by changing its name and adding an overlay of magic. Selden Edwards, bestselling author of *The Little Book*, gave me excellent advice on mixing historical details with imagination.

When I could not find any accounts on the invention of serinettes, I opted to give my townsfolk the agency to create a prototype. With the industry being based in Mirecourt, it's likely that local families did invent the serinette, though the traveling salesman who inspires them in *Singing Lessons for the Stylish Canary* is my own invention.

Canary breeding and song training information was gleaned from two helpful, now-defunct websites: ABirdintheHand.info and BirdChannel.com.

I learned about bobbin lace from members of The Portland Lace Society, who graciously answered my questions during one of their monthly meetings. Watching their fingers twist and cross the bobbins established a rhythm that I wrote into the novel.

The Life of Jullien: Adventurer, Showman-Conductor and Establisher of the Promenade Concerts in England, Together with a History of Those Concerts Up to 1895, by Adam Carse, helped me understand musical culture in France and the United States during the novel's time period. Its over-the-top storytelling tone influenced the level of playfulness in *Singing Lessons for the Stylish Canary*.

My fictional version of Le Havre owes its ambience to the German site Genealogisch-historischer Service, which includes an article on emigration through that port during the era in which Henri travels to New York.

Castle Garden and Battery Park by Barry Moreno (Arcadia Publishing) helped me imagine Henri's experience arriving in the United States, as did *The Hone & Strong Diaries of Old Manhattan*, edited by Louis Auchincloss.

Visiting the Raffin family in Überlingen, Germany, in the eighties influenced my decision to write about a family of organ makers.

And of course, I couldn't have conceived of this novel if I hadn't grown up around music boxes, street organs, and automata. For that, I thank my parents.

Acknowledgments

Bouquets and standing ovations to the following people: The fabulous Lanternfish Press team: Christine Neulieb, Amanda Thomas, and Feliza Casano. You've made my childhood dream come true. It's even better than I imagined all those years ago.

My agent, Laurie Fox, for your sharp editorial eye and for keeping a candle lit.

Joanna Rose and Stevan Allred: mentors, authors, friends. Finding my way to the Pinewood Table community is how I knew Portland was home. Steve Arndt, for getting me there. Kristi Wallace Knight, my first Pinewood friend.

Liz Prato, for holding your hand out to me, over and over again.

The Henry Writers have shared years of incisive feedback, laughter, and truffle fries with me: Dian Greenwood, Gigi Little, Liz Scott, Robert Hill, Kathleen Lane, and Steve Arndt.

These wise editorial guides helped me, at various stages of this project, to forge a path through the overgrown weeds of my imagination: Emma Burcart, Suzy Vitello, Shari MacDonald Strong, Sarah Cypher, David Cimonello, Denise Roy, and Naomi Hynes.

Jackie Shannon Hollis believed in my voice before I knew what I wanted to say. She also offered a quiet retreat space to work on *Singing Lessons for the Stylish Canary*, as did Mineral School and Mossy Rock Retreat. My cabin in the woods in Lincoln has allowed me to hold the whole story in my head for a week every summer. Over the years, I have written there alongside Kate Gray, Kathleen Postma, Christi Krug, Michelle Fredette, Melea Seward, Minton Sparks, Gina Loring, Julia Stoops, Martha Ragland, plus Dian, Jackie, Emma, Kathleen, and Joanna.

Every one of my Forest Avenue authors: you have taught me so much. So have these dear friends: Bess Kozlow (leading me by the hand since 1978), Priya Khanna, Crystal Wood, Piya Kochhar, Erin Bockelman, Vidisha Biswas, Christina Blanco, and Anisha Khanna. Mr. Bishé, my seventh-grade humanities teacher, believed I could grow up to be a writer before I knew for sure. Tamara McIntyre for suggesting Portland. Meriwether Falk for joining my Multnomah Village writing group. Nikole Potulsky, who asked, *Is that really your dream?* Tracy Stepp for always showing up for me. Chrysia Watson, the best secret reader in the neighborhood. Samm Saxby for speaking your truth and helping me do better. Grace Campbell: mama writers together. Anne Connell for lending her art to the novel's proposal package. Beth Kephart for the gifts of friendship and handmade journals; I do have more to say.

Independent booksellers and librarians are the very best; thanks for supporting my debut novel. You are all my favorites.

My parents: for everything, including a magical childhood full of music boxes, street organs, and carousels. I love you just the way you are.

My husband, Jonathan, for those early days of making dinner while I wrote scenes on your cozy teal couch, and all the days since. Our daughters, Hadley and Trixie, both excellent storytellers.

Thank you.

About the Author

Once upon a time, Laura Stanfill lived in a New Jersey house filled with music boxes, street organs, and books. She grew up to become the publisher of Forest Avenue Press. Her work has appeared in *Shondaland*, *The Rumpus*, *Catapult*, *The Vincent Brothers Review*, *Santa Fe Writers Project*, and various print anthologies. She believes in indie bookstores and wishes on them like stars from her home in Portland, Oregon, where she resides with her family and a dog named Waffles. Learn more at laurastanfill.com.